A
Desperate
HOPE

Books by Elizabeth Camden

A

Desperate
HOPE

ELIZABETH
CAMDEN

BETHANYHOUSE

a division of Baker Publishing Group
Minneapolis, Minnesota

© 2019 by Dorothy Mays

Published by Bethany House Publishers
11400 Hampshire Avenue South
Bloomington, Minnesota 55438
www.bethanyhouse.com

Bethany House Publishers is a division of
Baker Publishing Group, Grand Rapids, Michigan

Printed in the United States of America

Library of Congress Cataloging-in-Publication Data
Names: Camden, Elizabeth, author.
Title: A desperate hope / Elizabeth Camden.
Description: Minneapolis, Minnesota : Bethany House Publishers, a division of
   Baker Publishing Group, [2019]
Identifiers: LCCN 2018034268 | ISBN 9780764232107 (trade paper) | ISBN
   9781493417292 (e-book) | ISBN 9780764233142 (cloth)
Subjects: | GSAFD: Christian fiction.
Classification: LCC PS3553.A429 D47 2019 | DDC 813/.54—dc23
LC record available at https://lccn.loc.gov/2018034268

Cover design by Jennifer Parker
Cover photography by Mike Habermann Photography, LLC

Author is represented by the Steve Laube Agency.

19 20 21 22 23 24 25   7 6 5 4 3 2 1

Prologue

Summer 1896

Alex Duval's first hint of trouble was when Eloise failed to appear at their hideaway. For the past two summers they had met behind the ruins of an old cider mill in an overgrown orchard every Monday and Thursday. Those were the only days her guardian left town on business and she could get away without fear of discovery.

He propped the math book atop his knee and tried to concentrate. His only prayer of getting into college was if Eloise helped him master algebra. She was two years younger but a genius at mathematics. In exchange, he taught Eloise about the world around them, for he'd never met a girl so impossibly sheltered before he took her under his wing.

He swatted at a gnat circling in the warm air, worried that she was more than an hour late. Her guardian was a mean brute of a man, though Eloise claimed Mr. Garrett had always been good to her. She didn't know him as well as the people in the village, who called him "the Bone-Crusher" behind his back.

A bird startled, and a squirrel raced through the underbrush up on the hillside, which meant Eloise was probably on her way down. Alex scrambled to his feet and adjusted his collar. It was important to look respectable for her. He came from the finest family in the village, but that didn't compare to Eloise and her grandiose upbringing. He peered through the trees to catch a glimpse of her, but his brows lowered at the heavy tromp of footsteps.

It wasn't Eloise coming toward him.

He squatted back down behind the cider mill. If he was discovered, he'd need an excuse for being here that didn't involve Eloise. He peered over the rim of the stone wall but jerked down immediately. There were four men coming, all of them quarrymen who worked for Bruce Garrett.

"No use hiding, Duval," one of the men hollered. It was Jared Brimley, a stonecutter who was regularly thrown out of Alex's brother's tavern for rowdiness.

The worst thing Alex could do was act guilty. He affected a casual tone as he held the math book aloft. "I always hide when I have to study math. It's a terrifying subject."

The men didn't laugh. They just marched toward him without breaking stride.

Alex backed up a few steps. "What's going on?"

Jared didn't answer. He just hauled back a fist and swung.

Alex dived to the left. He wasn't very big, but he was fast. It was impossible to grow up with an older brother like Hercules Duval and not know how to fight. He sprang backward, both hands fisted to protect his face, but one of the men blocked him from behind while another punched him in the jaw, and he went down. The pain was bad, but he managed to brace a hand on the ground and push himself back up.

"Not so high and mighty now, are you, boy?"

Alex said nothing. With a last name like Duval, everyone knew he was from the founding family of Duval Springs. His father had been the mayor until his death earlier that year, and his brother owned the famous Duval Tavern.

Alex continued backing up. "I don't want any trouble," he said, embarrassed by the tremble in his voice. There were four of them, all bigger and stronger than he was.

"Then you never should have touched that girl, should you?"

Alex sagged, his worst fear coming to life. He'd done a lot more than just touch Eloise. He and Eloise had done *everything* together. And since she hadn't met him this morning, they'd probably already gotten to her.

"Where is she? What's happened to her?" he asked. *Please, God, don't let it be anything bad*. Eloise was his life. They were going to get married someday. Maybe they shouldn't have jumped the gun by meeting in the woods all this time, but he loved her.

"That's no concern of yours, boy," the man growled, hauling off for another punch.

Alex ducked and charged him like a bull, tackling him and shoving them both to the ground. He scrambled up and tried to make a run for it, but someone slammed into him from behind, and he got a face full of dirt. A storm of booted feet kicked him, and he curled into a ball, trying to cover his head.

The men finally backed away, and Alex rolled to his side, struggling to draw a lungful of air. Maybe it would just be a hard and fast beating. He could deal with that. He probably deserved it.

Someone hauled him upright, locking both his elbows behind his back. It took several moments for his vision to clear, and when it did, he was facing the man with tobacco-stained teeth.

"We know where you live," he said with a thick Irish brogue. "That nice place over the tavern where you bunk with your brother and his pretty wife and those three little kids. We can get to them too."

"Leave them alone," Alex said. "They didn't do anything wrong."

Hercules had done everything *right*. His brother had gotten married right out of school and was a good family man. The baby was only a month old. They didn't need trouble like this, but Hercules wasn't the sort to back away when threatened. He would fight fire with fire, and Alex couldn't let that happen.

"You want us to leave them alone, then you need to get out of town. Right, boy-o? Never show your face here again."

"Eloise . . ." Her name slipped out before he could call it back, and a fist landed on his jaw, filling his mouth with blood.

"Forget you ever heard her name," the Irishman growled. "Forget you ever lived in this valley. We catch you showing your mug here again, we go after you, and then we go after your family. Is that clear?"

Alex was slammed against a tree, banging his head so hard he saw sparks. The rumors about Garrett were true. Bone-Crusher . . .

"I hear you," he said, but his mouth was so swollen he could barely get the words out.

The Irishman stepped aside, and the biggest of the men took his place. A tiny sliver of pity was in his face as he made a fist.

"Where do you want it, boy? The face or the gut?"

The face would hurt more, but the gut could kill him. There wasn't going to be any escape, so he'd better take it like a man.

"Face," Alex choked out. The blow came fast and hard, breaking his nose.

"We're taking you to Kingston and putting you on a train," the Irishman said. "And you're never coming back to this valley, and you're going to forget that girl's name. You're going to forget what she looks like, where she lives, or that she even exists. You got that?"

Alex nodded.

The next few hours were a blur. He leaned against the window of the train while passing in and out of consciousness. He had no idea where the train was headed and had nothing but the clothes on his back, but he couldn't go back into town. Hercules had warned him against carrying on with Bruce Garrett's ward, and now Alex was paying the price. He wouldn't foist his problems on Hercules or the children.

He had failed Eloise. Instead of being her hero, he'd brought her to shame. He didn't even know what had happened to her. Tears pooled in his eyes.

"I'm so sorry, Eloise," he whispered. "May God bless and watch over you always."

Chapter
ONE

**Twelve Years Later
New York City, August 1908**

*P*lease, Eloise, I need your help."

Eloise Drake glanced up from her tax schedules. She'd only been an accountant for the State Water Board for two months, but her coworkers already depended on her, and it felt good to be needed.

"What can I do for you, Leon?"

Leon glanced nervously around the office. Almost a hundred architects, engineers, and accountants worked on this floor, and privacy was nonexistent. He hunkered beside her desk and leaned in close to whisper. "I forgot to calculate the abatement for the sewers into the operating expenses. Can you lend a hand?"

It was a damaging error that could skew an entire budget, but Leon's wife had just given birth to their third child, so maybe the oversight was understandable. Besides, Eloise was proud of her ability to grind through endless columns of numbers and spot the errors.

"I'll take care of it," she said, and Leon sagged in relief.

"Thanks, Eloise. You're the best," he said before darting away to collect the paperwork.

Her desk was already decorated with tokens of gratitude. The tin of peppermints came from the last time she had bailed Leon out. The paperweight of a green turtle was a gift from Mr. Trent when she stayed late to help complete payroll duties.

She twisted the whimsical paperweight to see it better. Bruce would grouse that she was letting people walk all over her. *"Men take advantage of women whenever they can,"* he'd growl in the voice that terrified her as a child. But he was her guardian and had always been overprotective.

And she loved working here, even if she wasn't quite part of the team. The other accountants often laughed and joked with one another, but as the only woman in the office, she was rarely invited to join in. It wasn't their fault. Being an outsider was normal for Eloise. She had always lacked that nameless ability to fit in and was grateful for the chance to be here at all.

Most people considered accounting a dull profession filled with endless columns of numbers, but when Eloise looked at those same columns, she saw stories. Those numbers spoke of financial gambles, triumphs, danger, and dreams coming true or being shattered. America was built on a foundation of finance, and without accountants to keep it all organized, business and innovation would grind to a halt. The people in this office were transforming New York City into a world of skyscrapers, subways, water tunnels, and bridges, and she got to be a part of that team.

It didn't take long to amend Leon's mistake, and then she returned to her own work. The latest expense report for the Duval Springs project was due by the end of the week. She opened a file to examine the statement submitted by the town for reimbursement, and her gaze zeroed in on the signature at the bottom of the page.

Alex Duval.

He was now the mayor of Duval Springs, and she routinely saw his name on official reports. It never failed to crack a tiny bit of her composure. She hadn't set eyes on him in twelve years. She and Alex had been harshly punished after Bruce discovered their clandestine meetings, but it appeared Alex had outgrown his reckless, daredevil ways. She didn't make a habit of following his career, but her job involved paying the state's bills for a lawsuit Alex had launched against their office. He'd been the mayor for five years and had clearly recovered from the damage Bruce inflicted.

For herself, she had received her accounting license and was flourishing in the most vibrant city in the world, the image of prim respectability. Each morning she smoothed her red hair into an elegant coiffure, then tugged on a smartly tailored jacket to project the air of unflappable confidence that had gotten her this far in the world.

It hadn't always been this way. As a girl, she'd been so madly in love with Alex Duval that she would have done anything for him. If he'd suggested they run away to join the gypsies, she'd have done it. Buy a boat and sail toward the sunrise? Flee to an attic apartment in Paris to live like bohemians? They had discussed all those glorious, improbable dreams. In the end, the only thing they'd done was lie in the grass behind the old cider mill. Bruce had been right. Young men wanted only one thing from a girl, and she'd stupidly given it away and asked for nothing in return but the chance to wallow in Alex's beaming attention.

Not anymore. Today she was governed by rules and respectability.

When the office clerk delivered the mail, she processed each form, putting the documents into her well-ordered files to be addressed in order of priority.

The last document in the mail contained a message that

robbed the breath from her lungs. It was an order from Mr. Jones, her supervisor. Normally she handled anything he sent her immediately and without question, but she could no more carry out this request than she could fly to the moon. There was a limit to her abilities, and it had just landed on her desk.

Fletcher Jones was the Commissioner of Finance for the State Water Board. Although he was as straitlaced as his lofty title implied, two weeks ago he had insisted she call him by his first name.

"There are three people with the last name Jones in this office," he had said. "Calling me Fletcher will avoid confusion."

Eloise hadn't pointed out that no one else in the office had been invited to use his first name, but she would be naïve not to sense the attraction humming between them. And Eloise hadn't been naïve since she was sixteen years old. Beneath Fletcher's carefully groomed exterior, he seemed to return her reluctant attraction, though he had never once made an improper comment or glance. Maybe he found romantic overtures difficult to grapple with too. She ought to be relieved he could awaken feelings she thought had been cauterized long ago, because she didn't want to be alone forever.

She stood and adjusted the hem of her jacket. She didn't have an appointment, and Fletcher's secretary made her wait twenty minutes before she was allowed into his private office.

He didn't even look up from his paperwork when she entered. "Our meeting isn't until tomorrow afternoon."

She didn't let the typically chilly greeting bother her as she set the note on his desk. "When I accepted this position, it was with the understanding that it would be in Manhattan."

"Yes. And now it's in Duval Springs."

She couldn't do it. If he asked her to go to Timbuktu, she'd find a way to get there and complete the job on time and under budget. But Duval Springs? No. It wasn't possible.

"Why me?" she asked calmly. "There are a dozen other employees with more experience on this project."

He finally looked up. With his neatly groomed blond hair and fine blue eyes, Fletcher had a patrician air that was easy to admire. "No one wants the Duval Springs assignment. It's a remote town without plumbing or electricity, the residents are hostile, and the assignment lasts four months. It's going to the lowest man on the totem pole, and that's you."

Duval Springs had just lost a five-year battle against the state. New York City needed water, and it was having to go far afield to find it. Duval Springs was almost a hundred miles north of Manhattan, but it was about to be wiped off the map so that the state could flood the valley and build a reservoir to serve the four million residents of New York City.

"Why can't I continue working on the account from here?" she pressed.

"In the interest of fiscal responsibility, I am combining the accounting work with appraisal duties. And property appraisals can't be handled from the city."

Eloise was taken aback. "I don't know anything about property appraisals."

"Can you count?"

The question was so absurd that the only response it deserved was the lift of a single eyebrow.

"Then you can do this job," he replied. "We've already had people in the valley demand unrealistically high valuations for their property, so I developed a simple formula to expedite the process." He presented her with a two-page chart, and as he outlined the technique, she warmed in admiration.

"Who designed this system?" she asked.

"I did."

It was a miracle of simplicity, so logical and efficient that her respect for him climbed higher. Although she'd never written a property appraisal in her life, this chart boiled the task down to clear, easy-to-understand principles, and the formulas removed all sentimentality from an inherently volatile situation.

"I like the way you think," she said simply.

He seemed surprised, but only for a moment. "You do? Most people find me horrible."

"Everything you just said makes perfect sense. I admire the straightforward rationality of it."

She thought she glimpsed a flash of pleasure, but he quickly retreated behind his austere demeanor. "But can you apply it?"

Her confidence surged. She'd already memorized the chart of simple mathematical equations and gave it back to him before scanning the interior of his office. She noted the wood paneling, the number of electrical outlets, and the arrangement of windows. It took less than a minute to apply the formula and perform the math in her head.

"The value of your office, stripped of furniture and moveable equipment, is $435."

That took him aback. He stood and glanced around the room, mental calculations going on behind his cool features. She hid a smile when he had to peck out a few numbers on his adding machine.

A look of admiration crossed his face. "The assignment is yours."

"I respectfully decline."

Fletcher leaned back in his chair, flummoxed by her refusal. "Are you . . . do you perhaps have mixed loyalties?"

Her eyes widened, but she kept her voice calm. "Why should I have mixed loyalties?" *He can't possibly know.*

"I gather you grew up not far from Duval Springs, correct?"

"Close. The house where I lived was at the top of the valley, but I've never actually set foot in Duval Springs."

She and Alex had met in an abandoned apple orchard halfway

between the mansion and the village. At the time, those summers had been magic, but now the memory brought only hurt and embarrassment. The years that followed had been brutally hard, but she'd survived. Her shattered heart had mended, and she covered it with a layer of smooth professionalism, but coming face to face with Alex might crack that hard-won veneer.

"I'm an accountant," she reminded Fletcher. "We do our work from an office."

"All the other accountants in the office work too closely with the engineers for me to send them upstate. You are the only person I can afford to send. Eloise, I need you."

They were the three words she was powerless to refuse. Some women might crave wealth or beauty or popularity. Eloise craved being needed, even if it meant she'd have to endure seeing Alex Duval again. Fletcher needed her, and she wouldn't let a disastrous, long-ago love affair interfere with her responsibilities.

"Then of course I shall go." Just saying the words made her cringe inside.

"Excellent. Please join the team for a meeting tomorrow afternoon to discuss logistics. Brace yourself. Claude Fitzgerald will supervise the team, and he doesn't like women. Figure out a way to cope with it."

She rose, smoothing her face into a look of cool composure. "I shall join the team tomorrow afternoon."

She just hoped she would be able to survive the next four months, for it would be a test unlike any she'd ever endured.

t two o'clock the following afternoon, Eloise joined a dozen employees in the Water Board's conference room to plan the initial stages of clearing the residents out of Duval Springs. Four of them would be stationed on-site for the preliminary work. The team consisted of two demolition engineers, a land surveyor, and an accountant.

They clustered around a conference table covered by a map of Duval Springs, and a lump of dread settled inside Eloise. Their mission was to obliterate this idyllic town. The buildings would be torn down, and thousands of people would be displaced. The trees would be chopped down, the roots dug up and grubbed. All vegetation and wildlife would be cleared away. Their mission was to literally wipe Duval Springs off the map.

Claude Fitzgerald, the team leader and chief demolition engineer, stood at the head of the table. Eloise had no doubt Claude was a competent engineer, but he fought hard to avoid living in Duval Springs during the assignment.

"I refuse to live in a backwoods village without decent plumbing and electricity for the next four months," he said. "Kingston is only twelve miles away and an easy commute to the town."

Claude was a bully, but she hoped his opinion would carry sway. It was going to be hard enough to work in Duval Springs without being forced to live there as well.

"It will save the state considerable funds to house the team in Duval Springs," Fletcher said. "Hotel rooms in Kingston cost nine dollars per night but only five in Duval Springs."

Claude whipped the cigar from his mouth. "Are you going to penny-pinch us over four dollars?"

"Miss Drake?" Fletcher asked, turning to her. "Please calculate the four-month cost differential between staying in Duval Springs versus Kingston."

She didn't want to live in Duval Springs, but Fletcher had asked a mathematical question, and it was impossible not to supply the answer.

"Since there are four of us on the team, it amounts to a difference of sixteen dollars a day," she said. "Multiply that by four months, and it comes out to $1,920. And that doesn't account for the cost of daily transportation and loss from compounded interest." She looked at Fletcher. "What is today's rate of annual interest?"

"Six-point-two percent."

She closed her eyes to run the calculations in her head. Fletcher had once called her a human adding machine, and he hadn't been off base.

"Adding in the cost of transportation and the loss of compounded interest, it comes to a total savings of $2,446," she said. "Of more value is our time lost during a daily commute. If we average the hourly salary of four employees, multiplied by—"

"For the love of all humanity, please shut up," Claude groused.

"Miss Drake was merely pointing out that it makes sense to live in Duval Springs, even though it may lack the comforts found in Kingston," Fletcher said. "The Water Board appreciates the sacrifices the team will undertake on behalf of the city, and you will be well compensated for the temporary discomfort. The demolition team shall live in Duval Springs for the duration of the preliminary assessment."

Despite her reluctance to see Alex again, Eloise was intrigued by the chance to finally venture into the town she'd always admired from the mountaintop mansion where she'd spent her summers as a child. Her bedroom had a telescope intended for astronomy, but it could also be directed to focus on the village nestled at the bottom of the valley. She had studied the residents of Duval Springs with a mix of fascination and envy. What would it be like to live in such a quaint village where there were other children to play with? She used to plead with her guardian to be allowed to explore the town, but Bruce always refused, which made the village even more intriguing. There were no other children at Bruce's house and little to do after finishing her daily lessons, so she aimed the telescope down into the village, studying its inhabitants like a scientist exploring remote life forms.

When she was fifteen, temptation got the better of her. How hard could it be to walk to the bottom of the valley and explore Duval Springs on her own? She'd waited until one warm Monday morning when Bruce set off for Kingston on business, then snuck outside and crept behind the high stone walls that ringed the estate. Bruce had wolfhounds, bodyguards, and heavy locks on all the gates, but there was a low opening where the dogs came and went, and she was slender enough to slip through.

It was frightening to leave the safety of the estate and venture into the forest blanketing the hillside. She'd never been alone in the woods before, but she swallowed her misgivings and pressed onward.

It should have been easy to keep heading downhill until she arrived at the town, but within an hour, she was hopelessly lost in the shrubs, brambles, and trees that all looked alike. She could no longer see the village and had started following a narrow path through the forest, assuming it would lead to someone who could point her toward Duval Springs. She later learned that she'd been following deer trails and had wandered miles away from home. If she hadn't stupidly followed those deer trails, she might never have met Alex Duval, the boy destined to change her life forever.

Slim, handsome, and with golden-blond hair, she recognized him immediately from the countless hours she'd spied on him and other young people in the village through her telescope. She could tell by the way others congregated around him that he was popular and athletic, but she didn't know his name until that afternoon when he found her while hunting for rabbits. She tried not to cry when she confessed she was lost.

"You're not lost anymore," Alex said with easy confidence. His smile felt like a sunbeam, and she fell a little in love with him in that moment.

From that day, they began meeting secretly in the woods whenever Bruce was away on business. She loved the way Alex talked about his family, which was the complete opposite of hers. He came from a rowdy and boisterous family that he adored. They were loud, passionate people who took delight in simple things like a game of darts or the annual apple harvest. She confessed terrible secrets about her own family that should never have been told, but she trusted him, and it felt good to finally confide in someone. All her life she'd been terribly isolated, and the chance to have a friend was irresistible.

That first summer had been thrilling as they secretly met behind the old cider mill. He taught her how to swim and smuggled books to her from the Duval Springs library. *Treasure Island*, *The Count of Monte Cristo*, *Robin Hood*—he introduced her to the great swashbuckling novels of the ages, and together they let their imaginations soar. More than anything else, Alex taught her to be brave. His indefatigable confidence rubbed off on the sheltered girl who never felt worthy.

Their relationship caught fire the next summer when she was sixteen and Alex turned eighteen. Back then Eloise didn't realize that little good could come from a boy and a girl who had lots of time and complete privacy as they huddled behind the crumbling stone walls of the mill.

Eloise dragged her attention back to the present as Claude proceeded to lay out the timetable for their mission.

"I want our work completed by the last day of December," he said. "We'll return to the city while the residents clear out of town, then go back in May to begin demolition."

The rest of the meeting outlined the steps necessary to evaluate the structural components of each building to be dismantled. It took hours to thrash out the plan, and it was late by the time Eloise returned to her desk. Everyone else in the accounting division had gone home for the evening, but she still had reports to file. The clatter of her adding machine echoed in the nearly empty room, and she was startled when Fletcher approached.

He set a slim blue box on her desk. "For your troubles," he said simply. "An advance token of thanks for the coming hardship."

They were alone in the office. Had he deliberately waited until they would have privacy? Fletcher was so straight-laced that he squeaked when he walked, so she wouldn't jump to any conclusions, but the box came from Tiffany.

Inside was a lovely silver pen and a matching letter opener. Hardly a token! The silver was embellished with elegant swirls of vines, the work of a master craftsman.

"I'm not certain I should accept such a gift," she said a little breathlessly.

"You can't accept office supplies?"

"Is *that* what they are?" A pause stretched between them for the space of a dozen heartbeats.

"If that's all you want them to be."

He hadn't moved a muscle, and yet she sensed that he had just tossed a ball into her court. It was buried under a layer of starch, but she liked his reserved formality. A gentleman seeking to court a woman offered a token of affection and hoped she accepted it. He would never bodily toss her into a lake because it was past time she learned to swim. He would never dare her to climb a tree to see what a woodpecker's nest looked like, or tug her down onto the grass and kiss her until they were both breathless.

She ran a finger along the silver vines. Accepting a gift of this magnitude would mean something. "Thank you," she said in a voice that mirrored his own reserved tone. "It's very generous of you."

Fletcher's face grew somber. "A word of advice," he said quietly. "Keep your dealings with the people in Duval Springs to a minimum. They are incensed, and it's an emotional quagmire in the valley. Rely on the formula for determining the value of their property. The moment you stray from it, they will bombard you with sentimental appeals that will be needlessly difficult for all sides. I know you to be a woman of sound logic. I wouldn't be sending you otherwise."

The mild praise from a man as reserved as Fletcher gave her a thrill she kept carefully hidden. The next four months would be challenging, and she must never forget that Alex Duval was her past but Fletcher Jones might be her future.

The only sound Alex Duval heard as he strolled up Mountainside Road was the breeze rustling through the oak and maple trees. The deep forest lining both sides of the road made it seem like a pristine, long-forgotten paradise.

It wasn't.

As mayor of Duval Springs, Alex had been summoned up here over the latest incident of sabotage to mar the valley. He rounded a bend and spotted a tractor tilted at a haphazard angle in a freshly dug trench. Half a dozen men stood by the side of the road, but Alex focused only on Bruce Garrett, the richest man in the valley and the only enemy he had in the world.

"A little mishap?" he asked cheerfully as he approached the group. If the glare in Garrett's eyes carried actual heat, Alex would have burst into flames, but he was no longer afraid of Bruce Garrett. The quarry owner once got the better of him, but twelve years, a battlefield commission, and the crucible of the Spanish-American War had taught Alex how to stand up to bullies.

Sheriff Dawson from the nearby town of Kingston stepped forward. "Thanks for coming up, Mayor Duval," he said. "We've got quite a mess on our hands."

"So I see." The trench was only a few feet deep, but the tractor had gone in headfirst during the predawn accident and was still stuck.

"That ditch is man-made," Garrett said. "This is sabotage, and it ruined a six-thousand-dollar tractor. Someone in your town did it, and your people are going to pay for it."

"You don't have any proof of that," Alex said in a casual tone that masked his concern. Garrett was a well-hated man in the valley, and someone from Duval Springs might have done it. The only people who used this stretch of road were workers from Garrett's quarry and some lumberjacks hired by the state to start clearing land for a work camp to house the thousands of construction workers expected to move into the valley soon. Both the quarry and the work camp were wildly unpopular.

"I don't have eyewitnesses because it was done in the middle of the night," Garrett said. "When my crew left yesterday, this road was in good shape. That trench happened overnight and was covered with pine boughs. It was sabotage."

The sheriff turned to Alex. "Mayor Duval? It wouldn't be the first time someone from your town sought a little rough justice from Mr. Garrett."

"That ended five years ago," Alex said. "As soon as the strike was settled, those minor disruptions came to an end."

They'd hardly been minor. The strike had been a ten-month standoff between Garrett and the workforce he treated like peasants. Alex led the charge, and the strike was finally settled in the workers' favor. It was Alex's leadership of the strike that earned him his election as mayor.

"Somebody from your town did this," Garrett snapped. "Now I have to order a crew of men to beat this road back into shape."

"But you're so good at ordering men to beat your problems."

The insult flew past everyone except Bruce Garrett, on whom it was a direct hit. Alex had plenty of reasons to despise Garrett.

His arrogance. His skinflint business practices. But mostly, he hated Garrett because of Eloise Drake.

His summers with Eloise seemed like another lifetime. A better, more innocent life. At first his attraction to her had been the thrill of the forbidden, but soon it was simply the thrill of *Eloise*. She was unlike anyone he'd ever met. Brilliant, book smart, but strangely unworldly and shy. Her adoration made Alex feel ten feet tall. Their love had been a shining beacon of light, but Garrett trampled on it, making it seem seedy and shameful.

The worst thing was that after all these years, Alex couldn't quite recall Eloise's face anymore, only the way she made him feel—like he'd captured a ray of sunlight that lit his whole world. Those summers were a time of innocence and joy, but they slipped a little further away with each passing year.

"At this point, it doesn't matter who did it. You've got to get that tractor out of the middle of the road," the sheriff said. "The lumberjacks plan on hauling out timber tomorrow, and this pass needs to be clear."

"The lumberjacks can cool it," Theodore Riesel said. "This road can't be repaired that fast for heavy use. It would be a safety hazard." Dressed in a dapper three-piece suit, Riesel looked out of place amid the others gathered on the mountain. His thirty-year-old son, Jack, stood beside him, looking equally formal except for the peppermint stick dangling from his mouth, which gave him a friendly, lackadaisical air. The Riesels owned the cement factory that processed Garrett's limestone, and Jack was the only man standing on this mountainside that Alex trusted.

Jack took the peppermint stick from his mouth. "What I don't understand is why the state is spending so much money on another work camp. The Kingston Work Camp is perfectly good and already in operation. Why build another?"

Alex agreed. All this construction was the result of the coming reservoir, which would move thousands of city workers to this remote rural valley. The Kingston Work Camp was built to house two thousand laborers, but the state had just announced they wanted a second camp outside of Duval Springs. Lumberjacks had been clearing the land for the new Timberland camp all week, and soon construction crews would arrive to erect the dormitories.

Jack paced the ground before the ruined tractor. "Planting a second camp so close to Duval Springs is waving a cape in front of an angry bull. If the state stops construction on the Timberland camp, I'll bet this pointless vandalism will stop. We all know someone from Duval Springs probably did this," he said with a sympathetic glance at Alex.

Throughout the lawsuit to stop the reservoir, Jack had been a surprising ally. He showed up to every court hearing to lend his support, even though his family's property lay well above the flow line. Most of the people who lived above the flow line thanked their lucky stars to have escaped the looming demolition, so Jack's support was rare and welcome.

Alex rubbed at the tension gathering in his forehead. He'd spent the past five years in a lawsuit to spare his town and had emerged tired, beaten, and demoralized. His final act as mayor was going to be closing down the town he loved. It was a job he never wanted, but he couldn't turn it over to anyone else. He loved this place too much to abandon it during its final days.

Soon his valley would swarm with thousands of outsiders. The lumberjacks had already moved into the historic hotel where Alex lived. They dragged in mud and left cigarette butts everywhere. And more workers were on the way. A team of businesspeople were coming this weekend, and he resented them even more than the lumberjacks. At least the loggers were hardworking people who sweat for every dollar they earned, not like the pampered office workers.

"Mayor Duval?" the sheriff asked. "Do you have any recommendations for getting this tractor removed and repaired?"

"Ask the state to get it out," he replied. "Let's see how much they care about anyone or anything in this valley."

He turned to start walking home, savoring the breeze and the first hints of yellow and scarlet tingeing the forest canopy. This would be his last autumn in the valley. To the outside world, he projected confident bravado, but in the quiet chambers of his mind, he mourned another good-bye. It seemed each day brought another "last." His last apple harvest, the last opening day of school.

Jack pulled up alongside him, joining him on the walk. "I'm sorry they dragged you up here to deal with state business."

Alex smiled and gave Jack's shoulder a quick affectionate clap. They'd become friends over the past few years, which was a surprise after the acrimony of the strike. Jack had been the company's chief enforcer and had hired a crew of strikebreakers, which had inflamed the valley. Yet after the conflict was over, Jack had been the first to extend a hand of friendship to anyone on the other side ready to accept it. Most hadn't, but Alex had.

"Sometimes I wish it were possible to turn the clock back to a time when the rest of the world didn't know this valley existed," Alex said.

Jack nodded. "I know it's cold comfort for you and everyone else in Duval Springs, but you've got my sympathy. I can't speak for Garrett's quarry, but I'll do my best to find work for anyone who needs a job after the town is gone."

"Thanks, Jack," Alex said as they continued walking. He didn't know what he would do after Duval Springs was gone. Closing down the town took all of his attention and energy.

All right, that wasn't really true. He just didn't *want* to think about it. The coming year would be a long and painful slog ending in the destruction of the town that was part of his soul. Thousands of outsiders would descend, each delivering their own special torment as they cleared forests, burned down homes, and evicted people who'd lived here for generations. The lumberjacks were merely the first wave. Next came a team of businesspeople to start planning the demolition.

The outsiders were on their way, and Alex would be waiting for them.

Alex worked late in his town hall office, for the lumberjacks at the hotel meant it was rowdy in the evenings. Living in a hotel wasn't ideal, but Alex had moved there six years ago after his brother's fourth child was born. It was too cramped for Alex to continue living in the family home over the tavern, so he moved into a room on the fourth floor of the historic Gilmore Inn, the landmark building in Duval Springs.

It was after dark when Alex headed back to the hotel, but a light still burned in the schoolhouse. That was odd. There was no cause for anyone to be in the building this late on a Friday night, and it worried him. The recent spate of vandalism had him on alert, and he slid alongside the building to peek inside the illuminated window.

It was only Marie Trudeau, the French teacher, still working at her desk. As mayor, Alex had keys to all the public buildings in town, so he let himself into the building and walked to her classroom. Mrs. Trudeau had been his favorite teacher when he was in school. She was *everyone's* favorite teacher, and he didn't like to see her toiling away so late.

"Please don't tell me you're still working," he said as he stepped inside the classroom.

She sighed as she closed her book. "My Latin is not what it used to be. I need to study each evening to keep ahead of the students."

He could only offer a pained smile. Last month their Latin teacher had left for a new position in Albany. People had been leaving town ever since Duval Springs lost its final appeal, and it was becoming a problem for the school. They no longer had a Latin, chemistry, or arithmetic teacher. Other teachers helped with the lower-level classes, but three students were aiming for college next year, and they needed a Latin teacher.

Mrs. Trudeau had stepped up to the plate. She never asked for a raise in salary or relief from her other duties. She rolled up her sleeves, stayed late, and got the job done. This nation was built on the tireless work of mild-mannered, middle-aged women like Marie Trudeau.

"I'm grateful to you for hanging in with us," Alex said.

A spray of wrinkles fanned out from her eyes as she sent him a sad smile. "After all this town has done for me? I will be loyal to the people of Duval Springs for as long as they need me. I know this isn't how either one of us wanted to end our time here, but I will be steadfast until the last hour of the last day."

He glanced away so she wouldn't see the sheen in his eyes. With all his heart he loved this place, and what an irony that his last act as mayor would be to dismantle the town. But he wouldn't have it any other way. The task should be done by someone who cared, not a faceless bureaucrat sent in by the state. His ancestors had founded this town two hundred years ago, and he would be the one to lead the exodus out.

There were eight more months until the end, and he would savor every day. It promised to be a hard, bittersweet time, but there would be joy as well.

"Hercules is hosting a send-off chicken dinner at the tavern tonight," he said. "Will you come? My treat."

Mrs. Trudeau seemed shocked. "Who is joining the army?"

"Vincent Gallagher. He always planned to inherit his father's sawmill, but that obviously can't happen. He's joining the army instead and will be off for Cuba soon."

And a send-off chicken dinner was a tradition in Duval Springs for any man shipping off to war. It had begun during the French and Indian War, when nine young men were treated to a farewell chicken dinner. At the end of the night, each man wrote his initials on the wishbone from his chicken, then hung it on the scrollwork railing behind the bar. That night set a precedent. The bone would stay on the rail until the soldier returned to take it down.

Tonight, it would be Vincent Gallagher's turn to place his wishbone alongside others from the American Revolution, the War of 1812, the Civil War, and dozens of other skirmishes. During times of war, the scrollwork was always heavily strewn with wishbones as the sons of Duval Springs left for duty. Most bones were claimed when the soldiers returned to a raucous celebration hosted at the tavern, but not all. Dozens still remained, each one representing a soldier who never came home. It was an odd memorial to their fallen soldiers, but a fitting one.

"Close up your books and come to the tavern," Alex urged. "This is likely the last chicken dinner send-off we'll ever have." Another *last*.

Mrs. Trudeau took his arm, and they headed toward the tavern, where friends and family of Vincent Gallagher had already gathered.

The tavern was lively as Alex and Mrs. Trudeau stepped inside, the atmosphere an odd combination of festivity, nostalgia, and sorrow. In the past five years, the people of this valley had grown tightly knit as they fought to save their land from the state's seizure. Now that the battle had been lost, it seemed each evening in the tavern carried a special sentimentality as people began moving away, the town's numbers dwindling a little more each month.

"Hey, Alex," someone in the back of the tavern bellowed. "Have you got a new chemistry teacher for the school?"

Since he had become mayor, people regularly brought up town business whenever Alex arrived at the tavern, but now wasn't the time. "This is Vincent's night, Elmer."

"But it's my boy's senior year, and he needs to get into college. And he's not the only one. What about your nephew?"

"Don't worry," Alex vowed. "No kid in this town will be held back for want of a chemistry class."

"Or a Latin class," Mrs. Trudeau added.

From behind the bar, his brother Hercules slammed down his mug. "My son is going to college next year," he vowed. "He's had a picture of the Harvard campus on his bedroom wall since he was twelve years old. I gave all my kids nice, normal names—John, Bill, Mark, and James. That way they can go wherever they want in this world without having to lug around a ridiculous name like Hercules. Good names for good kids! John Duval is going to be the first boy in the Duval family to go to college. That's *one* dream the state can't seize."

A few of the men gave hearty cheers of endorsement, but the applause tapered off as Sally, Hercules's wife, came out of the kitchen with a platter of roasted chicken surrounded by potatoes and vegetables. The platter masked her huge belly, for Sally was due to deliver her fifth baby soon.

"Where's the man of the hour?" she asked. It was a rhetorical question, for Vincent Gallagher sat at the center table in the chair of honor, surrounded by his family.

"I'm not going to be able to eat this whole chicken," Vincent said as the platter was laid before him.

"Make a dent," someone hollered from the back.

"Please eat," Vincent's mother coaxed, looking on the verge of tears.

At least the active fighting was over, but American troops

were headed back to Cuba for a second occupation after the government they installed following the Spanish-American War collapsed. Alex disapproved, for memories of sweltering in Cuba were still with him.

Would he have become the man he was today without his service in Cuba? He'd been a beaten, penniless kid when he joined the army, but the service taught him to be a man. What an irony that in banishing him from the valley, Bruce Garrett drove Alex toward the ultimate proving ground. Cuba and the army turned Alex into a leader so he could return home and stand up against his archenemy.

After dinner Alex stood on the seat of a chair and raised his mug. "A toast to Vincent Gallagher," he called out.

It took a moment for the crowd to settle down, but soon every eye in the tavern was on him. He cleared his throat and settled his nerves, for he got ridiculously sentimental over good-byes. He and Hercules could both be real watering pots during farewells.

"Vincent, we are proud to call you a son of Duval Springs," he said firmly. "I wish I could say the next years are going to be easy, but sometimes it's the hard things in life that make us great. The army will demand nerves of steel and a heart of gold, but you are about to join a brotherhood. War takes a man places no one else can follow, but we"—he nodded to the other veterans in the tavern, Dr. Lloyd, Dick Brookmeyer, and two of the quarrymen—"*we* understand, and we're going to be pulling for you. And we'll be waiting to welcome you home. Now go hang up that wishbone!"

There was plenty of foot-stamping and calls of approval, but a quiet voice sneered just behind Alex's shoulder. "So says the war hero who single-handedly won Cuba."

Alex let the insult glance off his back. The rivalry between him and Oscar Ott went back to their childhood when Alex had hidden Oscar's slingshot so he couldn't use it to torment stray cats. Oscar retaliated by planting stolen licorice sticks in Alex's schoolbag in a failed attempt to frame him for theft. Oscar was now an accountant for the Riesel Cement factory, but his resentment of Alex still smoldered.

For the millionth time, Alex wondered if it was Oscar who had snitched on him and Eloise all those years ago. It would be in character with Oscar's bone-deep resentment of anything Alex valued or accomplished in life.

Could Oscar have been behind the trench dug into Mountainside Road? If so, he'd probably try to frame Alex for it. Someone in the valley was out to cause trouble, and that person was willing to play dirty.

Alex needed to be on guard.

Eloise selected her wardrobe for the four-month assignment with care. The prospect of heading into Duval Springs was daunting, and she laid out her clothing like a soldier preparing for battle. She draped gowns, blouses, petticoats, and walking suits over every available surface in her apartment while her maid watched from the corner. Tasha Sokolov was a terrible maid but a welcome companion. For the most part, Tasha sat on a padded footstool and bounced baby Ilya on her knee while Eloise did the packing.

Tasha had arrived from Russia with no family, no husband, and no money, only a baby in her womb. *There but for the grace of God go I*, Eloise thought the first time she saw Tasha huddled outside a soup kitchen. Eloise brought Tasha home that very evening and gave her a job, and the young woman had been here ever since.

"Don't take the brown coat. Too boring," Tasha said in her heavily accented voice. "You must take the red one."

Eloise's crimson wool cloak with fur trim was warmer but

would look wildly out of place in a rural village. Her many years of peering down into the village had showed prosperous but plainly dressed people, nothing like the extravagant frills indulged in by the ladies of Manhattan. But Eloise enjoyed being finely turned out and added the scarlet cloak to the stack of things to take.

So far, she'd selected three tailored suits, four walking gowns, and an assortment of blouses with coordinating skirts in serge and wool. Then there were matching boots, scarves, and gloves. She had become a lady of consequence and wanted the world to see it.

The one thing she wouldn't take to Duval Springs was Tasha. It was probably time for Tasha to have Ilya on her own for a while, because Eloise had grown far too attached to the baby.

"Have you told the landlord you are leaving?" Tasha asked as she lifted the fussy baby higher on her shoulder. Little Ilya had been teething for days, and little pleased him.

"Yes, of course," Eloise responded. "I've already paid the rent through December, so you should have no difficulties."

"You must also pay the gas bill before you leave," Tasha said. "It will be cold by December."

"I've already taken care of it."

Tasha's smile was serene as she went back to rocking the baby. Eloise hated to acknowledge it, but Tasha had only become her friend because the work was minimal and Eloise paid well. It would be nice if she could develop friendships like other people, but it had never been easy for her.

Soon Ilya's whimpers morphed into wails. Tasha sighed and rocked him harder.

"Here, I'll take him," Eloise said, reaching out for the baby. Tasha handed him over without complaint, and Ilya immediately stopped crying.

"Sometimes I think he loves you more than me," Tasha said a little wistfully.

"Nonsense," Eloise said, even though it was probably true. She had been a part of Ilya's life since the hour he was born and had lavished adoration on him. Still, she wished that his lungs weren't quite so healthy. Did all teething babies suffer this terribly?

"I'll get some whiskey to rub on his gums."

Eloise gasped. "You can't give whiskey to a baby!" She turned away, adopting the pacing motion that seemed to give Ilya the most comfort. She would leave for Duval Springs in the morning and already missed the chance to soothe the baby.

"A little whiskey never hurt a baby," Tasha said. "In Russia my parents pickled potatoes in vodka and gave them to teething babies to suck. It can keep a baby happy for hours."

How different Eloise's childhood had been. Her first home had been a sprawling country mansion with thirty rooms and endless hallways and corridors, but no children to play with. She had been born late in her parents' marriage, and they never wanted anything to do with her. It was a lonely, isolated world. She amused herself by racing down the long hallways, stomping to hear the echoes reverberating through the vacant corridors. Eventually her father would emerge from his study and tell her to be quiet. *"Go back to your room, little cuckoo bird,"* he would say.

Back then she had loved it when he called her a cuckoo bird, for he'd always been so frosty, and she was thrilled he'd found a pet name for her. When she grew older, she learned that the cuckoo was a tricky creature that snuck into an unsuspecting bird's nest to lay its egg, then flew away, leaving the chick to be raised by someone else. It was a cruelly appropriate nickname for her, as she later learned that Thomas Drake had no role in her conception. Bruce Garrett was her real father, although to this day he insisted she was merely his ward.

The baby's wail shattered the old memories, and she resumed her rocking pace, patting Ilya's back.

"Shh, my precious boy," she crooned. "You are my brave Galahad, my Ivanhoe, my d'Artagnan."

"Who are those crazy names?" Tasha asked.

"Just some characters from novels." They were her heroes. Those swashbuckling adventure stories would always hold a place in her heart. How she loved those stories! Though they were wild, improbable, and completely unmoored from reality, she still escaped into an adventure novel every night. But in the morning she put on a starched collar, sharpened her pencils, and opened her financial ledgers.

The life of an accountant suited her down to the ground. It was a safe profession guided by strict rules and regulations that made perfect sense. Rules were like a trellis that supported a fast-growing vine, letting her thrive and find success in the world.

Tasha looked at the Tiffany box with the silver pen inside. "What about this fancy pen? Will you take it too?"

The Tiffany box was so plain, but it carried a world of meaning. Fletcher Jones was the complete opposite of Alex Duval's wild-hearted zeal for life. Even his characterization of the "office supplies" was typically understated and sedate.

"Yes, I'll take the pen."

The lovely, elegant pen would be a reminder of what she was fighting for. She wanted a baby of her own. It was time. And Fletcher Jones had the potential to be precisely the sort of stable, dependable man who would be an excellent father. All she had to do was survive the next four months in Duval Springs, and then she could return to her safe world of rules, regulations, and respectability.

*E*loise hadn't wanted to go to Duval Springs, so the surge of anticipation she felt as the carriage pulled into the center of town took her by surprise. How many years had she studied this town through the lens of that telescope? It was a place she secretly believed she had always belonged, and now at last she was here.

All four members of the demolition team were squeezed into a small carriage, but Eloise gazed out the window with delight as they rolled into the town square. A manicured lawn featuring a copper-topped bandstand was bordered by streets filled with shops, cafés, and a few homes so quaint that the people who lived inside simply had to be happy. The carriage drew to a halt before the Gilmore Inn, where they would stay for the duration of their assignment.

"Come along," Claude ordered in an impatient voice. "As soon as we've stowed our bags, we can start evaluating the town. We can still squeeze in a few hours of work."

"But it's Saturday," Roy Winthrop, their land surveyor, said.

"Yes, the first of many we'll be spending in this backwater town. Don't plan on a five-day workweek while we're here. The sooner we accomplish our task, the sooner we can get back to civilization."

"You haven't seen civilization until you've seen Rome, my friend." Enzo Accardi was the team's junior explosives expert. His thick Italian accent and cheerful demeanor made Eloise grateful for his company, even though the more Enzo smiled, the more it seemed to annoy Claude.

Bickering between Claude and Enzo commenced, but Eloise was too entranced by Duval Springs to pay attention. It was as though she'd stepped into the pages of a picture book she had learned by heart, for it was just as she remembered. Prosperous shops lined the streets, neatly groomed flower boxes brimmed with chrysanthemums, and the storefront windows sparkled in the sunlight. There was a library on one corner. She still had one of their books. Alex had once loaned her the library's copy of *Treasure Island*, and she still had it on that terrible day Bruce discovered them.

This town felt like home. It was a shame it was going to be dismantled, but oh, how lucky she was to finally see it. Its days were numbered, but she would touch, smell, and experience everything this idyllic town had to offer before it vanished.

"Miss Drake!"

The shout interrupted her reverie. Claude stood in the doorway of the hotel, beckoning her inside. The Gilmore Inn's four stories of white balconies made it look like a wedding cake when she gazed at it from afar. She had always wondered what it looked like inside, and now she was about to find out.

The spacious lobby featured an oriental carpet and lots of ferns in brass planters. Fine wood molding and wainscoting covered the walls, and mounted behind the counter was a charming clock that looked like a miniature Swiss chalet. Nobody manned the front counter, but an arched doorway led into a dining area crowded with rough-looking men and a waitress busily filling coffee cups and clearing plates.

Oddly, a well-dressed man slumbered on a padded bench in the lobby, a homburg balanced over his face. A gold watch chain dangled from his vest, but before Eloise got a better look, the clock above the front counter began chiming the hour. A flap on the clock swung open, and out popped a cuckoo. The screech of cuckoo calls interspersed with chimes made her wince. Would she ever outgrow those old childhood wounds?

The clock roused the slumbering man, who lifted the hat from his face as he slowly unpeeled himself from the bench into a sitting position.

"Someday I'd like to shoot that bird," he mumbled.

"Fine, but we need to check in," Claude told him. "We've got four rooms reserved."

The gangly man looked a little amused but made no effort to rise from the bench. "You'll have to speak with the manager for that. I only run the telegraph station."

Sure enough, he wore a nametag identifying him as Kasper Nagy, operator for Western Union. He was whip thin but handsome, with twinkling blue eyes and a healthy head of blond hair—unusual in a man who looked at least fifty years old. Unbelievably, he gracefully lay back down on the bench and replaced the hat over his face.

Claude wouldn't tolerate it. He banged the call bell on the front desk repeatedly, but no one came. Perhaps the hotel was understaffed, for despite its charm, mud trailed across the floors, and the ashtrays could use emptying.

Finally, the waitress from the dining room made her way to the lobby.

"We need someone to check us in, and *that man* is completely useless," Claude said.

"I'm afraid you're right about that," the waitress said with a gentle laugh as she consulted a ledger on the counter. "It looks like we weren't expecting you until this afternoon, but not to worry. Mr. Gilmore is just down the street at the tavern, if you want to go fetch him. He can check you in."

Before Claude could reply, the waitress disappeared into the kitchen. "What a fine, professional operation this is," he grumbled.

The man on the bench lifted his hat a few inches. "It's Saturday. Everyone heads over to the tavern on Saturdays."

"Let's go," Enzo said cheerfully. "I could use a mug of something after the dust of the road."

The carriage driver agreed to wait with their luggage as they set off for the tavern only a block away. Claude and Enzo started analyzing buildings as they strolled. Some of the buildings would be burned, some knocked down by bulldozer, and others would be dynamited. Claude suspected the tavern would be one of their more complicated jobs. Built of old weathered stone on the first floor, it had an overhanging wooden second story. Above the front door was a placard with ornate lettering: *Duval Tavern & Table, est. 1725.*

"Sledgehammers and a strong back are going to be required to bring this place down," Claude said as he stepped onto the landing before the tavern. "Explosives are too dangerous, as they'll send these rock fragments flying. We'll burn the top floor, but the ground level will be done by sledgehammers."

"Shh," Enzo said with a nod to the tavern's open door. "People inside might overhear."

"So? It's not like they don't know this place is going to be torn down."

Eloise shifted uneasily. This tavern was owned by Alex's older brother, and there was a chance Alex might actually be inside. She'd assumed their first meeting would be in the formality of an office, not a tavern. That complicated things. What would she say to him? He'd probably want to apologize for the way he'd taken advantage of her. Or, if Bruce was right, Alex wouldn't even remember her, for men rarely thought about the notches on their belt.

She tamped down her misgivings and stepped inside the tavern, a little appalled at the rowdy behavior so early in the day. A quick glance around did not reveal Alex, and she breathed a sigh of relief and approached the bartender, a giant of a man. She'd never met a Viking, but this man with his massive build and messy light hair could easily pass as one. She raised her voice to be heard over the din.

"I'd like to speak with the manager of the Gilmore Inn. Is he here?"

Alex concentrated on the heavy mug balanced on the center of his forehead as he leaned farther backward, both arms stretched wide for balance. Onlookers in the tavern roared to distract him, but he was going to win this bet. When he was in the army, he was famous for managing this ridiculously impossible backbend, leaning so far backward that his spine was parallel to the floor. The mug of beer balanced on his forehead added to the challenge, but he was up for it.

"He's even!" his nephew shouted.

"No, sir!" someone said. "He's got two more inches. Look! He's wobbling. That mug's about to spill."

Alex wasn't wobbling, but he wasn't horizontal yet either. Holding his breath, he leaned back another inch. Hearty masculine roars of approval mixed with groans filled the tavern.

Was that a woman's voice? It sounded like some lady asking for Willard Gilmore, but he ignored her as he tried for another inch. The mug tipped, sloshing beer across his face before it smashed to the ground. He toppled backward, slamming to the floor amidst howls of laughter and disappointment.

He grinned as he got to his feet. "Sorry about that, Bill," he said as he shook his nephew's hand.

"That's okay," the boy mumbled, but Alex felt bad for letting the kid down. All around him money was trading hands, and he'd be making plenty of apologies tonight.

He squinted to see what had caused the distraction at the front of the tavern, and it wasn't hard to spot her. A snazzy-looking lady gaped at him with an appalled expression on her face. He sent her a helpless shrug, a little embarrassed at his beer-soaked state, but everyone in this town had had a long week and was entitled to a little fun. She was still glaring at him, so he'd better go see what she wanted.

He wended through the crowd toward her, wondering how she could breathe in that wasp-waisted getup. It was dim, and he couldn't see much of her face, but she had piles of pretty red hair mounded on her head.

"Hello, Alex," she said primly.

"Can I help you, ma'am?" For some reason she seemed to be getting madder by the second. "Ma'am? We haven't been introduced. I'm Alex Duval."

Her eyes narrowed, and she looked ready to combust. "Oh, Alex. I think I'm finally seeing the real you, and it's a sad, sorry letdown."

He used the cuff of his shirt to wipe at the beer stinging his eyes, completely befuddled. They'd never met. He would remember hair like that. The last time he saw hair that red—

Recognition dawned, and a blast of delight ricocheted through him. "Eloise?" He lunged forward to grab her arms and pull her toward the window to see better. "Eloise! Is it really you?"

"It's really me."

And he hadn't recognized her. "Welcome back," he managed to stammer, then looked over his shoulder to Hercules, who watched from behind the bar. "It's Eloise Drake."

Hercules stilled. "*The* Eloise?"

"Yes, *the* Eloise," Alex said, turning his attention back to her. Then a terrible thought struck. "It is still Eloise Drake, isn't it?" he asked with a glance at her bare left hand.

"Still Eloise Drake," she confirmed.

He grinned. This was good. This was beyond good, this was *stupendous*. Eloise seemed miffed that it had taken him a minute to recognize her, but she had never dressed like that when they knew each other all those years ago.

"I'm not married either," he said a little breathlessly. Not that she was asking, but he couldn't stop smiling because she was here and she was beautiful and he wished he knew what to say to her. She seemed different.

She cast a chilly look at his nephew. "Perhaps the boy should step outside," she said. "This isn't the healthiest environment for a youngster."

He followed her gaze. Bill was trying to imitate his ridiculous backbend and not making much progress. "Oh, that's just my nephew, Bill. Don't worry, he's used to seeing crazy things."

"And how old is Bill?"

"Hey, Bill," Alex hollered across the tavern. "How old are you, lad?"

The boy straightened. "Fourteen!"

Alex turned back to Eloise. "He's fourteen, but more like forty. He's been helping at the tavern since he could walk. I've never seen a kid so eager to earn a buck."

"Gambling, betting, and drinking—all before lunchtime," she said in an artificially bright voice. She'd always been a lot fussier about the rules than he was, and it looked like that trait had grown with age.

"So what brings you to town?" he asked, keeping his voice pleasant.

44

"I'm looking for the manager of the Gilmore Inn. I understand he can be found here."

She sounded frosty, but maybe she was only nervous. Her sudden reappearance certainly made *him* nervous, but thrilled too. He kept his gaze locked on her as he shouted over his shoulder. "Willard? A lady wants to see you." He swallowed, both flustered and delighted. "I never thought I'd see you again. Whatever brings you back to the valley . . . I'm glad. Really glad."

Willard tore himself away from the dartboard. At least Eloise couldn't disapprove of Willard Gilmore, with his starched bow tie and handlebar mustache that was perfectly waxed and curled. He still carried a handful of darts from the game he'd been playing. "Ma'am?"

Eloise kept using that prim voice. "My supervisor has reserved four rooms at your hotel, and we would like to check in."

"We weren't expecting you until this evening, but I can check you in early."

She was staying in town? This was getting better and better. Maybe he'd have a stab at winning her back, or at least learning where she had disappeared to all those years ago.

Before he could say anything, a group of men entered the tavern, deep in conversation. They were all strangers, but the oldest scrutinized the underside of the balcony that circled the interior of the tavern, pointing out features to a younger man beside him.

"Those cantilevered brackets need to come down first," he said. "Then we take down the secondary beams. The load-bearing walls come last."

"Let's speak about this later, shall we?" Eloise said. It was obvious she knew them, and a cold feeling settled in the pit of Alex's belly.

"No, let's speak about this now," Hercules demanded from behind the bar. "Did I just hear you talking about how to tear down this tavern? Who are you people?"

The older man drew himself up to his full height. "My name is Claude Fitzgerald, and I am leading the demolition team charged with safely dismembering this conglomeration of rock and timber. It's going to be a monster of a job."

Behind the bar, Hercules slammed down a mug. "Then you can get out of my tavern. You aren't welcome here."

The entire bar fell silent, and the temperature dropped twenty degrees.

"Take it easy, Hercules," Alex said. He didn't want an ugly brawl in front of Eloise. She'd never had a chance to meet his family all those years ago, and he didn't want her seeing them at their worst.

"No, I won't take it easy," Hercules retorted. He planted a foot on the bar, then vaulted over it to land with a thump only a few feet from Claude. "Look at you," Hercules scoffed, flicking at the handkerchief in the older man's suit pocket. "City-slicker shoes and that prissy silk handkerchief. Walking in here like you own the place."

Claude tugged his vest down. "Keep your hands to yourself. Touching me is considered battery, and you can be prosecuted for it."

"Why don't you add it to the rest of the demands you trespassers are cramming down our throats?" With his clenched fists, Hercules looked ready for business, and Alex slid forward to separate the two men.

Claude retreated, as did Eloise. A niggle of dread cut through Alex's exhilaration at seeing her again. "Are you *with* these people?" he asked.

"I'm here as an accountant," she said coolly. "I'll be setting the values for the condemned buildings in town."

His confusion vanished, replaced by a searing sense of betrayal. "You're working for *the state*?"

"Yes, I'm working for the state," she said. "I'm also working on behalf of Duval Springs to ensure its citizens are fairly compensated for their inconvenience."

"'Inconvenience,'" he snapped. "Is that the word the state is using for throwing thousands of people off their own land?"

She lifted her chin. "It is for the betterment of all citizens in New York. The fact that a few people will be inconvenienced can't be avoided."

It was only his army training that kept him standing erect after this appalling blow. The old Eloise was gone. The woman before him looked like her but was a stranger.

"I wanted such wonderful things for you," he said in an aching voice. "I thought you'd be a great pianist or a poet or something grand. Not an *accountant*. Not working for the state."

"Another fine reason not to stay in this town," Claude groused. "We gave it our best, Miss Drake, but why should we stay in a place that doesn't want us, lacks all form of common courtesy, and doesn't even have running water or electricity? We'll be better off in Kingston, regardless of the expense."

"Did you expect us to throw rose petals in your path?" Alex directed the question to the surly leader, but Eloise answered.

"As the mayor of this town, I expected you to be sensible and help us," she said. "We are working toward the same goal, even if you find that goal abhorrent."

That scolding tone of hers was starting to grate. She turned to leave the tavern, the three men following, but Alex wasn't going to let her get away. Not again. He darted after the group as they made their way outside.

"I doubt we'll be able to find four rooms on short notice in Kingston," Eloise was telling the other men. "My guardian lives only a few miles from here and has plenty of space."

"You're staying with Garrett?" Alex asked incredulously as he pulled alongside the group.

"Why shouldn't I?" she replied calmly. "He has always been loyal to me."

"Maybe because he had me pounded to a bloody pulp when he found out what we'd been up to behind that old cider mill." He pointed to the crook in his nose. "See that? It's what a broken nose looks like. It has Garrett's signature on it."

She sent a fleeting glance to her coworkers before stepping closer to speak in a furious whisper. "Perhaps you could lower your voice so the entire valley doesn't learn our business."

She was right. The men she came with were already heading back toward their carriage, but a handful of people loitered outside the tavern, listening to every word. Maybe she could control herself and talk like the queen of England, but he actually had a beating heart and a pulse. Eloise hadn't come back to the valley for him. She came because she was bitter and vindictive.

"Is this fun for you? Showing up to help wipe us off the map?" Alex asked.

"Believe it or not, I have a meaningful career entirely free of personal vendettas. Good day, Mayor Duval." She headed toward a carriage across the street, her back stiff with anger, but he couldn't let it go at that.

"Eloise, wait." He grasped her arm, and she looked down at it as though a bug were crawling on her. He let go, dumbfounded. "What's happened to you?" he whispered.

"I grew up. I no longer run around behind people's backs. I don't break the rules. I'm sorry that seems to be a disappointment to you."

The other men boarded the carriage, and she followed. He stood, poleaxed as she walked away without a backward glance. Even after the carriage started moving and the wheels kicked up dust in his face, he couldn't move.

The weight of sorrow hit him hard. It was foolish to believe he could ever recapture those two summers, but this hurt. He was aghast at Eloise's chilly transformation, but he shouldn't have spilled their personal business in public. Willard and a few others still lingered on the tavern steps, and he closed the distance quickly.

"Willard, forget what I just said about me and Eloise behind the old cider mill, all right?"

The older man looked amused. "It's not exactly a state secret, Alex."

"Yeah, but it happened a long time ago, and she probably wouldn't want that old gossip stirred up again." Alex swiped a lock of hair off his forehead. Wet, beer-soaked hair from indulging in a stupid bet. Of all the times for Eloise to come waltzing back into his life!

Willard chuckled a little but nodded. "Sure, Alex. I didn't hear anything, didn't see anything."

Alex lived on the top floor of Willard's hotel, and the man was like a second father to him. He had no doubt Willard would keep mum, but he wasn't so sure about the other two men watching from the bench outside the tavern.

"You didn't hear anything either," he ordered them.

"Not a word," one said.

"I don't know anything about you and that girl from Garrett's mansion everyone was talking about all those years ago," the other said. "Marie Trudeau just left, but she probably didn't hear anything either."

Alex blanched. Having his favorite teacher overhear tales of his youthful escapades was like being caught out by his own mother. A glance down the street showed Mrs. Trudeau heading to her tiny saltbox house only two blocks away from the tavern. In five bounding steps, he was at her side.

"Mrs. Trudeau?" he implored. "Rumor has it you heard me shooting my mouth off about some girl I once knew. Please, if you could keep that quiet, I'll be forever in your debt."

She placed a gentle hand on his arm. "You need say no more, Alex," she said in her softly accented voice. His old French teacher had been in this country for almost thirty years but still had that lilting accent. "Of course I won't say anything. I am curious though. . . ."

"Yeah?" He braced himself. He adored Mrs. Trudeau and could deny her nothing.

"I always wondered why you never married. Is she the reason?"

"Don't read too much into it," he said with a shrug. "I got over her a long time ago."

Kind of. For years he had been frantic. After joining the army, he bombarded Hercules with letters, begging him to prowl around the Garrett estate, looking for signs of Eloise. Hercules was friends with the stable guy up at the mansion, who reported that Eloise was nowhere to be found. Alex used his first leave from the army to go to her fancy boarding school in Boston. He'd spent every dime he had bribing a few of the school employees for insight about what happened to her. All they could tell him was that she never returned to school after that fateful summer.

It seemed Eloise had vanished from the face of the earth. Having given up trying to find her, he concluded the best thing would be to let *her* find *him*. Even though he'd earned a battlefield commission and had a bright future in the army, he cut his military career short and returned to the valley. Battle-hardened by service in the Spanish-American War and tested through experience, he was no longer intimidated by Bruce Garrett. He led the strike, ran for mayor, and took out an announcement in every newspaper in New England to publicize his presence.

It seemed she didn't want to find him. At first he'd been miffed when she never tried to track him down. Then angry. Then he was merely bewildered about what had happened to the girl of his dreams.

Now he knew. She had become an ice princess.

Rather than gamble on their ability to find a hotel in Kingston, Eloise convinced the group to follow her to Bruce's house. The mansion where she had spent her childhood summers was only three miles away, and Bruce always told her she was welcome anytime. She'd been working as his accountant for years, and they were closer than they'd ever been, so she didn't feel too guilty leaning on his hospitality. He had probably never expected her to bring along three coworkers, but Bruce despised Alex and would gladly open his home if it meant keeping her away from Duval Springs.

The journey up the mountain was bumpy and tense. She clenched her teeth as she stole a glance at Claude and the others in the carriage. Had they heard Alex's reference to what they had done behind that old cider mill? Gossip like that could get back to Fletcher, an upright man who believed her to be a respectable woman. Not some foolish girl who gave everything to a boy in exchange for a little attention.

"I told you staying in Duval Springs was an idiotic idea," Claude growled as the carriage climbed the hillside.

"You're very wise, Claude," she said coolly. "We'll be far more comfortable at the Garrett mansion." It was halfway between Kingston and Duval Springs, plus it had the advantage of being free, which would please Fletcher.

"You seemed to know that man at the inn," Enzo said, politely waiting for a response. Claude and Roy both swiveled toward her, curiosity rampant in their faces. She looked out the window and scrambled for a truthful answer that remained entirely devoid of useful insight.

"I grew up nearby. So did he." She kept her gaze fastened on the towering pines outside the window, refusing to add even another word.

The carriage rounded the last of the hairpin turns, and Bruce's estate came into view. The roughly hewn stone mansion was perched on the side of a cliff and surrounded by wide terraces and towering walls, and it had an actual turret on one end of the house. A dozen smaller outbuildings were scattered behind the estate walls.

Eloise had only been eight years old the first time her mother brought her here one hot July morning. A combination of awe and fear had gripped her as she learned the Garrett mansion was to be her home for the rest of the summer. It looked like somewhere a king or evil wizard might live. Her mother had dropped her off on the front porch, not even accompanying her inside after the housekeeper answered the door. Eloise had to walk into that imposing mansion all alone, totally bewildered by why she had been abandoned here.

She was terrified of Bruce Garrett the first time they met. He was big, gruff, and ill at ease around her. That didn't stop him from insisting she join him at the massive dining table each night for dinner, even though she didn't know how to talk to grown-ups, for her parents mostly ignored her. Actually, she didn't know how to talk to children either, since there were no children at the country estate where she'd spent her first eight years. Bruce, as he insisted she call him, eventually filled the silence by talking about his quarry and how his workers used huge cutting machines to carve slabs of limestone out of the hills. She liked his stories and over time started looking forward to the dinners where she sat, silent as a mouse, and listened to the gruff man talk about his life.

She had never returned home again. During the school year she went to special conservatories because her mother wanted her to master the piano. During holidays and the summer, she went back to the Garrett mansion. She didn't ask why. Her parents had never wanted her underfoot, but when she learned about cuckoos in school and how they foisted their chicks on others to raise, suddenly her father's pet name for her made horrible, perfect sense. She and Bruce had the exact same shade of red hair, while her parents both had glossy black hair. She truly *was* a cuckoo bird, so no wonder her parents didn't want her around when it was so obvious she didn't belong.

The carriage halted before the mansion, and she stepped outside, breathing deeply of the crisp mountain air.

"How do you know Mr. Garrett?" Roy Winthrop asked as he looked at the castle-like fortress in awe.

"He was my guardian growing up," she said simply, a little wounded that Bruce still refused to acknowledge her. While her parents were alive, the charade was understandable, but they had both died within the last year, so now it was just hurtful.

One of Bruce's thickset bodyguards sat on the front stoop, whittling a lump of oak. She'd known Emil Lebenov since childhood, and his bark was usually worse than his bite.

"Weren't expecting to see you today," Emil said in his heavy Bulgarian accent as he continued whittling.

"Can I come in?" she asked.

"It's your lucky day. Riesel just left an hour ago."

Lucky, indeed. Bruce didn't have many rules when she was

growing up, but she'd been taught since childhood that when Theodore Riesel was in the house, she was to make herself scarce. Mr. Riesel owned the cement factory a few miles away, and he and Bruce were business partners. Bruce mined the limestone, and Mr. Riesel turned it into cement.

They were also related by marriage. Bruce had been married to Mr. Riesel's sister, Laura. A month after Laura's death, Eloise was delivered to Bruce's doorstep. At the time, Eloise was never sure why Bruce refused to let Mr. Riesel see her, but it was easy to understand now. Anyone with eyes could see their resemblance. It had been twenty years since Bruce's wife died, but he was still anxious to hide his infidelity from his brother-in-law and business partner.

"Can you tell the cook to expect four more people for dinner?" she asked Emil. "I'm sure it will be all right with Mr. Garrett."

The housekeeper, Mrs. Hofstede, took the others to guest rooms on the second floor while Eloise went in search of Bruce. By the time she reached the gathering room, she could hear him out on the terrace, shouting at one of his employees. Why did he always have to sound so bad-tempered? She crept forward, staying close to the wall as she approached the open French doors to listen in on the conversation. Old Mr. Jake, the man who could fix any of the mechanical equipment at the quarry, was getting a tongue-lashing.

Mr. Jake caught her eye and sent her a wink. Bruce whirled around and spotted her through the open doors.

"Eloise," he said, his voice flustered. "I wasn't expecting you today."

"I have some business to discuss. I can wait until you're finished." Bruce could provide valuable insight into navigating the dicey political situation in the valley. He was canny and shrewd, always thinking two steps ahead, and good at getting the upper hand. Given the demolition team's rocky start in town, they could use his advice.

Bruce dismissed Mr. Jake and beckoned for Eloise to join him on the terrace. From here she could see all the way down to Duval Springs nestled at the bottom of the valley. The moment she explained the situation to him, he almost exploded.

"I don't like the idea of you dabbling in Duval Springs," he said in a growl. "At least take a couple of bodyguards with you when you go into town. Don't roll your eyes at me, young lady! There's been a spate of sabotage lately, and that idiot mayor is nothing but a rabble-rouser. Have you seen him?"

"It's going to be hard to do business in Duval Springs without seeing the mayor."

Bruce clenched the arms of his chair so hard his knuckles went white. "That man is still a disrespectful hothead. He quietly sneers every time he sees me, and it's got nothing to do with the strike. It's all about thumbing his nose at me over you."

"You don't need to worry about Alex. He didn't even recognize me."

Bruce snorted. "I guess he's had so many women over the years that they all blend together."

She tried not to flinch, but the fact that Alex hadn't recognized her gave the accusation a ring of truth.

"Let me send some men down with you," Bruce said. "That hothead won't dare—"

"Was Emil one of the men you had beat up Alex?"

"Who said I had anyone beat him up?"

She sighed. "Please don't insult my intelligence. It would be foolish to inflame the situation by bringing anyone who participated in that incident into already tense circumstances."

"And why is the situation tense?" Bruce demanded. "It's because Duval is leading a campaign of sabotage against me. The whole town is bitter and irrational."

A part of her understood the lingering hostility from the villagers. Bruce and Theodore Riesel ruled over this valley with an iron first. At the time of the strike, they had demanded a sixty-hour workweek from their employees. They paid their workers in scrip that could only be redeemed at a company store. "Company towns" had a bad reputation for exploiting their workers, and under Alex's leadership, the people of Duval Springs revolted and won. After the strike, people worked a forty-hour week and were paid in cash, never scrip.

Alex had won the strike against Bruce but lost the bigger battle with the state. Bruce was probably secretly rejoicing that the demolition of the town would be planned in his own home. He invited Eloise and the rest of the demolition team to join him for dinner as they began the thorny task of deciding how best to empty the village.

The dining room was dominated by a heavy oak table imported from a monastery in Spain. The house had electricity, but Bruce preferred to light the room with dozens of candles, like it was a medieval castle.

Even Claude seemed impressed by the grandeur, but after dinner, he wanted to plan their first week of operations. "Roy will make a geologic assessment of the land, noting all possible sources of contamination. When we flood the valley, the basin needs to be pristine. Enzo and I will survey the buildings that will require dynamite and those that can simply be burned. Eloise, start making appraisals of residential structures and find out when people plan on moving. If we can get them out before May, we can start demolition early."

"Ha!" Bruce retorted. "The mayor has already got a court order saying the state can't touch a single building before May 1."

"But a third of the homes are already vacant," Claude said. "Why should he care if we start demolishing the abandoned buildings?"

"Because he enjoys being a thorn in the government's side," Bruce said. "They're billing the state for putting workers up at their hotels, using their telegraph service, even storing equipment in their empty buildings. They're charging twice the going rate for everything."

Eloise twisted the stem of her goblet as she studied him. "How do you know all this?" Bruce always seemed to know what was going on in the village, and given that he was the least popular man in the valley, he had to have someone on the inside feeding him the information.

"All you need to know is that I'm on your side and the mayor of Duval Springs is not, and he never has been."

Eloise sighed. She didn't want to be the kind of woman who dwelled on the past, but she had to admit that the only constant in her life had been Bruce Garrett. His punishment after discovering her trysts with Alex had been tough but fair. And in the long run, it had made her a better person.

All Alex had done was provide her with a cautionary tale of how life could go wrong. She must never forget that.

The first house Eloise planned to appraise was a modest, single-story clapboard home on the corner of Main and Cherry. She counted the windows and exterior features, noted them on the chart, then mounted the single front step and knocked on the door.

It was answered by a petite woman with fading brown hair and a spray of laugh lines at the corners of her eyes. She held a leather satchel, as though about to leave.

"Can I help you?" she asked with a faintly accented voice.

"You are Marie Trudeau?" Eloise asked.

"Yes."

"My name is Eloise Drake. I'm here on behalf of the state to determine a fair market value for your house. May I come inside?"

The woman's hand flew to her throat. "Oh dear, I did not expect this so soon. But yes, of course you may come in." She paused in the doorway, and Eloise had the feeling that Mrs. Trudeau was about to weep as she bowed her head. "Oh, Alfred," she whispered so softly Eloise could barely hear. "This is the beginning of the end."

Then she stepped aside and held the door wide for Eloise.

"Forgive me," the older woman said. "I came from France thirty years ago, but Duval Springs is the only real home I've ever known. Please make your assessment. I am due at school shortly, but I must know how much I am to receive for the house."

"Do you know what year it was built?"

Marie's brow wrinkled. "I have no idea. My husband was born in this house, and that was in 1845, but I don't know anything beyond that."

"Would your husband know?"

"He passed away eighteen years ago," Marie said. "I have been living in this house since my first year in America. It's hard to imagine that soon it will be no more."

Each word the widow spoke was laden with yearning. It made Eloise wonder what it would be like to have such a profound attachment to a home. Eloise had led an itinerant life as a child and never had the sort of bone-deep love for a place she saw on Marie Trudeau's face.

"I had my babies in this house," Marie continued. "Of course, they are young men now, but sometimes, late at night when I sit by the fire, I can almost hear those long-ago memories, as though they are embedded in the house itself. Alfred's footsteps coming home after a day at the quarry, or the whimpering of the babies. I still like to sit here and remember those sounds. It will be harder to summon those memories once I move to Saratoga."

"That is where you're headed?"

The widow shook herself and came back to the present. "Yes," she said briskly. "I understand prices are higher in the city, so please, make your assessment and let me know how much I can expect."

"It won't take long," Eloise said.

Fletcher's system was stark in its efficiency. As she traveled through the tidy house, she tallied the windows, doorknobs, and flooring material. The old floorboards creaked as she moved from room to room, and since there were only two bedrooms, a compact kitchen, and a front parlor that doubled as a dining room, the assessment didn't take long. In less than five minutes, her work was complete, but she stalled a little. It would seem rude to present the widow with the figure after only five minutes.

"Do your sons still live in Duval Springs?" Eloise asked as she pretended to jot notes at the edges of her form.

"Oh yes. They are quarrymen, just like their father was."

"And do they like working up at the quarry?" Eloise held her breath. She couldn't explain it, but she wanted good things for this soft-spoken lady, and having raised sons who enjoyed their work was important.

"It keeps their pantry full," the widow said. "Mostly they just like living in Duval Springs. We are a family here, no? My husband was sick for two years before he passed, and he could not work. My boys were babies, so I couldn't work either, but the town looked after us. People from the church brought baskets of food every week. Men came and shoveled our walk in the winter, and the doctor donated his services. They did these things for years until I could find my own way. I will be forever grateful."

The conversation stumbled to a halt, and Marie looked curiously at the chart. Eloise could delay no longer.

"The state will offer $2,010 for the house."

The widow gasped. "So little?"

But there could be no doubt. The compact house had no improvements, making it easy to tally the few factors in its favor and arrive at a valuation. Eloise tipped the clipboard so the widow could see.

"The state developed a formula for assessing fair value," she explained. "It is a straightforward mathematical calculation, based on the number of doorknobs and windows, the size of the rooms, and the composition of the materials."

The color dropped from Marie's face, and she sank onto an old chair, her hand clutched over her heart. "Oh, Alfred, how could things ever come to this?" she moaned softly.

Eloise struggled to find some comforting words to say, but she was useless in such situations. When she'd broken down in tears as a child, her father would say, *"Buck up, little cuckoo bird. Life isn't so bad."*

She didn't think such words would be any comfort, but before she could think of anything more useful to say, the thudding of boots and a rap on the door startled her.

"Mrs. Trudeau? Are you in there?" It was Alex's voice.

Marie rose, straightened her collar, and opened the door. "I'm sorry I'm late," she said.

Alex didn't notice Eloise as he stepped inside, concern on his face. He grasped the widow's shoulders. "Is everything all right? You're never late for school."

"I apologize. The state appraiser is here, and I needed to know what I will receive for my house."

Alex finally noticed Eloise standing beside the stove, and the muscles in his face tightened. "Miss Drake," he said. The formality of those two words hurt. He had lain on the grass with her, tickled her, called her Ellie. Now she was Miss Drake.

"Alex," she said with the tiniest of nods.

He turned back to Mrs. Trudeau with a reassuring squeeze of her shoulders. "It's all right. Lettie Cooper came to my office to report you hadn't arrived, and I came right over. Is something wrong? You look upset." His voice was tender, concern radiating from his eyes.

"The price they are offering for my house . . . it's not good." Marie jabbed a finger at the clipboard. "They are using some horrible formula that boils everything down to the number of doorknobs in a house."

Without asking permission, Alex grabbed the clipboard, his face hardening as he skimmed the printed page. "Calculated with all the tender compassion I've come to expect from the state."

"It's a very efficient method," Eloise defended, ignoring the scorn in his voice as he continued reading.

"You think a home's value can be boiled down to its component parts? Why do you care how many doorknobs are in a house?"

"Because an actual door with a closing mechanism connotes a room. Otherwise someone could claim this shared parlor with an archway leading to a dining area counts as two rooms."

"Why shouldn't it?" Marie demanded. "I am standing in the middle of the parlor." She took a large step. "And now I am standing in my dining room. Two rooms!"

The dining nook was not a separate room. This was exactly the sort of quibbling the chart was supposed to solve. Doorknobs were important.

"The formula is a fair way of quickly setting the value for all structures, whether it is a house, a barn, a factory, or a public building. The rules are transparent, and they are fair."

"But this house is less than ten yards from the public pump," Alex pointed out. "That makes it very desirable to people who need to lug water into their homes."

Eloise shook her head. "The chart adds value for installed plumbing, but there is no room in the equation for people who carry their own water."

"But you can see the town's pump is only footsteps from my door," Marie said. "It's what makes this house so valuable. And look at my view of the village green. It is wonderful to sit out on the porch on summer evenings. Over the years, many people have tried to buy me out, but I could never leave the home where my husband was born. Where we raised our children, where I nursed him during those final years that meant so much to us both." Her lower lip began trembling, but she wouldn't stop talking. "This house holds the best and worst of me. It is love and compassion and a thousand nights of laughter and tears. It's more than a collection of doorknobs."

It was impossible to put a price tag on the things Mrs. Trudeau valued. Fletcher was entirely correct in designing a formula to isolate the value of a home from the murky tentacles of emotion.

Eloise spoke as gently as she could. "I hope you sign the form, because otherwise the state has a right to claim you have refused payment, and then you will receive nothing."

Marie's shoulders sagged, but Alex wrapped an arm around her shoulders. "Don't let her push you," he said. "We aren't going to let the state bully us. If you don't agree with the value, we can sue."

"I don't want to sue. I just want to keep my home," Marie exclaimed. "I love it here. I thought I would spend the rest of my life here."

"Shh," Alex murmured.

The gentle warmth in his tone made Eloise flinch. It had been ages since someone had treated her so tenderly. The last person who offered to nurture or protect her had been *Alex*, back during those idyllic days when she wallowed in his unabashed devotion.

"There will be no need for lawsuits," Eloise said briskly. "If you sign the form, you can have your payment within a week."

"Don't listen to her," Alex said, not breaking his gaze with the widow. "She is only the voice of the state, trying to frighten you into giving up your rights. I'll make sure the town's residents are treated fairly. All I need from you is to go teach Latin class and get my nephew fluent enough to pass that Harvard entrance exam."

Marie nodded. "John is a bright lad. I can do that."

Mrs. Trudeau headed to the schoolhouse, and Eloise followed her outside. She was about to approach the next house on the street, but Alex blocked her on the front stoop of the widow's house. He planted his hands on his hips and looked down at her with a stern face.

"Why are you on this team? After all these years, why did you come back to the valley only to tear it down?"

Eloise hugged the clipboard to her chest. "It's not intended as a personal insult, Alex. I needed a job, and this is where they sent me."

He snorted. "You're rich. I heard that your parents died and you inherited a fortune, so you don't need to work."

It was true that she would inherit a tidy sum after her mother's estate was settled, but she didn't work for money. She worked because it was the only thing that gave her a sense of accomplishment. Alex couldn't possibly understand. He had hundreds of friends and a loving family; she had a desk at an accounting office. She'd give her eyeteeth if she could have the sort of easy relationships that seemed to come naturally to Alex, but for now, she would bring this project in on time and under budget. Fletcher depended on it.

"My finances are no concern of yours. You're being very rude. Is this how they taught you to treat women in the army?"

"They taught me to be a leader." There wasn't an ounce of sympathy on his iron face.

"It looks like they taught you to be a bully."

Anger flashed in his eyes. "I survived," he snapped out. "That's surely a disappointment to your loving guardian, but I fought and struggled and survived. I was slogging through the swamps of Cuba while you lounged in the lap of luxury."

She quirked a brow. "Is that what you call a convent in the desert?"

"A *what*?" he gasped. Apparently he knew nothing about what had happened to her after the catastrophic morning Bruce learned of their summer trysts.

"Saint Elspeth's," she said simply. "It was where Bruce sent me after he found out about us. A desert convent in Arizona. Eighteen women, two donkeys, and sixty goats. We made cheese. And prayed." A hint of guilt gnawed at her, because the way she described it made it sound bad, and it wasn't. It was hard, but it wasn't bad.

"A convent?" Alex asked incredulously. "It sounds so medieval."

She considered it. "I suppose it was," she admitted, for their life of barren simplicity wouldn't have been out of place a thousand years ago.

In the beginning she had hated the convent in the rugged desert. She arrived feeling used, dirty, and ashamed, with Bruce's harsh condemnations still ringing in her ears. In the early months, the grim women dressed entirely in black were intimidating, but over time they softened toward her, and she to them. What was supposed to be a punishment turned into a few years of blessed peace as her heart mended and her faith was restored. To this day she thanked God for the gift of Arizona and the wisdom she had learned in that scorching wilderness.

Alex sighed and dropped to sit on the front step, his head in his hands. "That's why I couldn't find you."

She sucked in a quick breath, surprised at the statement. "You tried?"

"Of course I tried!"

She could scarcely believe it as he recounted the dozens of letters he had sent to Hercules. He even visited her old school in Boston! She sat beside him on the stoop, stunned and bewildered. No boy who wanted only a quick roll in the hay would have done such things.

"Oh, Alex." Those two words carried the weight of twelve years of confusion. His impossibly blue eyes mirrored her own regret and heartbreak, and a dangerous surge of emotion welled up inside her. It threatened to pull her back into the wild, wonderful tumult of those sun-kissed days. Maybe Alex *had* cared for her, even though she'd been too young to be making life-altering decisions. He'd always been rowdy and impulsive, when all she craved was stability. Had they married, it would have been a disaster.

"Did you ever find out who told on us?" she asked.

"I think one of his bodyguards must have found out."

She shook her head. "The morning Bruce confronted me, he said someone from the town had been spying on us and told him everything." Bruce was many things, but he wasn't a liar.

"No," Alex said, rubbing his jaw as he stared into space. "I think it had to be someone on his payroll. Somebody from town might have told my parents or Hercules, but they wouldn't have snitched to Garrett."

Eloise swallowed hard. Although she hadn't breathed a word of their trysts to anyone, that hadn't been the case with Alex. In the tavern, Hercules Duval had asked if she was *the* Eloise.

She framed her words carefully. "Your brother . . . he knew about us."

Alex's face stilled. "Yes."

"Could he have been the one to tell? Maybe he didn't approve."

"Not Hercules. He would never have put us in danger like that. It had to be one of Garrett's bodyguards."

Alex pulled back a few inches, reluctant admiration on his face as he looked at her. She'd taken great care with her appearance this morning. After squeezing into the world's tightest corset, she had selected a tailored pinstripe jacket with a frothy lace jabot.

"You sure have changed," he said. "I almost didn't recognize you. The girl I remember had twigs in her hair and grass stains on her skirt. She never would have worn that torture chamber squeezing your waist."

Was he making fun of her? She couldn't be sure, but it wasn't prudent to get dragged into this conversation. She wasn't that rebellious girl anymore, but the way he smiled at her seemed uncomfortably familiar. She tried to stand, but he pulled her back down onto the step.

"Look, we got off on the wrong foot," he said. "I want you to know that I'm sorry. To the bottom of my soul, I'm sorry."

"For what?"

"Well, for everything," he said. "For what happened twelve years ago. For losing my head in there a minute ago. For the lack of electricity in this town. For the cloudy day." He spoke with teasing affection, and it stirred something inside her.

A bit of the starch went out of her. "Alex, can I ask a favor?"

"You can ask me anything in the world."

She always could. No matter how deep or vulnerable, she'd always been able to share anything and everything with this warm-hearted, funny man. But that was in the past. The town spread out before her. Hundreds of buildings, shops, and homes that needed appraising, and Claude Fitzgerald was waiting to pounce on her for the slightest mistake. Alex was a dangerous distraction on so many levels.

She swallowed hard. "Can we try to forget the past and treat each other like cordial acquaintances? I feel awful coming into this town to help pull it apart, and it's inevitable that we're going to run into each other over and over. It would be easier if we declare a cease-fire. I can't afford to botch this assignment. Claude Fitzgerald is a mean bulldog, and he'd like nothing more than to see me fail in spectacular fashion."

For a moment Alex seemed taken aback, then amused. He

leaned forward to speak conspiratorially. "You know that I'm the mayor. I can have him thrown into the stocks or banished from the town square."

"Doubtful."

"Tarred and feathered? It has a long and storied history in this part of the country. Just say the word."

It was hard not to laugh, but this sort of flirtation mustn't take root. "Alex, please. I'm here to do a job that neither one of us is happy about. I want to be civilized. I'd like us to behave like cordial acquaintances."

His eyes dimmed a little, but he still smiled. "Sorry, Eloise, my feelings for you will never be cordial. I think of you as the girl who set my wild boyhood heart on fire. Who I could tickle into—"

"No," she interrupted. "That's in the past. Buried."

"How far in the past? Maybe we could dig it up."

She'd just asked him to stop flirting, and he had ignored her. It was time to end this conversation and get down to work. With cool precision, she stood and smoothed the features in her face.

"It was another lifetime," she said coolly. "One that's gone and lost forever."

She didn't look back as she headed to the next house on her list, even though she felt Alex's gaze boring into her the entire walk. She had too much to lose by getting entangled with him again. There were only six female certified public accountants in the entire state of New York, and she was one of them. She had walked through fire to get her CPA license, and going forward she intended to be a model of efficient civility. Cordial acquaintances, nothing more.

No matter what, she wouldn't let Alex knock her off-kilter again.

*A*lex sat at the conference table in the town hall meeting room, surrounded by members of the town council. For the past five years, this had been their war room, where they'd desperately fought to save their town. So far, they'd lost every battle. Now the best Alex could do was negotiate favorable terms of surrender. This morning, that meant getting the upper hand over the government bureaucrats due to arrive in ten minutes to plan their demolition.

But Alex had a secondary motive. He needed to see if there was anything left of the old Eloise, the one who laughed and cried and shrieked with joy. The woman who recited legal codes and counted doorknobs was a stranger to him, but even so, he found her wildly attractive. Her steely, fierce demeanor was mesmerizing. He itched to crack through it, but he had to hand it to her—Eloise had come far in the world.

As in most town meetings, Alex worked closely with Willard Gilmore, the richest man in Duval Springs and by far the craftiest. People habitually underestimated the middle-aged man who sported a handlebar mustache and colorful suspenders. They thought he was nothing but a jovial, small-town innkeeper.

Willard could be jovial, but he also had a steel core of ambition and had amassed considerable wealth through the town's general store, contracting with Western Union for the valley's telegraph service, and operating the Gilmore Inn. This morning he was strategizing how to glean as much income as possible from the state.

"We can charge them triple for use of town meeting space," Willard said. "They've got no other choice unless they want to go back and forth to Kingston. We can also charge for stabling their horses."

Reverend Carmichael shifted uneasily in his chair. "That doesn't seem very Christian. Father Thomas told me before he left that people could use his church however they needed. There's no reason we can't let the state have that space for free. No one else is using it."

Both the Catholic church and the Lutheran meetinghouse had pulled up stakes earlier in the year, and their buildings sat vacant. Reverend Carmichael ran the only church left in town. Alex was grateful to have a man of God on the town council, but his endless goodwill could be frustrating.

"No deal," Alex said. "It's in our interest to require rental fees for every space they use. Not only for the cash, but it also lets us keep an eye on them. I don't want them wandering in and out of abandoned buildings."

"I agree," Dr. Lloyd said, making the final vote three to one. They were all that was left of the town council, as the others had moved away during the past year. Already the town was sinking into gentle dilapidation. Shop windows were empty, weeds took root in lawns, and each week they lost more residents.

At precisely nine o'clock, the state's demolition team arrived. Eloise glided into the room, as poised as a long-stemmed rose as she lowered herself into a chair. Wearing a gown of amethyst silk with a cinched-in waist, she looked as cool as the woman carved into the cameo choker at her throat. Claude Fitzgerald was with her, the buttons on his striped vest straining against his bulk. He wasn't fat, merely shaped like a brick and wearing an expression just as hard. He tossed a folder down on the table.

"Let's get this meeting underway," Claude said. "I want both sides to outline their position and—"

"I will be setting the agenda for the meeting," Alex interrupted. He was the only voice his people had, and he wouldn't let a city bureaucrat browbeat anyone. "Foremost of our demands is that all building inspections require a twenty-four-hour notice." If someone as mild-mannered as Mrs. Trudeau could be incensed by an unannounced visit from the state appraiser, it was only going to get worse unless Alex established some ground rules.

"Unacceptable," Claude said. "How are we to know how long each job will take? We didn't bring a scheduling secretary with us, and this sort of hairsplitting will hamper our progress."

"Do you know how to use a calendar?" Alex asked.

"I have a degree from Harvard and thirty years of engineering experience, so yes, I think I can figure out how to use a calendar."

"Excellent. Than use it to schedule a twenty-four-hour notice before you invade anyone's home or business."

Claude looked annoyed as he barked orders at Eloise. "Miss Drake, you now have secretarial duties. Draw up a calendar to keep these yokels happy."

"That's fine," she said, still refusing to look at Alex. Her aloof tone irked him. Eloise Drake was a girl who shrieked with laughter and danced in the rain. Now she calmly took orders like a doormat.

She took the cap from a fancy silver pen and prepared to take notes.

"Nice pen," Alex said before he could stop himself.

"Thank you," she replied tonelessly. Funny how a little

writing implement could underscore the gulf between them. That silver pen probably cost more than he earned in a month. It also served to redouble his determination to crack through her veneer of ice.

"We are agreed that no homes will be appraised without proper notice," Alex said. "What about commercial properties? Are those your responsibility as well?"

She nodded. "I have separate valuation formulas for retail and agricultural properties."

"What about apple orchards? There are a dozen below the flow line, some with old cider mills."

It was a deliberate provocation, meant to shake her composure, but it didn't work. She looked directly into his eyes as she replied. "Apple orchards are agricultural properties, and I have the forms to make an efficient assessment. Old cider mills are of no interest to me."

He admired her sangfroid even as he scrambled for a way to shatter it. "The land surrounding Duval Springs is famous for its attractions," he said. "Hiking trails, scenic views. Do you have a formula for those? There's a swimming hole only half a mile from here. I can show you."

"In September?" Claude asked incredulously, but Alex didn't take his gaze off Eloise.

"It's only for the brave," he continued, remembering those golden summer days when he taught her to swim. "Swimming holes aren't for everyone, but some people seize life with both hands, willing to embrace the good, the scary, and the challenging. What do you say, Miss Drake? Can you be tempted by a bracing autumn swim?"

She lifted a brow. "You might call it a bracing autumn swim, but to me it sounds like a flirtation with pneumonia and an unwholesome association with mud."

"Speaking of mud," Willard Gilmore said, breaking into

the conversation and steering it back to the business at hand. "Lumberjacks from the state have been littering and making a mess of my inn. Tracking in mud and using foul language in front of the maids. They've also been loitering in the town bandstand, smoking and scattering cigar butts. They're leaving trash all over the village green."

"How is that our fault?" Claude asked.

"It's Miss Drake's fault," Alex said impulsively.

"Me?" she asked incredulously. "I've never seen a lumberjack in my life."

"Precisely. But your office sent them here and didn't pay for an on-site supervisor. You should have anticipated the problem." Why was he doing this? If his mother was alive, she'd box his ears, but the compulsion to crack through the ice and down to the real Eloise was irresistible. The old Eloise wasn't dead; she was just buried beneath a layer of permafrost.

She frowned at him. "You're really grasping at straws, Alex."

"The floor of the bandstand is a disgrace," he continued. "It will be demolished soon, so maybe the state doesn't care if the lumberjacks ruin it with cinder marks, but we'll be using it for the next eight months, and I want it in good condition."

Pounding footsteps interrupted the conversation, and the door to the meeting room was yanked open. Alex shot to his feet at the disheveled appearance of Rebecca Wiggin, the young woman who had recently inherited the creamery from her father.

"Alex, you need to order Zeke to hold up his end of the bargain! He's trying to worm off the hook."

Zeke Himmelfarb, a dairy farmer from the county, sauntered in behind her, a stubborn look on his leathery face.

"What's going on?" Alex asked. He was no lawyer, but people often asked him to settle disputes, and this looked like a big one.

"Zeke said he wasn't moving out of the valley until the

spring," Rebecca said. "Now he's trying to back out of our deal."

"I changed my mind," the dairy farmer said. "I found a farm for sale outside of Newburgh, and it can't wait. Today is my last delivery to you."

"How am I supposed to operate a creamery if I don't have milk?"

"Not my problem, girlie."

"Don't call me *girlie*," Rebecca snapped. "We have a contract! I've been paying top dollar for your milk because you promised to stay in the valley until the May deadline."

"She's got a point," Willard said. "If you break the contract, you'll need to reimburse her for the premium she's been paying."

"I don't want to be reimbursed, I want to have milk!" Rebecca shouted.

Alex held up his hands. "Calm down, let's think this through." But this was going to be bad. If the dairy farmer left, the creamery couldn't stay in business. Zeke was the largest dairy farmer in the county, supplying more than half the town's milk.

"Come sue me in Newburgh," Zeke said. "I suspect we all have better things to do than sue over an extra three cents for a gallon of milk." He left the room, leaving Rebecca with a crestfallen look on her face.

"Don't panic," Alex said to her. "We'll figure this out."

"Would you stop saying that?" Rebecca said in a choked voice. "You've been telling us not to panic for years, but things just keep getting worse!"

He swallowed hard, for she was right. He'd lost every court case and appeal. Steel bands constricted around his chest, making it hard to breathe. He rubbed his neck and looked away—straight at Eloise, who witnessed his helplessness in the face of this latest defeat. Everyone else had heard too. Claude was smirking.

Alex turned away as if burned. He'd once been so confident about this battle. David was supposed to defeat Goliath if only he was steadfast and had faith. For five years, that image had sustained Alex, but now it was ordinary people like Rebecca Wiggin who were drowning, and he had precious little to offer her.

"I'll find a dairy you can contract with higher up in the valley," he said. "You're going to be okay."

"Just stop!" Rebecca shouted. "Stop raising our hopes and stop telling us to trust you, because I can't anymore!"

She stormed out of the meeting room, slamming the door so hard that the windows rattled in their frames.

"That's some arm she's got!" Claude chuckled. "If she'd thrown a bit more muscle into it, she would have helped us knock this old building down."

Heat flooded Alex's body. It wouldn't hurt so badly if everything Rebecca had just said wasn't true. He'd give anything if he could avoid the next eight months, for things were going to get more difficult as May drew near. He swallowed hard as he sat back down. He had another two hours of scheduling ahead of him, and it had to be done no matter how awful.

Across the table, Eloise looked at him with pity in her eyes. Somehow, the loss of her respect was hardest of all.

After the excruciating meeting concluded, Alex turned to the only person with whom he could truly be himself. He and Hercules were more than just brothers. They shared the same blood, the same lawless sense of adventure, the same sentimental streak a mile wide. Growing up, they had shared a bedroom above the tavern. Even after Hercules got married and moved into a bigger room, Alex welcomed Sally into the fold and took part in raising their boys. Neither of them had ever planned to live anywhere else.

They walked out onto the footbridge on the outskirts of town. Standing in the middle of the bridge above the swift-moving brook guaranteed there would be no eavesdroppers. Ever since the flurry of sabotage began, Alex had grown increasingly concerned about who was behind it and why. The circle of people he implicitly trusted was growing smaller.

"I really hate this," he whispered to Hercules as he leaned his elbows on the railing, staring at the water rushing beneath the bridge. Some days the weight of despondency made it hard to even stand upright. "This has been the biggest battle of my life, and I've failed."

Hercules clapped him on the shoulder but said nothing. What was there to say? They'd lost on all fronts, and their entire world was about to be wiped off the map. He didn't even know where he would go after the town was pulled down.

On the opposite side of the bridge, a train rumbled past. These trains were becoming more common as forest was cleared and construction workers started erecting aqueducts stretching across their valley. The slow train lugged earthmoving equipment and concrete blocks. A flatbed car carried a pre-built dormitory up the mountain to the new work camp. It was one of dozens being delivered to the valley to house thousands of construction workers.

Alex stared hard at the boxy dormitory as the train carried it to higher ground.

An idea hit. The vision was so powerful it drove the air from his lungs. He couldn't move; he could only stare in dumbfounded astonishment at the train lugging the dormitory to higher ground. Elation filled him as the vision rapidly took shape.

He knew how to save this town. It was possible. He could do it.

"Hercules," he whispered, "why can't we put our houses on

a platform and lift them out of the valley just like that train is carrying a dormitory up to the work camp?"

"What are you talking about?" Hercules asked. "To what end?"

Alex straightened and pointed to the train still snaking around the bend. "Mrs. Trudeau's house is smaller and more compact than that dormitory. I think we can move her house." It was hard to keep talking when he was smiling so wide. "And after we move Mrs. Trudeau's house, we move the tavern. And then the creamery. The school. We can move the whole town."

"Move the town *where?*" Hercules asked, his tone half-amused, half-appalled. "To Kingston?"

"No!" Alex laughed. "We're not moving to Kingston or any other city. We are going to pick up Duval Springs and move it to higher ground right here in the valley. Everything—the church, the tavern, all the houses. We'll build a new town square. We'll take the bandstand. I'll order those city workers to quit smoking on it because we're going to save it all. We're going to cart it up the mountain and build a new town. We'll have running water and electricity."

He smiled as the final detail clicked into place. "And we're going to make New York City pay for it."

*I*t didn't take long for word of Alex's plan to race through town. Within an hour the tavern was packed to capacity. The town council was present, as was every teacher in Duval Springs. As soon as Alex's idea took shape, he had run to the school and dismissed the classes, for he needed as many brains on this task as possible. In all likelihood, school had just had its last day of class in its present location. The move to higher ground would require the planning, organizing, and manual labor of every able-bodied person in the town, and that included the students. This move would give them a priceless education in real-life civics, math, and engineering.

Marie Trudeau sat at the front table, her face a combination of delight and trepidation. "But where?" she pressed. "We can't just plant a new town in the middle of wilderness."

"The old Hollister farm is for sale," Reverend Carmichael said. "Six hundred acres of buckwheat and rye that have been laying fallow ever since the old man died last year. It would be a start."

It would. The Hollister farm was above the flow line and already clear of trees. It had a rudimentary road leading to it, suitable for the construction of a railway, for they would need one to transport the buildings.

"How much will buying that land cost?" someone shouted from the back.

Alex had no idea, but the town was going to be paid for their public buildings. They were owed for the school, the town hall, a post office, a railway station, and the library. That money could be used to purchase land, but that was only the beginning of their expenses. They'd have to build a railway from here to the new place. They'd need platforms and pulleys and cranes to get buildings on and off the train. The people of the town might donate their labor, but they'd still need to hire engineers for specialized planning.

Willard shifted uneasily in his seat. "There's no way a four-story hotel with thirty-six rooms can be loaded on a train and moved up the hill."

The Gilmore Inn was the grandest and most distinctive building on Main Street. It was hard to imagine a new Duval Springs without its most elegant feature, but there were going to be hard choices ahead.

"I was in Paris when they moved a sixteenth-century cathedral," Mrs. Trudeau said. "If they can move a cathedral, why can't we move a four-story hotel?"

Mrs. Trudeau was the last person Alex expected support from. She looked as frail and timid as a wren, but as the idea of moving the town took root, she seemed eager to be part of it. And who was to say she wasn't right? Maybe they *could* move the hotel.

"What about the tavern?" someone asked.

"We're moving the tavern!" Hercules vowed. "We've still got unclaimed wishbones on that rail, and as long as there is breath in my body, this tavern will be here for any man who wants to come home to Duval Springs." He cleared his throat. "Even if we have to move the town a few miles."

"It seems like a lot of work," Rebecca from the creamery said. "It will be cheaper and easier to take the payout and move somewhere else."

Alex didn't want a town without a creamery and was determined to change Rebecca's mind. "Have you seen what New York City is building in its work camps? Those men have dormitories, canteens, and recreation buildings. They will have running water and electricity. I'm going to demand the city put our new town on the lines for water."

"Would they do that?"

"They'd better," Alex said. "We're losing our valley so that people a hundred miles away can drink our water. We'll insist the city build the necessary lines so that we have access to the new reservoir. They're doing it for the other nearby towns above the flow line, and they'll do it for us too. Sewer as well. No more outhouses. While they're at it, they can build us one of those electrical plants. I'll see to it that every house and building in the new town gets power and water lines supplied by the state."

The prospect of water and electricity sent a pleased murmur throughout the crowd, but Willard wasn't convinced.

"I still don't think we can afford it," he said. "We'll have to buy a lot of land, and even if we get the city to pay for some of it, what about labor? It's going to take an army of men."

"Look around you," Hercules exclaimed. "We've got an army! I'd rather go down fighting than sit here begging for scraps from that girl the city sent to assess our property. This town is worth saving. *We* are worth saving."

There was a shift in the air. For years a pall had hung over Duval Springs as their prospects for salvation dimmed. That soul-destroying sense of helplessness robbed a person of dignity, but not today. As he looked out at his friends and neighbors crammed into the tavern, Alex saw the beginnings of hope. The people in this room were strong and loyal, and together, they were going to save this town.

～❦～

Eloise spent the day evaluating farms that had the misfortune to be located only a few acres below the flow line. Luckily, Fletcher had devised separate formulas for barns, silos, even pigpens. Before today, Eloise had never even *seen* a pigpen, but she was now intimately acquainted with stalls, watering, and drainage systems. It was late in the afternoon when she returned to the town square to meet the other team members. They would be sharing a carriage back to Bruce's house, and she hoped she didn't still smell like pigs.

The town square seemed strangely deserted as she arrived, but the demolition team stood before the general store, staring at a notice posted on the door. She joined them, not certain what to make of the page of work groups and room assignments fluttering in the breeze.

"What's going on?" she asked.

"They are moving the town," Enzo said in a dazed voice.

She glanced at him in confusion. "Well, of course they're moving. That's why we're here."

"No, Miss Drake," Claude said, a note of impatience in his voice. "These hillbillies think they can pick up and move their town to a new location. All of it! The houses, the stores. They have no idea what they're up against."

"Oh dear." Had some shyster sold them a bill of goods? Marie Trudeau couldn't even speak about leaving her house without tears, and now someone was raising her hopes with a bizarre scheme to move the village?

But Enzo seemed intrigued. "I think it's a possibility," he said, pointing to the narrow gap between the general store and the pharmacy. "Look, these are freestanding structures, just built side by side. If they jack the store up off its foundation, slide it onto a—"

"The time for that is long past," Claude interrupted. "Moving a town takes years, and we've already begun plans for the demolition. Who is going to pay for the work we've already done if they decide they want to move the town instead? You don't invite a highly respected demolition team into your town if you don't want it torn down."

Except that no one in Duval Springs had *invited* them in. These people had been fighting the demolition of their town for years.

The page tacked to the door listed teams and meeting places scheduled for this evening. A signature at the bottom of the memo identified the leader of this irresponsible mess: Alex Duval.

The breath left her in a rush. Alex had always been reckless, but now it looked like he was ready to lead the entire town over a cliff. For once in her life, she agreed with Claude Fitzgerald. This was a terrible idea.

"I think we should attend the meeting," she said.

Enzo nodded. "We will surely be as welcome as wasps at a picnic, but maybe we can help."

Enzo's prediction was accurate. By the time they arrived at the school, the meeting was already underway. Alex stood at the front of the room, fielding questions from townspeople crammed into the desks. The blackboard behind him was filled with dates and assignments. Every seat was taken, and others stood along the walls three people deep. The only place for her and Enzo to stand was directly inside the door at the front of the room. Every face swiveled toward them, conversation sputtered to a halt, and the temperature in the room dropped a few degrees.

"Get them out of here," someone grumbled. "Spies," someone else shouted.

"We're here to help," Enzo said. "Maybe that means paying you a fair price for your property and then dismantling it, but if you decide to move the town, I don't see why we can't help with that too. The city is paying us either way."

An old farmer with skin like leather scowled. "The city wants us to curl up, die, and blow away like autumn leaves." The preposterous statement rubbed Eloise the wrong way.

"Do you think the city cares what happens to you?" she called out over the rumble. "They don't. They aren't thinking about you at all. All they want is to clear the valley so they can build the reservoir. They don't care if you plow the town under or move it to the surface of the moon, but on May 1 they will be here to start building their reservoir, and no starry-eyed delusions of moving the town will stop them."

"It's nice to know I can depend on you for a bottomless supply of good cheer," Alex said. "Now, let's get back to our starry-eyed delusions. We can't move anything until we get the railroad built. Boomer, you were up at the quarry when Garrett laid his newest line. How long did it take?"

Eloise recognized Boomer McKenzie as Bruce's lead explosives expert.

"Laying the rails only took a couple of days, but a team from Pittsburgh did all the steel work in advance. We'll have to commission that, but I can help lay the rails. I know half a dozen other guys up at the quarry who'd quit in a heartbeat."

"Can you afford to quit?" Alex asked.

Boomer snickered. "It might hurt my pocketbook, but it would do my soul good to quit working for the Bone-Crusher. I'm tired of sliding up the mountain on my belly to kiss that man's ring."

The comment was greeted by a rumble of laughter and foot-stamping.

"We are going to need a lot of manpower," Alex said. "Any

quarryman who wants to quit working for Garrett will have plenty of work here in town. I can't afford to pay wages, but if we pool our resources, no one will go hungry. The town will provide food and supplies for any man who throws his lot in with us."

"Garrett won't rehire anyone who quits," someone warned. "If moving the town doesn't pan out, anyone who quits might as well leave the valley. He'll put the word out on you."

"I'm not afraid," a man with a wiry build said. He stood and held a newspaper aloft. "My cousin lives in New York City, and he sent me this announcement from the newspaper." He slipped on a pair of spectacles and read from the newspaper. "'The State Water Board is looking for two thousand able-bodied men to work as land grubbers, cooks, oxen drovers, machinists, water boys, pipe fitters, pump men, plumbers, stonemasons, powder men and general laborers.'" He put the newspaper down. "Does anyone think you'll be out of a job if Garrett won't hire you back?"

"I don't mind the cut in pay," Boomer said. "I'd rather salvage my dignity than be that man's paid lackey."

Others joined in to recount the indignities Garrett had foisted on them during the strike five years ago. Eloise stared at Alex, growing ever more disillusioned. Why did he let these people ramble on? While they were unleashing their vitriol against Bruce, they weren't accomplishing a lick of progress toward the monumental schedule on the blackboard, and Alex showed no inclination to rein them in. Even to her uneducated eyes, the timeline seemed terribly unrealistic.

She thought of the young woman who owned the creamery. Rebecca Wiggin had been in tears as she shouted at Alex, castigating him for building up her hopes all these years. Alex was about to ruin more than a young creamery owner's future. He was on the verge of destroying the livelihood of everyone in this town.

Eloise approached Alex. "Would you please step out into the hallway?" she asked quietly.

"I'm busy, Eloise." All he was doing was listening with a faint smile on his face as people bellyached about Bruce.

She stepped closer and turned her back to the crowd so only Alex could hear her. "How can you hope to lead this town to a new location if you can't even lead a meeting? You're building castles in the air for these people, and yet you've got no money, no expertise, and precious little time."

The only sign that he heard her was a tightening of his jaw. "The people will help me."

"The people will *gamble* with you. I did that once, and it didn't work out so well."

"I'm pretty good at what I do, Eloise."

"And what is that?"

A look of fierce determination she'd never seen before transformed his face. "Building castles in the air," he retorted, throwing her own words back at her. "If a cause is worth having, I'll fight for it and make it happen. I can motivate people and drag them across the finish line. Your accounting ledgers don't have a column for the size of a human heart. That's where I come in."

She shook her head. "It doesn't matter how badly you want something. If the numbers don't add up, it won't happen." She turned to look at the people crowded into the schoolroom, all so hopeful as they clustered into groups and talked over one another in their excitement. It was hard not to pity them.

"You're leading these people over a cliff," she said softly. "I followed you once and have regretted it ever since. Think carefully before you ruin these people too."

She turned and left the room.

loise was ashamed. There had been a time when Alex brought out the best in her: the brave, the funny, the curious. But at last night's school meeting, she'd been mean and short. It wasn't the sort of person she wanted to be. She needed to heed Fletcher's warning and stop allowing emotion to cloud her judgment.

But it was hard when Eloise rode out to appraise Alex's apple orchard. The orchard was his only form of income. While Hercules had inherited the family tavern, Alex received a sprawling two-hundred-acre orchard that had fallen into disuse decades ago. She had been dreading the appraisal, as it meant putting herself back in the overgrown orchard where they once met. She remembered it choked with brambles and shrubs, and over-topped by fast-growing oaks that dwarfed the apple trees and starved the fruit of sunlight.

She rode out alone, unwilling to venture into this dangerous territory alongside Alex. At first, she couldn't believe her eyes. It looked like a completely different orchard, with neatly pruned trees stretching as far as her eye could see.

She looked in vain for the old cider mill, but where it had once stood was now a two-story building of brick and timber. Was she in the right place? She dismounted, went to the building's front door, and wiggled the handle, but it was locked. Peeking through the window showed her nothing but empty, unfinished rooms. What was this place? And what had happened to the tumbled-down cider mill?

Only Alex could provide the answers.

After counting the number of healthy apple trees and making note of a fine pump-irrigation system, she headed back into town. She already had an appointment to discuss the valuation of his orchard, so he would be expecting her, but they had scheduled the appointment before she groused at him in the schoolhouse. Would he even be willing to see her?

He was, but he eyed her with a guarded expression as she appeared in the doorway to his office.

"I come in peace," she said, still embarrassed by her loss of temper last evening.

The corners of his eyes crinkled in humor. "Too bad. I kind of like crossing swords with you."

She set her paperwork on his desk, refusing to be drawn in to a flirtation. "I've drafted the appraisal for your apple orchard. Nothing so exciting as swords or pistols at dawn."

"Oh, Eloise, you underestimate yourself. The sight of you in that riding habit is enough to excite any red-blooded man."

She sat in the chair opposite his desk, wishing she didn't enjoy his flattery so much. She pushed her ledger toward him and sank into the safe discussion of finances.

"Your trees look healthy and obviously productive. The irrigation system is an excellent feature for which you will be handsomely paid. The new building on the property was locked, so I couldn't perform a full appraisal. What can you tell me about it?"

His humor fled, and he got down to business. "It was supposed to be a fruit-drying facility. Apples, dates, pears, grapes. I bought kilns and commercial dryers. I would have been able to process fruit for hundreds of farmers. It should have made a fortune."

"What happened?"

"The *reservoir* happened," he said sourly. "When the state announced the location of the reservoir, the bank pulled my funding. They repossessed the kilns and ovens. The building was useless after that. I lost three thousand dollars on it."

Eloise was surprised. Somehow she had never imagined Alex as a man of business, but he'd had an ambitious plan for capitalizing on his orchard that collapsed through no fault of his own. Nor was she sure he could be fully compensated, as the formula didn't account for potential value, only what actually existed.

She took out her clipboard and form. "You still have four thousand healthy apple trees."

He nodded. "I sell the fruit to a distributor in Albany. Fresh apples don't earn half what I could have made from dried or canned, but it's a living."

She wasn't so sure about that, but another question itched for an answer. It was dangerous even touching the subject, but she needed to know. "What happened to the old cider mill?"

He looked at her in amazement. "You don't know?"

She shrugged and shook her head.

"Garrett tore it down. Hercules said a bunch of his thugs came and knocked the last of it down, dumped kerosene on it, and set the place on fire. It killed a bunch of the apple trees too. I had to clear the rubble before I built the new place."

"*Oh, Alex*," she whispered, shocked by the wrath Bruce had unleashed against the boy she once loved without limits or restraint. The crook in Alex's nose would be a lifetime reminder of that terrible day.

There was nothing she could say to heal those old wounds, but Alex didn't seem bitter, merely wistful as he gazed at her.

"I really missed you, Eloise." His face was open with honesty. "Is there any chance left for us?"

His voice was a strange combination of hope and curiosity, and it hurt to hear. Even as a girl, her fling with Alex had been out of character. She craved the safety of a predictable world. That wasn't Alex and never would be. She owed him the truth.

"Bruce was right to separate us," she said. He looked flabbergasted, and she rushed to explain. "We were too young and too reckless. I had no business meeting you like that, but I was consumed with the fires of some unquenchable yearning, and nothing else mattered to me when you were near. Bruce said you were only after what any eighteen-year-old boy wanted."

"It was more than that," he insisted.

"Maybe, but if Bruce hadn't intervened we could have gotten into much deeper trouble. I will forever be sorry about the way he did it. You didn't deserve what he did to you, but it was right to separate us."

Alex looked like she'd punched him in the gut. He stood and held out his hand, palm up. "Come with me."

"Why?" His serious tone put her on guard. She didn't know what to expect, and that was always dangerous where Alex was concerned.

"Just come with me," he repeated.

She stood but refused to take his hand. He didn't insist, merely turned to stalk out of the office, and she followed him down the hallway and out the door of the town hall. He marched across the village green to a towering, twisted old elm tree. The ground at its base was lumpy with gnarled roots. He pointed to a spot in the bark a little higher than his shoulder. Her eyes widened when she read the weathered scar carved into the silvery bark of the tree:

A.D. loves E.D. forever.

"Is that . . . did you do that?" she asked.

"Yep. Twelve years ago. I thought you and I were going to be one for the ages."

She had too, but wasn't it normal for people in the throes of love to believe it would last forever? An oddly wonderful ache bloomed in her chest as she pressed her fingers into the scar on the bark.

"I wish I'd known," she finally said.

"I told you often enough."

"I didn't believe you." Over time, Bruce's harsh words had taken root. *He took advantage of you because he could.* She lifted her fingers off the old trunk and spoke from the heart. "I was so hungry for affection during those years that I would have given you anything and everything. I can't blame you for taking it, but afterward I was so ashamed. It was the only time in my life that I broke the rules, and given the way it ended . . . well, I've been a stickler for rules ever since."

He grabbed her hand and laid it flat over their initials on the tree. "I loved you back then and *still* love what we had. You call what we did back then a mistake, but I will always, *always* love the memory of us together. I'm even delirious enough to hope that we weren't wrong. That we can find our way back to each other."

This conversation hurt. For twelve years she had believed she'd been seduced by a boy eager to take advantage of her, but that wasn't true. He had cared. He had suffered too.

But that didn't mean he was the right man for her. Fletcher Jones was solid and dependable, and she was counting the days until she could get back to her safe, normal world in the city. She didn't belong here amidst these boisterous people. She craved a secure home, and perhaps she and Fletcher could build one, but she needed to put Alex and their wild, glorious summers behind her before that could happen.

"Alex, we aren't those people anymore. It's time for us both to move on."

The hope in his eyes dimmed. "Is there someone else?"

"Yes," she said simply, hating the pain that flashed across his face before he masked it with a reluctant smile. No matter what, Alex could always put a good face on things.

"Whoever he is, he's a lucky man. I still hate his guts, though." His deadpan tone was belied by the affectionate humor lurking in his eyes.

She smiled and touched the back of his hand. "We're going to be okay, Alex."

He rotated his palm and squeezed her hand. "Thanks for that," he said, but his shoulders sagged as he ambled back to the town hall with a little less dynamism than before, and she couldn't help but mourn losing him all over again.

lex never worried about tedious matters like finance, but even he was dismayed at how rapidly the town's pooled funds dwindled over the next two weeks. The state had compensated them for the loss of their school and library, but most of it went to purchasing the old Hollister farm. He used the rest to hire two engineers to make a list of recommendations for how to accomplish the move. He felt physically sick as he listened to their report. The good news was that moving the town could be done; the bad news was that it would take two years.

The Hollister farm was uphill from Duval Springs, so they'd need to install an expensive rail line to transport the buildings. They would need to rent a steam engine to do the hauling. Under normal conditions, it took a week to move a single building. They had eight months to move two hundred.

Alex sat in the meeting room of the town hall, resting his forehead in his hands as the engineers continued talking, but a blinding headache made it hard to think. Eloise's accusation about leading the town over a cliff stung worse than ever. Had he been feeding the townspeople a pipe dream? The post office and town hall would bring more revenue, but most of it would be spent on building the railway. Their money was mostly gone before he'd laid a single street in the new town. Although he'd hoped to let people keep a portion of their state payouts, it now seemed increasingly unlikely. Anyone intending to move their house or business to the new town would need to donate their entire payment.

And if he failed, they would be left with nothing.

"What about building foundations in the new town?" he asked. "How much will that cost?"

The engineer shrugged. "It depends on if people want a basement or not. Basements need to be dug, framed, and then lined with either concrete block or stone. Concrete is faster, but the mortar won't cure well over the winter, so you'll want to get that in place now. And take my advice, get an excavation contractor who knows what he's doing. Otherwise you'll face a slew of problems if you plop a house on a lousy foundation."

The man's voice droned on, but it was hard to keep listening. Everyone wanted a basement, didn't they? But it was a cost few of them anticipated. He needed to know exactly how much the state intended to pay for each house, business, and farm, and Eloise wasn't exactly moving at top speed. He'd hunt her down and light a fire under her to get those appraisals completed and paid.

Thanks to the meticulous schedule she had designed, he knew exactly where she would be. He headed to the west side of town and watched from a distance as she stood outside the home of Peter and Hazel Mason, showing them the papers on her clipboard.

An accountant, he thought with a roll of his eyes. Where had their wild dreams of sailing the seven seas or living in a garret apartment in Paris gone? But fondness overwhelmed him as he gazed at her, so prim as she held the clipboard before the

Masons. Eloise loved those blasted rule books as much as he loved teasing her over them. And maybe the garret apartment in Paris sounded better than the reality would be.

Accounting suited her. It was painful to admit, because it meant they would never run away with the gypsies or swing from the halyards, but she seemed to like the work. He'd rather pull out his own teeth than stare at accounting ledgers all day, but Eloise was happy, and wasn't that all he'd ever really wanted for her? Jealousy gnawed at him, knowing there was another man in her life, but he could accept that. He could. He wasn't an envious man who wanted the woman he loved to languish in lonely solitude. And he'd probably get over her eventually.

He waited until her business with the Masons was finished, shook off his gloom, and intercepted her before she could reach the next house on the street. When he slid onto the sidewalk in front of her, her friendly expression became guarded.

"Hello, Eloise," he said pleasantly. "How can I get you to speed up the appraisals?"

"I intend to deliver on the schedule we all agreed upon. No faster, no slower."

He gestured to a bench in the yard outside the schoolhouse. "Let's chat," he suggested as he guided her toward the bench. He didn't waste any time once they were both seated. "I'm planning a budget for the move and need to know what I've got to work with. I'm burning through cash pretty fast."

"How fast?" There was no judgment in her voice, and talking numbers with her reminded him of those long-ago summer days when she tutored him in math.

"I've spent eighty percent of what's come in. I need to know what else the town can expect."

She sighed, but instead of attacking him, she looked at him with all the sympathy in the world radiating from her face. "Alex, you can't afford this move. The bills are going to be astronomical. I managed the books for a road-building project a few years ago. A small stretch of road will cost thousands, and you need to build two miles. Plus a railway! And that's before you've moved a single building."

"I'll make it happen," he said grimly. Her roads hadn't been built by volunteers, and he had hundreds ready to pitch in.

"But have you really planned for everything?" she asked. "Forgive me if this is a stupid question, but how will each house get from its foundation onto your railroad?"

"Oxen. We jack the house up off its foundation, slide metal beams and a platform under it, and then oxen haul it to the rail yard. The engineers say they've seen three- and four-story buildings moved this way."

Eloise still looked pained. "But you can't afford it. The only way I see to finance a project like this is to float a municipal bond, and I don't think . . ."

Her voice trailed off, and he was caught by the surprised expression on her face, as though she were staring at a revelation unfolding before her eyes.

"What does that mean?" he asked. "What's a municipal bond?"

"It's a way of getting outside investors to fund a project. The townspeople must vote to approve the bond, because it will be their duty to pay it back, but they usually get twenty or thirty years to do so. It's a quick way to get a lot of money. That's how the big cities pay for major projects. Not by passing a hat and asking people to turn over their life savings."

A seed of hope took root. "How do I get one of these things up and running?"

"You create a budget, have it audited for accuracy, and then the town votes on it. If it passes, it will go up for sale to investors. There are companies in New York that handle the sale of municipal bonds."

"Have you ever done that sort of work?"

"Two years ago, the nuns at the convent asked me to design one for a new church. They're building it as we speak."

His heart sped up as he leaned closer. "Okay, can I hire you to do that? Be an agent or auditor or whatever? I can draw up a budget. I can persuade people to vote for it. Whatever it takes."

She stood. "Slow down. These things take time and—"

"I don't have any time. How do I get this thing done immediately?"

She sat back down, and he hung on every word as she outlined the process. Maybe he didn't understand fully, because it didn't sound all that difficult to him. He and Hercules could stay up all night making a list of everything they needed to buy or build. He'd get Reverend Carmichael to write the fancy language to make it sound good. They could vote on it tomorrow or the next day. That meant all he had to do was find an auditor and get the bond listed on the securities exchange.

"You can be our auditor, can't you?"

She looked taken aback. "I can't work miracles. I've already said I don't think you have a prayer of getting this done."

"I'm not asking for miracles, I'm asking you to volunteer some auditing services. I'm going to need a lot of favors to pull this off, and I'm not afraid to ask. Beg. Bargain. What do you want?"

Eloise sighed, leaning back to gaze wistfully at the town. "I want to believe that dreams really can come true," she said simply. "I would like to believe that hope and heart is all it takes to make anything happen, but it isn't."

"Try me." If she wanted pearls from the bottom of the ocean, he'd find a way to get them for her.

She still looked skeptical as she closed her eyes in resignation. "I know you're not going to give up unless you can see it for yourself. And you've always been so terrible at math, Alex."

"No, I haven't."

"If I hadn't tutored you all those—"

"But you did!" He grinned. "And it took. If you tell me to write up a budget, I'll do it."

She arched a brow at him, probably just like one of those scary nuns she'd told him about. When she spoke, all softness had vanished, and her voice was rock hard.

"Before I even consider helping you, I need to see a realistic budget. I want a list of supplies and their cost. For every task you intend to assign to volunteers, I need to see their names and their signatures guaranteeing they will deliver on their promise. And those oxen you intend to buy? I want to see costs for harnesses, tackle, nine months of feed, where they will be stabled, and who is going to care for them. An allowance for veterinary services too. I want to see fuel costs for the locomotive. I want a budget for food to serve the volunteers. On top of everything else, I need you to factor in a ten-percent reserve."

He swallowed hard. Her demand was hard, but not unreasonable. She had just flung a challenge in his lap, and he loved it.

"I'll do it." Because deep in his soul, there was nothing he loved more than tackling impossible dreams.

Eloise had agreed to attend the meeting Alex called for that evening at the tavern. Her stomach was a mass of knots. Maybe she shouldn't have uttered the word *bond*, for Alex had seized on it and set the wheels in motion with breathtaking speed. Dozens of townspeople were already gathered to hear her explain how a municipal bond would work. This was her fault. She would be responsible if their hopes came crashing down because Alex underestimated the difficulty of getting a bond measure passed and funded.

At least Enzo had agreed to come along so he could escort

her back to Bruce's house after the meeting. She didn't want to admit it, but traveling alone after dark was frightening. Years of living in the city had made her forget how dark the forest could be at night.

The tavern was crowded as they stepped inside, and to her surprise, she knew most of the people here. How different than in Manhattan, where she rarely bumped into the same people from day to day.

"What can I get you?" Hercules hollered from behind the bar. "It's on the house. Anything for the woman who's going to get this bond thing off the ground."

"It's not a done deal," Eloise cautioned, hoping that Alex hadn't told everyone a municipal bond was an easy solution to their problems, but as she drew a breath to say so, Enzo cut her off.

"Whatever smells so good would be wonderful. We are famished," he said.

A moment later two bowls of fragrant beef stew were set before them, and Eloise had to admit that the food in this tavern was every bit as good as that in Manhattan.

A young boy about five years old approached, a mug of apple cider held carefully in both hands. "This is for you," he said with a shy smile. He looked so eager to please as he brought her the drink.

"Thank you," she said as she took it from him. He blushed furiously and darted behind the bar to get another mug for Enzo.

"That's my nephew, James," Alex said as he joined her at the table. "He's the reason I had to move out of the tavern. There wasn't room here anymore."

Eloise couldn't take her eyes off the boy as he returned with another mug for Enzo, carrying it as though it contained liquid gold. Such concentration! Would she ever have a child so adorable? It would be wonderful to come home to a sweet child every evening instead of the occasional chance to admire other women's children.

She took a bite of the stew. The paprika and cloves seasoning the meat made for amazing flavor, but it felt awkward to eat with everyone staring at her. They all looked as eager as children on Christmas morning. Farmers with leathery faces, shopkeepers still wearing their work suits, stonecutters with a pale film of limestone dust still in their hair—all of them watched and waited.

After a few bites, she pushed the bowl away and looked at Alex. "What do you need from me?" she asked politely.

"I need you to explain to everyone what a municipal bond is and how we can get one." His sentence was followed by a few hoots of excitement and the stamping of feet. It was exactly what she had feared. Alex had already raised these people's hopes, and they had no idea of the regulatory hurdles and difficulties ahead. Alex painted such magnificent visions, but it was her responsibility to reel them back down to earth.

She explained how they needed to design a budget that would pass a strict external audit. Even more important, the town would have to demonstrate its ability to pay the investors back with interest. It was not a quick and easy solution to their problem.

To her surprise, Alex smoothly took over the meeting and began assigning tasks. He asked the owner of the hardware store to estimate the cost of moving supplies and a team of laborers to set a price for the materials to lay building foundations. He and Reverend Carmichael agreed to write the narrative portion of the bond proposal.

"None of your flowery language," she cautioned. "The bond will be marketed to bankers and stockbrokers. You'll need to convince them this is a rock-solid investment."

Alex grinned. "It's more than solid, it's a crusade. We're

leading the Israelites out of Egypt to the promised land. We are Columbus setting sail for the west, armed with hope and a compass. We've got drive and determination, we've got—"

"We've got too much extravagant language," she interrupted. "I don't want speeches to light a fire under the troops, I need numbers that will make bankers open their checkbooks."

Willard Gilmore's normally jovial face looked grim. "This scheme is too risky," he warned. "Our timetable could be ruined by a harsh winter, or the engineers could say the move will be too tough."

"Willard, you've been taking risks all your life," Hercules said. "After the court ruled that Garrett's company store was illegal, you took it over even though you didn't know a thing about retail. You spiffed it up and invested a fortune in fancy imported spices and tobacco. Now you're making money hand over fist."

"Wrong," Willard said. "I *never* gambled. I bought an ordinary general store that the whole town depends on, and I expanded it slowly, monitoring it at each step along the way. I never put all my chips on a single hand of cards, and Alex, that's what you're doing."

Alex didn't lose an ounce of momentum as he stood to respond to the innkeeper. "Willard, I hope you come to the new town, but if you think it's too big a risk, take the state payout. Those who want to follow me can sign on for the bond. I'm going to make this new town happen if I have to crawl across broken glass to get there."

By the end of the meeting, dozens lined up behind Alex, eager to peruse the list of jobs needing volunteers. It was dark by the time Dick Brookmeyer, the owner of the local stables, brought two horses to the tavern so Eloise and Enzo could ride back to Bruce's house. She looked with apprehension at the end of the street where the path disappeared into the darkened forest.

"I'll ride up with you," Alex offered.

A piece of her wanted to accept the offer, which was ridiculous since Enzo was riding with her. She still couldn't say with certainty how Bruce would respond if Alex dared set foot on his land.

"We'll be okay," she said, glad to see Enzo nod with confidence, but she regretted her decision the moment they left town and the road snaked into the woods.

It was dark. And the forest made noise—the rasp of rustling leaves and the sound of crickets. The horses must have had better eyesight than she did, for they trotted along at an alarming clip, not hesitating at all. She startled and nearly fell from her horse when an owl swooped across the path.

"Are you all right back there?" Enzo asked, and the smile in his voice helped unknot a bit of her tension.

"I'm fine. I'll be glad to get home."

She *was* glad when they arrived home. One of Bruce's men saw them coming and opened the gate. Thank goodness for the lanterns burning inside, illuminating the courtyard with a warm glow.

Bruce stood on the landing before his front door, hands braced on the railing and a hard look of disapproval on his face as she mounted the steps. She'd asked Claude and Roy to explain to Bruce why she'd be late, and he wasn't pleased.

"A bond?" he said, mocking disbelief dripping in his voice.

"It's just an idea," she said. "I doubt Alex will be able to pull it off."

Only storybook heroes could deliver the impossible in the space of a few days, and despite all the radiant optimism in the tavern tonight, Alex didn't fully grasp the magnitude of either launching a municipal bond or moving the town.

Bruce followed her inside the house and all the way up the stairs, never letting up on his torrent of disapproval.

"If you link your professional reputation to this wild-eyed scheme, you'll pay for it when he can't deliver. New York may seem like a big city, but your reputation will be in tatters if this thing goes south. Alex Duval is nothing but trouble. And both experts he hired are civil engineers. He should have had a structural engineer on the team for better insight."

Bruce continued with his litany, and the worst thing was that almost everything he said was correct.

But how did he know so much about this, anyway? Roy and Claude must have conveyed a lot of information, but when she asked them about it the next morning, they denied telling Bruce anything about what kind of engineers Alex had consulted. They didn't even realize he'd consulted experts at all.

Which meant Bruce still had a spy in Duval Springs.

Eloise arrived at Alex's office on Friday morning to review the budget proposal. She braced herself for an anemic document swelling with overblown language but few concrete facts.

"Are you all right?" she gasped upon seeing him slumped behind his desk. He was unshaven, with shadows beneath his eyes and lines she'd never seen before.

He straightened immediately and summoned a grin for her. "We've been working on this budget around the clock," he said. "My hand to God, I don't know how you accountants can stay awake juggling all those awful numbers. But we got it done! Here."

She held her breath while flipping through the stack of papers he handed her. It was written according to the example she'd provided. Page after page listed the town's expenses, and the volunteer work was assigned to people who promised to donate their services for no compensation. The timeline looked tight but was in order. His narrative summary of the project was straightforward and soberly written. A smile tugged at the corner of her mouth. She hadn't really thought he could do it, but at first glance, it looked good.

"I'll need a few days to double-check your numbers," she said.

"Double-check them now. I want to get moving on this thing."

She slanted him a glance. "A complete audit takes time and shouldn't be rushed."

"But I want to hold the vote tomorrow. Can you get it to me—"

"Absolutely not. You can't vote until the townspeople have at least two weeks to review the proposal."

Alex gestured to the window. "Don't you see what's going on outside? The railway bed is almost fully dug. We've received a delivery of pebbles and plan on laying it down tomorrow. Everyone wants this to happen."

She folded her arms across her chest, prepared to do battle, for it looked like Alex was going to be intransigent. "You don't know that until a formal vote is held. That means no hand-raising at a town hall meeting where people feel pressured by their neighbors. I'm talking about a closed ballot vote with an informed electorate. You need several hundred copies of this proposal printed and distributed." She flipped through the document to study the list of incidental supplies. "I don't see any allocation for the cost of printing and distributing this proposal. That will cost—"

"I'm not printing a copy for everyone. My secretary will type five copies, and they'll be available for review at the public library."

"That's not how it's done—"

"It's how we do it."

"Everyone needs their own copy for private study. This sort of decision takes proper consideration."

"Maybe people in New York have money to splash around on documents no one will read, but as a working man, I have more respect for my budget. Five copies on reserve at the library. And if you look at the list of volunteers, you will see that my secretary has already agreed to donate typing services for correspondence and paperwork."

Eloise wondered if this was what he had sounded like in the army. He projected forthright command and firm determination. She didn't want to admit it, but it was a tiny bit thrilling.

"Ten copies," she countered.

"Done! And we vote tomorrow."

She found her backbone again and shook her head. "Absolutely not. Maybe no one else will read this document, but I will, and I need a few days. I'll have it back to you on Monday, your secretary can type it up, and then you can vote on Saturday. That is as far as I will budge."

His face was a combination of amused frustration and anticipation. This was exhilarating for both of them, even though it shouldn't be.

"Fine!" he agreed. "I want you to be here for the vote, on the town square as we read out the results. We can set off fireworks when it passes."

"*If* it passes."

But in her heart she desperately hoped it would, for somehow the quest Alex envisioned was the most exciting adventure story she'd ever taken part in. She only hoped the ending would be a happy one, for with Alex, there were no guarantees.

The Saturday evening vote was going to be a triumph, and Alex had planned a grand festival to celebrate.

His motives were twofold. First, the town deserved a party to mark the official beginning of their move. More importantly, he wanted Eloise to be a part of the festivities. Years ago she had confided to him how eagerly she watched their town festivals through the telescope in her turret bedroom. Fourth of July holidays, autumn harvests, even the barbershop quartet concerts held on the bandstand during long summer evenings were fascinating to her. He'd always taken such gatherings for granted, but the lonely girl on the mountaintop craved the chance to attend.

This would be the last festival ever held in Duval Springs, combining the town vote with the traditional autumn harvest festival. Eloise loved maple candy, and on Friday morning, he commandeered the hotel kitchen to make a huge batch that would be given away for free at the festival. He kept the kitchen doors open so he could hear when Eloise arrived to send her weekly report to her supervisor in the city.

The scent of maple enveloped the kitchen with its warm, sweet aroma as he stirred the simmering liquid, but the instant he heard her voice, he moved the pot to the back burner. He strolled down the hallway to watch as she dictated her message to Kasper at the hotel's front counter. She looked spectacular, decked out in another of those fancy city getups, this time in peacock blue. It gave him pleasure just to watch her primly report the status of her work and the fact that she was ahead of schedule. She was so good at everything she did, and he couldn't help being proud of her.

"Come on back to the kitchen," he coaxed the moment she paid Kasper for the wire. "I've got maple candy on the stove."

She quirked a brow at him. "Maple candy is my weakness."

"I remember." He instantly regretted the comment. Eloise was prickly about protecting their private business, and he shouldn't have alluded to their past, especially since Kasper was paying full attention. Kasper Nagy might be the laziest man in the entire valley, but he loved gossip.

"Come on back," he urged, and to his relief, she followed. He set the pot back over the heat and resumed stirring, then invited her to tip in the chopped walnuts while he updated her on the progress of the festival. "Hercules went to Kingston to buy fireworks, and a couple of farmers brought in wagons for hayrides. The barbershop quartet will sing. Those pies on the cooling rack over there are ready to go, and of course . . ." He tipped the pot so she could see inside. "The world's best maple candy. Can I convince you to come?"

She looked pensive as she watched him pour the first batch of maple into the candy molds. "I've always envied those festivals," she said, the wistfulness plain in her voice.

"I know. This will be our last one, and you should be there."

She still looked reluctant as she shook her head. "It would cause trouble with Bruce. He and I have grown very close over the past year. Especially since my mother died."

Alex set down the pot to give Eloise his full attention. "I saw her obituary in the local paper. I'm sorry." The obituary hadn't even mentioned Eloise's existence, yet another slight for the redheaded child who'd never been wanted.

"It's okay," she said quietly.

"It's *not* okay. I know you weren't close after she sent you to live with Garrett, but her death had to hurt, and I'm sorry."

Eloise hugged herself and stared at the floor, looking like she was struggling to form a question. She finally peeked up at him and spoke in a hesitant tone. "Did you hear anything about the circumstances of her death?"

He shook his head.

"A few weeks before she died, she approached me to do some accounting work for the family business. It was right after her husband died, and I thought she might be trying to reach out to me. Make amends for having cast me aside all those years ago. I was *so happy*—thrilled, really. I agreed to help without a second thought."

Her face was troubled, and he ached, knowing that this reunion with her mother had somehow been disastrous. "What happened?"

"The financial books she gave me were fraudulent. She was trying to get revenge on my cousin Nick over some ancient grievance, and she used me to do it. The police got involved, and when everything unraveled, I was left holding the bag." At his appalled look, she rushed to explain. "I don't think she meant for it to happen that way."

"Don't defend her. She's not worthy of your loyalty." He couldn't wrap his mind around the concept of a mother putting her own daughter in such peril, but the humiliation on Eloise's face made it impossible to doubt her. "What happened?" he finally managed to ask.

"Well, I was fired from my job," she said. "No one wants to employ an accountant accused of fraud. Nick knew I'd been duped, and he pulled a lot of strings to get me this job with the state. Anyway, my mother committed suicide, and it was a messy death. It was almost two days before she died, and Bruce went with me to the hospital. Even after everything she'd done to me, I couldn't abandon her at the end. She was an unhappy person with no hope and no faith. I felt sorry for her."

Alex covered her hand with his own, wishing he could offer better comfort, but Eloise hadn't finished.

"Bruce stayed with me at the hospital the whole time, and we were never closer. I knew he could never acknowledge me as his daughter while my mother was alive, but she's gone now, and I hoped that might change. I still hope for that."

Her voice trailed off, and Alex's heart split wide open. How could he fix this for her? Part of him wanted to take out an advertisement in a newspaper and spill the truth to the world. It was in his nature to fight for the people he loved, and standing aside while Eloise accepted the atrocious treatment by her family violated his every instinct.

"If you want Garrett to acknowledge you, ask for it. Demand

it. If you want, I'll go up that mountain and demand it on your behalf."

She choked back a gulp of laughter. "Oh good heavens, no!" she gasped. She looked partially appalled but mostly amused, and pure, clean laughter bubbled out. Why was she laughing? He was serious.

"Say the word and I'll go right now," he offered.

"Oh, Alex," she finally said. "Thank you for your willingness to help, but your plan would be a howling disaster."

"Not howling," he corrected. "Maybe a little disastrous, but howling?"

"It would howl," Eloise assured him with amusement still lurking in her eyes, and he was at least grateful he could lighten her mood.

"I would do anything in the world for you," he said. "Always. Show me a dragon to slay. A mountain to climb. Just ask."

She hadn't moved from her position against the back wall, but her entire countenance had shifted. Pleasure flushed her cheeks, and she gazed at him with undiluted happiness.

"At the very least, come to the harvest festival," he prompted. "The vote is going to be a landslide victory, and you deserve to be there. None of this would be happening without the work you did for us."

"All right," she said. "I'll come."

She still hadn't moved, but he closed the distance between them and leaned in, almost touching his forehead to hers. A connection hummed between them, and the longing to tug her into his arms was almost unbearable. Her face was only inches from his, and if he lowered his head just the tiniest bit . . .

A clicking rattle drifted down the hallway, a message coming into the Western Union telegraph station. Eloise pulled back and looked down the hall, where Kasper Nagy roused himself from the bench to start receiving the message.

"I'd better go see if that's for me," she said. "It could be a reply from my boss."

She was gone before Alex could stop her. He battled an almost irresistible urge to yank her back to the privacy of the kitchen and away from anything having to do with New York. For a few minutes, the magic of what they'd once had was here again. The old Eloise was back, and he'd do anything to keep her here for good.

He swallowed hard and planned carefully. Eloise might have loyalties to the city, but for now she was here in the valley, and that meant he had a home-field advantage.

And this time, he'd fight hard.

loise looked forward to the harvest festival with un-seemly anticipation. Maybe it was a little foolish, for these events seemed tailor-made for children, but she so desperately wanted to attend. She kept it a secret from Bruce. It might endanger their fragile relationship, and she could probably escape the house without him even noticing.

It was the first weekend of October, and most of the demolition team had returned to the city for a visit with their families. Fletcher had promised them all a monthly trip home, and she had been looking forward to seeing baby Ilya again, but the chance to attend the festival in Duval Springs won out. Claude, Roy, and Enzo all had wives and children they were eager to see and left for the city first thing on Saturday morning.

She would settle for a telephone call back home to hear baby Ilya's voice again. Bruce had a telephone in his home, but the closest one to Eloise's apartment was in the pharmacy on the first floor of the neighboring building. She had instructed Tasha to delay placing the call until Ilya could be on hand. It was ridiculous, because he only knew two or three words, but even hearing his jabbering was something she craved.

Tasha didn't call until late in the afternoon. Eloise raced to the back hall, where the telephone had been installed on the other side of the electrical box. She grabbed the receiver in excitement.

"I'm so sorry," Tasha said about the tardy call. "First the baby was throwing up his lunch, and then he took a nap. I didn't want to wake him."

"Of course not!" Eloise said. "But he's all right now? Can you hold the receiver to his face so I can hear him?"

"I am," Tasha said. "He's not making any noise."

"Tickle him a little."

Tasha must have obeyed, for a moment later her precious boy made some gulpy squeals that sent Eloise's heart soaring. Someday she would have a baby of her own. As soon as she returned to New York City, surely this unwelcome fascination with Alex would fade, and she could concentrate on finding a solid, dependable man like Fletcher Jones.

It had been unusually generous of Fletcher to fund monthly trips for the team to go home. Normally he was such a stickler for every dollar. As she hung up the telephone, she wondered if he had expected to see her this weekend. Perhaps it had been a mistake to stay. Harvest festivals were for children, and she was a grown woman.

But she rushed to get ready because she didn't want to miss a single moment, and the telephone call had delayed her longer than expected. As soon as she tidied her hair and put on a dash of powder, she slipped out the back door and headed to the stables. The horse had made plenty of journeys between Bruce's home and the village, and she didn't need to guide it as they set off through the woods. It was so different from the city. There was no bustle of traffic or vendors hawking their wares. Only a faint rustle in the trees and the dull thud of horse hooves on the autumn leaves carpeting the ground.

She crouched over the horse's neck to ride beneath a low-hanging branch. Pain slashed across her back, followed by a loud *crack*. The horse panicked, breaking into a gallop, and she started sliding out of the saddle. She grasped the horse's mane to keep from tumbling to the ground. A searing pain, like a line of fire, slashed across her back. Had she been shot?

Oh good Lord, she'd been *shot*!

She tried to pull herself back into the saddle, but the scorching pain made it impossible. The horse kept galloping, and she slipped a little farther with each hoofbeat.

Gravity won and she fell, hitting the ground hard before tumbling down the hillside. The speed of the tumble left her breathless. She couldn't stop. Grass and dirt flew in her face until she rolled against some kind of outcropping and crashed to a halt.

She lay flat on her stomach, praying she hadn't broken anything on the way down. She couldn't move, couldn't breathe.

What happened? The pain felt like fire at the top of her back, but she couldn't twist around to see. What was she supposed to do now? The horse was gone, and she'd fallen a long way down the ravine. She didn't think she could stand, let alone climb back up to the road.

Maybe a hunter had shot her, but didn't they usually hunt at dawn? Bruce always traveled with bodyguards, and tensions in the valley were hot. But why would someone shoot *her*? She was helping these people, everyone knew that.

A twig snapped somewhere. "Quiet!" a hoarse voice whispered.

Eloise held her breath and listened. It sounded like someone creeping through the woods up near the road. Part of her wanted to summon them for help, but she was pretty sure she'd just been shot. Could she trust them?

"Do you see her, Pomo?" a different voice said. "I think we missed."

The breath froze in her lungs. Maybe they were talking about a doe or some other animal, but she'd be stupid to assume that. She'd fallen a long way down the ravine and lay atop a bunch of ferns, her yellow dress making her a bright target in the mossy forest. Fear gave her strength. She shoved herself forward, aiming for the lumpy outcropping of limestone a few yards ahead.

She was on Bruce's land and knew these woods well. There were often hollows beneath these ledges, and it would be a perfect place to hide. The irony! She remembered asking Alex about these overhangs but had always been too frightened to explore them because she was afraid of bears.

She feared those men more than bears and crawled until she reached the rim of the ledge, then peered below. The gap was narrow, only about three feet deep. She held her breath and slid inside, water from the wet moss soaking through her dress.

"There's blood here," a voice called from up near the road. "We got her."

"Then be quiet," the other voice urged.

They could still be talking about a deer, but she didn't think so, and she held her breath as the footsteps came tromping through the underbrush. They were getting closer.

"Come on out, chickadee." The footsteps were directly overhead, so close she could smell the pungent scent of tobacco. It was a strong, sickeningly sweet smell, like cedar and cigars. She clamped a hand over her mouth, fighting not to gag.

Their footsteps faded into the distance, but terror kept Eloise huddled in the cave.

Alex was at the front of the crowd as Reverend Carmichael stood on the bandstand and counted the votes in full view of the town. It was a simple *yes* or *no* referendum to endorse the bond, and after announcing each vote, the reverend held the ballot aloft to ensure no one doubted him.

As he read the first ballot, the reverend stood and majestically shouted "Yes," and the crowd roared. They stamped and clapped and hugged, giving Alex little doubt about the ultimate outcome of the vote. Part of him wanted Reverend Carmichael to simply count the ballots and announce the final tally. It would have taken five minutes, but the reverend's methodical announcement of each vote had been going on for nearly twenty minutes. So far the vote was 267 to 19 in favor of the bond.

"Come on," Hercules grumbled. "Even if every remaining vote is no, we still win. Can't we speed this up?"

Alex shook his head. "Eloise said the investors in New York put stock in things like a landslide victory. And I want everyone in town to see how united we are. It's a necessary step."

But people were already lining up for ice cream. Casks of both hard and soft cider were flowing, and no one paid any mind to the reverend as he kept announcing votes, his voice going hoarse.

All evening long, people came by to shake Alex's hand or clap him on the shoulder. It was hard not to feel over the moon. After tonight, the proposal would go to a New York securities company to put the bond up for sale. It would take a while for that to happen, but Eloise assured him she knew what she was doing.

And where was Eloise? She had promised to be here for the vote, but he'd been looking all evening, and there was no sign of her. None of this could have happened without her, and he wished she were here.

On the bandstand Reverend Carmichael banged a gavel. "My friends, I am holding in my hands the last ballot. And it is a vote for Yes!"

The applause was deafening. People hugged and cheered.

Hercules put Alex in a headlock and tried to wrestle him to the ground, but he grinned and twisted his way out of it.

"What's the final vote?" he called out.

"486 to 29," the reverend announced. "The municipal bond is endorsed."

For about five minutes Alex allowed himself unabashed celebration. He crept up behind Hercules and returned the headlock, pulling them both to the ground in exuberant horseplay. Dr. Lloyd began setting off fireworks.

Tonight was only the first of many battles. Eloise needed to get cracking on launching the bond to investors, and then they needed to hire a crew from Pittsburgh to build them a railway. Oh, and then move two hundred buildings, a church, a school, and a bandstand. It was going to be a tough slog through the winter months, and the hard work would begin tomorrow, but tonight was for celebrating.

After he'd brushed off the grass from his tussle with Hercules, Alex's nephews wanted in on the action. He had to kneel so five-year-old James could imitate the headlock, and Alex obligingly rolled over with a mighty roar.

Someone rapped him on the shoulder. Hard. "Get up, Alex. We've got a problem."

Alex snapped to attention. Dick Brookmeyer, owner of the local stables, had a grim expression on his face. "What's wrong?"

"The horse I lent to Eloise Drake just came trotting up to the stables. No rider, but there's a smear of blood on the mare's saddle."

The comment was so incongruous with the general spirit of excitement that for a moment Alex thought he was dreaming. Then he forced down the surge of fear as an eerie calm settled over him and battle mode kicked in.

"Let's saddle up some horses and ride out," he said.

"But it's already dark," Dick warned.

"All the more reason to go looking for her." Alex rounded up five other men willing to join the search party, and ten minutes later they were all saddling up at Dick's stable.

Hercules swung into his saddle. "Does she know how to ride?"

"Yes. She also knows these woods pretty well, so something is wrong."

The only way to get between Duval Springs and Garrett's mansion was Mountainside Road. Could it have been more sabotage? The horse could have been spooked by damage to the road and thrown her. She could have broken her back, her neck. . . .

This was no time to panic. He murmured a prayer as he nudged his horse faster, and the men followed as the road gradually rose through the thick forest. He called Eloise's name, as did the others. She'd have to be deaf not to hear them as they moved deeper into the woods. Unless she was unconscious. The lanterns they carried didn't cast much light beyond a few yards, and he peered fruitlessly into the darkness.

Frustration clawed at him as he stood in the stirrups. "Eloise!" he bellowed, his voice echoing in the woods. Nothing! He exchanged a worried glance with Hercules and swallowed hard. "Let's keep moving."

His voice was gravelly from overuse by the time they rounded the old miner's pass, but now they were only a mile from Garrett's house. Either they'd already passed her, or they'd come upon her soon. Alex drew in a lungful to start hollering again but stopped when a thin voice came from somewhere in the distance. He drew his horse to a halt.

"Quiet, everyone." He held his breath to listen.

"Alex?"

He nearly doubled over with relief, because it was Eloise's voice, coming from far down in the ravine. He vaulted off the stallion, grabbed a lantern, and scrambled through the brush as he hustled down the slope.

"Where are you, Eloise?" he called. Mud made the hillside slippery, and he grasped at saplings and tree branches to steady himself as he lurched farther down.

"I'm here."

Her thin voice sent a new wave of concern through him. She must have taken quite a beating on her way down to sound so bad. Even so, he smiled as she crawled out from beneath a ledge of limestone jutting from the soil.

"Find any bears in there?"

"No bears."

But she didn't sound good, and he rushed to her side. A scarlet splotch marred the back of her yellow dress.

"What happened?"

"I think somebody might have shot me." Her voice sounded as bewildered as her expression looked. The bloodstain and a rip on the back of her dress made it hard to conclude otherwise.

"Are you hurt anywhere else?" There was no trace of panic in his voice as his battlefield training came to the surface with remarkable ease. After assessing her condition, he ordered two men to Garrett's house for a wagon. Hercules came down the ravine to wait with them until the wagon arrived.

"Could it have been hunters?" Hercules asked.

"I don't think so," Eloise said, still lying on her stomach in the dirt. She went on to relay a conversation between at least two men speculating on whether "they got her" or not. She hadn't seen the men but thought one of them might be named Pomo or maybe Cuomo. Their voices had been muffled, and she couldn't hear well.

Alex exchanged worried glances with Hercules. "We'll figure it out once it's daylight," he said.

Hercules had his rifle at the ready, and they both scanned

the woods for any hint of danger. In the meantime, Alex kept up a constant stream of chatter to keep Eloise distracted from the pain.

"We held the vote tonight," he said, unable to block the pride from his voice. "We won, 486 to 29. The bond is a go."

He was rewarded by a genuine smile from Eloise as she lay weakly in the dirt. He spoke of the festival and the maple candy, and of how Oscar Ott's professional pride had been offended when he wasn't trusted to tally the votes. "He's an accountant too. What's with this weird fascination with numbers you people have?"

He continued the rambling steam of pure nonsense to keep her distracted. After the longest thirty minutes of his life, the men returned with a wagon. It would be impossible for them to maneuver the wagon down the ravine, and once again Alex's army training came to the fore. After helping Eloise stand, he and Hercules faced each other and grasped arms, forming a makeshift chair with their arms.

"Go ahead and sit," he urged. "We're going to carry you up to the road like a princess on a throne."

"I think I can walk." A grimace of pain crossed her face as she took her first trudging step up the hillside, but others on the road hollered encouragement as she got closer. She even managed a smile as she reached the road, and Alex helped her into the bed of the wagon.

"Let's go," he ordered as soon as the tailgate was closed. He walked alongside the wagon all the way to Garrett's house. It galled him that he had to turn her over to that man's care, but this wasn't the night for a confrontation, and he needed to do what was best for Eloise.

When they reached the gate outside the mansion, he asked the driver to stop the wagon. He leaned over the wagon bed to get as close as he could to Eloise.

"I need to leave you now. You're in good hands, but I don't see any point in asking for trouble by setting foot on the property."

She tilted her head to see him in the dim light. "Probably for the best," she said.

He reached in to squeeze her hand, wondering when he'd be able to touch her again. A couple of men opened the gate leading up to the mansion, and he stepped back, watching them lead the wagon through doors that then closed with a clang and a thump as the bolt thrust into place.

It *was* probably for the best that she would be cared for by Garrett, as the place was swarming with guards.

Because there was one thing Alex knew for sure about what had happened. Whoever had shot Eloise wasn't a hunter.

loise was a little miffed at the doctor's belittling of her wound.

"It's only a mild graze," he pronounced after cleaning it. It was three inches long and so shallow that it didn't even require stiches. After spreading on a thin layer of ointment, he covered it with a bandage and declared her fit.

In truth, the physical wound wasn't serious, but the fright still held her in its grip. If she hadn't bent to avoid a low-hanging branch, that bullet could have killed her. Spending hours huddled alone in a muddy overhang had only magnified her fright.

Despite this, she felt well enough to join Bruce for breakfast the next morning. She gingerly descended the staircase, a model of poise because it was impossible to slouch or even lower her chin without aggravating the wound on her back. Were grazes supposed to hurt this badly?

Bruce nearly choked on a mouthful of coffee when he saw her approach the breakfast table. "What are you doing out of bed?" he roared.

"Since it is impossible to lie on my back, and I hate being on my stomach, I thought I'd join you for breakfast."

Bruce filled a plate with scrambled eggs from the sideboard, then brought her a cup of coffee. Two of his bodyguards were at the table with him and had been huddled in a furtive discussion when she entered. The bodyguard she knew simply as Moose stood up and held a chair for her.

An uncomfortable silence reigned after everyone was seated. None of the men made any attempt to resume the conversation that had them so engrossed when she entered the room. She tasted the eggs, wondering when one of them would speak, but the three men seemed uncomfortable, fidgeting in their chairs.

The silence was unbearable, and she finally set down her fork. "I'm feeling much better this morning. Thank you all for asking."

"I can see that," Bruce said. "Do you have any additional insight about what happened yesterday? Do you remember any other voices?"

Before she could answer, a trio of men clomped into the room. One of them held a rag to a cut beneath his eye, but the others looked triumphant. Emil Lebenov, the head of Bruce's security team, tossed a burlap sack on the floor.

"That foreman squealed like a baby," Emil said. "We got all we're going to get—"

"Ahem!" Bruce rose to his feet. He sent a pointed glance at Eloise, and the newly arrived men instantly sobered.

"That breakfast sure smells good," Emil said. "It looks like Mrs. Hofstede outdid herself. Do you think there's enough left for us?"

Bruce gestured for the men to serve themselves from the sideboard. He had never been a stickler for formality, and she'd known most of these men since childhood, so it wasn't unusual for them to join him at the breakfast table.

"Fill your plates, and we can talk later," Bruce said.

"I'd prefer to talk now." Eloise stared at the man with a cut beneath his eye. "Where were you this morning?"

"Eloise," Bruce said in one of his warning tones, "the men were doing a little business, and you needn't concern yourself."

"You're feeling better?" Emil said. "We heard it was only a graze, but those things can hurt."

"Ha!" Moose pulled the collar of his shirt open. "See that scar? That's where I had shrapnel dug out without anesthesia. *That* hurt."

The man with the cut on his eye lowered his handkerchief to hold up a hand with only three fingers. "I had two fingers blown off in a mining accident. *That* hurt."

Lowering the handkerchief revealed a cut on his lip too. And Moose had a smear of blood on the knee of his pants.

"What sort of business were they on?" Eloise demanded of Bruce.

He rolled his eyes. "Hang it all, Eloise. They were out at the Kingston work camp, trying to find who shot you. There was a drunken bash last night, and I need to know if any of them thought it would be a good idea to shoot off some guns in the woods."

Her mouth dropped open. "And you thought beating people up was a good way to find that out?"

"No one was going to volunteer to it," Emil said reasonably. "And besides, we learned a bunch of construction workers placed bets on who could shoot more squirrels in the space of an hour. We'll have their names soon."

"Not if you have to beat it out of people," Eloise said.

Before Bruce could protest, the housekeeper entered the room, a hint of panic in her face. "Mr. Riesel is on his way in," she said.

Everyone in the house knew what that meant. When Bruce's most important business associate entered the house, Eloise needed to make herself scarce. As a child, she had been insatiably curious about Mr. Riesel, probably because she was forbidden to have any contact with him.

Bruce stood and offered a hand to help Eloise rise. "Come along," he prompted when she didn't budge.

Was he really going to make her clear out of the room? Yesterday she had been shot. Maybe it was only a graze compared to the horrors suffered by the others in the room, but the wound was fresh, and it hurt to stand. Even worse, it would hurt her soul to scurry away and hide because Bruce Garrett still refused to acknowledge their relationship.

"I'm not moving," she said quietly.

Bruce waved his hand impatiently. "Come on, Eloise. It will only be for a few minutes."

"How long are we going to keep playing this game?" she asked. "I've been shot, I'm in the middle of breakfast, and I don't feel like leaving."

"Go and ask Mr. Riesel to wait," Bruce ordered the housekeeper, but it was too late.

Two men already stood behind the housekeeper—a stocky, middle-aged man and a younger man with a peppermint stick dangling from his mouth. Both looked at Eloise with curiosity.

Bruce straightened. "Jack!" he boomed in an artificially bright voice. "I didn't expect you to be joining us today. Come in! I'd like to introduce Eloise Drake. Miss Drake is my accountant. Eloise, this is my oldest business partner, Theodore Riesel, and his son, Jack."

The older man looked stonily at Eloise, but Jack seemed intrigued. "Eloise Drake," he said in a pondering tone. "I've heard the name recently. Aren't you the one placing a bond up for sale? I saw a woman named as the placement agent and thought that very odd. Is it you?"

Good manners dictated that she should stand, but she remained seated at the dining table. "Yes, that's me. The people of Duval Springs need a rapid influx of cash if they're to get their town moved ahead of the demolition crews."

Jack tutted. "The fact that a town needs money doesn't justify a risky investment scheme."

She ignored the condescension in his tone and relied on logic for her reply. "The municipal bond will bring a 5.25-percent rate of return, compared with 2.6 percent for treasury bonds, and it is far safer than commodities. It is an excellent investment."

A roguish smile spread across Jack's face. "You should keep this lady on the payroll," he said to Bruce.

"I intend to. Come, let's head out to the quarry, and I can show you the proposed blasting zone."

Eloise watched as all three men disappeared down the hallway. Did Bruce mean to hide their relationship for the rest of his life? It would have been awkward to acknowledge an illegitimate child while his wife was alive, but Laura Riesel Garrett had died twenty years ago, so why did it still matter? She twirled her coffee cup, wondering what it would be like to have a real family.

Emil and the other bodyguards began conversing in Bulgarian. She met Moose's gaze across the table. Moose was from Quebec and his native language was French, so neither of them could join in.

"Would you please speak in English?" she asked the Bulgarians.

"Sorry about that, Eloise," Emil said. "We were just talking a little business. Didn't think you'd be interested."

More likely they were discussing the rough justice they'd been dispensing in the labor camp this morning.

She pushed her coffee cup away and turned to Emil. "Why does Bruce only hire foreigners here at the house?"

Emil shrugged. "You should probably ask him that."

"I have. He never answers." Bruce was cagey and defensive whenever she asked questions along those lines.

"Well, I suppose it's because foreigners are loyal," Emil finally said. "Not like those people down in Duval Springs whose first loyalty is always to their family. All of us came here on a ship with nothing but what we could carry. No family. No divided loyalty. And Garrett has always treated us decently. Why shouldn't we be loyal?"

"What about the Russians?" Moose said.

"What Russians?" she asked, and Emil answered.

"Garrett brought in a bunch of Russians fresh off the boat to work at the quarry during the strike. They were willing to work for pennies, but it only lasted a few months. They left, and that was the straw that broke the strike."

"They were lousy workers," Moose said. "None of them had worked in a quarry before, and it took weeks to get them trained. Production slowed, contracts were canceled. Then they up and quit. We never did see those Russians again."

Eloise sighed. Why couldn't decent people get along with each other? She liked and respected almost everyone she'd met in the valley, and yet mistrust and old hostility seemed to haunt so many relationships. And those old grudges might very well have prompted someone to take a shot at her last night.

Her thoughts were so worrisome that after breakfast she sought escape in a favorite novel, following the rollicking tale of Jim Hawkins in *Treasure Island*. She found a cozy chair in Bruce's study to await his return. She had read *Treasure Island* countless times, yet she still loved the grand adventure.

It was nearing lunchtime when Bruce returned, and she was still waiting for him. He looked tired as he strode into the study.

"How are you feeling?" he asked.

"Fine." She closed the book and hugged it against her chest. "I'd like to continue the discussion we started this morning before the Riesels arrived."

He sighed. "Not that again."

"Yes, that." It hurt too much to even state the problem. "Do you intend to hide it forever? I need to know."

Bruce was silent as he pulled out his desk chair and sat. He steepled his fingers and took a deep breath. "I intend to formally recognize you as my daughter, but I want to get Riesel's signature on some contracts first. The quarry and the cement factory are tightly linked, and we've got ironclad trusts that dictate how things are done. We agreed from the outset that when we die, the assets would be divided equally between our living children. If one of us had no children, the entire lot would go to whoever did."

The puzzle pieces were falling into place. Theodore Riesel was a widower with one son, so Jack Riesel had probably come of age believing he would someday inherit everything.

"Were you really intending to leave me out in the cold?" she asked.

Bruce snorted. "You would hate running a limestone quarry," he pointed out. It was true, but it still seemed a little uncaring. "I'll see that you get your fair share, but Jack is a hardworking young man who has been fully engaged in the business. He's the right man to run the cement factory *and* the quarry. Acknowledging you as my daughter will complicate things. Let me work with my lawyers to figure out an equitable distribution of the assets before upsetting the applecart by acknowledging you."

"I understand," she said softly. Corporate agreements could be a complex nightmare to untangle, but she still wished she meant more to Bruce than an applecart.

Who shot Eloise?

The question plagued Alex incessantly throughout the next day. Hercules's friend in Garrett's stable reported that Eloise felt well enough to go downstairs for breakfast that morning, so she must be getting along okay.

That didn't mean she was all right. She'd been petrified when he found her in the woods, and knowing Eloise, she'd locked that anguish beneath an ivory mask while pretending to be cool as a cucumber. He needed to see her for himself, but knocking on Garrett's front door and asking for a visit was out of the question.

Which was why he was cutting through the woods to Garrett's mansion at two o'clock in the morning. His breath turned into white puffs in the chilly night air, but he was grateful for the thin moonlight that illuminated the stone wall surrounding the estate. He grinned as he found footholds in the roughly hewn stone and hoisted himself up and over. It was going to be a challenge to get into the mansion, but this sort of danger thrilled his blood.

He waited for a cloud to cover the moon before crouching low and darting toward the house. He hadn't indulged in this sort of escapade since his army days, and it stoked a long-dormant craving for adventure.

As much as he wanted to see Eloise, he had a secondary motive. The municipal bond needed to get posted. Visiting a woman on her sickbed to get her cracking on town business was a little callous, but it had to be done.

He dashed up the staircase that led to the balcony spanning the entire back of the house. Eloise's room was in the turret, which surely had all sorts of symbolic irony attached to it. He cupped his hands against the French doors leading to her bedroom and peered inside. There was the telescope Eloise had told him about, and even from here he could see her braid of long red hair on the coverlet. It didn't take long to pick the lock and push the door open, but he winced at the metallic squeak of the hinges. He left the door open and crept to her bedside.

"Eloise," he whispered as he hunkered down beside the bed. "Eloise, wake up."

She didn't. If the doctor had given her something to sleep, it would be a problem. He needed her to be alert when they discussed the bond. He glanced at the bedside table, but there were no signs of any medicines, only a single book. He tilted it to see the cover.

Treasure Island, with the label of the Duval Springs Public Library still affixed to the spine. A surge of old memories welled. Hercules had said that after Alex was run out of town, the librarian came looking for the book, but since Alex had loaned it to Eloise, there was no sign of it. Hercules paid the fee long ago, but it delighted Alex that she still had it.

After a few more futile attempts to wake her with a whisper, he reached out to jostle the mattress. She jolted awake with a gasping, half-strangled shriek.

"Shh! It's only me."

She clutched the bedsheets to her chin and gaped at him, barely able to speak. "What are you doing here? Are you insane?"

"Maybe," he agreed with a grin as he reached inside his coat pocket. "Here. Maple candy. You missed the festival, so I saved you some. How are you feeling?"

"I'm furious," she said in a harsh whisper. "You need to leave before Bruce finds you here and kills us both."

"Let's not exaggerate. He might kill me, but never you." Her breathing was ragged in the dark, and he felt a little guilty for scaring her. "I'm sorry for startling you."

"I'm not going to say it's all right, if that's what you're hoping."

All he hoped was that she had recovered from the fright of the previous evening. Not knowing what happened after she disappeared behind those gates had been killing him. He pulled a chair to her bedside and sat.

"You were brave in the woods last night. I was proud of you."

She shook her head. "I was scared out of my wits."

"You can be brave and scared at the same time. A little fear is a good idea when people are shooting at you." He held up the copy of *Treasure Island*. "Filching library books? As mayor, I feel duty-bound to report you to the authorities."

"You *are* the authorities," she said, trying to repress the hint of laughter in her voice. "And I'm not giving it back. I took that book to the convent with me and had to hide it from the nuns. For a while it was my lifeline."

"And then what happened?"

"Then I grew up and put childish adventure stories behind me."

"And yet there it sits."

"But at least now I understand the distinction between a novel and real life."

He grinned. "Please, Miss Certified Public Accountant, characterize the last twenty-four hours of your life. Did it involve dodging bullets, moonlit flights in the dark, and infiltrating bear-infested caves?"

"Yes, it did," she said in exasperation. "I've now had enough adventure to last a lifetime. I want nothing more than to return to my boring accounting ledgers."

He tried to affect a casual tone. "Speaking of which, how is the bond coming along?"

"I got shot, Alex. I haven't done a single thing."

"Which is why I'm here to offer my services. Do you need me to deliver paperwork to New York? Make some telephone calls? Tell me what you need, and I'll get it done."

"The documents are in the top bureau drawer. The name and address of the securities company are on the second page. All that's needed is to deliver the paperwork with a notarized copy of the election results, and they will offer it for sale."

He retrieved the paperwork, tilting it toward the weak glow of moonlight to verify everything was as she said, and his knees went weak with gratitude that this was actually happening. He glanced at her from across the room, where she watched him with a guarded look. He didn't understand what launching a municipal bond required, but it looked complicated and riddled with charts, codes, and regulations. For Eloise to be so comfortable navigating this mathematical quagmire made his respect for her soar.

"You should be very proud of this," he whispered as he held the papers aloft.

"Thank you. Now you need to go."

"What if I want to stay?" And he did. Everything in him longed to indulge the growing bond between them. When they were younger, they had lain on the grass and daydreamed about what life could be. Now they were living it. They'd rolled up their sleeves to work in tandem on a daring, desperate quest, and there was no one he'd rather have beside him.

"I have a reputation to maintain, and if anyone finds you here, it will be ruined." It was impossible to miss the panic in her voice, and his nascent fantasies crumbled, for Eloise already had someone else in her life.

"Who's the guy?"

Eloise knew exactly what he meant. "He's someone I respect and who respects me. I can't have you here. Now please go."

It was the answer he dreaded, but the first step in any battle was to figure out your enemy. "Did he come visit you? After you were shot?"

Her look turned stony. Still, he wouldn't get far without respecting her wishes. Before he left, he glanced at the battered old copy of *Treasure Island* on her bedside table. Buccaneers, buried gold, and derring-do. She wasn't quite so prim as she pretended. He still had hope.

He held up the paperwork. "Thanks for this," he whispered as he tucked it into his coat pocket, then stepped through the French doors into the cold night air. He held his palm over the squeaky hinge to muffle the noise as he closed the door, then turned to leave.

"Hello, varmint."

Bruce Garrett stood five feet away with a pistol aimed at Alex's chest.

Alex stuck both hands in the air. "I didn't touch her."

"If you had, you'd be dead right now." Garrett's voice was calm, so perhaps he could be reasoned with. Garrett would be idiotic to shoot him only yards away from Eloise. If Garrett meant real harm, he was going to force Alex away from this terrace to someplace where he could do the dirty work in private.

"What are you going to do now?" Alex asked, his heart pounding so hard he could hear it in his ears.

"I want you to stay away from Eloise. She has a good man in New York City."

The easiest thing would be to agree. Or even lie. He could always back out later, because promises made at the point of a gun weren't worth much. But he was in this for the long term, and that meant he had to play the game a little differently. He rolled the dice and tackled the problem head on.

"Then where is he? The good man from New York? She's been shot. What in New York City is more important than rushing to her bedside?"

A series of emotions flitted across Garrett's face. It seemed to take forever but was probably only a few seconds before Garret spoke.

"That may be the first intelligent thing you've ever said."

Garrett lowered his pistol and casually strolled toward Alex. Every instinct urged Alex to kick the pistol away and make a quick escape into the darkness, but he stood his ground. Garrett stood only inches from him. When he spoke, his voice was eerily calm.

"If I ever catch you sneaking around my daughter's bedroom again, you'll have a bullet between your eyes. Now get out of here."

Chapter
FOURTEEN

*E*loise was in trouble. Over the next three days while she recuperated at Bruce's house, she could do little but remember the thrill of Alex's midnight visit. It was as if the past twelve years had rolled away and they were once again two lovers trading secrets and daydreams in clandestine meetings. His dead-of-night visit was such classic Alex—irreverent, dangerous, and fun. It stirred a treasure trove of old memories that were better left behind. Youthful romantic flings were a thing of the past. It was time to buckle down, get her work done, and return to New York City, where she might kindle a relationship with a man of character and rectitude.

Four days after the incident in the woods, it was time to return to work. Moose drove the buckboard with the four members of the demolition team squeezed onto the two benches.

"What on earth is that?" Eloise gasped as the wagon rolled toward the town square. A monstrous shed looked incongruous in the middle of the charming village green.

"It's a pole barn to shelter the oxen they bought to help with the move," Enzo said.

"It's an eyesore," Claude added. "And those animals stink."

Eloise didn't think so. Six lumbering oxen, their coats a shiny black, grazed on the sparse grass of the village green. The scent of the animals and newly cut hay was earthy but nice.

The oxen weren't the only change. A railbed cut through the center of town, and half a dozen men unloaded supplies outside the stables. As Moose navigated the buckboard around a mound of gravel, a couple of workers straightened, dropped their shovels, and began applauding.

"Welcome back!" they hollered.

Were they talking to her? She wasn't the sort of person to garner attention, but they were all looking at her and smiling as they clapped.

"The mayor has been talking you up," Enzo said. "He keeps reminding everyone of the heroic work you did in launching the bond."

Rebecca Wiggin from the creamery came scurrying toward her with a bouquet of daisies. "We've all been praying for you!" she said. "Alex said none of this would have happened without you."

The man who ran the Main Street café joined in. "Coffee and cake is on the house for the rest of your stay in Duval Springs," he called out. "I doubt you'll pay for another meal in this town ever again!"

Eloise was baffled and amazed. Being feted like this was strange and overwhelming. What was she supposed to do with these flowers? She'd never been given flowers in her entire life, and a sheen of tears began to form in her eyes. She battled it back. She'd die of mortification if Claude saw her getting weepy, but oh, this was wonderful.

Moose pulled the wagon to a halt outside the Gilmore Inn, where her first appointment of the day was to appraise the grandest building in the village. She walked inside, the daisies balanced atop her accounting forms so they wouldn't get crushed.

There was no sign of Willard, but Kasper Nagy was at his station, hunched over the telegraph machine as it rattled away. He flagged her down as she entered the foyer.

"A telegram arrived for you just a few minutes ago," he said as he extended the card to her. The message was from Fletcher.

Best wishes for a speedy recovery. FJ

That was all? It had taken Fletcher four days to send a message, and it was so succinct it could be written on a postage stamp. Then again, it was far more proper than a midnight ambush in her bedroom, so she shouldn't mind. And Fletcher's thrift had always appealed to her. He hadn't squandered money on a single extra letter on this message, not even to spell out his name.

"Want to send a response?" Kasper asked with one ear still cocked to the incoming beeps from the telegraph sounder.

"Aren't you in the middle of receiving a message?"

He shrugged. "Just eavesdropping on gossip. All I have to do is open the sounder, and I can hear what people are wiring all along this line. And apparently . . ." He paused to listen to the cascade of beeps. A curious range of expressions flashed across his face as the message rattled on for over a minute. When the beeps finally stopped, Kasper leaned forward to whisper conspiratorially. "Apparently the manager of the Brooklyn Dodgers is in a salary dispute with the team's owner. Very nasty. You should hear the language that just crossed that wire."

Eloise fiddled with the daisies. "Don't you feel guilty, eavesdropping like that?"

"Not in the least. I'd die of boredom if I couldn't tap into a juicy message now and then." He looked pointedly at the card in her hand. "Do you wish to send a response?"

Now that she knew Kasper paid unseemly attention to every

message, she'd be a little more careful about what she sent. "No. I'd better get down to business."

She passed the daisies to a hotel maid to put in a vase, then found Willard. Over the next hour, the innkeeper accompanied her as they walked every room of the impressive building. He pointed out countless special features, from the imported banister to the hand-carved moldings in the rooms and hallways. The innkeeper grew sadder with each room. As he showed her the double-glazed windows in the third-story hall, he suddenly paused, a troubled look on his face as he gazed at the volunteers working in the village green below.

"I didn't expect saying good-bye to be so hard," he said, his voice laden with pain.

"So you will be leaving?" she asked.

He nodded. "I'm not a gambler. I love this town, but I fear for every person who pins their hopes on this scheme. They would be safer taking the state payout and moving somewhere else."

"I agree."

Willard threw up his hands in frustration. "Then why are you helping them? Why raise their hopes with a bond that will give them the fuel to dig themselves deeper into debt?"

It was a valid question, but as she looked at the dozens of volunteers on the village green laboring to get the railway built, the answer was obvious. She was coming to admire the risk-takers who were brave enough to reach for the stars.

"The people who need safety will take the payout and move somewhere else, but the risk-takers will follow Alex. I can no more stop them than I can stop the sun from rising tomorrow morning. It would be insanity to even try."

As much as she craved safety, others longed for the chance to grapple with whirlwinds. It was simply the way God had made them, and the world needed both sorts to succeed. Tonight she would go home to the safe haven provided by Bruce, but a piece of her envied those who followed Alex.

Alex hefted another shovelful of dirt from the trench that would someday support the foundation of Reverend Carmichael's house. Land preparation for the new town was going slower than predicted. Thirty men worked on preparing roads, while teams of four worked on foundations for individual homes. Each foundation required a three-foot trench along the perimeter, and the foundations were proving to be more work than anticipated. Everyone was dirty, exhausted, and demoralized by the snail's pace of their progress. The gloves Alex wore no longer protected the oozing blisters he had on both hands.

"We need real equipment," Oscar Ott muttered from a few yards away. "Stupid garden spade. This isn't what professionals use to build anything."

Alex glowered as he hefted another load of dirt. Their equipment had been donated by the residents of Duval Springs. It had taken two full days to prepare a foundation for Mrs. Trudeau's tiny saltbox house, and every other structure they planned on moving was significantly larger.

"How long is it going to take to dig a basement for my house?" Oscar grumbled loudly enough for everyone to hear. "I ought to run for mayor. I'd have made arrangements for proper equipment. An excavator. A steamroller. I'd have a couple dozen professionals shipped in from the city to do all this grunt work."

"And you'd have blown the budget in less than a week," an old apple grower said. "Quit complaining and get back to work."

Oscar straightened, spreading his arms wide. "I'm not complaining! Did anyone hear me complain? I'm just trying to be helpful by pointing out how this operation could be improved."

Alex hated to admit it, but Oscar was right. As he walked

back to town at the end of the day, his back ached and the blisters on his hand began to bleed. They needed to triple their speed to stay on schedule, and donated household equipment wasn't up to the task.

He headed into the tavern for a mug of cider and an hour of sulking. He'd lost Eloise to some city slicker, he was failing the town, and for once in his life, Oscar Ott had the better of him.

His gloomy stream of thoughts was cut off by rowdy laughter as a gang of quarrymen stumbled into the tavern led by a grinning Boomer McKenzie.

"We quit!" Boomer proclaimed. "We waltzed into Bruce Garrett's creepy fortress and told him what we really think about his lousy quarry. And we did it in style. Have a look at *that*!" Boomer slammed down a section of the *Kingston Daily Freeman*, folded into quarters to display a large advertisement.

It was a double-bordered announcement saying that the following men would no longer be indentured laborers to the Bone-Crusher. A dozen men had put their name to the advertisement.

A few months ago Alex would have laughed and congratulated each man, but not now. Leading the town's move forced him to become a different person, one who was less impulsive and more likely to ask for favors rather than burn bridges.

"Maybe he can hire a bunch of Russian scabs to replace you," Hercules joked. "Although that didn't work out so well the last time he tried it."

One of the jubilant men danced a little jig. "No more driving a steamroller and choking on the dust! No more risking my life with that excavator."

"Or that crane!" Boomer added.

The newspaper passed from hand to hand as hoots of laughter filled the tavern, but Alex couldn't join in the hilarity.

A steamroller, a crane, and an excavator. Rich men like Bruce Garrett had earthmoving machinery, while Alex had to rely on the muscle power of the townspeople to get their land leveled, basements dug, and buildings moved. They'd spent a week getting the land at the Hollister place perfectly graded for the future town square. Garrett's steamroller could have done it in a day.

Alex said nothing as Hercules grabbed the old chair hanging on the tavern wall, plunked it down, and ushered Boomer into it. That chair had once been sat on by George Washington when he moved through the valley on a slushy December night during the dark days of the revolution. It was taken down only for special occasions such as this. The celebrating continued unabashed, but Alex watched the quarrymen from a distance.

Those men were professionals. If he could get earthmoving equipment, they would know how to use it to speed up operations in the new town. A slow smile curved his mouth. Money from the municipal bond would be flowing into the town soon. There was no allocation in the budget for heavy equipment, but he would figure out a way around that. Eloise would be auditing their expenditures, and she was a stickler about rules, but he'd figure something out. He was going to get these men the equipment they needed, even if Eloise tried to stand in his way.

Eloise sat at a dining table in the hotel, finalizing her schedule for next week's appraisal appointments. As soon as Claude and the others arrived, they would head back up to Bruce's house. She startled in surprise when a chair pulled out and Alex plopped down opposite her with a mischievous smile.

"Good evening, Eloise. Can you tell me when the bond money is going to come through?"

She went on immediate alert. Alex knew exactly when that money was due, and his charming smile was meant to disarm her. Whatever he wanted, she wasn't going to budge.

"The first installment will arrive in two weeks."

"Can I get an advance?"

"What for?"

The answer was exactly what she expected. It was a struggle to remain calm as he discussed taking a hatchet to the budget before the first payment had even arrived. It was unthinkable.

"That budget is your bible," she explained. "Investors are making a loan based on the budget the town voted on. As the auditor, I can't permit any deviation, and expensive earthmoving equipment isn't in the budget."

"Come on, Eloise, don't turn into an annoying pencil pusher on me," he wheedled. "We can build a new town, but not without that equipment."

"Too bad. Buying an excavator will break your budget, and you need to trust me on this." She'd been managing Bruce's accounts for years and knew exactly how much an excavator cost to buy and maintain. "Alex, I've spent the last eight years as an accountant. I've worked for a shoelace factory, a fish cannery, and a limestone quarry. None of them were as ambitious as building a new town, and they still inevitably had cost overruns. You can't afford an excavator."

He pierced her with an exasperated stare. "Balancing the books for a shoelace factory has nothing to do with inspiring people to fight for a cause. You think I don't know how hard it's going to get? I do. That's why I intend to deliver what these people need to keep them fighting through mudslides and snowstorms and setbacks. Inspiring people to imagine the future is entirely different from managing an accounting ledger."

"Those accounting ledgers are your lifeblood!" She must have raised her voice because people at the neighboring tables swiveled to peer at them, but she needed to make Alex understand. "I know they don't look glamorous, but they supply the food in your mouth and the clothes on your back. Dreamers build castles in the air, but you need boring accountants to buy the bricks for the foundation. Go ahead and poke fun at my tedious job, but you dreamers would never survive without boring pencil pushers to keep your fantasies afloat."

She slumped back into her chair, crossing her arms over her chest. Almost everyone in the dining room was eavesdropping, and she shouldn't have lost her temper. Normally she plastered a brave face over hurt feelings, but she was proud of being an accountant, even if the rest of the world thought it dull.

"I'm sorry I called you a pencil pusher," he finally said.

She sniffed. "But I *am* a pencil pusher. You just never learned to appreciate people like me. You'll have your money in two weeks. And Alex—I'll be watching how you spend it. Don't you dare try to buy an excavator."

He rocked back in his chair, a speculative look on his face. She didn't like it. He had another card up his sleeve, and she braced herself.

"You're right," he said. "I shouldn't buy an excavator. Why buy one when I can borrow one instead? How about you get me a meeting with Bruce Garrett so I can convince him what a good idea it would be to loan us the equipment?"

"Bruce! Now I know you've lost your mind."

"He's got earthmoving equipment. Boomer McKenzie says the northwest corner of his quarry has just been blasted and cleared, so he won't need his heavy equipment for another three months. It will cost him nothing to loan it to us and earn him a lot of goodwill from the town. I can see that he gets it."

"Bruce doesn't care about goodwill. He wants an explosives expert, and if you read the *Kingston Daily Freeman*, you know that Boomer has parted ways with the quarry."

Alex shifted, rubbing his jaw. "Yeah, taking out that ad wasn't the smartest thing. Look, if Garrett needs Boomer back on the job, I'll make it happen. We need that equipment, and all I need from you is to get me a meeting with Garrett. And you've got to admit, it makes more sense than buying it all."

Alex would rather pry out his own teeth than ask Bruce for a favor, but the fact that he was willing to do it was a sign of maturity. It also made a lot of sense, if they had a prayer of getting this town moved in time.

"I'll try," she said cautiously. But she wasn't a miracle worker, and getting Bruce to loan them that equipment would require one.

lex sat on a hard bench in the foyer of Bruce Garrett's house. Eloise had succeeded in getting him an appointment to discuss the loan of the equipment, and Alex arrived on time for the six o'clock meeting but had been informed that Mr. Garrett was at dinner and would see him after he finished.

That was two hours ago, and from the sound of laughter down the hall, dinner was still in full swing. It grated on Alex. It wasn't the fact that he hadn't eaten yet and the scent of simmering meat was so tempting it made his mouth water. It wasn't even that Garrett had ordered him here at a time when he knew Alex would be forced to wait before being ritually humiliated by pleading for the loan of his equipment.

It was the sight of Emil Lebenov sitting on the bench directly opposite him that made his temper simmer. Emil was one of the thugs who had beat him up all those years ago. Some of Garrett's bodyguards had just been carrying out business, but Emil seemed to have enjoyed it. Even now, as he whittled a chunk of wood in his beefy hands, he had a creepy half-smile on his face as he kept Alex pinned on the hard bench.

A half hour later, the door of the dining room opened, and the footman approached.

"Mr. Garrett will see you now."

Instead of a private meeting in Garrett's study, the footman led Alex into the dining room. Apparently the lord of the castle wanted an audience while Alex groveled, but Alex needed this equipment and would do whatever was necessary to get it.

A long dining table dominated the center of the room, laden with platters of food and dozens of flickering candles. Members of the demolition team sat at the table with Garrett at the head, but all Alex could see was Eloise, sitting at Garrett's right hand. Dressed in silk with her hair mounded atop her head, she looked like a duchess. But he couldn't let her distract him.

He squared his shoulders and met Garrett's gaze from the far end of the table. "Thank you for seeing me."

Garrett took a long sip of coffee before wiping his mouth. "What do you want?"

"I have reason to believe you might be willing to loan some of your equipment to the town. Your steamroller and new Otis excavator."

Garrett took his time as he poured himself another cup of coffee. Silence descended as he stirred in cream and sugar. A bead of perspiration trickled down Alex's back, but he remained motionless.

Garrett's demeanor appeared relaxed, but contempt simmered in his voice. "Why would I would loan thousands of dollars of equipment to a passel of ingrates?"

This wasn't going to be easy. Alex wished Eloise weren't here to witness his humiliation. Garrett was going to make Alex lick his boots, but he couldn't let his pride get in the way.

"The gesture would go a long way toward easing relations between the town and your business. Boomer even agreed to come back to work if you extended such a gesture of goodwill."

Garrett toyed with his coffee cup, slowly rotating it in his hands. "I'm surprised Boomer would be willing to slide up the mountain to kiss my ring."

Alex didn't move a muscle. He'd heard that phrase before, but it took a moment to remember that Boomer had said it that first night of planning during the schoolhouse meeting. Someone in that room had carried a detailed report of the conversation to Garrett. There were hundreds of people at that meeting, but knowing a snitch was among them was disconcerting.

Alex swallowed hard and blocked twelve years of hostility from his voice. "I know how generous the loan of the equipment is, and I will take personal responsibility for the equipment."

Garrett quirked a brow. "*Personal* responsibility? You'd be willing to sign a document to assume *personal responsibility* for the equipment?"

He opened his mouth to agree, but Eloise cut him off.

"Alex, don't," she said, a note of warning in her voice. Her admonition surprised him, but it stunned Garrett, who looked at her as though his lapdog had just bitten his hand.

"Why shouldn't he?" he demanded of Eloise. "If I am to send a fortune in earthmoving equipment into hostile territory, I need a guarantee my investment will be secure. If the mayor of the town can't insure it, who can?"

"Don't do it, Alex," Eloise continued. "This could ruin you. Last week a steam shovel at the Timberland camp had its chain cut. It was sabotage, and it's getting worse." She turned her attention back to Garrett. "Until we know who is responsible for the ongoing sabotage, it's not fair to make Alex assume responsibility for the equipment."

Garrett was unmoved as he looked at Alex. "Well?" he asked silkily. "Can you keep your men in line and guarantee the safety of my equipment?"

Alex hesitated. He hadn't heard about this latest incident

of sabotage at the new Timberland work camp, but that was hostility against the reservoir. No one in Duval Springs would undermine their own cause in moving the town.

"I'll sign for it," he said, trying to ignore the pained resignation on Eloise's face.

A hint of a smile curved Garrett's mouth. "Send a note to my attorney to arrange a meeting," he said to one of the servants. "Although why I should waste my time with this ridiculous crusade is beyond me. You have no idea what you're up against."

It was true. He was no engineer or builder, but he had an army of people ready to figure out a way to make it happen. "I have nine hundred people who have agreed to supply labor."

"No," Garrett countered. "Your nine hundred people includes old men, women, and children. You need able-bodied men and a skilled workforce. You need engineers, surveyors, and builders. Your town can't even find someone qualified to teach your grammar school classes."

If Alex worried about the magnitude of the task, it would stop them in their tracks. This war needed to be waged one battle at a time. "I will find a way," he vowed. "We've got the most important element on our side. We've got hope, and hope can build bridges and tame storms and fuel our muscles until we drag ourselves across the finish line. We aren't quitters."

"I can help." Eloise's voice stunned him.

"What?" The outburst came from Alex and Garrett simultaneously, but Eloise was already on her feet, sending him a tentative smile.

"I'm good at math," she said, looking a little surprised at her own audacity. "If you need someone to calculate building loads or costs, or whatever . . . I can help."

"I can too." This was Enzo, the young Italian demolition expert, who leaned back in his chair with an expression of admiration and surprise. "I like this idea of moving a town. I've never done it, but if you need an engineer, I can help. In fact—"

"Pipe down!" Claude Fitzgerald smacked his fist on the table, causing the silverware to rattle on the plates. "We are being paid to dismantle this town, not move it. Don't forget who is paying your salary, Enzo. I refuse to squander state resources on this dangerous gamble."

"Then I shall help in my own time," Enzo said. "We've been complaining this mountaintop is a boring place to live, and it is." He glanced apologetically at Bruce Garrett. "I'm sorry, but I've spent my whole life in Rome and Manhattan. I live on a diet of Mozart and Michelangelo and the poets of the ages. There's not much to occupy my mind up here once the workday is over. I want to sink my teeth into something *big,* so yes, this crazy idea to move the town speaks to the poet in me. I can work on the project during long winter evenings and on the weekend."

Alex reached out to grab the back of a chair. Without it, he would have collapsed. An *engineer* was ready to donate his time? And Eloise? That she might join in this incredible adventure was staggering.

"Not so fast," Claude said. "We have a job to complete, and I demand your complete loyalty. The state deserves nothing less."

"Not after five o'clock," Enzo said. "After five o'clock, our time is our own, and I can devote a few hours each evening."

"I'm in too," Roy Winthrop said. "I'm a land surveyor, so I can't help with moving the buildings, but I can show you how to get that old farmland into shape to support roads and a town."

Hope bloomed inside Alex. He had come up the mountain in search of some equipment, and he was going to leave with priceless skilled labor. He had to think how best to take advantage of it.

"The town will put you up at the Gilmore Inn," he said.

"That way you won't need to use your free time traveling back and forth. It will save over an hour each day."

Both Enzo and the land surveyor looked pleased at this prospect, and even Eloise agreed to the move, though she still looked worried at the prospect of him signing the note guaranteeing the safety of the earthmoving equipment. He wasn't worried, for no one in Duval Springs would do anything to hurt their own cause.

He left the mountaintop with the promise of skilled labor and a fortune in heavy equipment. Sometimes all the stars in the sky came into perfect alignment, and tonight was such a night.

Eloise was stunned by the way her life changed overnight. Alex showed up at the crack of dawn with a wagon to move her, Enzo, and Roy into the hotel. Willard greeted them all at the door and agreed to donate their rooms for free.

"I've been against this move since the beginning, but I have to congratulate Alex. Having you folks on board is quite a coup," Willard said.

Maybe Eloise shouldn't have brought so many clothes with her, for it was a little embarrassing to have this many trunks and hatboxes. Alex and Hercules each lugged a trunk upstairs, but she had three hatboxes and only two hands. Kasper Nagy read a newspaper at his favorite spot on the lobby bench.

"Can you help me with this hatbox?" she asked.

Kasper tipped the newspaper down to peer over the edge at her in surprise. *"Minulle? Vitsailetko?"*

"Pardon me?" she asked.

Kasper laughed as he folded the newspaper onto his lap. "Forgive me. When I'm shocked, I revert to my native language. Everyone knows better than to ask me for help."

"Where are you from?" she asked. "You speak English perfectly."

"Yes, but I spent my first sixteen years in Finland. It took me a few decades to thaw out after I arrived in New York. I learned English, then Morse code, and I earn a living with my mind. The work for Western Union is so taxing, I simply have no energy left for anything more strenuous than reading a newspaper." Kasper lifted the newspaper again, and the conversation ended.

Eloise looked at Willard in baffled amazement.

"Don't look at me," Willard said. "I'd have fired him decades ago, but he works for Western Union, not me. Hand me the hatboxes. I'll carry them up."

Eloise obliged. It didn't take long to get settled in, and she soon came to appreciate the advantages of living in town. Now, instead of traveling in a bumpy carriage up the mountain each evening, she and the others could simply walk over to the tavern to plan how they could help with the move.

"Come inside," Hercules boomed on their first night of work. It was a much warmer greeting than the first time they'd entered this tavern two months ago. He pulled out a chair at a table and gestured for her to sit. "What can I offer the three of you?" he asked. "Ale? Cider? My firstborn child?"

Enzo grinned. "How about some of your wife's shepherd's pie? I had some last week, and I still can't stop thinking about it."

Hercules disappeared into the kitchen with their order while his oldest son, John, joined them at the table, his mathematics textbook at the ready. Ever since the school had closed, the students had been working with various teams to get an unconventional but excellent education.

"I figured out the size of the footprint for Dr. Lloyd's house," John said. "Now I need to calculate how much cement its foundation will need. I don't know the right formula for that."

Eloise did, and she worked with John while Alex and Enzo worked on scheduling. Before long, a pretty blond woman with an immense belly waddled out of the kitchen, carrying a tray weighed down with shepherd's pie. Alex rose to relieve her of the tray and introduced his sister-in-law to Roy and Enzo.

"Sally is the glue that holds our family together," Alex said as he began distributing the plates. "She's the mother of all these young Duval scamps."

Enzo's smile was broad. "And you are expecting another soon, I see."

"Any day now," Sally said. "We've already got four boys, so my husband is hoping for a girl, but I doubt it will happen. I can tell by the way he kicks that I've got another rowdy one in here."

"Bite your tongue!" Hercules called out from behind the bar. "That little girl is going to be a blessing to this family. The prettiest, sweetest, and daintiest girl to walk the earth. Daisies will spring up in her path. Birdsong will follow wherever she walks."

Sally rolled her eyes. "Listen to him daydream! There hasn't been a girl born into the Duval family in the past four generations. Not since Esmerelda Duval—"

"That's because some crazy fool named her Esmerelda," Hercules said. "If I am blessed with a daughter, she will have a nice, normal name. Mary or Ann. No Esmerelda or Persephone or idiocy like that."

Eloise glanced over at Alex. "How did *you* get such a nice, normal name?"

Her question triggered a round of snickering from others in the tavern, and Alex flushed in embarrassment.

"Go on, tell her, Uncle Alex!" John said, his face breaking up with laughter.

"Confess, Sir Lancelot," someone shouted.

There was clearly a joke that she didn't understand. She looked at Alex in curiosity.

"My real name is actually Lancelot," he admitted. "My mom

was furious, but Dad got to the town hall before she could stop him, and he made it legal. She insisted on calling me Alex after her father, but everyone in town knows the truth."

"We all know you for the brave and gallant soul that you are," Sally said with a wink. "We've learned our lesson, and all the children in our family have normal names. This one inside me kicks like he's strong enough to bring down the walls of Jericho. Start lining up another boy's name, Herc."

The door of the tavern opened, and a gust of chilly air blew in.

"Close the door!" someone hollered, but Eloise nearly choked.

What on earth was Fletcher Jones doing here? He was flawlessly attired in a long wool coat and scarf, but his hair looked disheveled, and annoyance was stamped across his features as he spotted her across the tavern.

"I'd like to know what in the name of all that is holy is going on up here," he demanded.

She rocked back in her chair. "Welcome to Duval Springs," she said in an artificially calm voice. "I hope your journey here was agreeable."

"No, it wasn't agreeable," he snapped. "I gave myself an ulcer wondering why the team I sent here has been sidetracked into an impractical scheme to move a town."

She'd never seen Fletcher angry before, and she was partly responsible for it. Not long ago she would have been appalled at her own behavior, but in the past weeks, some of the stalwart vigor of Duval Springs had sunk into the pores of her skin and changed her a little.

She reverted to common sense to pacify Fletcher. "It's not worth giving yourself an ulcer," she said calmly. "All we're doing is donating a little of our personal time."

Alex rose to stand before her in a protective stance. "It's none of your business what Eloise does with her free time. Who are you, anyway?"

"I'm the person underwriting the salaries of the people charged with the smooth demolition of this town," Fletcher replied.

"The words *smooth* and *demolition* don't belong in the same sentence," Alex said tightly.

This wasn't going well. Fletcher could cause trouble for them if he wanted, and she needed to get him on their side.

"Pull up a chair," she said. "Let's discuss this like rational people."

Fletcher made no move to join them, but a little of the starch went out of him. He focused his entire attention on her and spoke calmly. "I warned you against getting emotionally involved with these people. This is a volatile situation, and I need employees of sound logic on the job. A solid block of granite. That's why I sent you."

Being described as a lump of rock pricked her feminine sense of pride, but wasn't he right? She had indeed gotten carried away by one of Alex's reckless schemes.

Fletcher continued in his firm, unflappable manner. "If the people of Duval Springs choose to use their state payouts to move their homes to higher ground, I won't stand in their way. But let me be clear. Any structure remaining in the valley on May 1 will be torn down and burned to ash. Our timetable is firm, and there will be no exceptions."

"We already know that, Mr. Jones," Enzo said.

"But do the people of Duval Springs know it?" Fletcher asked, raising his voice loud enough to be heard all the way to the corners of the tavern. People put down their mugs and stilled to listen. Fletcher spoke with clinical precision. "Everyone in this town must understand that when they accept payment from the state, the deal is done. Finished. They won't receive another dime, no matter how much the cost of moving their home escalates. Snowstorms, mudslides, equipment breakdowns—none of it will buy another day beyond the deadline. Any home or business still here on May 1 will be demolished."

Eloise glanced at Alex, whose face looked like it was carved from stone. She and Alex understood better than most how big a gamble the homeowners were taking. Their money was *gone*. Everyone who threw their lot in with Alex risked complete financial devastation if he couldn't get their homes moved out in time.

Alex stepped forward. "Do you think we are ignorant clodhoppers?" he asked, matching Fletcher's volume. "Do you think because we don't have a college degree that we can't read a calendar?" Murmurs of approval rippled through the tavern, but Alex wasn't finished. "Let me tell you something about the people in this valley. We've got strong arms and big shoulders and hearts that won't give up. We can deliver a calf, repair broken machinery, and replace a roof, all with our own two hands. We do all that and still get to church on Sunday morning to thank God for the blessing of being born in a place like Duval Springs, where we laugh and work and cry together. And we *will* get this town moved in time, because we aren't quitters."

It looked like Alex wanted to keep talking, but the stamping of feet and a healthy round of applause drowned him out. This was the big-hearted dreamer she'd fallen in love with all those years ago. She glanced at Fletcher, worried that he could somehow throw a wrench into this plan. His face was skeptical but not angry.

"Here's something you need to know about *me*," Fletcher said once the applause died down. "I don't dispute anything you just said, and I wish you well. No one will cheer louder if you succeed, because I don't relish the prospect of coming back here to burn down homes that people risked their livelihoods to save. But I'll do it."

Fletcher buttoned his vest and picked up his traveling case, then directed his attention to Roy and Enzo. "I've come to inspect the Timberland camp before we officially open it for business next week, and then I'm heading back to Manhattan. I'll expect the timetables and the list of necessary supply expenditures on my desk Monday morning. How much longer do you anticipate before the work is complete?"

"We'll have it done by the end of December as planned," Enzo said.

"Excellent. You are clipping along at an admirable pace." Fletcher's tone had reverted back to the formal man of business—safe, logical, and easy to deal with.

Just as Eloise was about to relax, he shifted his attention to her.

"Six more weeks, and then you can come home," he said, looking only at her. "I'll be waiting for you."

Alex silently fumed as he watched Fletcher Jones leave the tavern. This was the man who'd captured Eloise's affection. The stranger's parting words to Eloise couldn't have been more blatant if he'd hung a placard around her neck.

Alex leaned over to whisper in her ear. "That's the guy, isn't it?"

Eloise didn't deny it as she stared stonily ahead. It had been easy to pretend he didn't have competition over the past weeks as they'd worked and laughed together, but he wouldn't forget it again.

And of all the worries and threats he had looming over his head, the one that kept him awake at night was the fact that they hadn't caught whoever had shot Eloise.

Most people had concluded it was drunken workers from the main camp, but Alex wasn't ready to let it rest there. Bruce Garrett's thugs had already done a shakedown of the camp, looking for anyone who answered to the name of Pomo, and come up empty, but threats and intimidation weren't the best way to glean information. Alex had paid his own visit to the Kingston camp and spent more time than he could afford glad-handing the workers and asking after anyone named Pomo or anything that sounded like it. When that failed, he quietly offered a cash reward to company supervisors, but that turned up no leads either.

Which was why he was trudging toward the Riesel Cement Factory, the only other employer of any size in the valley. Jack Riesel had already told him there was no one who answered to the name of Pomo at the factory, but Alex wanted to look around himself.

The factory was a three-story structure that heated, ground, and pulverized limestone into cement dust. A cacophony of noise and heat engulfed Alex the moment he stepped inside. He spotted Jack on the factory floor, examining lumps of rock traveling on a conveyor belt toward an open kiln. The ever-present peppermint stick dangled from Jack's mouth. The moment their eyes met across the factory, Jack waved and headed toward Alex.

"You'll get used to it," Jack shouted above the noise. The cavernous room was filled with kilns and huge rotating drums that made a thundering noise that could surely deafen a man. Windows propped open high in the walls alleviated some of the heat, but not enough. Alex's nose twitched at the chalk in the air, and he had to respect Jack for working in a sweltering, gritty environment like this.

To his relief, Jack motioned for Alex to follow him toward the offices to escape the noise and heat. Even so, Alex's ears continued to echo with the rumble of the churning drums.

"Thanks for meeting with me," Alex said. "I won't take much of your time. I'd like to look at some of the company's records to see if someone named Pomo worked here in the past. Maybe while you were in college? It could also be a nickname."

"I don't think so, but let's ask Oscar. He's been here a long time and has a good memory for that sort of thing."

Alex nodded. As the factory's accountant, Oscar Ott had an eye for detail and dealt not only with factory employees, but with suppliers too. The office where Oscar worked was small, lined with stacks of ledgers, and barely had enough room for a desk.

"Coming to mingle with the peasants?" Oscar asked.

Alex ignored the taunt and asked after insight into who might have shot Eloise.

Oscar just rolled his eyes. "I heard it was just a rip in her dress. She probably faked the whole thing. Women do stuff like that for attention."

"She didn't fake it," Alex said tightly.

Oscar held up his hands. "Okay, okay. She got shot. Just like I'm sure she got that accounting job up at the quarry on her own merit and not by being Garrett's ward. Everyone knows women are bad at math."

"She's a CPA," Alex said, which was more than Oscar was.

"Only rich people can pay for all those fancy classes and tests," Oscar said. "I managed to learn everything all on my own."

It was a frustrating conversation, but in the end Oscar proved unable to think of anyone answering to a name or nickname sounding like Pomo.

"Sorry about Oscar," Jack said afterward as he walked Alex back to the hitching post. "He's annoying, and we only keep him on because . . ." Jack's voice trailed off.

"Because why?" Alex prompted.

They walked a few more paces before Jack replied. "His father was our accountant for years. I know Oscar isn't the brightest man on the planet, but we like to reward loyalty, and he's been loyal. That's worth something."

Alex said nothing as he untied his horse.

"Anyway, I'm sorry we couldn't be more help," Jack continued as he put the peppermint stick back into his mouth. "She doesn't remember anything else about that night?"

"She remembers everything, she just didn't see the men or catch much of what they said. Most people think it was drunks from the main camp." Quite frankly, it was the only thing that made sense, since there seemed to be no motive for anyone to shoot Eloise. Oscar Ott's professional jealousy was the only thing Alex could think of.

"Let's hope so," Jack said, worry in his eyes as he twirled the peppermint stick. "Let me know if there's anything I can do to help."

"Will do," Alex said as he mounted the horse, but unless new information surfaced, he doubted this mystery would ever be solved.

They were ready to move the first building on Saturday, November 7, and Marie Trudeau's compact house was the logical choice. Marie was terrified that her beloved home was being used as a "practice house," but Enzo tried to put her at ease. "Your house is tiny. A *piccolo*," he said in his thick Italian accent. "And since it is first, everyone will take extra care."

Eloise had no formal responsibilities during the move. Her contribution had ended after calculating the weight and size of the house, but it was impossible to stay away. Real-life adventures like this were rare and wonderful, and she wanted to be a part of it.

People began gathering outside Marie's house before sunrise, stamping their feet and blowing into cupped hands. Someone set up a large carafe of coffee in the neighboring yard, and bystanders helped themselves. Hundreds of people were here to witness their first building move to the new town.

Marie looked pale and weak as she sat on the front porch of her house. One of her sons sat on the step beside her while the other carried a box of dishes out to a wagon loaded with the household furniture.

Eloise walked up the path and smiled down at Marie. "You look cold. Can I get you some coffee or a hot muffin?"

At the mention of food, Marie looked ill. "No," she whispered. "I couldn't get anything down."

"Come on, Ma," her son urged as he wrapped an arm around her shoulder. "No matter what happens, it's better than seeing the old place burned to the ground, right?"

Eloise stepped away to get a mug of coffee for herself, then watched from a distance as Alex strode toward Marie, his face somber as he gave her a swift hug. Eloise loved watching his competence, first as he comforted Marie, then when he consulted with Enzo.

At last all the required workers arrived, and Reverend Carmichael stood on Marie's front porch to lead them in a prayer.

"Our dearest Lord," he began. "We've spent the last few years in fear and doubt, not certain what you intend for us, but today we know exactly where we are headed. We ask for your blessing as we begin our journey to a new town, where we will do our best to build a city on a hill, one where we shall lean on each other in times of need, celebrate times of joy, and welcome strangers as friends. In your name we pray."

After the prayer, Alex crossed to Eloise's side, his face solemn. She wasn't used to seeing him nervous, and it was contagious. She clenched her hands to stop them from trembling as the work crew circled Marie's home.

Workstations were set up at each corner of the house. Each station had a brick pad, a hefty jackscrew, and four men. The jackscrews were the size of a horse saddle and had a handle the length of a baseball bat, long enough for two men to use it in tandem.

Once the men were in place, the onlookers pulled back, and Enzo stood at the front of the house, a whistle at the ready.

This was either going to be a disaster or the start of something magnificent. Without thinking, Eloise reached for Alex's hand. He grasped it with surprising strength. They didn't look at each other, just stood shoulder to shoulder as they watched the culmination of all their planning draw near.

"At the whistle, give the jack a quarter turn," Enzo hollered.

The crowd collectively held their breath as a pair of men at each station hunkered down, their hands grasping the cranks. The whistle pierced the air, and all four teams cranked their handles in tandem.

A whimper escaped from Marie, but Enzo blew the whistle again a few seconds later to signal another turn. The first few rotations showed no progress, but Enzo had said it would require several rotations to take the "give" out of the house, and on the eighth twist, the house moved a bit. A collective gasp raced through the crowd. It was a minuscule lift, but it happened again on the ninth twist, and again on the tenth. After a few minutes, the jackscrew teams stepped aside, and fresh crews replaced them to continue the lift.

Eloise glanced at Marie. The older woman's eyes were wide as saucers, and a hand was clamped over her mouth as she gaped at her house, now almost a foot off the ground.

"She's terrified," Eloise murmured to Alex.

"Me too," he admitted. She tightened her grasp on his hand. He still didn't look at her, but the slightest curve of his mouth indicated he felt her support.

The men raised the house another foot, as they needed a full twenty-four inches to slide a set of rolling metal rails beneath the house. Then they would lower the house onto the wide-bed platform, and the oxen would pull it to the railyard. Eloise glanced toward the team of men holding the oxen and caught her breath at the sight of Bruce Garrett on his favorite chestnut bay as he cantered toward them. This wasn't going to be good. Bruce was a distraction this town didn't need.

When Alex noticed where she was looking, his entire body stiffened. "What is *he* doing here?" he said between clenched teeth.

"I'll find out." She dropped Alex's hand and angled through the crowd. Plenty of other people had noticed the unwelcome arrival and muttered under their breaths. She reached Bruce just as he arrived at the corner of the street. "What brings you here?"

Bruce dismounted, his face calm, as if he didn't notice the tension rippling through the crowd. "I came to show my support for the community," he said loudly enough for the nearby bystanders to hear. "It's my equipment making this possible, after all."

"And everyone is grateful for it," she said, hoping the cluster of former quarry workers standing only a few yards away would be respectful. It would have been better if Bruce had stayed home, but how could she tell him that? She took his arm and guided him a few steps back. "Let's keep out of the way," she urged. "As soon as they get that house onto the rollers, the team will need a clear path to the railway."

And the move was imminent. The custom-built rails and platform had been positioned beneath the house, and Enzo signaled for the crew to begin lowering the small building. It took a while, but as the house settled, the old boards let out plenty of creaks and groans.

Marie clamped both hands over her mouth, and a wail cut through the air. Jasper did his best to comfort his mother, but her whimpering was loud and obvious.

"What's that woman caterwauling about?" Bruce asked.

"Shh! It's her house that's being moved," Eloise said.

He snorted. "Then she ought to be grateful it's getting out of the valley ahead of the deadline. I doubt if even half these places can be moved in time." Bruce set off before Eloise could stop him, striding to Marie's side. "No need to worry, ma'am," he said. "This isn't all that big of a job, and in a few hours your house will be safely relocated."

The words failed to crack Marie's anxiety as she stared, fixated, at the men now scrambling to secure cribbing blocks to stabilize the house on the platform. The moment the blocks were in place and the cables were tied down, the oxen would begin towing the house down the street.

"I need to check," Marie said, her voice choked with anxiety. "Jasper, come. We need to be sure those blocks are secure."

Bruce shot out an arm, blocking her from getting any closer to the house. "Let the men do their jobs, ma'am. You'll just get in the way."

"That is my home, and my responsibility," she retorted. "I can't let it be damaged."

"It's just planks and boards, ma'am. Anything that gets broken can be fixed."

Instead of providing comfort, Bruce's words caused Marie to explode. She gave him a solid shove, pushing Bruce off the walk and into the road. "Those planks and boards hold the dreams and memories and fabric of the human experience!" she roared. "They are my life. My history, my family."

Now Bruce was angry too. "You think planks and boards are what make a family? Look around you, woman! I see two hundred people who turned out to help you. *They* are your family. Not a run-down wreck of a house that ought to have gone to the slagheap long ago."

Angry murmurs rippled through the crowd, and Jasper stepped forward. "You can't talk to my mother like that."

Bruce rounded on Jasper, but whatever he was about to say was cut off as he narrowed his eyes to scrutinize the younger man. "I know you," he said. "You're one of the Trudeau boys. You're a cutter up at the quarry."

"I *was* a cutter," Jasper retorted. "I just quit. I won't work for a money-grubbing parasite another day."

Bruce's face reddened, but Reverend Carmichael intervened before it could escalate. "Pipe down, Jasper, and help your mother. It looks like she's about to faint."

The young man shot Bruce a surly glare but obeyed. To Eloise's relief, Bruce also stepped back to join her at the curb. Enzo gave the signal, and the oxen began their work, slowly hauling the house toward the street. Eloise stood spellbound, watching the boxy home roll forward.

"Rabble-rousing idiots," Bruce muttered.

"Wild, magnificent idiots," she said in reluctant admiration as the house inched down the street. It was impossible not to be thrilled with what was happening. That house was actually moving! "It was a good thing you did, loaning that equipment. There are plenty of hotheads here, but most of the people in this town understand the gift you've given them."

Bruce peered down at her. "I didn't do it for them, Eloise."

He had done it because she'd asked him. Bruce was a hard and aggressive man with no soft edges. He didn't know how to back down from a fight, and he was lousy at showing affection, but he was a decent man.

She laid a hand on his forearm. "And I thank you for it."

She wasn't very good with words either. She stepped closer and laid her head on his shoulder. Only for a second before pulling away. They'd never exchanged a hint of affection, and it was probably stupid to do it in public, but it would be nice to have a family, and every now and then, the weakness got the better of her.

Alex couldn't stand the tension any longer. It was nerve-racking watching Mrs. Trudeau's creaky old house be jacked up and moved, but with seventy able-bodied men on the crew and another hundred onlookers, no one needed him here.

He turned away to head up to the old Hollister farm. He walked alongside the newly installed railway, its twin bands of steel still shiny and new against the bed of gravel. Twenty minutes later, he rounded a bend of spruce trees to see the expanse of freshly graded acres that would someday be their new town. It didn't have a blade of grass or a single tree, only hundreds of little flags demarcating future streets, a town square, and individual plots for houses and shops. In a few hours, this blank canvas would have its first house. And in a week? A month? So many unknown details were still in the air.

To his surprise, a handful of people lined the road as he drew closer to the site. The Timberland work camp was less than a quarter of a mile farther up the hill, and last week the first construction workers and their families had arrived. It looked like they had come to watch. Half a dozen men plus a few women loitered near the new town.

One of the women bounced a toddler on her hip. "We heard a house is being moved," she said in a thick Irish accent. "We thought it might be exciting to watch."

Alex let out a nervous laugh. "I'm hoping it will be as dull as watching paint dry."

It was only eleven o'clock in the morning, but already he was exhausted. He glanced through a break in the trees at the path cutting through the woods that led to the new work camp. By the end of the year, the Timberland camp would house at least five hundred workers, most of them Irish immigrants. They would have their own school, canteen, and recreation building. Construction of the reservoir was going to take five years, so such infrastructure was necessary.

"How are things at the camp?" he asked.

One of the men hesitated before answering. "Okay, I guess.

Last weekend a new pump was installed alongside our well. The water has tasted bad ever since."

Alex didn't comment. The state supplied these people with running water, and still they had the nerve to complain. The cold, clean water of the Hudson River Valley was so pure that it could be bottled and sold. It was the reason the state had come here in the first place.

One of the women continued complaining about the water, and Alex was about to give her a piece of his mind when he spotted a movement around the bend of trees. A cluster of men carrying shovels on their shoulders was heading this way, and behind them came the train, slowly pulling Marie's house, inching along at a snail's pace.

Alex sucked in a breath, dumbfounded that this moment was actually happening. Tears pricked at his eyes, but he blinked them back as he sprinted across the field, waving his handkerchief.

"Over here!" he shouted. Stupid, because the men knew down to the inch where they needed to go, but he couldn't restrain himself. This was the best moment of his entire life. The relief, the joy—all of it threatened to swamp him.

Dozens of townspeople trailed after the house, carrying rails and shovels. Dick Brookmeyer walked alongside the slow-moving train, for the oxen had been loaded onto it as well and would soon be put into service again.

Eloise walked alongside the train too, carrying one end of a basket. Rebecca Wiggin held the other. The basket came from the tavern and was filled with sandwiches and apples for everyone's lunch. Eloise sent him a blinding smile as she walked toward him, and he smiled back. The prickling in his eyes was back, and he hoped he wouldn't start bawling like a baby, but sometimes moments of blinding joy came out of nowhere. He swiped his eyes with his cuff so she wouldn't see. This barren, blank field of dirt was about to get its first house. It was the start of their town.

It took an hour to get the oxen offloaded and the house shifted onto the rolling platform and ready to haul the final yards. By the time Dick guided the oxen toward the blank foundation, at least three hundred people had gathered. As the house moved its final inches, they began to clap and cheer, pounding each other on the back. Even people from the Timberland camp applauded as they watched.

Unloading the house went more slowly, as getting it settled in perfect alignment with the foundation took longer than simply lifting it off. At least Mrs. Trudeau didn't look ready to faint anymore. She managed some weak smiles and accepted congratulatory hugs. Meanwhile, most of the townspeople grabbed shovels and yardsticks to start working on the foundations for other buildings to be moved in the coming months.

Hercules soon arrived with a wagon carrying Mrs. Trudeau's furniture. "What, not finished yet?" he asked with a grin as he vaulted from the driver's bench.

Alex tossed him a hoe. "Come help us lay the foundation for the tavern."

Hercules caught the hoe with one hand. "You think that's really going to happen, baby brother?"

"It will happen."

They could do anything. Enzo had warned them the tavern would be a challenge, but on a day like today, with hundreds of men streaming into their new town, and everyone flushed with good cheer and boundless energy, anything was possible.

The moment of truth arrived when Enzo declared the house properly installed on its foundation. He approached Mrs. Trudeau, who stood a few yards from her front door, gazing at her house in a mix of trepidation and joy.

"Not a pane of glass broken," Enzo said with pride. "Do

you want to go in first, or shall I? I believe it to be safe, but if you'd feel better with someone else going in first . . ."

"No," she said. "I would like to be the first to welcome my home to its new town."

Alex felt the tears prickling again as Mrs. Trudeau cautiously opened the front door and went inside. Hundreds of people surrounded the house, watching and listening. A few moments later, she peeked out the front window, lifted the sash, and poked her head out.

"This view looks very different," she said.

"That's because Dick Brookmeyer's ugly mug is messing up the scenery," someone shouted, and Mrs. Trudeau's smile transformed her whole face into radiant joy.

"It is a beautiful view," she said. "Come! Jasper, come inside and tell me what you think. You too, Joseph."

The house met with the approval of her sons, for they soon began carrying furniture from the wagon into the house. It didn't take long. The house was tiny, and with two young men lifting and carrying, Marie was welcoming people inside within the hour. Hercules lugged a barrel of apple cider into Marie's front parlor. Throughout the afternoon as people needed a break, Marie kept her door wide open and invited them inside for something cool to drink.

It was a long day as Boomer used the excavator to dig more basements and others poured concrete for foundations. The sun was setting as people began drifting home. Every muscle in Alex's body ached as he walked alongside Eloise. He was tired and dirty but thoroughly happy. It had been a good day.

He reached out to clap Enzo on the shoulder. "You're a good man, Enzo. We couldn't have done this without you."

The Italian gave a tired smile. "I hope you will say the same thing tomorrow. It will be a bigger challenge."

No doubt, for tomorrow they were moving Dr. Lloyd's house,

and it was a two-story structure. Enzo wanted to move a variety of buildings during the short time he was in the valley. Once he returned to the city, the people of Duval Springs would be on their own, and every building had unique challenges, quirks, and potential for disaster.

"What about the tavern?" Alex asked, for it was the building he cared about the most. It was the heart and soul of this community, the place where people gathered to celebrate, to plan during a crisis, or simply to enjoy the blessing of a long summer evening.

"You will need to have a structural engineer on the scene for that one," Enzo said after a long pause. "It is too challenging for my skills."

But Alex had to believe everything would work out as God intended. He would worry about the tavern another day. This evening was too precious to squander on fear or anxiety. Their first move was a triumph. In the months ahead, there would surely be setbacks and problems, but for tonight, it was time to celebrate the blessing of a truly perfect day.

After the tension of moving Mrs. Trudeau's house on Saturday and their first two-story house on Sunday, Eloise thought the rest of the week would be easier.

She was wrong. Each evening Alex accompanied her and Enzo as they consulted with people who planned to move their buildings. During the meetings Alex was professional, competent, and helpful as they drafted plans for a safe and efficient move.

And that was the problem.

This businesslike side of Alex was something Eloise had never seen before, and his confident leadership was irresistible. It was the first time she sensed real depth beneath his daredevil charm. Now she had witnessed him in action as a leader who balanced management issues with the perfect dose of compassion. It had been easier to resent him when he was wild and irresponsible, but now she understood why people in this town were ready to follow him.

The new town was starting to take shape. Bruce's steamroller and excavator made quick work of land preparation, and little flags covered the barren field to outline future streets and the foundations for the two hundred houses and shops that would someday become a town called Highpoint. The new town needed a new name, and Highpoint was selected by popular vote.

The next three weeks were the busiest of Eloise's life. During the day she continued evaluating properties for the state, but in the evenings she threw her lot in with the residents of Duval Springs to shift the town. She and Enzo calculated the loads for each structure to be moved. Roy advised the volunteers on grading the streets and preparing the lots. Farmers, shopkeepers, and schoolteachers got busy plowing under stubbles of rye and leveling the ground. School had been canceled for the rest of the year, but the children got a real-world education in team work. Older children helped mix concrete and maintain the equipment while younger children helped prepare meals and carry supplies.

On Friday evening, Alex insisted on buying her, Enzo, and Roy dinner at the tavern. They were finishing the meal when Sally came out from the kitchen, rubbing her back. "Can I get you folks anything? I'll bring one more round before heading upstairs for the night."

Enzo was about to ask for another mug of ale, but Alex cut him off. "I'll get whatever they need. Are you okay, Sally? You look done in."

Hercules must have thought so too as he eyed her from behind the bar. "Let me finish washing the glasses, then I'll walk you upstairs, Sally-lass."

Sally shook her head. "I think you'd better go for Dr. Lloyd. We're going to need him."

Hercules let out a streak of curse words as he bounded to his wife's side. "How long has this been going on?"

"An hour. I wanted to be sure before we dragged Dr. Lloyd over."

Hercules sent a harried glance over his shoulder. "Help your-selves to whatever you want from the bar. It's going to be a long night. John, go get Dr. Lloyd," he told his oldest son.

Alex remained standing while Hercules guided Sally toward the staircase, then sat back down. "Let's work on the town hall move. How do you recommend we proceed?" he asked Enzo.

"Alex!" Eloise said. "You can't seriously think we're going back to work."

"Why not? We've got a deadline to meet."

"But—but . . . your sister-in-law *is in labor*." She clasped her suddenly clammy hands together. Wasn't there something they should be doing to help? Shouldn't the world stop?

But Alex seemed mildly amused as he gestured for her to sit again. "Sally's been through it four times before, and trust me, it's going to be a long night. We may as well take advantage of it."

Alex and Enzo went back to studying the timetables, but she couldn't join them. Delivering a baby was too important, and she kept glancing toward the upstairs balcony in case Hercules appeared and needed something. Everyone else in the tavern had gone back to their business.

"Eloise, sit," Alex said gently. "It's going to be okay. And if it's not, save your energy until it's needed. Okay?" Humor crinkled the corners of his eyes, and she sat, but it was impos-sible to concentrate. Didn't these men realize the magnitude of what was happening upstairs?

Twenty minutes later Dr. Lloyd arrived, and he ousted Hercu-les and all the boys downstairs. Dr. Lloyd was an old-fashioned sort who refused to tolerate fathers or children anywhere near the delivery room. At seventeen, John was the oldest boy and had been through this before, but Mark was only eight and seemed alarmed.

"How come we have to leave?" Mark asked. "What if Ma needs us?"

Hercules ruffled the boy's hair, then grabbed a handful of darts. "She's got a pair of lungs on her that can shake the rafters. She'll let us know what she needs. Come on, let's see if we can work on your aim."

Hercules took a position before the dartboard, then threw a dart that hit the board sideways and clattered to the floor. Alex noticed and frowned. He turned back to the timetables, but his hands were clenched, and he shifted uneasily in his chair. Mr. Brookmeyer lounged in the corner but fingered a string of prayer beads.

They were *all* nervous and just trying to pretend they weren't! Why were they pretending?

She didn't realize she'd spoken aloud until Alex reached over to squeeze her hand. "Of course we're nervous," he said. "But hand-wringing isn't going to help. Sit down, and let's work on these schedules."

She couldn't concentrate on schedules while Hercules kept throwing darts that didn't stick to the board. Mark Duval sat on the piano bench, kicking the instrument with hollow thuds.

A prayer would be helpful right now.

"Would you mind if I played the piano?" She'd always considered "Jesu, Joy of Man's Desiring" a form of prayer. Same with "Amazing Grace" and *Salve Regina*. Playing hymns on the piano was the most useful thing she'd been able to contribute to religious services when she was at the convent.

Alex gestured to the old upright piano in the corner. "Be my guest."

She joined young Mark on the bench and settled her fingers on the cool ivory keys. The timeless music of Bach filled the tavern, and Hercules set down the darts. Bach lifted her up and peeled away worldly concerns. At the end of the hymn, she launched into a rendition of "Amazing Grace." By ten o'clock Enzo and most of the townspeople had drifted home, but Eloise didn't leave. It felt like she was finally being useful by filling the tavern with wholesome, spiritual music.

Somewhere around midnight, Reverend Carmichael and his wife arrived at the tavern with a freshly baked apple pie still warm from the oven. Mrs. Carmichael knew it was Sally's favorite and had started baking the moment she heard Sally was in labor. It was the kind of thing people in this community did for one another.

Finally, Eloise reached the end of her repertoire of hymns and turned to the others. "Is there anything you'd like to hear?"

"Do you know any Stephen Foster?" Hercules asked. "He's Sally's favorite, and she'll be able to hear."

It seemed a little discordant to play "Oh! Susanna" after the majesty of Bach, but this was Sally's night, and Eloise played the song with gusto. Then she played "Gentle Annie" and a rousing rendition of "Camptown Races."

Reverend Carmichael requested "Nearer, My God, to Thee," but Hercules disagreed. "Sally really likes Stephen Foster," he said.

Reverend Carmichael disagreed. "But I think given the occasion—"

"Look, I've been married to that woman for nineteen years," Hercules said. "I know exactly what she likes, and if she hears 'Nearer, My God, to Thee,' she'll think we're singing her into the grave. She loves Stephen Foster."

Reverend Carmichael and Hercules bickered, but the debate came to an abrupt end when Dr. Lloyd stepped out onto the upstairs balcony. Hercules shot to his feet in expectation, but the doctor spoke only to Eloise.

"Mrs. Duval would like to hear more Stephen Foster," he said.

"But I've already played the only songs I know," she replied.

"Then play them again," Hercules said. "Please."

Eloise launched back into her three Stephen Foster songs. She repeated them several times, fearing the relentless cheer of "Oh! Susanna" would become branded in their minds for eternity. She finally gave in to Reverend Carmichael's urging for more Bach, but it didn't take long for Dr. Lloyd to step outside again.

"I am passing along a request for Stephen Foster," he said in a tired voice.

It was two o'clock in the morning, and if Eloise never heard another Stephen Foster song, she would fall to her knees in thanks. Hercules could sense it.

"Just do it. Please," he implored. "You can have my firstborn child."

"Dad, you've got to quit saying that," John said, clearly tired of hearing that promise all his life. Eloise conceded and played another round of "Gentle Annie."

Ten minutes later they heard the mewling cry of a newborn baby. Hercules bounded up the staircase, and the boys tried to follow, but Mrs. Carmichael sprang up with surprising agility and tugged on the back of John's collar to stop him from vaulting upstairs.

"They've got their hands full with your baby brother," she said. "Be patient. Your father will be down in good time. Go have a piece of pie."

Hercules emerged less than five minutes later, carrying a bundle in his arms. The baby was quiet, but Hercules openly wept.

"It's a girl!" he sobbed. "We've got a baby girl. A beautiful, sweet, blessed baby girl."

Eloise's heart grew twice its normal size, and a lump filled her throat, but even more surprising was Alex's reaction. He looked both stunned and joyous.

"I don't believe it!" he managed before giving Hercules an awkward hug so as not to crush the baby. The boys gathered around, eager to see their only sister.

"What's her name?" Bill asked.

Hercules gazed in rapture at the tiny scrap of humanity nestled in his arms. "All my life I've dreamed of having a little girl," he said in a teary voice. "I swore I'd give her a nice, normal name like Ann or Mary . . . but no, I just can't."

"Stick to your guns, Hercules," Alex said.

Hercules smiled wide, laughter mingling with tears as he gazed at his baby. "This sweet girl is Blessed Joy. That's exactly who she is, and no other name will do. She is Blessed Joy."

Alex nearly choked. "You can't saddle an innocent baby with a name like that. As your brother, it's my duty to stop you from doing stupid things. Give her a solid name, a normal one. Mary sounds good."

The smile on Hercules's face was blinding. "Nope. We can call her Joy, but it's a puny word for what I feel right now, and her real name is Blessed Joy. That's what I will write on her birth certificate."

Hercules held up the baby so each person in the tavern could pass by and admire the miracle. Some reverently gazed at the tiny bundle, although most couldn't resist touching her nose or stroking her patch of light brown hair.

But Eloise clung to the back wall of the tavern and watched from a distance. If she got any closer, the emotions welling inside would swamp her. Painful longings for a baby roared to life the moment she saw Hercules step onto the landing, his face bathed in tears, but this groundswell of emotion was more than that. Since she was eight years old, she'd watched this town from afar, and tonight she had been one of them. It was a heady feeling that made her both happy and profoundly sad. This town's days were numbered, as was her time here.

If only she could put a word to this emotion. Poignancy? Bittersweet? Neither word quite captured it. Her soul cried out for something she had never actually possessed but desperately wanted.

Alex noticed her standing apart, and he closed the distance

between them. "What are you doing all the way over here? Have you seen the baby?"

"I can see from here," she said. "And I should be getting back to the hotel. We've got a long day tomorrow."

Alex gave a weary nod and helped her into her coat, then held the door for her. It was cold outside after the warmth of the tavern, and she pulled her coat tighter.

"He won't really name her Blessed Joy, will he?" she asked as they headed toward the inn.

Alex could only shrug. "So far he's been good about naming the boys, but I can't put anything past him. Tomorrow I'll head over to town hall and warn the clerk not to let Hercules file a birth certificate until the euphoria wears off."

"Thank you," she said gently.

"For what?"

"For intervening on that baby's behalf. For being so good-hearted these past months. For being nice to me when I got lost in the woods all those years ago."

She had to stop babbling, or this unwieldy emotion was going to sweep her away. But would that be so terrible?

Alex stopped and turned to face her as they reached the old elm tree in the center of the town square. His face softened, warmth and regret blazing in his eyes. "I really did love you back then," he said. "I keep wondering what would have happened if we hadn't been separated."

She didn't need to wonder, for she already knew. They would be married. They would have children. She never would have earned her accounting license or developed a backbone to stand up for herself.

She looked at him with sad affection. "You would have grown tired of catering to the insecurities of a needy cuckoo bird, and I would forever carp on you to become the kind of serious, sensible man you were never meant to be."

"That's not true!"

"We both know it is." The kind of man a woman chose at twenty-eight was very different from the sort who dazzled a sixteen-year-old girl.

His shoulders sagged and he looked away, for he had no answer. This cascade of emotion was hard to grapple with. Even now she longed for the comfort of her apartment and her predictable job back home, for her time in Duval Springs had been exhausting. Fletcher was perfect for her. He was sensible and accomplished and was the safe harbor Alex could never be. A piece of her would always love Alex, but they weren't right for each other.

"I'm so sorry," she said gently. "I wish it were otherwise."

The raw pain in Alex's eyes haunted her the entire night.

piece of Alex wanted to lie in bed and mope over Eloise's rejection. She was imprinted on his soul as the partner he wanted to laugh with, take to bed each night, raise children with, and grow old alongside. To know she imagined a different man for that role was crushing. Even with the sounds of breakfast percolating from the dining room below, he couldn't force himself downstairs, where he'd have to see her and pretend all was well. It was cowardly, but he knew his limits and loitered in his room until he saw Eloise and the rest of the demolition crew set off for the day.

The ache sapped his energy, making it hard to be cheerful as he greeted others in the hotel dining room, but he did it. He smiled as he announced the arrival of Blessed Joy and accepted hearty congratulations and teasing over the ridiculous name his brother intended to saddle her with. Rumor had it Hercules filed the paperwork at the crack of dawn, and Alex probably never stood much chance dissuading him anyway. Soon people wanted to know when their houses would be moved and if they could have a basement. Normal town business came to the fore, and he loved it.

He loved it. He must never lose sight of that. Maybe Eloise preferred someone else, but God had given him a huge and wonderful blessing of a town to move and friends worth fighting for. By the time he mounted his horse to head up the hill, his mind was already strategizing how to restructure the production schedule so more people could get a shot at the excavator for basements.

It had been three weeks since Marie's modest house had been moved, and during that time they had moved an additional ten houses and a café. A hand-cranked pump had been installed, and it was in almost constant use as men mixed concrete, workers slaked their thirst, and the café made coffee by the vat. Over a hundred people were already at work on dozens of plots as he rode into town, but his eye was drawn to a movement behind Marie Trudeau's house.

Mrs. Trudeau stood huddled close to another figure. Misgiving descended as Alex recognized Bruce Garrett's hulking frame. This couldn't be good. The last time Garrett spoke to Mrs. Trudeau, it had ended in a shouting match, so Alex prodded his horse into a canter, heading straight to the back of Mrs. Trudeau's house. Garrett had better not dare breathe one harsh word toward the woman who was beloved by everyone in town.

"What are you doing here?" Alex asked as he swung down from the horse.

Garrett shifted his weight and shot Alex a surly glare, and Mrs. Trudeau seemed anxious as she took a step back. She pulled her coat tighter and gave a nervous smile.

"Mr. Garrett came to apologize for what happened on the day my house was moved," she said. "I have accepted his apology."

Alex glanced between Mrs. Trudeau and Garrett, who had never struck Alex as the apologizing sort.

"That's all?" he asked skeptically. "An apology?" The way

they'd been huddled so close behind her house almost seemed as though they wanted to avoid attention.

"Would you rather I was here to inspect the equipment I loaned you?" Garrett said. "There's mud caked all over the steamroller."

Alex held up both hands. The gift of the earthmoving equipment had been a boon beyond measure, and he couldn't endanger it.

"Look, I came down here to speak with you as well," Garrett said. "I've been at the new work camp. A bunch of Irish workers there are getting sick. They think there's a problem with their water. People are having stomach problems, and there's a baby that's had diarrhea for a week." He glanced at the pump a few acres away and then back at Alex. "Have there been any problems with the water from that pump?"

The water had tasted fine every time Alex drank from it, but he didn't live up here yet. "Mrs. Trudeau? Have you noticed any problems?"

"It's cold and clear, just like all the water here," she said, but Garrett wasn't finished yet.

"People up at the Timberland camp think someone might have tampered with their well," Garrett said.

"*No one* in Duval Springs would poison a well," Mrs. Trudeau said, and Alex instinctively agreed. Roadside sabotage was one thing; poisoned water was something else entirely.

But Garrett didn't seem convinced. "You sure about that?"

Mrs. Trudeau looked so indignant she could barely speak. "It is an insult to even suggest it!"

If anything, her response amused Garrett. "You don't let me get away with anything. I like that. And I wasn't accusing Duval Springs. I'm wondering if it might be workers from the main camp over near Kingston. The best jobs are going to the Irish crew, and they're angry, so keep an eye out for trouble.

The state already knows about the water issue and is sending someone to test it. In the meantime, I've sent for a doctor to look at that baby."

"That's very kind of you," Mrs. Trudeau said.

Garrett rolled his eyes. "If we wait for the state to send a doctor, the baby will be in school before he gets treated."

Mrs. Trudeau looked as if she wanted to say something more, but Garrett had already turned to mount his horse, and he cantered off toward Mountainside Road.

As Alex headed to the first of the morning's inspections, a terrible thought intruded. Maybe someone from Duval Springs *had* done something to the water up at the Timberland camp. Duval Springs had lost every legal battle to stop New York City from seizing their land, but what would happen if the water was foul?

Bad water would be the only way to stop the reservoir in its tracks.

Eloise thought it would only take an hour to appraise the town's general store, but she was continually distracted by the alluring goods on display. Crates of teas, tobacco, imported herbs, and spices gave the store a heady aroma. The front counter was lined with large glass jars filled with peppermint sticks and jelly beans. Colorfully wrapped soaps and perfume filled the shelves. It was a feast for the senses.

"You have an impressive store here," she told Willard, who had bought the store after Bruce lost it as part of the strike settlement.

"It's been a sound investment," Willard said modestly, but it was impossible not to be impressed with the variety of goods. She wandered over to the gallon-sized stoneware pots containing blends of tobacco. On another shelf were vibrantly decorated boxes of cigars. The artwork on the boxes was impressive, and she slowed to admire a sultry-eyed woman in a Grecian toga ironically named "the Queen of Havana."

Unease trickled through her, for through the haze of other scents in the emporium, this one made her hackles rise. She lifted the Queen of Havana box and sniffed. The pungent scent of cedar and tobacco made her recoil. This was exactly what she had smelled the night she was shot, and it turned her stomach.

"Is this a popular brand?" she asked Willard.

"Our bestselling cigar," he replied. "People claim to like the taste, but I think they like the box more."

The bell over the door dinged, and she was surprised to see Enzo enter the shop, his face narrowed in concern.

"You are needed at the hotel right away," he told her. "Claude has a plan to speed up our work so we can be back in the city in two weeks."

They weren't supposed to leave so soon! Alex was counting on them to be available through December. Enzo had supervised every building moved so far, and the townspeople weren't ready to start moving things on their own. Leaving early would be a disaster.

"I'm coming," she said, dropping the box of cigars and heading outside.

They had to cut around the construction rubble blocking much of the village green but made it to the hotel dining room in short order. Claude sat with Roy, slicing into a plump breast of duck with cherry sauce.

"Good news!" Claude announced the moment he saw her. "I'm cutting a full month off our schedule." He went on to say that since so many buildings would be moved rather than demolished, they were ahead of schedule.

"I'd like to stay until the end of December as originally planned," Eloise said. "Enzo? Will you stay as well?"

"Yes, if possible, of course I want—"

"Well, you can't," Claude snapped. "I've had enough of the crude hinterlands and am ready to return to the comforts of the city and somewhere we don't have to listen to that infernal clatter," he said with a glare over his shoulder, where Kasper Nagy transcribed an incoming telegraph message.

Eloise scrambled for an excuse to stay. "Helping the towns-people with their move will buy the state tremendous goodwill. It would be a genuine sign of compassion."

Claude's sigh was pained. "Here comes the torrent of ir-rational female hysteria."

"Female hysteria?" Enzo asked in his thick Italian accent. "I'm not sure what that term means, but maybe I have irrational female hysteria too. I want to stay."

It was too early to panic, for this sort of timetable shift could only be made by Fletcher Jones, not Claude. "I shall send a telegram to Mr. Jones and ask for his input," she said.

"There's no need," Claude said. "He and one of the other commissioners are headed up here for an inspection. There's trouble up at the new work camp. They suspect more sabotage."

The scar on her back began to tingle and itch, and the stink of the cedar-scented cigar came back to her. "What is it this time?"

"Something about bad water," Claude said with a shrug. "Whoever drilled their well obviously didn't know what they were doing, and Drake is coming up to check it out."

"Nicholas Drake?" Her cousin was the commissioner of labor for the water board and the person who got her this job in the first place.

"Drake and Jones both," Claude confirmed. "Everyone needs to be on their best behavior, and I want all our re-ports and assessments done when they arrive. The sooner they sign off on our work, the sooner we can get out of this awful place."

"Shh!" Roy said in a harsh whisper. "Kasper might overhear you. He's coming this way."

Sure enough, Kasper had completed transcribing the telegram and was heading their way with a grim look on his face.

"This just arrived," he said as he passed Eloise the card. Her eyes widened at the length of the telegram, and it was hard to make sense of the cascade of legal terminology. Downgrade. Deteriorating water quality. Massive reduction in payments.

She clamped a hand over her mouth and read the telegram three times before she made sense of it. The note was from the securities firm handling the municipal bond. They had heard about the problems with the well at the Timberland work camp and believed it would affect the long-term viability of the new town. Skittish investors began withdrawing their commitments, and the town's bond rating had plummeted.

Which meant the money flowing into the town was about to dry up.

lex was in the middle of helping a team pour concrete for the town pharmacy when Eloise came striding across the blank field toward him. He swiped the dust from his face, worried by her grim expression.

"What's wrong?" he asked.

Eloise pulled him a few yards away, although there was no such thing as privacy in this open field swarming with two hundred workers. His disbelief rose as she explained the bond's downgrade and how the money to keep fueling the move was hanging by a thread.

"The bank can't change the rules on us," he snapped. "We're owed another payment next Friday, and I intend to get it."

She shook her head. "A bond is a long-term investment, and the rules can change. If the investment starts to look shaky, the bond gets downgraded and your payments shrink."

"Fine," he said. "Where do I go to fight this?"

"You can't fight your way out of this. The best we can do is prove the water in the valley is pure, and trust me, New York City wants the same thing. For once, you and the State Water Board are on the same side."

Joining forces with the state was appalling, but he would do it. Eloise reported that the state had hired a water specialist to test local samples, and the results would be presented at the town hall tomorrow. The Timberland camp was less than a mile from Garrett's quarry and even closer to the cement factory. It was possible one of the companies was the source of the contamination, and Alex expected them to be on hand for the state's meeting too.

On Friday morning he met Eloise in the lobby of the hotel so they could walk to the meeting together. He'd never gotten along well with Nicholas Drake, the commissioner of labor for the water board. As far as Alex was concerned, Nick Drake was the face of the state that had turned his world upside down. But Nick was Eloise's cousin, and he'd gone out on a limb to get her this job, so Alex would swallow his resentment and try to get along for her sake.

"You already know Nick," Eloise said as they walked toward the town hall. "The scientist in charge of the water test will be here too. Rosalind Werner has a doctorate in biochemistry and specializes in water purification. She's also engaged to Nick."

"Oh, that's convenient," Alex muttered as they trudged up the final few yards to the town hall. Anxiety was making him irrational, but everything about this situation aggravated his nerves.

"Please be respectful," Eloise cautioned. "I adore Nick. When I was little, he was the only person who was ever nice to me."

"He's the only person who has ever evicted me and two thousand other people from our homes."

Eloise sighed. "I know you resent the state for what's happened, but today we are all on the same side."

The meeting room was crowded. Alex recognized Cormac McIntire, the foreman up at the Timberland camp. Bruce Garrett was here, as was Jack Riesel, representing the cement factory.

Both men came armed with a lawyer, and Alex wished he had thought to bring one as well. Going unarmed into a meeting like this spelled trouble.

Nick Drake strode across the room and offered Eloise an affectionate hug. "You remember my fiancée, Rosalind Werner?" he asked as he presented the only other woman in the room.

Eloise nodded. Dr. Werner was as pretty as they came, petite and slender with silvery blond hair, but Eloise kept glancing around the room.

"Fletcher Jones isn't here?" she asked.

Nick snorted. "Your penny-pinching boss is saving a few bucks by traveling on the Saturday train," he said. "Just as well. We can talk about water quality today and work on finance once Fletcher gets here tomorrow."

Alex filed that bit of information away. It seemed the thrifty Mr. Jones cared more about saving two dollars than showing up to support Eloise when the bond fund she had sponsored was heading south in flames.

Nick called the meeting to order, and everyone took their seats around the table. It was hard to sit still and listen when Alex would rather stand up and fight, but Eloise was right. All that mattered today was getting a clean bill of health for their water.

Dr. Werner began with a presentation of her findings. "I was asked to test the well at the Timberland camp because of illnesses that are consistent with waterborne disease," she said. "In addition to the Timberland camp, I took samples from Duval Springs, the new well at Highpoint, and nine additional samples from groundwater where the new reservoir will be built."

"And?" Alex asked. A prickle of sweat broke out over his body at the prospect of a tainted well at Highpoint.

"And I found a shocking amount of barium carbonate at the Timberland camp. All the other sites tested pure."

"What's barium carbonate?" Jack asked.

"It is a naturally occurring element in soil," Rosalind responded. "If ingested, it can cause neuromuscular and gastrointestinal problems. Especially in children. We sometimes see traces of barium contamination next to mining operations—"

"My quarry is clean," Bruce interrupted. "And why would it show up at the Timberland camp and nowhere else?"

Rosalind offered a helpless shrug. "I can't answer that. All I know is that the concentration is extraordinarily high. So high that it doesn't seem like a naturally occurring incident, because there is no trace of it elsewhere in the valley. The state has been testing the water quality in this valley for years, so it is odd for it to suddenly appear in only that single well."

"Then we move the camp," Jack said. "I can't have a sick population on my conscience, in case it's coming from the cement factory. There is a perfectly good work camp already in operation outside of Kingston. Move the workers there."

Nick looked at the foreman from the Timberland camp. "Mr. McIntire? How would your people feel about pulling up stakes and bunking over at the Kingston work camp?"

Cormac McIntire didn't look happy. "Some of us lived there when we first arrived. It didn't go well."

"How so?" Jack asked.

"Oh, you know," McIntire replied in his thick Irish brogue. "Italians who resent the Irish. Irish who like to thumb their nose at the pasta-eaters. A couple of fistfights, a couple stolen wallets. We like having our own place better, but we're not so keen on drinking out of that well."

Jack rose and began pacing. "The state is paying a fortune to build an entirely new camp. It means additional plumbing facilities, more roads, and ugly power lines once the electrical plant is built. It's a blot on our valley and a misuse of taxpayer funds."

"Fletcher Jones certainly thinks so," Eloise said. "He asked me to do a cost analysis of that second camp, and he thinks it's an appalling waste."

"Fletcher Jones is a skinflint and doesn't understand what goes on out in the field," Nick said. "I ordered a second camp for a good reason. As soon as the Irish teams are done building the roads, they'll move out and I'll use that camp to house the engineers."

Right now the engineers were living at the hotel, a blessing, since tourists no longer visited the valley. After the hotel was torn down in May, the engineers would need someplace nearby to live, and they expected better conditions than could be found at the first work camp.

"Besides, something about this doesn't smell right," Nick continued. "The Highpoint well is only half a mile away, and it's clean. This sounds like sabotage to me, and I want to get to the bottom of it. Barrels of clean water will be delivered to the Timberland camp, and I'll send in security guards. I don't like being pushed around."

Alex had no problems with protecting the Timberland camp, but that wouldn't help their plummeting bond rating. He turned his attention to the water scientist.

"I need you to write a report giving the well at Highpoint a clean bill of health," he said to Dr. Werner. "We're getting a raw deal over this whole mess."

"I'm afraid I can't do that," she replied. "Since I don't know what caused the contamination, I can't guarantee that it won't eventually taint the new town's water too."

This was ridiculous. Hadn't she just pronounced the well clean? "I need the bank to know our water is good. If you can't do it, I'll find someone who can."

That triggered another round of arguing, and the fate of the bond was still in limbo at the end of the meeting. Alex wanted to hire his own scientist to pacify nervous investors, but Eloise was adamant that he join forces with the state.

"Cooperating with the state is the only logical thing to do," she urged as they walked back to the hotel. "Highpoint can be saved, but not if this bond falters. The state is your most powerful ally for ensuring the water in this valley is clean. Work with them."

He sighed, rubbing at the tightness that gathered in his chest every time he was forced into a corner like this. She was right. If he'd learned nothing else over the last five years, it was that unleashing passion against the legalistic strictures of the state was a losing battle. Eloise had gotten them further along on this quest than he could have gotten on his own. He'd always thought the world would stop spinning on its axis before he ever willingly cooperated with the state . . . but it was time.

loise began Saturday morning on her knees, hands clenched in prayer. She was drowning. The bond needed her to save it. The town needed her to persuade Fletcher to let the demolition team stay another month. The people of Duval Springs balanced on a precipice, and she had helped put them there.

"Dear Lord, please show me the right thing to do," she whispered.

It had been so much easier at the convent, where she prayed for cool weather and forgiveness and the chance to be needed someday. Now she had everything she once prayed for and was still drowning. A longing to escape back to the barren simplicity of the desert convent tugged at her.

Buck up, little cuckoo bird.

She straightened. Had God just told her to buck up, or was it merely a remnant of the cruel taunt Thomas Drake had so often told her? Either way, it wasn't bad advice. Now wasn't the time to wallow in doubt or flee back to the safety of the convent. She could only tackle one problem at a time, and today that meant convincing Fletcher to allow her and Enzo to stay until the original deadline. The town was counting on it. Enzo was essential for training the crews on moving a variety of building types.

Today they were moving Reverend Carmichael's church. It was the largest building they'd attempted to move so far, and if Fletcher arrived in time to see the actual move, he would surely be impressed and grant permission for them to stay.

Activity was already underway outside the white clapboard church. The long nave and lack of internal supports made it a problematic move, and Enzo wanted the church stripped of as much weight as possible. The bell was brought down from the steeple, and the stained-glass windows had already been taken out and wrapped in cloth. The pews had been removed the previous day, but they needed to be carried to a neighboring lot to clear a path for the oxen. Eloise paired with Dick Brookmeyer to carry a pew, taking tiny steps to avoid banging her shins, but it was fun. She'd never done manual labor before coming to Duval Springs, and it made her feel like part of the community.

By lunchtime the jackscrew teams had the church hoisted two feet off its foundations, and a crew was preparing to move the rails into place when Eloise spotted Fletcher disembarking from a carriage at the end of the street. How handsome he looked, his blond hair carefully groomed and long wool coat swaying as he walked toward her in long, confident strides.

She left the church and headed down the street toward him, gathering her thoughts. She needed to sell her proposal to him, which meant balancing the complexity of the task with the town's likelihood of success. It would be the only way he'd authorize Enzo to stay. She reached him a block away from the church.

"Hello, Fletcher," she said brightly. "Have you ever seen a church roll down the street? Because you're about to!"

He didn't return her smile as he paused in the middle of the road. "I came to town hoping to sign off on the preliminary stage of the demolition team's work, but what's this I hear about a request for an additional month?"

"Actually, we're only asking to stay through our original deadline."

His eyes were stern with disapproval, but she was going to win this battle.

"Look across the street," she said, gesturing to the empty lots where Marie Trudeau's house and four others used to be. The gaps in the row of buildings made the street look like a smile with a bunch of teeth missing. "Those lots are where houses used to be. They've all been safely moved to the new town. Come! Let's head to the church, and you can see how Enzo leads the team in lifting it from its foundation."

"I'd rather have Enzo show me his beautifully completed plans for how to dismantle these buildings," Fletcher said wryly, but at least he followed her.

This was the most complex part of the operation, and Fletcher needed to see how crucial Enzo was to its success. She watched with pride as Enzo strode from station to station, inspecting the cribbing blocks that secured the building to the rails. "He's been magnificent," she said to Fletcher. "The men are learning more and more with each building. This one is a challenge because the bell tower adds so much weight on one end. Enzo says it's a stability issue, but he's shown us how to secure it."

When Enzo noticed Fletcher's arrival, he gave a long blast of the whistle to signal a break, then jogged across the street to join them. Alex followed closely behind.

"Impressive work," Fletcher told Enzo with a nod toward the church. Eloise appreciated his economy of words. All it took was two words along with that infinitesimal nod to convey a world of meaning. It was an acknowledgment of their accomplishment but still laden with skepticism.

Enzo rubbed his hands on a handkerchief. "How can I help you, sir?"

"I came to ensure that the two of you will be back in Manhattan next week."

She sucked in a quick breath. "You're already rejecting my request? I'd like a chance to speak with you about it first."

"I received it and rejected it. You need to be back to work a week from Monday." Fletcher nodded toward the church. "This is a volunteer project, and while your service is commendable, the state has strict timetables. If you can't meet them, I need to know now."

Enzo shifted on his feet. "This isn't interfering with our work. Since so many buildings are being moved instead of demolished, we are way ahead of schedule. Please, we can still meet the original schedule if we stay through the end of December."

"If we can speed up the schedule, we will," Fletcher insisted. "It would be a misuse of state funds to do otherwise."

Enzo looked uneasy, and Eloise felt sick at the prospect of moving more buildings without him. She couldn't back down.

"We would like a one-month leave of absence," she said daringly. "It won't cost you a dime, for I will personally fund Enzo's salary." Enzo and Alex both gaped at her. She'd built a respectable bank account over the years and didn't mind drawing on it to cover Enzo's salary. One day the funds from her mother's estate would replenish it, but for now the town needed Enzo's help.

"A leave of absence was never in the cards," Fletcher said.

"I've seen you approve such requests for other employees. The people in this valley have had their entire lives disrupted, and helping them move will go a long way toward salvaging wounded feelings. I suggest the water board grant Enzo and me a one-month leave of absence."

It was an audacious request, but Fletcher's expression was typically calm. "Declined," he said simply.

"Why?"

"Because the rules dictate that such requests be submitted months in advance. Both of you have responsibilities in the city. You will be back in the office a week from Monday, or you will be terminated."

She blanched. That was a lot blunter than anticipated, and it annoyed her. "When we accepted this assignment, you said the city would be flexible in accommodating our needs."

"I repeat: The two of you will be at work next Monday, or you will be fired."

Behind them, all twenty men on the crew stood idle, awaiting Enzo's return. Those men needed Enzo. They needed her.

Enzo drew a heavy breath as he met her eyes. "I have a wife and two daughters back home," he said. "I can't afford to lose this job. I'm sorry, Eloise. I'll do the best I can to show people what to do, but I can't lose my job."

She hated the way Alex grimaced at Enzo's words. He recoiled and turned away, as though from a body blow. Their plan had no room for delays or setbacks, and this was a huge one. It would take weeks to find another skilled engineer.

She turned back to Fletcher. "You could grant us the leave if you wanted."

"Not without a significant adjustment to our timetable."

Her gaze tracked to the men working at the church. Enzo had rejoined them, and they returned to their stations, hunkered over to begin the move. All of them had donated their time and money to save this community. She couldn't let them down. Her heart brimmed with an inexplicable emotion, and she turned her attention back to Fletcher.

"Sometimes there are more important things in life than timetables or profit margins, and those things are called *dreams*.

Wild, impossible dreams that are normally only the fantasies of poets and playwrights, but sometimes ordinary people seize upon them, join forces, and fight to make it happen."

She hoped she wasn't destroying any chance she had for a future with Fletcher, but if she let him bully her into returning home, it would plant a seed of resentment that would never heal. For once in her life she had stepped into an adventure tale and become part of it. She wasn't ready to leave yet.

Fletcher hadn't moved a muscle as he scrutinized her. "You never struck me as such a person."

"I'm not," she admitted with a helpless smile. "I want to do it for the next month and then go back to timetables and rule books and my safe, predictable life." Could he understand that? She scanned his face, searching for a hint of sympathy. For the first time since they had met, she showed Fletcher the raw, vulnerable piece of her soul she normally kept under lock and key, and prayed he could understand. They would be brilliant together if he could accept her for who she truly was.

"It doesn't work that way," Fletcher replied. "You need to decide where your priorities are. If you aren't at your desk by nine o'clock next Monday, I will fire you."

A piece of her appreciated how firmly he stuck to his convictions, but it felt like the foundation was crumbling beneath her. It didn't matter. She couldn't give up.

"We don't need to wait until next Monday," she said calmly. "I'm staying in the valley. If you want to fire me, do it now."

She finally got a reaction out of him. He blanched in surprise but recovered quickly. "Don't be a fool. Don't throw your livelihood away over an ill-conceived pipe dream."

"Eloise, maybe you shouldn't do this." Alex's voice was pained. For once in her life, she didn't want Alex to be reasonable. She wanted his support. She kept her gaze locked on Fletcher.

"Go ahead," she challenged. "Fire me."

She didn't really expect him to do it, but he did. "You're fired," he said flatly, no trace of heat beneath the words. He turned away and headed back toward the carriage. It would be easy to catch him if she chose. Did he want her to? Fletcher never once looked back, but his pace was uncharacteristically slow as he strolled toward the carriage.

"Eloise, I'm sorry," Alex said. "I didn't expect this to happen."

She hadn't either, and as Fletcher walked away, the first regrets rose up and threatened to choke her. She loved that job. It wasn't that she needed the money; it was Fletcher's rejection that hurt. She hadn't expected him to walk away so easily.

It suddenly felt very cold on this street corner. She drew her cloak tighter, but her teeth started chattering anyway. "Don't worry about me. I'm used to starting over."

She'd done it her entire life, but this was the first time it was of her own making. It was both empowering and terrifying.

Without thinking, she turned and ran toward the hotel. There was something she needed to do.

❧

Alex was torn between darting after Eloise and getting back to the church. Losing Enzo was a disaster. The crushing weight of disappointment made it hard to breathe, but everyone in this town depended on Alex. They had entrusted him with their life savings, and he couldn't let them down. He needed to glean what he could from Enzo about moving a lopsided building like the church, for there were other buildings with weight distribution problems.

But Eloise had just allowed herself to be fired on behalf of this town. His rigid, rule-following CPA had just thrown her lot in with him because she had been seized by a vision she wanted to fight for.

He stood in the middle of the street, torn between returning to Enzo and going after Eloise. She had just scurried up the hotel steps and slammed the door behind her, probably already regretting her decision. He looked at the church, where Hercules and Dr. Lloyd conferred with Enzo as he gave them instructions. That building was ready to roll, and he needed to be there.

Or . . . he could trust Hercules and Dr. Lloyd to learn what Enzo had to teach. It didn't all have to be on his shoulders. In fact, it shouldn't be. If they were going to move this town, it was going to require teamwork, and he'd have to start leaning on others to help.

He sprinted toward the hotel, dirt and sand flying up behind him. He dashed up the stairs and through the front door. Eloise stood at the front counter, her eyes alight with determination as she filled out a telegram form.

"What are you doing?" he asked.

"I'm sending a telegram to my maid."

"You have a maid?" he asked.

She set the pen down and turned to face him. Her expression was still inscrutable. He couldn't tell if she was shattered or ecstatic. "Yes, I have a maid. Since I won't be returning to the city this month, I'd like to have her here."

"If you need help, you should have asked. We've got maids at the hotel who can—"

"Tasha is a friend. And I miss Ilya."

His brows lowered at the man's name. "Who is Ilya?"

"He's a baby. He just turned eight months old, and he cut his third tooth right before I came here, and I miss him. It's ridiculous. He's my maid's baby, not mine, but I miss him and I want him here."

And then the most amazing thing happened. An uncertain smile began tugging at the corners of her mouth.

"Alex, I've never been a very bold or brave person, but I think I've just crossed the Rubicon. I keep waiting to burst into tears over what Fletcher just did, but it isn't happening. I think I made the right decision."

A sense of elation began building inside him. He'd never been prouder of her than he was at this moment. "You did, Eloise."

"You think so?"

"I *know* so. I've known you were this brave since I was eighteen years old."

Pleasure made her cheeks flush red. "Oh, Alex, sometimes when I'm with you, I feel like I can fly. Like we can pull the sword from the stone. We can break the man out of the iron mask. And in my heart, I know that we can move this town."

His heart was so full it threatened to split wide open. "Eloise, I wasn't wrong when I carved our initials into that elm tree. We really *are* one for the ages. I've got the vision, and you've got the ballast."

She gulped back laughter. "Is that the best you can do? I've just flung caution into the wind over you, and the best you can call me is ballast?"

A sheen of tears threatened to unman him. "Yes, my love, you are the ballast in this particular story. And I thank God for it! I thank God for your pencil-pushing ways and your hidebound regulations. I'm even coming to appreciate the way you make me toe the line. You are my ballast." He drew her into his arms.

"Okay, Lancelot," she murmured before kissing him full on the mouth.

He kissed her back with all the bottled-up longing of twelve years, then picked her up and whirled her around, giving her an extra squeeze before setting her back down. She was here, back in his arms, and nothing had ever felt so right.

"Let's go change the world," he said, and at this perfect moment, he was certain they could.

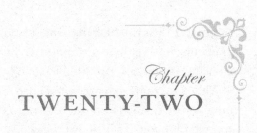

The night before the demolition team returned to the city, Hercules hosted a farewell bash at the tavern. Paperwork kept Alex late at his office, and it was dark before he could get away. A storm was coming, and he tugged a scarf higher against the sleet beginning to fall. It was December 3, and the weather was going to get rough, but plenty of people had already gathered by the time he stepped into the warmth of the tavern.

To his surprise, Claude Fitzgerald was here. So far, the team's lead engineer had shown only disdain for their town, and Alex had assumed he wouldn't come. On the contrary, Claude looked well into his cups and was in the middle of a good-hearted farewell speech.

"You people are maniacs to move this town without professional help," Claude said. "But I have inspected every building in the valley, and by golly, most of them were built without the help of professionals." His voice was a combination of bewilderment and sloppy drunkenness, as though he was amazed people without a college degree could wield a hammer. He stamped his foot on the plank flooring, wobbling a little as he did so. "Take this place," he said. "Obviously cobbled together by complete amateurs, and yet here it stands, two hundred years later, still a fine and noble place to hold a party."

That got a round of cheers, and Enzo rushed to catch Claude's mug before it sloshed more beer onto the floor. Alex finally spotted Eloise sitting in one of the windowsills beside her newly arrived maid and the little baby she adored. The maid flirted with one of the Trudeau boys while Eloise bounced the baby on her knee.

In the week since her maid had arrived, Eloise and that baby seemed inseparable. She lugged him down to breakfast and then took an hour each evening to give him a bath. Alex would be a little jealous except for the unmitigated delight she took in the baby. It seemed Fletcher Jones had been entirely banished from her heart, for which he gave daily thanks. He wove through the crowd and to her side, pleased at how her face warmed when she spotted him.

"Has Claude been rambling a long time?" he asked.

"At least ten minutes." She made room for him on the window seat, but when he tried to link his hand with hers, she scooted a little farther away. He didn't mind. Part of Eloise's charm was her prickly sense of decorum.

At the center of the tavern, Claude kept running off at the mouth as he alternately praised and insulted the town. "Look at those chicken bones," he said over a hiccup. "Completely impractical. Those boys are never coming back—"

"Bite your tongue," Mr. Gallagher shouted from the back of the tavern. "One of those wishbones belongs to my boy!"

Claude bowed in concession. "Aside from that *one* wishbone, that is a wall of failure, and yet it still holds a place of honor. But you know what? I love that wall! This tavern has it all, the good and the bad, the failure and the triumphs. And possibly the best ale—" He hiccupped again. "And possibly the best ale outside of Manhattan."

It was a backhanded compliment, but Alex was surprised to get even that much from the surly engineer.

Claude raised his mug high. "To Roy and Enzo!"

A roar went up from the crowd, as much for the conclusion of the overly long speech as for the toast to Roy and Enzo. Those men deserved more than a sloppy tribute from a drunken man.

A rush of sentimentality seized Alex, and he launched himself up to stand on top of a table. Eloise cringed, no doubt appalled by his gauche behavior, but they were all friends here.

"Enzo Accardi and Roy Winthrop, you are now honorary citizens of Duval Springs," he pronounced. "And five months from today, that citizenship will be good in Highpoint too. Your generosity will never be forgotten. When you come back to this valley, you will both see streets named in your honor."

The cheers were deafening, and Alex hopped off the table to pull Enzo into a bear hug. In a better world, they would have been lifelong friends. As it was, their lives had only intersected during these stress-filled weeks, but their camaraderie flourished as if they'd known each other for years.

Enzo accepted the toasts with a hearty, flushed face. "Next time I come I shall bring my daughters," he said. "I don't think my girls really believe their father is off doing work when I leave for months on end."

"You'd better keep a close eye on your daughters," Oscar Ott hooted from the back of the tavern. "Everyone knows Alex likes young girls."

Alex shoved a chair aside and went to confront Oscar. "What's that supposed to mean?" he snapped.

"Oh, pardon me." Oscar smirked, his breath stinking of liquor. "It's not like everyone doesn't already know how you got caught fornicating with Garrett's ward when she was only sixteen," he said with a leer at Eloise.

Alex held his breath, for Eloise had just gone stark white. It looked like she hadn't realized that everyone in town knew their business. Alex had never learned who snitched on them all those years ago, but he'd always suspected Oscar.

He grabbed Oscar by the lapels, shoving him against the wall. "That woman walks on air. She's given us her time and talent, all for free. You've given us nothing but a load of bile."

Murmurs of approval rumbled around Alex, but it wasn't unanimous. A few people cast sidelong glances at Eloise, who looked ill as she handed the baby to her maid and bolted for the door. People parted to let her through. Oscar deserved a face-bashing, but Alex wasn't going to waste his time with a drunken man when Eloise was hurting. He shoved Oscar aside to rush after her.

The sleet storm had deposited a layer of ice on the ground, but Eloise was heedless as she scurried toward the hotel.

"Slow down!" he hollered, following as quickly as he dared. It was early for a storm this bad, and he only caught up to her at the hotel porch, where she turned her horrified eyes on him.

"The whole town knows? You let me live here and didn't tell me that they all *knew*?"

It stunned him that she hadn't realized that. It was a small town. He'd been beaten within an inch of his life and had to flee town to join the army. Everyone in Duval Springs knew what had happened, but Eloise was from the city, where things were different.

"We don't have scarlet letters in this town. We have imperfect people who sometimes make mistakes."

Her lips twisted with bitterness. "Those people were all judging me."

"So? I've judged you and think you're spectacular." He injected a little humor into his voice. "What do you care what the small minds think?"

She wrapped her arms around herself, and her voice shook with anger and embarrassment. "I care that you didn't bother to warn me. I let Fletcher fire me because of you. I thought you had changed and could be the kind of man a woman could depend on, who wouldn't—"

"Of course you can depend on me!"

"You kept a *big* secret from me."

He folded his arms across his chest. "You're being unreasonable. You can't control the world like a timetable or an accounting ledger."

"Leave my ledgers out of this."

He held up his hands and struggled to keep a straight face. "I'm sorry I insulted your ledgers." Laughing would be the kiss of death right now, but she was being ridiculous. No one cared what they had done behind the old cider mill twelve years ago. But she didn't know these people as well as he did, and her pain was real. He took a breath and spoke straight from the heart. "It's going to be all right," he said gently. "You can trust me on this."

She turned her back on him and headed inside, marching up the stairs without even breaking stride. He heard the door slam on her third-floor room with enough force to rattle the windows.

Eloise was tempted to leave with the rest of the demolition team. She didn't owe the people of this town anything. While she had deluded herself into believing she belonged, half of them had been snickering behind her back the whole time. She could board the train and be safely home in Manhattan by lunchtime tomorrow.

Would Fletcher rehire her?

Sleet battered the windowpanes all through the awful night,

and her thoughts kept straying back to Fletcher. He wouldn't have been flippant like Alex had been last night. Fletcher never would have compromised her to begin with!

She was still conflicted when she ventured downstairs at six o'clock the following morning. It was frigidly cold, and she needed a cup of coffee to clear her head. She'd just taken a seat in the dining room when Enzo came downstairs, lugging his bags.

"What time are you leaving?" she asked.

"Not until the 8:30. Why? Are you joining us?"

It was now or never. "I'm not sure. You were there last night. You know everything."

Enzo crossed to the sideboard to get himself coffee. They were the only ones in the dining room, and his voice was straightforward. "So you wish to run away?"

She shrugged and slumped back into her chair. "It would be safer."

"Yes. It would have been safer for me to stay in Italy. There was no work and no prospects, but it would have been safe. I have been through some rocky times in the past few years, but I don't regret any of it. It is in tackling the new and the scary that we become who we are meant to be."

"I've been venturing into new places all my life," she defended. Getting dumped off at Bruce's house as a child hadn't been easy. Then there was the convent, and college, and a series of assignments in Manhattan where she was constantly new and required to prove herself.

But she'd never been part of a family before, and there wasn't a rule book for how to behave when people hurt her feelings. She drew her wool shawl closer as the cold seeped all the way to her bones, and tried to speak without her teeth chattering.

"Everything in me wants to run away," she confessed. Because the longer she stayed, the more it would hurt when she ultimately had to leave, for she truly didn't belong here.

206

Constant exposure to new people and unfamiliar tasks was wearing her down, making her brittle and tired. She wanted a normal job in an office where duties and expectations were clear. The temptation to go home where she belonged grew by the minute.

Enzo seemed to be reading her mind. "You'll regret it for the rest of your life if you run," he said simply.

He was right. It wasn't going to be easy to face everybody today, especially since she'd made a spectacle of herself by fleeing the tavern like a frightened rabbit. Maybe it had been idiotic to imagine she had the guts to become part of this adventure story, but she'd already signed on for it and didn't want to be the sort of person who ran away.

Two hours later, she waited in the hotel lobby as townspeople poured inside to await their assignments. They were supposed to move the Belmont house today, but maybe work would be canceled due to the sleet storm. The windows had a layer of ice on them, and Eloise couldn't imagine how they would get anything productive done.

The front door opened, and Rebecca Wiggin entered, along with a gust of icy wind. "Alex says the move is a go! We need all hands on deck today. Line up for your assignments," she said.

Eloise slid to the end of the line and tried to avoid meeting anyone's gaze. No one had spoken to her, which was a relief. When she reached the front of the line, Rebecca gave her a genuine smile.

"You're assigned to the team clearing ice from the rails. Are you game?"

"Of course."

"Good! Get your warmest clothes; you're going to need them."

Eloise headed upstairs and opened her wardrobe, and there it was—her scarlet coat. Lined with fox fur and sporting brass buttons, it was the most conspicuous garment she owned. It hadn't been cold enough to wear it yet, and the glamorous coat would look terribly out of place in this rural valley.

But it was her warmest, and it was going to be a long, frigid day. She gritted her teeth and pulled it on, then headed out to the lumberyard to join the crew. At least it had stopped sleeting, and snow now fell in fat, puffy flakes.

The Belmont house had been jacked up yesterday, and Alex already stood in the front yard. The cold air made voices carry, and she clearly heard him calling out instructions to the crew.

"I need two people to go door to door and collect any portable heaters to be had. Kerosene heaters, smokers, coal-burning cans—whatever you can find. The rest of us will disperse them along the rails and then—"

He stopped the instant he saw her. His eyes flicked down to take in her coat, and a faint smile graced his mouth.

That smile irked. He'd better not think that her presence here meant she forgave him. She was here because she was *loyal,* nothing else.

"—and then we move the Belmont house as soon as the rails are clear," he concluded. The crowd dispersed, each going to their respective positions. A dozen kerosene heaters already sat on the supply table.

"I'm glad to see you here," Alex said as he handed her the wire handle of a heater. It was almost two feet tall, and the tin chimney was covered with soot. Her crimson coat was going to take a beating today.

She grasped the handle. "I'm freezing. Give me another heater; I can carry two." She wasn't going to budge an inch toward that easy smile.

Ice forced her to take mincing footsteps as she inched toward the rails. The freezing cold sapped her energy. How could people work in conditions like this? She delivered her two heaters to spots along the railway. They were being allocated every ten feet, and hopefully they'd soon soften the ice.

Eloise returned to the lumberyard, where brooms, shovels, and spades were distributed to the volunteers to start chipping the ice from the rails. She kept her head down as she grabbed a spade and trudged after a group heading back to the railway. Hercules led the group, appointing someone every ten yards to start clearing the ice. She cringed a little when she was assigned to work only one station away from Reverend Carmichael.

Did the reverend know too? He hadn't been at the tavern last night and had never treated her with a hint of disrespect, but he still might now. He probably *did* know.

She started working close to a kerosene heater. Her spade knocked away slivers of softened ice, but only two feet away, the ice was still frozen solid. She moved the heater, but it was slow going as the spade chipped powdery white scars into the ice. She got winded quickly. Was it the cold that made this so challenging, or being hunched over? With each hard-fought inch of liberated rail, she got a little closer to Reverend Carmichael. She sank into a rhythm, attacking the ice as though it were a personal affront, and it felt good to vent her anger against it. She might be a fallen woman in the eyes of this town, but she knew how to work and would clear this stretch of railway if it was the last thing she did. The noise of her spade made a rhythmic clink, echoed by the reverend's similar cadence as he closed the distance between them. Soon their shovels were only inches apart. His shovel banged into hers as the last of the ice chipped free.

His good-hearted laughter was contagious. "We did it!"

Her back ached as she straightened, surveying the stretch of freshly cleared railway line. Up and down the line, others were still stooped over and hard at work. Her crimson coat was smudged with soot and water stains, but she didn't care, for the sense of accomplishment felt good.

"Let's go help the others," she said, leaning over to collect her kerosene heater.

Her good mood evaporated as she passed Oscar Ott. "A woman in scarlet!" he chortled as he plugged away at his own stretch of ice.

"Knock it off, Ott," the reverend warned, a pretty good indication that Reverend Carmichael knew all about her tarnished past.

"I was just complimenting her coat," Oscar said defensively. "It suits her perfectly."

Eloise sank her spade into a pile of snow beside the rail and lifted it high. "Hey, Oscar, this is for you," she said, and hurled a load of wet snow smack against his chest.

"What did I do to deserve that?" he asked, but everyone else smothered their laughter as they turned back to their work.

Alex sighed with relief as the crew sent to clear the rails returned. The ice had put them several hours behind schedule, but with luck they could still get the Belmont house moved today. A second team had gone up to Highpoint to be sure the foundation was free of ice and ready to accept the house.

"All clear!" Hercules hollered as he drew near, and Alex nodded to Dick Brookmeyer to harness the oxen.

In her red coat, Eloise stood out like a poppy in a field of rye. He'd heard about the shovelful of snow she'd hurled at Oscar Ott. That little morsel of gossip spread fast, and everyone thought it hysterical, but given the way she stood aloof from the others it looked like she was still upset.

"Eloise!" he called out. "Come help with the Belmont house. We need you."

"Yes, come help!" old Mr. Belmont beckoned. "I don't trust this lad to know anything about math. I tried like the dickens to teach it to him in school, but none of it stuck. I hear you're much better with numbers."

Alex's smile tightened. Back in the day he'd often told Eloise how much better a teacher she was than Mr. Belmont, and given her spotless memory, she surely remembered.

She looked torn, and he strode over to see her. "Don't let what happened last night ruin everything," he said quietly.

"Why didn't you tell me the whole town knew?" Her voice was frostier than the air. "Looking back, I can see the times people were teasing you and me, but it all flew over my head. I feel like such an idiot."

"No one in this town thinks you're an idiot."

"I still don't like that everyone knows." Her teeth chattered, and they hadn't been a moment earlier. It made his heart turn over that she was beating herself up over something like this.

"Yes, they all know," Alex said, hating that she flinched at his words. "They know we weren't perfect and that we acted like young, impulsive fools. In a town this small, we all know each others' business, and no one is perfect. Do you want me to tell you what I know about Dr. Lloyd?"

"No!" she burst out.

"Because there's some pretty rich scandal there. And the war between the Talbots and the Gallaghers is epic, all rooted in a snub over a wedding invitation. No one here is perfect, and yet we all still live and work together. We still hold our heads high."

The sound of her chattering teeth cut through him like a pickaxe. It was his fault she still suffered over their wild-hearted idiocy. "Eloise, I'm so sorry," he said gently. "I know you care what people think, and if I could somehow shield you from this, I would."

She clutched her arms around her middle. "It just seems so

sordid. The way Oscar sneered at me. And good people like Reverend Carmichael probably think the same."

"It wasn't sordid," he said.

"But *they* don't know that."

"They're about to."

He grabbed her hand, tugging her back toward the group of people preparing to shift the house. Behind him, Eloise sputtered, tugging at his hand, but he knew what he was doing. If Eloise worried the people in this town didn't respect her, he was going to disabuse her of that notion.

He jumped atop the empty wagon bed. "Gather around, everyone. I have an announcement!"

Eloise let out a whimper, but it wasn't possible to squelch unsavory gossip by burying her head in the sand. People swiveled to look at him curiously, and he took a deep breath and began.

"I have been in love with Eloise Drake since I was eighteen years old. I should have married her back then, and the only reason I can't today is because she won't have me. Mercifully, I've now got a second chance. I intend to pull out all the stops and win her back. If that means shooting down gossip or stomping on people who look at her the wrong way, I'm ready to stomp."

"Tell it like it is, boy!" old Mr. Belmont shouted. Plenty of others nodded in approval, while others didn't understand what all the fuss was about. But Eloise did, and that was all that mattered.

He looked back at the crowd. "When I was eighteen, I was an irresponsible idiot, and I snuck around behind closed doors. No more. I'm proclaiming my love and admiration openly. Without shame." He looked her directly in the eyes, speaking only to her but loudly enough for everyone to hear. "I love you, Eloise. I did back then, I do today, and I expect I'll love you a dozen years from now, even if you go back to the city and marry that stuffed shirt. Which I sincerely hope you don't."

He hopped down from the wagon and walked toward her. It looked like she didn't know if she wanted to laugh or run and hide. At least she wasn't ashamed anymore. "You're making this very hard," she finally said.

"That's the idea," he said. "I saw that guy. You deserve better than that."

Her teeth still chattered, and standing here so long was making him cold too.

"Let's go move the Belmont house," she said.

He reached for her hand. "Friends again?"

She didn't need to say anything. She just slipped her glove-encased hand in his as they walked toward the Belmont house, and he let out a sigh of relief. Today everything was fine; that might not be the case tomorrow. So many unknowns loomed on the horizon, but he'd battle those dragons when they came.

TWENTY-THREE

loise slipped into a routine over the next month. Each morning she and four other women headed out with shovels and brooms to clear the railway lines of snow and other debris on the track. It took an hour each morning, then they repeated the task every evening. It was tiring work, and the cold meant her toes were blocks of ice, her nose red and hands so frozen she could barely hold her pencil as she and Alex reconciled their budget at the end of each day. Their tentative courtship was fresh and new and wonderful. She could be herself with Alex. As they embarked on the biggest challenge in their lives, it was a blessing to have a person with whom she needed no artifice.

The municipal bond was back on track. Contamination at the Timberland camp plummeted immediately after Nick's security guards arrived to patrol the grounds. If it had been sabotage, it seemed the guards were sufficient to stifle it, and the tainted water was regarded as a one-time fluke.

By the end of December, they were on schedule despite the snow. Forty-five houses, six shops, the library, and the church had all been moved. Today they were moving the schoolhouse. The compact building had a small footprint, but its brick construction and two stories made it the heaviest building they would move. Before he left, Enzo had provided a list of special concerns for each building. He said the small classrooms lined up like matchboxes on each floor made the building very stable and a good candidate to move despite its weight.

Christmas was in two days, and in acknowledgment of the holiday, a pine wreath with a big red bow had been placed on the school's front door. The steamroller had made several passes over the ground leading to the main road to ensure it was perfectly level, and the building was already jacked up and ready to be lowered onto the rails. Members of the work crew were bundled into thick coats and scarves, making them all look alike, but even from a distance Eloise could spot Alex. Something about his energy as he darted across the worksite was distinctly him.

Dozens of people had gathered to watch the school make its historic journey to its new home. Marie Trudeau stood a few yards away, her face a combination of anxiety and wistfulness.

"Enzo said this is one of the easier buildings to move," Eloise told her, hoping to reassure the older woman.

Marie nodded but couldn't tear her gaze from the schoolhouse. "I still get nervous with each one of these moves. I taught school in that building for twenty-three years. God willing, I will do so again next year."

Eloise reached out to squeeze Marie's hand. Marie squeezed back, the unspoken communication needing no words. It would have been nice to have a mother like Marie Trudeau, whose gentle compassion extended to everyone around her.

Alex gave a quick blast of the whistle, and the jackscrew teams began lowering the school onto the platform. It took an hour to get it lowered and secured, but then the building was ready to move. Dick Brookmeyer guided the oxen toward the road, the harnesses jangling in the cold air. As always, the oxen came to a halt as the slack pulled tight, and then the building moved. Eloise caught her breath. It was always astounding to see a building in motion, and her heart swelled with pride. She'd had no part in arranging this engineering marvel, but it was still a privilege to be part of it.

A crack split the silence, and the wagon abruptly stopped. Mr. Brookmeyer dropped the lead rope and ran to the side of the wagon to see what was wrong.

"Broken axle," he called out.

Eloise gasped. How could they possibly fix the wagon with a building on top of it? Even worse, the right corner of the wagon sagged. As the wagon tilted, so did the school.

"Everybody move back," Alex yelled. People ran to the other side of the road. Alex and Mr. Brookmeyer worked to free the oxen, for if the wagon collapsed, it would take—

The back wheel splintered to pieces, and the platform lurched to the side. The schoolhouse tipped at a dangerous angle. Alex and Mr. Brookmeyer abandoned the oxen and ran. Eloise stood frozen in shock. No one knew what to do. She and Marie clutched each other, and the whole world seemed to freeze.

The platform's front wheel collapsed next, and the school crashed into the dirt. The frame of the building caved in, windows shattered, and roof tiles smashed to the ground. Bricks came tumbling down, rolling over the embankment and burying the steamroller in rubble.

Alex didn't know what to do. In an uncharacteristic move, he asked people to clear out of the tavern so he could speak freely with the town council and a handful of others whose opinion he needed. All he knew was that he had to come up with a plan to replace their equipment and get the move back on schedule.

Outside, a huge mound of bricks, broken boards, and shattered glass was all they had left of their schoolhouse. The chalky smell of mortar dust hung in the air. Their school was gone, their wagon smashed beyond repair, and he was personally on the hook for a twelve-thousand-dollar steamroller. He would probably go to his grave still owing on it.

At least the oxen were unharmed, but they would need to buy another wagon, platform, and bracing rails before any more buildings could be moved. It was going to destroy their budget and their schedule.

He braced his forehead in his hands, trying to rub away the tension. He couldn't bear to look at Eloise, but he needed her guidance.

"How much money do we have left from the bond?"

"Some, but it's all been allocated for building the roads up at the new place."

"And the reserves?" He held his breath, clinging to that last hope.

"It won't be enough to buy a new steamroller. Your only hope is if Bruce somehow forgives the debt and loans you more equipment. I don't think he will."

The words were gently spoken but a body blow nevertheless. A quarter of the town was safely moved, but six hundred people and their homes remained stuck in the valley. He'd already spent their money and had no way to get their houses out. The easiest thing would be to run away and start over somewhere else. He'd done it once before, but he couldn't leave these people to face the wreckage he'd created.

"Perhaps if I approached him?" Marie asked, her voice timid. Alex swiveled to look at her. Marie Trudeau was as dainty and delicate as a hummingbird, and just as persuasive. Unless she had some connection with Garrett he didn't know about.

"Were you once his teacher?"

"I'm not *that* old," Marie said. "I think you need a neutral party to make the appeal."

Eloise shook her head. "I'm your best shot at getting mercy. Bruce respects my opinion. Since I was the bond's auditor, it will look bad if the town goes under. He might be willing to intervene to spare me from that."

This made Alex feel even worse. He hadn't even considered what this catastrophe might do to Eloise, but it seemed his destruction knew no end. Everyone he cared about in the world was getting sucked down into this quagmire.

Marie wouldn't give up. She laid her thin hand atop his. "Forgive me, Alex, but I think everyone knows that Mr. Garrett took your . . . your youthful indiscretion with his ward badly. If Eloise appeals for debt forgiveness, he will assume she is asking on your behalf, not for the good of the town. I don't think she should go."

Reverend Carmichael spoke up. "I would be willing to do it." He sounded like a frightened man facing a firing squad. "As a man of the cloth, my endorsement might carry sway."

Eloise stood. "I'm the best person to do this. Of course he's going to be angry. And of course he'll assume I am asking on Alex's behalf—he's not stupid. He's going to be furious, but he appreciates direct dealing. I'm the best person to make the appeal."

Alex's headache intensified. Everything she said was correct, and being forced to depend on her help was agonizing. But he needed her, and if she failed, this town was doomed.

Eloise headed up to Bruce's house first thing the following morning. It was the morning of Christmas Eve, but Bruce hadn't eased up on his schedule and was already at the quarry when she arrived.

"Can you send someone to fetch him?" she asked the house-keeper. "It's important."

This wasn't going to be easy. If she had the money from her mother's estate, she could simply buy a steamroller for Alex, but it could be years before that money came through. She waited in Bruce's study, where a massive desk dominated most of the space and a stone wall housed a fireplace. She plopped onto the hearth and waited. When she was growing up, this was where she always sat whenever anything of importance needed to be discussed. Sometimes it was when she begged not to be sent away to boarding school, or when she fruitlessly pleaded to visit her parents. It didn't matter that they didn't want her; she had simply been so lonely during those years.

Bruce entered the study ten minutes later, a look of mild annoyance on his face. He wore a rugged canvas coat with work gloves. While some rich men managed their investments from an office, Bruce supervised from the field. He still carried his gloves in one hand, impatient to get back to work.

"Eloise," he said as he closed the door. "What can I do for you?"

"There was an accident during the move yesterday. An axle broke on the transport platform, and a building tumbled over."

Bruce froze. "Was anyone hurt?"

"No. I suppose we were lucky, all things considered. But the schoolhouse is a complete loss, and I'm afraid the rubble buried your steamroller. It's ruined."

Aside from the clenching of a muscle in his jaw, she could detect no change in his expression. He opened a desk drawer, took out a cigar, and clipped off the tip. She quaked inside but waited patiently as he prepared the cigar. When it was lit, he took several puffs, then leaned back in his chair to scrutinize her through narrowed eyes.

"I suppose you're here to appeal on Duval's behalf for me to go easy on him." It was a statement, not a question.

"Yes."

"That was a twelve-thousand-dollar steamroller."

"Yes. And we need to get another. Either buy one or borrow one. I know you've placed a lien on his property until all the equipment is safely returned. If you forgive the debt, Alex can apply the money from his orchard toward more equipment, but only if you withdraw the lien."

She held her breath as she awaited his answer. She didn't have long to wait.

"If I forgive the debt, it will be throwing him a lifeline," Bruce said, not without compassion. "It might save him today, but what about the next disaster? The next long-shot investment? The faster you distance yourself from this entire scheme, the better off you'll be."

She clasped her hands, trying not to remember Alex's dejected face in the tavern last night. If she had to return to town and tell him of Bruce's refusal to help, she knew exactly what Alex would do. He would pretend it didn't hurt, send her a reassuring smile, and make a joke, but inside he would be in agony.

"I love him," she said softly. Bruce flinched but didn't seem all that surprised by her declaration, so she continued. "You don't need to fear that I'll throw my lot in with Alex Duval forever. I know I don't belong here, but I can't walk away just yet. It ended badly before, and this time I want to leave on my own terms. This is the greatest, hardest, and the most remarkable thing I've ever done in my life. I've learned what it is to test my heart and mind and muscles against an epic challenge. But in the end, I know I'll go back to my normal world. That was always the plan."

Memories of her apartment back home triggered a surge of longing. A long, hot bath whenever she wanted one. Electric lights and an indoor job where her boots weren't caked with mud and melting snow didn't leak down her neck. Where expectations were clearly set out, and snooping neighbors didn't know her business.

But she couldn't leave while Alex and the town still needed her. "I'm staying until the town is moved. I have to see this through, even if it breaks my heart all over again."

Bruce set down his cigar. "For an intelligent girl, you seem reluctant to learn from experience. Don't expect me to support you in this madness."

"So you won't help us?"

"I will help *you*, but never him," Bruce said. "Alex Duval showed me who he is when he was eighteen years old."

There wasn't a trace of sympathy in Bruce's expression. This was a man who had indulged in at least one extramarital affair, yet he had never showed her the slightest indication that he understood what it meant to be in love. Suddenly it became vitally important to know if he could understand how she felt about Alex.

"Were you ever in love?" she asked. "You betrayed your wife with my mother, but when she returned to Thomas Drake, I never saw any gnashing of teeth from you."

He shrugged. "You were still in the womb, so that would have been unlikely."

True, but she'd once stolen a peek at her mother's diary and knew about the circumstances of her conception. Feeling neglected, her mother had indulged in a foolish affair while her husband was on a six-month business trip to Europe. Thomas returned home to a pregnant wife who had no possibility of passing the child off as his. Her mother wept and confessed everything. Thomas took his wife back, and in return she was slavishly loyal to him for the rest of her life, even going so far as to banish the redheaded child who clearly did not resemble her husband.

"But why did you do it?" she asked. "You risked your marriage, even your own business, to dally with a married woman. Why?"

"Because I could," Bruce said bluntly. "Alex Duval took liberties with you because he could. That's the way men are."

She dropped her head. Bruce always tried to paint her summers with Alex in a tawdry fashion, but it didn't feel that way to her. Not anymore.

"I loved him then, and I love him now," she said. "His fire, his vision, his unquenchable optimism. When I'm with him I feel limitless, like the sun will never set and we can live in Eden forever."

"Oh, Eloise," Bruce said in a voice aching with tenderness. "I would give my entire fortune if I could buy that for you, but the real world doesn't work that way. Bills come due, accidents happen, and idealists fail to plan. I could forgive that debt, but it won't solve the problem. It will only give him a shovel to dig himself further into a hole. I can't do it."

She left the mansion feeling like a failure. She dreaded telling Alex, but when she arrived at the lumberyard she was met with the strangest sight. The yard was a mess, with wheels, metal siding, and tools scattered everywhere. A blacksmith hammered a wheel onto what looked like the bottom of a railcar. Most odd was Alex, wearing a dress suit, vest, and tie, with an exuberant expression on his face.

He waved to her across the staging area. "Eloise! Come see our new flatcar trailer."

It was huge, as large as any full-sized railway car, but it was only a metal bottom, with no sides. She looked at Alex with questions in her eyes.

"We should have done this from the beginning," Alex said. "Trains use flatcar trailers to tow heavy loads, so they're built to handle the weight. Solid steel! I hired a blacksmith from Kingston to overhaul the wheelbase of this one, but it can still be fitted on the railway for transporting up the hill."

With its metal wheels and undercarriage, it certainly looked like a much better platform than the one that broke, but where had Alex gotten the money for this?

She pulled him aside. "How are you going to pay for it?"

"I'm diverting some of the money for roads," he said. "We can pave the roads later, but we need this trailer now. Plus, the guy's father runs an inn up in Kingston, and we're going to supply them with free cider for the next year. I'm guessing you failed with Garrett?"

She nodded, stunned that his buoyant mood didn't dim.

"No matter," he said. "We're still going to get this town moved. We'll just have to go without paved roads for a while."

"Why are you wearing such fancy clothes?" And he wasn't the only one. Most of the villagers in the lumberyard also wore their Sunday best.

"Because it's Christmas Eve, and tonight is Blessed Joy's christening. Do you want to come?"

"Alex! How can you be so nonchalant about all this?"

His eyes watered as he smiled at her, but it was a genuine smile with only a little sorrow behind it. "Because I made a good deal on a solid steel platform, which means we'll be back in action soon. And in an hour my beautiful niece is going to be baptized. Sally has baked a dozen spice cakes, and three Irish fiddlers are coming down from the Timberland camp to help us celebrate. How can I *not* be happy?"

This was what she'd always loved about Alex. He had a bottomless well of optimism that let him walk between the raindrops without getting wet.

"You're right!" she said, surprised at how quickly her own mood lifted. No matter how many problems loomed on the horizon, tonight was perfect. It was a blessing that should not be squandered.

The baby's christening was unlike anything she'd ever seen.

The ceremony took place in the bandstand, for the church had already been moved. Loving, tired, and joyous people welcomed the baby into their community on this most holy of evenings.

Afterward the celebration moved to the tavern, where the fiddlers played lively tunes that lit up the night. Eloise served the spice cake so Sally could enjoy the evening, and it was good to be needed. Alex sat huddled with a group of men indulging in animated conversation. Across the crowded tavern, he met her gaze and flashed her a wink before going back to the men.

Tomorrow was Christmas, and they would all share a day of rest, but after that would come an avalanche of bills, problems battling the snow, and deadlines to meet. But not tonight. Looking around the warm interior of the tavern, Eloise saw a hundred reasons to keep pushing through the exhaustion and bills and anxiety. She saw a community worth fighting for.

lex had never been an early bird, but in the next months, the hour before dawn became his favorite of the day. It was in that quiet hour when he and Eloise met to plan their work objectives for the day. They were the only two people in the hotel dining room as they prioritized a list of tasks and budgeted for supplies.

With the rising sun, they sweated alongside the others in the tough physical labor of moving the town. And in the evenings, they stole kisses and dreamed about the future. Maybe someday they would have the luxury of courting like normal people, with roses and moonlit serenades. Instead, he and Eloise had budget meetings, kitchen duty, pouring concrete, and turns cleaning the oxen pens. He wouldn't have had it any other way.

By the end of February, their new town was shaping up. Most of the buildings had been safely relocated, and only forty more needed to be moved. There had been no additional accidents after the disaster with the school, but without a steamroller, street construction had ground to a halt. It was something he would have to worry about once the town was entirely moved, for he could only fight one battle at a time.

On March 1, Alex and Eloise spent the entire day in Kingston, making arrangements to draw down bond money to keep paying for the relocation. It was past dark by the time their work was completed and they arrived back in Duval Springs.

"The town looks so sad and bewildered," he said to Eloise as they rode down the main street toward the stables. As more buildings moved to Highpoint, the remnants of Duval Springs looked ever more dilapidated, littered with construction waste, vacant lots, and untended lawns.

"A town is an inanimate object which can be neither sad nor bewildered," Eloise said primly.

He pointed to the buckled sidewalk that had taken a beating from months of heavy construction carts. "Sorry, Eloise, but that sidewalk is sad. So is the mud pit where the bandstand used to be. Even the oxen avoid it."

Eloise nodded in concession. "I suppose you're right, but I'd rather dream about what Highpoint will look like someday."

He would too. Soon they'd be able to plant grass in the new village green. They'd add trees and fill the flower boxes and do their best to recreate a vibrant, healthy town square. Once the new town started greening up, it would look more like home.

Dinner was long over by the time they arrived at the hotel, and most people had already turned in for the night. With all the physical labor, few people indulged in late-night carousing anymore. Alex kissed Eloise on the forehead and prepared to wait in the lobby for a while after she disappeared upstairs. Only Kasper and a handful of men were still here, but Alex didn't want rumors to take root by heading up with her.

Kasper was closing up the Western Union stand for the evening. Each night he set up a Morse inker to capture brief messages that might come in overnight until he was back on duty in the morning. Alex glanced at the men in the dining room, who were engrossed in a hand of cards but still within earshot. He needed to speak to Kasper confidentially.

"Follow me into the office as soon as you wrap up here," Alex said.

Kasper looked curious but finished setting up the overnight Morse inker and appeared in Willard's empty office a few minutes later. Alex closed the door. He didn't like reading someone the riot act, but it was time. He cleared his throat and spoke calmly but directly.

"I know you take your duties manning the telegraph seriously, but I need you to contribute more hours to the move each day."

Kasper drew himself up to his full height. "But I am contributing," he sputtered. "I send and receive plenty of move-related telegrams every day."

"At the beginning of the move, everyone agreed to contribute twelve hours of manual labor per week. Ever since your house was moved, you barely show up at all." With so many homes now safely relocated, Alex feared that people whose homes had been moved might slack off. So far Kasper was the only one who had tried.

"Who will man the telegraph station if I'm not here?"

"Use the Morse inker. That's what we bought it for."

Kasper launched into a series of excuses for why he couldn't work, but Alex refused to be drawn into the argument. He simply laid out the consequences. "Our new town is going to have water and electricity supplied by the state. People who didn't contribute their fair share to the move will be excluded from the services."

"You can't do that," Kasper snapped. "Those lines are coming from the state, not you."

"The state is running lines from the reservoir and the power plant to our town, but service to individual homes is on us. And I won't order our volunteers to lay utility lines to your house unless you continue contributing your fair share."

Kasper was incensed. Whenever he got this angry, traces of his Finnish accent came to the fore. "I can afford to pay for my own service. I don't need town charity."

"It's your decision, but I'm letting everyone know that getting added to the public utilities depends on contributing to the move all the way to the end."

Kasper shot him a hostile glare and left without another word.

Lethargy weighed on Alex as he trudged upstairs. He was asleep almost before his head hit the pillow.

The clang of the town bell penetrated the fog of his sleep, but Alex punched his pillow, rolled over, and tried to ignore it. He dragged the pillow over his head—and then his brain kicked in.

The town bell! He bolted upright. If someone rang that bell in the middle of the night, it meant trouble. He stumbled to the door of his room and yanked it open. Other lodgers had straggled out into the hotel hallway as well. No one knew what was going on, so he raced downstairs in nothing but his skivvies, jerked open the front door, and ran across the frozen ground toward the bell. By the time he got there, he didn't need to ask what the problem was, because he could see it.

A fire. Up near the new town. An orange glow illuminated the night sky, and smoke tinged the air. He raced back to the hotel and up the stairs.

"Fire!" he shouted. "Get everyone up," he ordered one of the bewildered men, who obeyed without question and began banging on every closed door.

Alex ran to his room and pulled on his clothes, but fear gripped his heart. They had no way to fight a fire up at Highpoint, only a single well, and it looked like an inferno up there. This was going to be bad. Others stumbled out of their rooms, rubbing sleep from their eyes, but there was no time to waste.

Two minutes later he was on the street, glad to see others gathering with whatever equipment they could grab. This fire would be fought with axes, shovels, and dirt, and they needed every able-bodied person in the fight. Within a few minutes, he had a buckboard hitched and ready to go. He prodded the horse to move faster as they joined the line of other wagons heading up the road. Before he reached the end of Main Street, Hercules ran alongside the wagon and vaulted aboard.

"What's happening?" Hercules panted.

"I don't know, but this doesn't look good."

The reek of smoke worsened as they got closer to Highpoint. Specks of floating cinders sparked smaller fires in the brush along the road. For once Alex was grateful for the snow that blanketed the dead underbrush, but men still hopped off the wagons to beat at the glowing cinders. Alex didn't slow his wagon. He needed to get up to Highpoint and see what was going on.

The strangest sight met his eyes as he rounded the bend. The people at the new town were already awake and beating at a line of fire, their silhouettes outlined against a low rim of flames. None of the buildings were on fire. The flames seemed confined to the brush along the roadside.

Alex leapt from the buckboard. "What's happening?"

Dr. Lloyd straightened. Trails of sweat cut through the soot on his face. "The fire is in a straight line," he said, still panting. "It's burning between here and the Timberland camp. As soon as we get this end put out, we need to head up there. They've got it a lot worse than we do."

The scene made no sense. The fire was no more than a yard wide, but it trailed all the way to the forest line, then up the mountainside, where acres of trees were fully engulfed. And right in the middle of those trees was the Timberland camp.

"I'm heading up there now," he told Hercules. People could be trapped inside buildings, and that mattered more than whatever structural damage they might suffer down here.

He ran up the hillside, and Dr. Lloyd's assessment was confirmed. The fire blazed along an inexplicably straight line, continuing to burn despite the absence of vegetation. There had to be some kind of fuel on the ground to feed this fire and connect Highpoint to the work camp.

Hot air choked his lungs as he drew near. A cluster of children huddled on the outskirts of the Timberland camp, but inside the camp were dozens of men beating at the flames and clearing brush away. A man worked the handle of their single water pump to fill buckets. The rudimentary canteen and supply shed were completely engulfed, but the other buildings were safe for now.

"Can I help?" Alex bellowed to the nearest man.

"Grab a shovel and start throwing dirt," the man panted.

He obeyed. After an hour his back hurt, the blisters on his hands bled, and his throat was coated with soot, but the fire was partially contained. No one had been hurt.

The night watchman supplied by the state said the flames had come roaring toward the camp in a straight line. Whoever set this fire must have known that guards patrolled the Timberland camp, but that Highpoint wasn't guarded. The culprit must have soaked the ground with an accelerant ahead of time, then lit it from the relative safety at Highpoint.

Hercules and a handful of other men from the new town arrived after an hour, carrying buckets and shovels.

"How are things at Highpoint?" Alex asked Hercules.

"The flames are out, but we've got men combing through the forest, looking for smoldering ash."

"Anyone hurt?"

"Just a dog that got hit by a falling branch."

The biggest problem at Timberland were the burning trees. There was nothing to do but wait for them to burn themselves out. Men stood in a wide circle around the camp, everyone on the lookout for falling branches that could scatter more flames.

Alex was tired and demoralized as he shuffled back into Highpoint, too exhausted to continue down the road to Duval Springs. Once the sun was fully up, he'd need to inspect every inch of their railroad to be certain it was unharmed.

The stink of smoke hung in the air. Men patrolled the area in a line, inspecting the underbrush to stamp out cinders. Others stood in a cluster near the entrance to the town square, heads together and faces grim.

Eloise looked up from this group, and he couldn't suppress a smile. No matter how bad the day began, she was still here and fighting alongside him.

But she looked awful. She broke away from the group, her face white with fear.

"Thank goodness you're back," she said in a shaking voice. "Marie Trudeau is missing."

Eloise hated to bring him the terrible news, but he needed to know.

"What do you mean, missing?" Alex lashed out in his commander's voice.

"She's not here, and we've looked everywhere," Eloise said. "Her sons said they had dinner at her house last night, but that was the last time anyone saw her. It doesn't look like her bed was slept in."

And her sons were frantic. Ever since discovering their mother was missing, Joseph and Jasper had been tramping through the forest, hollering her name.

Reverend Carmichael jogged over to join them. "No one saw her during the fire. The boys left her house at eight o'clock last night, and the fire woke us up around two. She's been gone for at least five hours."

Eloise hurried after Alex as he headed toward Marie's house.

Several people had already scoured the compact house for clues. There was no sign of foul play, but Alex might spot something they'd missed. She was about to follow him inside when a shout split the air.

"Here she comes!" Dr. Lloyd hollered, pointing toward the main road. Eloise gasped as she recognized Bruce Garrett riding on his chestnut mare, with Marie perched on the horse behind him. Both looked stunned to see the charred remnants left by the fire. Bruce sprang off his horse, then lifted Marie down.

"What's going on here?" he demanded.

Eloise recognized that tone. Whenever Bruce felt backed into a corner, he lashed out. She stepped in front of Alex and explained as calmly as possible.

"There was a fire. No one could find Marie, and we panicked. Her sons are out searching for her."

"Well, call them back in," Bruce said. "As you can see, she's fine."

"But where were you?" Reverend Carmichael asked in a bewildered tone. "We've been searching everywhere."

"I'm home now," Marie said. Her face was tense, and she didn't meet anyone's gaze. "I see grimy footsteps all over my porch, so I'd like to take care of it." She scurried toward her house and disappeared like a mouse running for cover.

Eloise stood beside Bruce, still appalled by what appeared to be going on. It didn't seem possible, but it looked like Marie Trudeau had spent the night with Bruce.

Eloise shot him a questioning glare. "Because you could?" she asked pointedly.

Bruce's face tightened at the reminder of how he'd blackened Alex's intentions with the same phrase. "Mind your own business, Eloise."

Others had seen Marie's arrival and came running, asking questions it was obvious Bruce had no intention of answering, and he was growing angrier. She knew all the signs—the glower, the clenched fists. She had to defuse this.

"Everyone, go back to your jobs cleaning up," she said. "There's no problem here. I understand we're moving the Gunderson house today. It would be best if some of you scrubbed the foundation so we don't set a house atop a layer of soot."

Her efforts were futile. A cluster of women whispered behind their hands, and when Oscar Ott approached Marie's house, pressing his face against a window to peek inside, Bruce's temper snapped.

"Get away from that window, you pervert." He dragged Oscar back by the collar of his coat. Oscar slipped in the mud and went down.

Eloise glared at Alex. "Would you please help?" she whispered fiercely.

"What do you want me to do?" He sounded almost amused. "Part of me wishes I had a pack of Bulgarian bodyguards that could pay him a visit, but that's been done before. It's probably best handled by Marie's sons. Speaking of which . . ."

She followed his gaze and spotted Jasper and Joseph, both of whom must have been alerted to their mother's return. They came careening across the field, not looking at anyone as they made a beeline to Marie's house and burst through the front door.

"Mom?" Jasper hollered. "What's going on?"

The door slammed shut behind them, but people continued gathering before Marie's house. Ten seconds later, Marie's door flung open, and Joseph barreled straight at Bruce.

"Why was my mother at your house?" he demanded.

"That's none of your business, sapling."

Joseph drew back a fist, ready to punch, but Alex stepped between them before it could land. Bruce knocked Alex out of the way and cuffed Joseph on the shoulder.

"You want to throw a punch at me, whelp? Go ahead and take your best shot." Bruce pointed at his jaw. "Right there. Go on, do it! But after that, I'll be returning fire, and you'd better be man enough to stand up and take it."

By then Jasper and Marie were running down the steps, Jasper looking ready to join the fight. Dozens of people gathered in a ring around the family.

"Stop it, all of you!" Marie ordered, her voice strong for so tiny a woman. She cast a furious glare at Bruce, imploring him to lower the tension. He didn't.

When one of the thickset bystanders picked up a rock, Bruce turned on him.

"Do you want a job Monday morning?" he snapped at the man.

The thickset man froze, fingers still clenched around the rock. The state had completed its hiring for the reservoir, and any man who lost his job at the quarry would be in trouble.

Bruce dialed up the heat. "If you want a job, you will set that rock down. Not drop it—you will *set* it down."

Murmurs of discontent rumbled through the crowd, and the thickset man looked ready to snap, but after a moment he bent his knees and set the rock on the sooty ground. The smirk on Bruce's face was one of pure satisfaction.

Marie looked ready to weep. "Why must good people be so horrid to one another?"

Eloise had heard enough. She needed to take over and get the teams back on schedule.

"Hercules, go get some water to refill the trough. Dick, I need you to head back to town and be sure the oxen are fed and watered. We've got a house to move today."

"But did you hear what Mr. Garrett just said?" one of the young men sputtered in outrage.

Eloise gave him a frosty glare. "Did you know we have forty

buildings still to move and we're behind schedule? Now get to work over at the Gunderson plot. No arguing."

Marie had already raced back into her home, and Bruce aimed a final scorching glare at the townspeople before mounting his horse and leaving.

Schedules, timetables, and budgets were sacred if they were going to get this town moved on time. They had enough real problems without letting tempers and gossip take root. They were six months into an eight-month project. They had come so far, but exhaustion was beginning to take its toll. As their deadline drew near, tempers were growing thin, room for failure had evaporated, and this morning's events would only make things worse.

loise still simmered with anger as she rode in a wagon with ten other people back to Duval Springs. Despite her efforts to use the time to discuss practical matters, all people wanted to talk about was this morning's scandal.

"Did anyone notice if Marie was wearing the same clothes as she had on last night?" Oscar asked.

Mr. Gallagher opened his mouth to reply, but Eloise cut him off.

"Are you suddenly fascinated with women's fashion, Oscar? Because if you are, I have an extensive wardrobe featuring the latest trends straight from New York, and you're welcome to peruse them."

"I just want to know if she took a change of clothes up with her," Oscar said. "Because if she did, that's pretty good evidence—"

"It's evidence of nothing," she said in her frostiest tone. Alex choked back a laugh, which angered her even more. Didn't he understand how agonizing it was to have your most intimate secrets flaunted before the entire town? Was this how people talked about her and Alex behind their backs?

"You have to admit they looked pretty cozy on their way down the mountain," Mr. Gallagher pointed out. "How long do you suppose they've been carrying on?"

"I think it's revolting," another man said. "She ought to know better than to take up with a man like that. Can you imagine what her dead husband must be thinking?"

Eloise had heard enough. "Her dead husband isn't thinking anything *because he's dead*. You don't know what went on at that house, and neither does anyone else. But let's assume the worst. So what? Who here is perfect? Is it you?" she demanded of Mr. Gallagher.

"Heavens, no," he stammered, looking like he wanted to crawl beneath the wagon to hide.

"In ten minutes we'll be back in Duval Springs, and we all have jobs to do. If I hear anyone spewing gossip at the hotel, they won't be welcome for the communal meal." She looked at Alex. "I expect you to back me up on that."

Alex merely shrugged. "I've never been a big fan of telling people what they're allowed to think or say."

She planted her hands on her hips and glared at him. "Then start learning. We have a timetable, and I won't let pointless gossip throw us off schedule."

The wagging tongues continued even after they got home, but she did her best to ignore it as she opened the town's accounting books to track the daily expenditures. She was still working on it when Alex emerged from his room, freshly bathed and wearing a clean suit of clothes. She always loved the way he looked when newly scrubbed and shaved. An involuntary smile tugged at the corner of her mouth. She tried to tamp it back, but he saw it and wended his way through the tables to her.

"Still angry?" he asked.

It was the wrong thing to say. The humor in his tone indicated he saw no parallel between this morning's scandal and what had happened to them. "I'm doing my best to ensure the town's money is properly accounted for, and it takes considerable concentration, so I'm sorry I can't join everyone in rehashing the humiliation of two decent people."

"*One* decent person, anyway."

She threw down her pencil. "When will you grow up? I wish him and Marie well."

"I don't know exactly where he was last night, but I'll wager my bottom dollar that it looked a lot like an old cider mill."

Half the people in the room were eavesdropping, and his comment triggered a round of giggles from the next table. Eloise's eyes narrowed, and she leaned forward to speak in a low tone.

"You don't have a bottom dollar to wager because you're in debt past your eyeballs to Bruce, who hasn't called in the lien on your apple orchard. He could squash you like an insect, and the only reason he hasn't is because he's a decent man."

Alex rolled his eyes, and Eloise had had enough. She'd been going cross-eyed scrutinizing columns of financial data on behalf of this town and was tired of being taken for granted. Keeping her face entirely calm, she gathered the receipts, tucked them inside the accounting ledger, closed the book, then whapped it against Alex's chest.

"Here. See if you can find another accountant willing to work for free," she said. She turned and made her way to the front of the dining room.

A row of customers waiting to be seated all stared at her. To her mortification, at the front of the line were Fletcher Jones and her cousin, Nick Drake.

"Hello, Eloise," Nick said in an annoyingly cheerful tone. "Have we arrived at a difficult time?"

She swallowed hard. How much had they heard? Given the shock on Fletcher's face, probably everything.

"Wh-what are you doing here?" she managed to stammer.

"We came as soon as we heard about the fire," Nick said. "Apparently the security guards we hired aren't stopping the sabotage, and something more needs to be done."

"I agree," Alex said as he strode up to join them, all signs of his irreverent teasing gone.

Fletcher didn't even glance at Alex. He merely looked at her with all the sympathy in the world in his gaze. "Emotions continue to run hot in Duval Springs," he said. "I warned you about that."

"You did. I shall certainly heed your warnings in the future." She reached out her hand, offering a conciliatory handshake, but Fletcher raised it to kiss her fingers.

"Stop worrying," he said. "I am amazed at the progress I see outside. All is well. You're doing a good job up here, and they're lucky to have you." His voice was pure kindness, and she drank it in like a cactus parched in the desert. It felt so good to be appreciated.

"You're too kind, Fletcher."

You're too kind, Fletcher.

The words still galled Alex more than an hour later as he guided both commissioners up to the Timberland camp. He needed their help, but surveying the fire damage in the clear light of day was stomach-churning. Most of the Irish workers had gone to their jobs at the road-building project, leaving the wives and children to clean up the camp. It reeked of soot and despair.

Nick and Fletcher looked grim as they surveyed the camp, but Alex didn't feel any sympathy. "These people shouldn't have been housed in an isolated camp if the state can't protect them."

"Who set the fire?" Fletcher asked.

"I have no idea."

"And yet the odds are good it was someone from your town," Fletcher retorted.

"I don't think so," Alex said. "It was probably one of your workers from the other camp."

Nick held up his hand. "We aren't here to figure out who did it. That's the sheriff's job. We're here to get this camp back into operation and keep it safe."

Nick gestured for them to follow him down the trail to the road. When they were out of earshot of the camp residents, he spoke in a low voice. "The guard reported that he saw the fire traveling up to the camp along a line of dirt soaked in accelerant, probably kerosene. It came from somewhere near Highpoint. Whoever set the fire knew the work camp was being patrolled overnight, and that's why the fire was set from Highpoint. That person prepared carefully. He was able to move around during the day, planting the kerosene, and not arouse suspicion."

It made Alex physically ill to believe someone from his town could have set this fire. Whoever it was had probably poisoned a drinking well too.

"I'm hiring undercover detectives," Nick continued. "I'll station them at various points throughout the valley. I'll assign them a reservoir job, but in actuality they'll have their eyes open and ears to the ground. I'm planting two at the main camp, two at the Timberland camp, and two will cover Highpoint and Duval Springs."

"Spies?" Alex asked.

"Yes, spies," Nick said without hesitation. "If your people are innocent, you've got nothing to fear."

Most of the people in Duval Springs were salt of the earth, but not all. Alex wouldn't trust Oscar Ott if the man said the sun rose in the east. If there was a snake in their town, he needed to know.

But Fletcher balked at the suggestion. "Who's going to pay for this?"

"You are," Nick and Alex both answered simultaneously.

"I only have funds for people gainfully employed by the water reservoir," Fletcher retorted.

Nick's face split into a smile, but it was a wolf's smile. "Oh, you're paying," he asserted, then swiveled to glower at Alex. "On my way into town this morning, I passed the cemetery, with hundreds of gravestones looking serene and untouched."

"That's right," Alex replied.

"I want all the graves disinterred and moved. We aren't building a reservoir over dead bodies."

It was a gauntlet. Last spring when Nick had first announced that all bodies buried in the valley needed to be disinterred, a mob had attacked him. It wasn't the town's finest moment. Alex's mother had died only six months earlier, and when Nick insisted she needed to be dug up and buried somewhere else, Hercules threw the first punch. Alex regretted the fight, but he wouldn't order anyone to do the abhorrent task of digging up their own relatives.

"Moving the bodies is the state's responsibility," he said. "We've got more urgent work to do." Between the schoolhouse accident and the fire, they were badly behind schedule.

"I'll have the undercover men start the disinterment process," Nick said. "People who died within the last decade probably still have family living in the area. That will give my men an excuse to circulate among the residents, asking where they want the body moved, poking around for gossip or resentment toward the reservoir. They're professionals. They'll know how to pry out information before anyone knows the prying is even happening."

Alex had to admit it would be a perfect cover story, and Nick delivered on his promise. Three days later, six private detectives arrived in the valley. Two went to the Timberland camp, two to the main camp, and Alex found room for the two men covering Duval Springs at the Gilmore Inn.

Willard gave him an odd look when he learned the state was paying for gravediggers to stay at the hotel rather than up at the main camp with the other manual laborers.

Alex was nonchalant as he provided a justification. "These men will need to consult with people in town about where they want their relatives moved. It makes sense for them to stay here."

Alex wouldn't tell anyone about the detectives' real purpose. Not Willard, not Eloise, not even Hercules. It went against his nature to withhold information from his closest friends, but there was a saboteur somewhere in the valley, and until he knew who it was, he'd keep his cards close to his chest.

*A*lex lunged out of the way when the boom arm of the excavator swung straight at him.

"Sorry!" Cormac hollered, his teeth shining white in a wide smile. "The left and right is all backward on this rig."

The detectives wanted a security fence built around the Timberland camp, the kind with concrete posts sunk deep into the ground so it would stand up to vandalism. Cormac McIntire, the foreman at Timberland, had asked to borrow the excavator to speed up the process, and Alex agreed, even though the machine belonged to Garrett, not the town. Alex had already signed his life away to borrow it, so he figured it was his to loan.

He turned his attention back to Cormac. "Let's give it another try," he hollered and held his breath. Learning to operate the boom and the pivoting bucket was a delicate operation, and Cormac had been practicing all afternoon on this patch of land a few acres outside the Timberland camp.

The bucket smashed against the ground harder than necessary, but the machine didn't seem damaged as Cormac wiggled a stick to turn the bucket's teeth into the earth and scoop up a load of soil. The hole he dug was around four feet deep, but it needed to be six. Cormac lined up the bucket for another scoop.

A clang pierced the air, and the excavator shuddered to a halt. Alex winced, for something had just gone badly wrong. Cormac vaulted out of the driver's bench to squat beside the hole. The excavator's arm and bucket tilted at an unnatural angle in the hole. This entire valley was riddled with limestone deposits, the kind that could break equipment with one bad strike.

"Let me get down there and see how bad the damage is," Alex said grimly.

The earth crumbled as he slid down into the hole and landed with a thump at the bottom. He squatted beside the bucket. Sure enough, the connecting rod between the bucket and the cylinder had broken off. Was this a ten-dollar fix or a ten-thousand-dollar fiasco?

"How bad is it?" Cormac asked.

"I don't know."

Something was strange. It wasn't limestone the bucket had hit. The teeth of the bucket had left furrows in the soil, revealing something bright blue and glossy. Metallic. Alex scraped the dirt away, his hand rubbing against smooth, cold metal.

"We hit something," he called out. And it seemed big. He walked to the other side of the hole and toed the soil away, revealing the same blue sheet of metal. This made no sense, but everywhere he moved away the dirt, he hit the same thing.

"Send a shovel down," he called out.

They had just found something very odd.

Despite her threat to quit, Eloise couldn't walk away from Duval Springs, not when she was still needed. As much as she longed to get back to a safe office job in the city, the move wasn't finished, and loyalty compelled her to stay.

Just like everyone else in town, she was completely fascinated by the strange discovery up at the Timberland camp. Throughout the day, she listened to the volunteers as they came in to the hotel for lunch and dinner, bringing updates about the strange discovery. The excavator was broken, so the digging was now being carried out by hand, and it was slow going. By the end of the day, they still had no idea what they'd found.

Digging had started again at the crack of dawn this morning. The Pollard house was supposed to be moved today, but that was on hold because so many workers had gone to help dig at the Timberland camp. It now looked like they'd found a large metal structure buried in the dirt.

Eloise was on kitchen duty and peeling potatoes when Tasha came in with an update.

"Dr. Lloyd says it looks like a railway car," Tasha said as she bounced Ilya on her hip. "The top is the same shape and size, but why would anyone bury a railway car?"

"Smugglers?" Eloise guessed, but it seemed like a lot of work to bury something so deep when there were caves all over the valley.

A rapid thud of footfalls in the lobby of the hotel was followed by a man shouting. "It's a boxcar! They're about to open it."

Eloise met Tasha's gaze across the mound of potatoes. "Let's go!"

A March snow was falling, and they bundled Ilya into his warmest clothes before heading out. Dozens of people were heading up Mountainside Road, and she and Tasha scurried as fast as they could. It was easy to get out of breath as they trudged uphill, but now that she'd succumbed to curiosity, Eloise couldn't bear to miss the actual opening of the car.

At least a hundred people gathered at the rim of the pit to watch the final bit of excavation. Eloise nudged through the crowd for a better look. A metal boxcar, painted blue but with huge patches of rust marring its surface, tilted at an incongruous angle in the pit. A dozen men with shovels and pickaxes scrambled to clear the last of the hard-packed dirt. The railway car had no lettering on the outside, and the double sliding doors were firmly closed. One of the grubby men swiveled to flash her a wink. It took a moment for her to recognize Alex, his face grimy with dirt that couldn't mask his anticipation.

She returned his smile. It *was* exciting. There could be anything in that boxcar—long-forgotten treasure or smuggled goods.

Most of the car was still mired in dirt, but the area around the sliding doors was clear now. Alex tossed his shovel aside.

"I'm ready to give it a try," he said. He grabbed a metal clamp on the rim of a door, trying to release the mechanism. Eloise heard the scrape of rusty metal as he tried to pry it open.

"It's rusted shut," Alex said, and Hercules jumped into the pit with a pickaxe to scrape rust from the mud-caked tracks. When Alex tried again, the door budged a fraction with an awful sound of metal on metal. Hercules joined in, slipping his hands into the narrow opening and lending a hefty push. The screeching was awful, but applause broke out when the door was finally open.

Alex took a huge step up to get inside the car and froze.

"What do you see?" someone called out.

Had Alex heard? She didn't think so, for he hadn't moved a muscle or made a sound. He just stood motionless and stared. After a moment, his entire body swayed, like a tree about to topple over. Hercules jumped inside the car to steady him, then looked about the interior of the car himself. A moment later he turned away, his face white.

"We're going to need the sheriff," he said. "This car is filled with dead people."

Alex had never been so revolted in his life as when he stepped inside that boxcar. At first, he couldn't understand what he saw. It was dim, and the car seemed empty except for some lumpy padding on the ground. As his eyes adjusted, he saw woolen clothing, hair, and boots. It took a moment to realize he was looking at desiccated bodies. A lot of them.

He'd cleared out of the boxcar quickly, but the image was seared onto his mind. The bodies had been dressed in thick clothing, with coats, boots, and scarves. They were curved around one another, as though huddled for warmth.

The sheriff took charge of the scene and ordered everyone away except Dr. Lloyd, whose cursory examination showed that the bodies were in good shape, perfectly preserved, and bore no sign of bullet wounds or violence. There was no blood on their clothing.

Alex wanted answers. They had just uncovered a very good motivation for the ongoing sabotage up at the Timberland camp. It wasn't resentment against Irish workers or the reservoir; it was probably an attempt to prevent the discovery of that boxcar. People in the valley had been angry about the reservoir for years, but sabotage hadn't started happening until construction on the Timberland camp began last September.

Every seat in the tavern was filled with people batting around ideas about the dead bodies. Eloise and Tasha arrived, the maid carrying the sleeping baby over her shoulder. Alex flagged Eloise's attention and made room for her on the window seat. They hadn't been on the best of terms lately, but when he reached for her hand, she didn't reject it. Which was a blessing. The sight of those bodies had shaken him more than he cared to admit.

Everyone had an opinion about what had happened. "I think

they froze to death," Jasper Trudeau said. "Doc Lloyd said he saw scorch marks on the floor of the car, like they'd been tending a fire to keep warm."

"Or starved," someone else chimed in.

"Were they buried alive?" Oscar Ott asked, his voice rich with excitement. "That means they would have suffocated."

Alex wanted to punch the enthusiasm off Oscar's face, but it was more important to gather people's theories about what had happened.

"I think whoever is behind this crime was also committing the sabotage," Alex said. "Almost all of it was near the Timberland camp. It was probably an attempt to stop any digging or development near the site of that boxcar."

"What about who shot Miss Drake?" someone asked. "That doesn't play into your theory."

Eloise disagreed. "I was about to file paperwork for the bond," she said. "The new town is half a mile from the Timberland camp. If Highpoint succeeds, sooner or later it would grow large enough to reach that burial spot."

A wave of guilt swamped Alex, for what she said was correct.

"I'll bet those bodies are the Russian strikebreakers from five years ago," someone said. "It never did make sense that the whole lot of them up and left."

"How many bodies did you see?" another person asked Alex.

"A lot," was all he could respond. He'd been so appalled that his mind froze as soon as he realized what he was staring at.

"There were twenty-three strikebreakers," Reverend Carmichael said. "I've been doing research on the town history for a book I'd like to write someday, and there were plenty of articles about the labor unrest in the valley. Twenty-three Russian strikebreakers came in 1903, but they left after only a few months."

There would be more details soon, for the "gravediggers"

had been sent to assist the sheriff. The fact that everyone believed the detectives were gravediggers was a perfect alibi for wanting their assistance at the crime scene. They would remain undercover to everyone but the sheriff.

"But who buried the boxcar?" Alex pressed.

"Gee, Alex, who do we know who has heavy earthmoving equipment?" Jasper Trudeau asked. Jasper's hostility toward Garrett knew no bounds since his mother had been caught out with the valley's most hated man.

Eloise stood, hands fisted on her hips. "If owning heavy equipment is all it takes to be guilty of mass murder, we will need a lot more jail cells in this state."

Alex grabbed her hand and tugged her back down. He wanted to hear as many ideas as possible, not get bogged down in squabbling. Eloise sat, but every muscle in her body trembled.

It was fear, not anger, that made her shake. As much as he loathed Garrett, Alex hoped he wasn't behind this. It would destroy Eloise.

The tavern door opened, bringing a gust of frigid wind into the room, and a trio of people entered. Alex rose when he recognized Sheriff Dawson and the detectives. He angled his way through the crowd to the door.

"Can I help you?" he asked.

The sheriff leaned in close and spoke in a low voice. "I understand there is a Russian woman in town. Someone's maid?"

"Tasha Sokolov," he replied. "She's here. Do you need her?"

The sheriff nodded. "We've found a note in the boxcar that looks like it's written in Russian. We need someone to read it. We'll need some privacy."

Alex glanced at Tasha and Eloise, still huddled on the window seat. He beckoned them forward. By now almost everyone in the tavern had noticed the arrival of the county sheriff, and the noise dwindled.

"Nothing to see here," the sheriff announced in a gruff voice. "You can all go back to your business."

A few disgruntled murmurs rose up behind them, but no one followed as they stepped outside and down the tavern steps. It was pitch dark and cold as they made their way toward the hotel. There were only a handful of people in the dining room, and Kasper Nagy slumbered on the bench in the lobby, a gentle snore coming from beneath the hat covering his face.

Alex led the group toward the empty office on the main floor. They all filed inside, and Alex closed the door, but no one sat. It took a moment to light a kerosene lantern. Someday their new town would have electricity, but for now all they had were lanterns. A small circle of light soon lit the room.

"What have you found?" Alex asked.

The sheriff looked grim. "Almost all the bodies had scrip from the Garrett quarry in their pockets," he said grimly. "There are twenty-three bodies. It's hard not to conclude these were the men Garrett hired to replace his workers."

Eloise looked sick but said nothing as the sheriff held out a single piece of scrip. It was the size of a dollar bill but printed on white paper and marked with *Garrett Company Store* on the front, along with a serial number. Alex knew those notes well, as they were one of the main bones of contention during the strike. Unlike a dollar bill with its lavish engraving, the scrip notes were mostly blank, with plenty of room for a validation stamp on the back.

Except this note wasn't blank. The back of the note was covered in minuscule, shaky handwriting. The tiny letters looked sloppy to his untrained eye, but perhaps it was written by a man dying of cold.

The sheriff handed the note to Tasha. "Is that Russian?"

She nodded.

"What does it say?" the sheriff asked.

Tasha passed the baby to Eloise and held the note close to

the lantern to read. It took a while for her to scan the note. Her accent was heavy, and her voice shook as she spoke.

"It is very bad. Very wrong," she said on a shattered breath. "It says they work at the quarry. They complained to Mr. Garrett about the camp he built for them. The tents are cold and the pay is bad." She paused again, scrutinizing the note as she scrambled to find the right English words. "This is hard to read," she said. "The writing is shaky and spelling is bad, but it says Garrett made them sleep in this boxcar. He locked them in to teach them a lesson. He taunts them from outside and won't let them out. It has been two days, and Sergey, who is only seventeen, has already died of the cold."

Tasha looked up, holding the note away from her as though it burned. "That is all it says."

Eloise looked sick, passing Alex the baby before collapsing into a chair. "I don't believe it," she said in a shaking voice.

The despair on her face made him ache, but how much more proof did she need? He wished it were possible to shield her from the hurt this was going to cause.

"Twenty-three men are dead," he said gently. "That note was written by someone who wanted their story told."

"Do you think Bruce would have ordered me shot?" she asked incredulously.

No. Of all the things Alex could believe of Bruce Garrett, he wouldn't have tried to kill Eloise. But maybe the shooting incident had nothing to do with this. "It could have been hunters. Or drunks from the other camp."

"This note is a dying declaration," the sheriff said. "It will carry a lot of weight with the court, and I will secure a warrant for Mr. Garrett's arrest in the morning."

The sheriff opened the door, and Jasper Trudeau almost fell into the room, having had his ear pressed against the paneling.

"I was about to knock and check on Tasha," he said with

a guilty flush. A dozen others also congregated in the hallway. Even Kasper Nagy had managed to rouse himself and join the other eavesdroppers.

Tasha took her baby back, then raced to Jasper's side. The two of them had been mighty cozy ever since she arrived. The other eavesdroppers scattered to spread the gossip. The sheriff and detectives left, taking the damning note with them.

Eloise stood motionless in the back of the office, her face stark white.

Alex closed the door. He wished he could comfort her, assure her that everything would be all right, but they both knew it wouldn't be. All he could do was tell her the truth.

"You're going to survive this," he said quietly. "It's going to be tough, but you are tougher. No matter what happens to Garrett, you are going to pick up the pieces and build a strong and honorable life." His heart was full to breaking. She didn't deserve more pain and loss.

"I don't accept this," she said, her voice still shaking.

"How can you deny it? Locking those men in to teach them a lesson? Taunting them? It's completely in his character."

"Maybe. But I still don't believe it, and I won't accept this without a fight."

"What choice do you have?"

She ignored him as she left the office and headed outside, tugging her coat tighter around her. She was heading toward the stables.

"Tell me you're not going up there," he said.

"I'm going up there."

He raced to catch up with her. "Eloise, start distancing yourself now. Bruce Garrett is a sinking ship, and you don't want to be on board when he goes down."

"I'm not going to abandon him, even if he's guilty." Two fat tears rolled down her face to splat on her coat. "I don't know what to think or believe, but I can't abandon someone, even if the worst is true. *Especially* if the worst is true."

Her words stopped Alex in his tracks, but she continued marching toward the stables. Everything in him wanted to drag her back to the hotel and shake some sense into her, but it would be useless.

This was a lesson she would have to learn on her own.

TWENTY-SEVEN

loise arrived at Bruce's house a little before midnight. The first time she'd come here, she'd been only eight years old, and Bruce had welcomed her into his home even though she was a stranger to him. It was the first place she'd ever felt safe.

Bruce was still awake and surprised to see her. The orange glow from the flickering fireplace cast shadows on the rugged contours of his face. There was no way to soft-pedal the news, so she delivered it bluntly.

"Everyone believes the bodies are the Russian strikebreakers," she said. "They had scrip from your quarry in their pockets." It was hard to look at him as she relayed the message scribbled on one of the notes. It turned her stomach to even think of the horrible way those men had died.

Bruce remained impassive as he digested the news, but a muscle throbbed in his jaw. "Do you believe it?" he demanded, his voice the same hard tone he often used with his workers but never before with her.

"I can't," she said, although her words didn't seem to give him much comfort. "They're coming to arrest you in the morning. You should get a lawyer."

"They'll make an arrest without even speaking to me?"

"Oh, I'm sure they'll want to talk to you. If you're smart, you won't answer."

Eloise stayed at the mansion that night. The town was turning against Bruce, and by staying here, she was announcing whose side she was on.

As expected, the sheriff and two officers from his department arrived shortly after sunrise to question Bruce. Eloise insisted on being present. Bruce was a hothead who could fly off the handle, but she never did. She had an eye for detail and would be on the lookout for any clue that might exonerate him.

Neither of them expected to see Marie Trudeau alongside the sheriff. "I've heard the rumors, and I'm here to testify to what I know," she said.

"No, you won't," Bruce said brusquely. "You can't help, and I don't want you here."

"I tried to tell her the same thing," Sheriff Dawson said. "She spotted us heading up the mountain and stuck to our side the whole way but refused to hear a word we said. She doesn't listen."

A glint of amusement flashed across Bruce's face, but it vanished quickly as he led the team of investigators into the main room. He sat in a chair before the fireplace like a king on his throne and gestured to the others to sit.

"Those Russian strikebreakers came and disappeared within the space of two months," Bruce said. "I didn't have anything to do with their going missing."

"Except they aren't missing anymore," the sheriff pointed out. "They're dead, and they pointed a finger at you on their way out."

"I remember those men," Marie said. "Four or five of them came to the school, wanting to learn English. They offered me money to teach them."

Eloise straightened. "Money or scrip?"

"Money," Marie said. "I remember being surprised, because my sons hated how all the workers were paid in scrip. I was surprised to see these men had cash."

"That's because I paid them in cash," Bruce said. "I didn't want to, but they were still in debt to the agency that paid their transportation from St. Petersburg. My scrip was no good anywhere outside the valley."

This changed things. If those dead bodies all had scrip on them, it could have been planted. *The note* could have been planted.

"Can you prove that?" the sheriff asked.

"Of course I can. I've got records."

"Can you *independently* prove it," Sheriff Dawson pressed. "Anything from your own office could be rigged to provide you with cover."

"I just told you the men tried to pay me in cash," Marie said. "I am certainly independent of his office."

"Did you ever provide tutoring to them?"

Marie shook her head. "They were hated. I would have tutored them, because I know what it is to be a stranger in a foreign land, but when word got around, the town council voted and said I was to do nothing to make life easy for the strikebreakers. The town paid my salary, so perhaps they had the right to make that demand, and I did not help those men. I'm sorry for it now."

"It's obvious to me what's going on," Bruce said. "Whoever buried that boxcar needed it to stay hidden. They terrorized anyone who got close to it. The road damage. The tainted well. The fire."

"And I can testify he had nothing to do with the fire," Marie said as she rose to her feet. "He was—"

"That's enough, Marie," Bruce said.

"But I can exonerate you."

"I don't need you to."

Everyone in Duval Springs knew what Marie had been doing that night, but the gossip probably hadn't spread to Kingston. If Marie was required to testify in court as to where she'd been that night, it would make news across the state.

"Please," the sheriff prompted, "if you have something relevant, we need to know. Because right now, the case looks grim for Mr. Garrett."

Marie lifted her chin, ignoring the glare from Bruce as she continued. "I was here in this house. I was with Mr. Garrett all night, and I can testify that he never left until dawn. He could not have set that fire."

The sheriff's brows rose, and it looked as if he choked back laughter. "We never thought Garrett actually lit the match. That's the sort of thing a rich man orders his henchmen to do, just like he ordered them to beat up Alex Duval all those years ago. He paid someone to set that fire, and *you* were nothing more than his alibi, ma'am."

The color drained from Marie's face, and she reached for the back of a chair to steady herself. Eloise hurt for her, but what could she do? It was horrible to witness this good woman's humiliation before the three officers from Kingston.

Marie regained strength quickly. An angry flush of color stained her cheeks, and she straightened her shoulders. "Take him!" she ordered the sheriff. "And throw away the key."

In the end, Bruce was arrested and carted off to jail in Kingston. Eloise borrowed a wagon to drive Marie back to Highpoint but was surprised by the older woman's demeanor when she climbed onto the buckboard. Instead of anger, Marie seemed anxious but not the least bit offended.

"You don't think he's guilty," Eloise said.

"I *know* he's not guilty, but the sheriff doesn't need to know I'm in Bruce's corner."

Eloise breathed a sigh of relief, knowing Bruce had at least one additional ally in town. On the drive home, she listened to Marie recount how she'd fallen in love with the most hated man in the valley. They first met the morning Marie's house was moved when she lost her temper. Bruce came the next morning to apologize. She invited him inside, where an apology that should have taken only a moment stretched into a three-hour conversation about her life in France, the work at his quarry, and why leaves turned colors in the fall.

"He gave me this," Marie said, pulling a chain out from her bodice to reveal a silver acorn pendant. "He said I remind him of an acorn. Something that has existed only a stone's throw from his front door all these decades, but he never realized it until one day he spotted me, and then it was like a mighty oak tree had sprung up in his path. Maybe it isn't the most romantic of notions, but I feel the same way. I don't mind a little gruffness in a man, and in his heart, I see his good. Not a day has gone by when we have not managed to steal an hour or two."

"But why has he kept it a secret?" Eloise was outraged on Marie's behalf. Bruce's life was full of secrets, and he *still* hadn't completed the legal work to have her recognized as his daughter.

"That was at my request," Marie said. "I feared how my sons would react. Now I'm embarrassed for that. I should have shouted it proudly and let my sons think what they will." She reached a gentle hand to cover Eloise's own. "Just as Bruce should have shouted how proud he is to be your father."

"You know?"

Marie nodded. "We have no secrets from each other. I don't

know how we can prove his innocence, but perhaps between the two of us, we can figure something out."

Eloise smiled. It was a long shot, but at least she had an ally.

After dropping Marie off at Highpoint, Eloise drove back to Duval Springs. The once quaint town now looked even more battered, shabby, and sad. The village green had been shorn of grass and trampled by the oxen. More than a hundred buildings had been moved, leaving a ragged collection of vacant lots. Construction materials lay scattered everywhere. The iconic town hall was gone, having been safely moved last week.

A sudden inspiration struck her. Marie said the town council had forbidden her to tutor the Russians. If Eloise could find a record of that vote, it would validate Marie's story that the men had cash with them, not scrip. Alex could help her get those records.

She was breathless after running up the stairs and into the lobby of the Gilmore Inn. Inside, the world continued to operate as though everything was normal. A maid poured coffee in the crowded dining room, Kasper manned the telegraph machine, and Alex sat behind mounds of paperwork at a table. He looked distracted as she raced up to him.

"Alex! Where are the old records of town council meetings?" If she could find them today, it might be enough to get Bruce released from jail.

"Somewhere up at the new place, probably," he muttered without looking up at her. "I have no idea."

"I need to find them. It's important."

He gathered the papers into a stack and stood. "It will have to wait. I've hired two engineers from Boston to design a plan to move the tavern. They're due any moment, and it's going to be a challenging job."

"Yes, but I need to find those records. They've arrested Bruce."

A group of men at a nearby table overheard and started applauding at the news. She didn't expect people to mourn Bruce's arrest, but she had bent over backward for this town, and a little support would have been nice. Instead, Alex exchanged good-natured winks with the cheering men.

"*Now,* Alex," she stressed.

"It's not going to happen, Eloise. Hercules and I are paying a fortune for these engineers, and I can't dash off on a wild goose chase."

"Marie said the Russians were paid in cash instead of scrip. Do you know anything about that?"

"It was a rumor. Yes, I heard it."

Hope took root. If the mayor of the town could testify that Bruce had paid the Russians cash instead of scrip, it might help prove Bruce was being framed.

"Can you come with me to Kingston and testify to that?" she asked.

"I just told you I'm meeting with the engineers to save the tavern."

"And I'm trying to save a man's freedom," she snapped. "I've never asked much of you. In fact, I've never asked *anything* of you, but I'm asking now. Will you come to Kingston and testify that Bruce paid the Russians in cash, not scrip?"

Her arrow must have found its mark, for his shoulders slumped a little, and when he spoke, his voice was calmer. "Eloise, you're so desperate for that man's approval that you'll do anything, even if it means overlooking twenty-three dead bodies."

"I'm asking because I love him."

Alex frowned as he shuffled paperwork into a satchel and closed the buckles. "I can't help you," he said bluntly. "This town has put up with a lot from that man over the years, and frankly, what I saw in that boxcar doesn't come as a huge shock, so forgive us if we don't rush to his rescue."

The bell above the front door dinged, and two older men carrying traveling bags and yardsticks stepped inside. Alex's engineers, probably. He brushed past her to offer a hearty handshake to the men.

"Let's head over to the tavern where we can talk," he said.

She stepped in front of him. "Alex, please don't go. Kasper is right here. He can send a telegram up to Kingston testifying that you knew Bruce paid the Russians in cash, not scrip."

Kasper stood behind the lobby counter, his hand at the ready atop the telegraph sounder. The two engineers took a respectful step back, and she plowed ahead.

"Please, Alex. It will only take two minutes." She hated the way her voice wobbled, but Bruce was sitting in jail and might hang for something he hadn't done. "I don't think you understand how much I need—"

The door on the cuckoo clock flapped open, and the annoying bird popped out, its rhythmic chirps interrupting her. It would be useless to talk over that racket, and she waited until the bird retreated into its cubby, the flap closing over it.

Alex didn't even let her finish her sentence. "I'm trying to save this town," he said. "You're like that cuckoo bird, begging for scraps. Willing to do anything to win approval."

The accusation poured salt into a raw, unhealed wound. She'd always been the poor little cuckoo bird—picking up work for her colleagues, dancing attendance on Tasha. Giving her virginity to Alex.

He opened the door, preparing to lead the engineers to the tavern.

"Alex, don't leave!"

He didn't even acknowledge her as he headed outside, followed by the two men. She ran after him, but he never looked back.

She'd given everything to this town, and the first time she asked for help, Alex waltzed off with his precious engineers.

She had once intended to stick it out in Duval Springs until the town was fully moved, but why should she stay where she wasn't appreciated? The comforting security of her normal life in New York City beckoned. Alex didn't need her, and Bruce did.

This poor little cuckoo bird was going to prove Bruce paid those men in cash, not scrip. She didn't know how to do it, but she knew who did.

She marched back into the lobby and approached the telegraph station. "Kasper, please send a telegram to Fletcher Jones, requesting an appointment for tomorrow morning."

Fletcher was an expert in the world of finance and might know how to prove Bruce paid the Russians in cash. She wasn't too proud to ask for his help, and the moment the telegram had been sent, she raced upstairs to pack her bags.

It took the engineers four hours to assess the tavern, and it was nearing dinnertime before they were ready to present their findings. Alex sat at a table with Hercules and Sally, all of them grim as they awaited the verdict. Nathan Richards, the lead engineer, gave them a sympathetic smile as he told them the bad news.

"This building has been modified over the years, with additions and a second floor tacked on. That makes it unstable for moving." He went on to say that the wall of river rock stretching across the back of the tavern would crumble if they tried to move it. The mortar was too old, and the fireplace in its center a destabilizing force.

"The only way to save this tavern is to disassemble it," Nathan continued. "It will be expensive, and it would make more sense to simply build a new tavern of similar dimensions and materials."

Hercules lit up. "We can save it by taking it apart?"

Sally looked equally delighted, and Alex couldn't stop the grin from spreading across his face. While he didn't relish the thought of taking this old place apart, it would still be their tavern.

"How do we go about disassembling it?" Alex asked.

The engineer shook his head. "It will cost a fortune."

"I know, you said that. How do we do it?"

Both engineers explained the impractical task of pulling the building apart, numbering and transporting each piece, then reassembling it—but they didn't understand the Duvals' bone-deep love for this place. If it was possible to save the tavern, he and Hercules were going to do it, even though the engineers estimated it would cost at least fifteen thousand dollars.

"We'll find the money somehow," Sally vowed. "This is our home and our business both. How can we have a new town without the Duval Tavern?"

Alex grinned at her enthusiasm and turned to the engineers. "Who do we need to hire to help us with this move?"

Before they could answer, Willard entered the tavern and strode toward Alex. "I thought you'd like to know that Eloise checked out of the hotel a few minutes ago."

Alex shifted. He felt lousy for dismissing her so abruptly earlier today, but she was being completely unreasonable. "Where's she going? A visit to the city?"

"No," Willard said. "She *checked out*. Took all her bags and belongings. Took her maid and the baby. She said they weren't coming back, and we should put the room up for rent again."

Alex rocked back in his chair, stunned that she'd take off so abruptly when the legal case against Garrett would take months or years, while he had so little time to move the rest of the town.

He pinched the bridge of his nose, a headache beginning to pound. Eloise was sending him a message, but he would deal with it later. He had four weeks to clear out the last of the buildings, hire a specialized crew, and get the tavern moved. Finding records of an old town council vote wouldn't do anything to prove Garrett's innocence. He was guilty, and Alex wouldn't put the move at risk to go on a wild goose chase. For once, he was going to be just as calm and logical as Eloise.

"Then go ahead and put the room up for rent," he said.

It was dark by the time Eloise arrived back in Manhattan, but it felt good to be home. Everything felt natural and normal here. It was easy to slip back into the world of anonymity where no one knew her private business or judged her. She couldn't blame the town for letting her down; it was Alex who had done that. A part of her was still a pathetic cuckoo bird, always desperate to belong.

Well, she belonged in New York City. It was safe here, where office jobs had predictable hours that never involved working through sleet storms or getting caked in mud or climbing into pigpens. Her first night home, she sank into a hot bath and let the heat unwind the tension of the past few months.

Fletcher seemed pleased to see her when she arrived at his office the following morning. He held his office door wide, gesturing her inside and guiding her to a chair.

"What can I do for you?" he asked as he took a seat at his desk, but he didn't close the office door. While she would have preferred privacy to discuss the pending criminal charges against Bruce, Fletcher had enough respect for her reputation to leave the door open. He was always proper, and she ought to appreciate it.

"I've run into a problem reconstructing some old accounting records, and I don't know how to handle it."

Aside from a single raised brow, he showed no change of expression as he asked her to elaborate. As quickly as possible, she filled him in on the discovery of the dead Russians and the scrip issued by the Garrett quarry as the primary evidence against Bruce.

"Bruce swears he never paid them in scrip and the note is a forgery planted by the real culprit."

"As an insurance policy should the boxcar ever be discovered," Fletcher added.

"Exactly." How nice that Fletcher drew the logical conclusion instead of rehashing a litany of old grievances against Bruce. "Is there any way to track old scrip? The notes all have serial numbers on them."

Fletcher shook his head, a sour expression on his face. "Scrip is impossible to trace. It's a completely unregulated industry, and a shady one at that."

"What about old bank records?" she pressed. "If we can prove Bruce drew out large sums of cash to pay his workforce, wouldn't those records still exist? The documentation would need to be from a bank, not the company's records, because the police want independent verification."

"Those records exist, but I don't think they'll help you," he said. "The bank will have records of the withdrawals, but not what it was expended on. How did someone get a boxcar onto the side of a mountain, anyway?"

The question stumped her. Bruce and Theodore Riesel shared joint ownership of a private railway to transport their materials from the quarry to the cement factory, and then all the way to the Kingston depot. She'd never seen the cars go off the rails, but obviously someone had accomplished it. The boxcar was discovered a mile from the railway line. Five years ago that spot of wilderness would have seemed a safe place to bury an inconvenient reminder of a terrible crime.

"It appears we are both woefully ill-informed about railway operations," Fletcher said. "Fortunately, I know who we can ask. You said it was a Manchester railcar?"

"Yes, all the railcars they own are Manchesters."

Fletcher smiled. "Rudolf Manchester is an old college classmate of mine. I expect he can provide an answer for how railcars are moved in the absence of tracks."

He crossed the room to a telephone mounted on the wall beside the window and calmly asked the operator to connect him to the Manchester Railcar Company. Fletcher casually gazed out the window at the cityscape as the telephone call was patched through a series of exchanges.

"Rudy, good of you to take my call. Jillian is well, I take it?" At first Eloise thought Jillian must be Mr. Manchester's wife, but as the conversation continued, it seemed Jillian was a dog who'd suffered a mishap the last time Fletcher went duck hunting with his old college friend. Pleasantries were exchanged for a few minutes before Fletcher brought the conversation to the matter at hand.

"Tell me, if I had a boxcar I needed to move without the benefit of railway tracks, what would be the best way to do it?"

Not being able to hear the other end of the conversation was frustrating, but after a long pause, Fletcher broke into some hearty laughter. "If it was easy, I wouldn't have called you! Yes, if I wanted to move it over rough land, how could it be done?"

She leaned forward but still couldn't understand the faint, tinny voice on the other end.

"And where would I purchase an industrial dolly like that?" Fletcher asked, casually bracing his foot on the windowsill as he gazed outside. "You do? And is it profitable? It sounds like a financial sinkhole to me."

The temptation to leap out of her chair and grab the receiver from Fletcher's ear was intense, but at last he placed the receiver in its hook and turned to her with carefully concealed triumph on his face.

"The answer is an industrial-sized dolly built specifically for that purpose. Manchester makes them, plus a sliding mechanism for moving across uncertain terrain. They sell poorly, but the company feels compelled to produce them as an option. Does Mr. Garrett own one?"

"I know Bruce doesn't. I have no idea if Theodore Riesel does."

Fletcher smiled. "Rudy is willing to open his archives to us. We shall soon see if either man ever bought one."

Fletcher's prediction was overly optimistic. Although they arrived at the modest building in Queens shortly after lunch, the Manchester Railcar Company's archivist had difficulty locating records for dolly sales, since it was such a minuscule portion of their business. The archives waiting room was in the basement, its cinderblock walls covered in exuberantly bright yellow paint. It was a perfectly awful room, and time stretched endlessly.

"I'm sorry to be destroying your afternoon like this," she said.

"Nonsense. It's no trouble at all." Fletcher shifted in his chair and seemed to be groping for words. "Your cousin Nick is getting married next week," he finally said.

She knew about the wedding, of course. As a child she had idolized Nick, but after her parents banished her to Bruce's house, she didn't see him for almost twenty years. Nick hadn't even recognized her when they met again last year, but he'd gotten her the job at the water board, and she was grateful for it.

"I was wondering if you would like to accompany me to the wedding," Fletcher asked.

She stilled. This was what she had once been hoping for,

right? A chance to begin a proper courtship with an eminently suitable man. A safe man who couldn't hurt her.

"I think that might be a little awkward," she stammered.

"Why?"

"Well . . . being fired and all." The wedding would be swarming with employees from the water board. How could she possibly show her face among them?

A flush stained Fletcher's cheekbones. "I never actually pulled the trigger on that. Your desk is still awaiting your return. When you accomplish whatever it is you hope to discover in Duval Springs, you can come back at any time."

She swallowed hard. Did Fletcher know about her ties to Alex and Duval Springs? Should she choose to pursue a relationship with Fletcher, she would need to disclose what had happened when she was sixteen. As poised and proper as she tried to appear, she hadn't always been so.

The door to the archives opened, and the clerk lugged in a heavy box and a stack of files. They landed on the table with a thump. "Here's the box for the dolly sales," he said. "And files on the sliders. Hardly anyone buys those."

It didn't take long to locate the file for the year the Russians went missing. There had been only three purchase orders for dollies. Two were for companies on the West Coast, but one was from a New York company. It was dated three days after the Russians disappeared.

And had been paid for by the Riesel Cement Factory, and signed for by Oscar Ott.

The breath left her in a rush. While it couldn't prove that Bruce had no part in the affair, it was enough to point a finger of suspicion toward Oscar and the Riesels. She dropped the document and impulsively hugged Fletcher.

Ever the gentleman, he grasped only her forearms and held himself away as quickly as possible, but he still smiled at her.

"Thank you!" she gasped, for she could never have managed this on her own. "This means the world to me."

"Is it enough for me to earn a companion to your cousin's wedding?"

"Oh yes . . . yes, I think so!"

It was only after she returned to her apartment that the sadness hit her. Stepping out with Fletcher would change things. It would symbolize a break with Duval Springs and with Alex.

But hadn't she always known this day was coming? Her foray into Duval Springs was merely a chance to dip her toe into a real adventure story, and then retreat back to her normal world. The ending was coming a little faster than anticipated, but Bruce needed her and Alex didn't.

Duval Springs was already gone. Most of its buildings had been moved or abandoned, and soon the rest would be burned to the ground. The town viewed through her telescope would forever linger in her memory, an idyllic place she had always longed for but that didn't really exist. And Alex was a huge part of those memories, where he loomed larger than life with his flashing grin and eager curiosity, the prince of her forbidden kingdom.

There wasn't time to wallow in painful memories while Bruce languished in prison. Eloise marched to the nearest telegraph office and sent news of what she had learned to Bruce's attorney in Kingston.

Once Bruce was free, she could cut her final ties to Duval Springs and set down roots in New York.

Hopefully with Fletcher Jones.

ere's to the successful move of the post office!" Alex said as he raised a glass high.

"Hear, hear!" Hercules replied from his position behind the bar. Only a dozen men and Hercules's four boys were on hand tonight. Almost everyone else had already moved up to the new town.

But these daily gatherings were important. The physical labor and emotional toll of the past few months were catching up with people, but they were back on schedule. The only things left to move were four houses and the tavern. They should have no problem getting them moved ahead of the wrecking balls, and now Hercules's second-oldest son had a plan to make a little extra money.

"The state is paying six dollars for each body that gets dug up from the cemetery and reburied above the flow line," Bill said. "I could borrow a wagon and round up some kids, and we could make a lot of money. Uncle Alex says we're too young to work on moving houses, and those two gravediggers the state hired never got anything done."

That was because the undercover detectives had been pulled

from the job and sent to work on proving the case against Bruce Garrett.

"Boy, have you ever dug up a dead body?" Hercules asked.

At fourteen, Bill had the irrational optimism of youth and was not daunted. "They'll be in coffins, so it won't be too bad."

Alex had always thought one of the biggest indignities of losing their town was the removal of their cemeteries. Not only were the living to be kicked off their land, but the dead as well. Digging up a grave was a lot of work, and Alex suspected Bill had no idea what he was getting into.

"Okay, you can do it, but first you need to come up with a plan and a budget," Alex said, knowing he sounded remarkably like Eloise. "You'll need shovels, ropes, and a wagon. You'll have to borrow a pair of horses too, and I doubt you'll get that for free. Don't forget to factor in the feed for the horses."

"I've already got it," Bill said, whipping out a scrap of paper with everything from how much the horses would rent for, to who would loan them the wagon and the pulley. Four neighborhood boys were listed, with wages for each.

"How come you're paying the Jansen kid less?" Alex asked.

"He's only twelve and won't be as much help. I figure we can move two graves a day, and after expenses, I can clear five dollars a day."

Alex had to admire Bill's initiative. Before he could say so, the door to the tavern opened, bringing a gust of chilly air and the silhouette of a man he did not recognize. He was old, with a stooped frame and careful gait as he stepped into the tavern, looking around the interior as if in a daze.

"Can I help you, sir?" Hercules asked.

The stranger's face was weathered and lined with age, his expression carrying an echo of sadness as he stepped farther into the tavern. Then he stopped, his gaze fixed on the iron scrollwork behind the bar.

"I've come for my chicken bone," he said in a gravelly voice.

Everyone froze. The old man wore the hat of a Union officer, and Alex closed the distance in three strides to shake his hand.

"Second Lieutenant Alex Duval, Seventy-first New York Infantry," he said, citing his regiment from Cuba. After a brief exchange of salutes, the old man replied.

"Captain Eugene Franks, Third Brigade, New York Infantry. I heard this town was on its last legs, and if I was ever going to claim my wishbone, I'd best hurry."

Alex stood aside and gestured to the scrollwork. Eight wishbones from the Civil War still hung on that rack, but no one had imagined there were still men alive to claim them. The tavern was silent as the old soldier approached the wall, carefully lifting each bone to check for initials. After a few tries, he held one over his head and turned toward the crowd. His face was proud, but his lower lip wobbled furiously with emotion. He couldn't even speak, but everyone in the tavern stood and applauded. Cheered. Stomped their feet and roared.

Hercules grabbed George Washington's chair from the wall and held it for the old soldier to sit. Sally brought a mug of ale and bowl of stew. Everyone gathered around to hear the man's story, which came out in jerks and starts. He'd seen hard service for two years before he broke his leg in 1864 and was invalided out for the duration.

"I felt like a failure for not being there at the end," he said, which was met with murmurs of protest. Captain Franks held up his hand. "Plenty of good soldiers fought in worse shape than me, and I let those men down. I heard their voices in my head for years. I wasn't in my right mind. Instead of coming home after the war, I figured it would be better to head out west. I didn't want my parents seeing me like that. And then after they died, I didn't see much point in ever coming back.

But I heard a rumor this town was getting plowed under, and I figured it was time to make peace."

"We're glad you did," Sally said warmly, but Alex wasn't sure the old soldier felt the same. His emotions seemed to career from nostalgia to gloom to anxiety.

"The town square sure looks different," Captain Franks said. "I'm glad to see the Gilmore Inn is still here. I could see it from almost a mile away."

"It's too big to move," Alex said. "We'll have a room there for you tonight. On the house." It was impossible to know the old man's financial situation, but his clothes were a little shabby, and he could use a new pair of shoes.

The old solider nodded. "I'd be grateful for it. What about the tavern?"

"We start taking it apart this weekend," Hercules said. "We'll reassemble it up at the new place."

For the first time, a genuine smile lit Captain Franks' face. "Good! There may be others out there who still need to claim their wishbones."

"And we'll be waiting for them!" Hercules roared, causing a renewed round of foot-stomping and clapping.

Alex walked Captain Franks to the hotel and got him settled in a room. It had been a joyous evening, but sad too. While the old soldier seemed to appreciate the veneration of the people in the tavern, he was on shaky ground, tormented by memories and regrets that had yet to heal.

Alex didn't want to follow in his footsteps. It was impossible to know what his life would be like once he moved to Highpoint, but he didn't want regrets tormenting him in his old age.

That meant he had to do something about Eloise. He'd acted like an impatient idiot the other day, but if he had to choose between saving the tavern and saving Bruce Garrett, the tavern won every time.

But Eloise cared about Garrett, and that meant Alex would do whatever was necessary to help her. He didn't have time to dash off to New York, but he could write her a letter to tell her she was the cornerstone he wanted to build his new world around. They belonged together, like earth and sky. Beneath her starchy façade, her dreams were as wild and audacious as his. They were better people when they were together. He needed her tedious, pencil-pushing ways to drive them both across the finish line and into a glorious future. She needed him too. If she surrendered to her crippling need for security, she would never soar the way God intended for her.

He returned to his room, pulled out a sheet of paper, and began to write.

Eloise's official courtship by Fletcher Jones began with an awkward visit to the New York Botanical Garden. It was a blustery morning, and they managed only stilted conversation during the carriage ride to the park. Fletcher commented on the weather, and she asked if he enjoyed the outdoors. He didn't, and after that they struggled to make conversation.

Bruce's legal quagmire was still at the forefront of her mind, and Fletcher had already been a tremendous help in that area, so perhaps the topic would break this awkward silence. She turned away from the carriage window to provide an update.

"Mr. Garrett's attorney is optimistic that the evidence you helped me find will be enough to get him released until a trial," she said.

"And what about the accountant who bought the dolly?"

"He's been arrested." Oscar Ott initially denied knowing anything about the dolly, but when shown his signature on the purchase form, he backpedaled and stumbled through half a dozen explanations. When none of his excuses held water, he bolted and tried to run. The sheriff had him arrested on the spot.

"The state has several detectives on the job," Eloise continued. "They have also questioned the cement factory owner and his son but haven't been able to pin anything on them yet."

Fletcher nodded sagely. "I'm sure the truth will emerge in the end."

Their conversation reverted to stiff formality as they stepped through the stone gates leading into the botanical park. They wandered through acres of forest in the middle of the city. A fortune had been spent to preserve this stretch of land for its beauty and history. Eloise couldn't help but think of Duval Springs, whose trees were just as old, but they would all be torn down to keep this city in operation. Soon an ancient elm tree where Alex once carved their initials in a rush of youthful enthusiasm would be cut down and burned. Only the memory would remain.

A light drizzle drove them toward the conservatory. The glass building had soaring white arches and looked like it belonged in heaven, but their conversation did not improve as they wandered beneath the towering palm trees and jungle ferns.

Everything brightened the moment they turned a corner toward a new wing in the conservatory.

"Cactuses!"

She lifted her skirts to scurry toward a wing different than everything else they'd seen this morning. It had rocky borders and hard-packed sand, and even the air seemed different as she stepped into the arid gallery filled with barrel cactus and prickly pear. She hadn't seen anything like this since her Arizona days. She reached down to finger the plump petals of a stonecrop plant, its flesh cool between her fingertips.

"How I've missed this," she murmured. "I used to cultivate cactuses."

There had been a cactus garden surrounding the convent in Arizona, and looking after it had been one of her chores. There wasn't much to it, but over time she felt a deep affinity for those tough, prickly plants.

"That's a curious hobby," Fletcher said. "How did you come to have a fondness for cactuses?"

She supposed most well-bred ladies had never lived in a desert convent. She could evade the topic, but if she and Fletcher were to have any hope of a future, she would need to tell him about the convent and why she'd been there.

"When I was sixteen, I was sent to a convent in Arizona for a few years." Her fingers grew cold as she kept talking. "There were all types of cactuses there. Pests and scale sometimes infect them, so I took care of that. Sometimes I watered them if things got too dry."

She continued down the stony path. Fletcher walked beside her, but cowardice kept her staring straight ahead so she couldn't see his expression.

"That seems a little strange," he finally said.

Now would be the perfect opportunity to tell him. They were the only people in this part of the conservatory and had complete privacy. But she couldn't bring herself to do it. They barely knew each other, and this was so intensely personal.

"Oh look, they sell them!"

She moved toward the table where a variety of potted cactuses and succulents were available for purchase. Her mind raced as she pretended to survey the variety. Fletcher stood only inches away, waiting for a response she wasn't prepared to give.

"So . . . the convent," he prompted.

She straightened. One of the things she had always admired about Fletcher was his calm logic and straightforward dealings. It was time to test that aspect of him. She turned to look him in the eye.

"Fletcher, why do you suppose any sixteen-year-old girl is banished to a desert convent two thousand miles from home?"

He lifted a brow, but there was no other change in his expression. "One would suppose that wayward conduct would be the primary reason."

"Correct." Memories of her "wayward conduct" with Alex crowded the edges of her mind, threatening her composure.

Fletcher absorbed her statement with typical nonchalance, indulging in neither outrage nor surprise. He had a two-word response.

"Please continue."

She didn't want to, but it was a fair request. "There was once a boy, and I was once a wild and reckless girl. We used to meet secretly in the woods where no one would find us. I think you can imagine how that scenario played out. Especially since I ended up in a convent."

She kept staring at the cactuses, the muscles in her neck so tense it made her whole body hurt. She counted ten heartbeats before Fletcher finally spoke.

"And did it work? Did it turn you onto a different path?"

"I've never done anything else to justify incarceration in a convent."

This was exquisitely awful but necessary if they were to pursue a serious relationship. There might not even *be* a relationship after this discussion, so she decided not to share any additional details and turned her attention back to the table of cactuses.

"I think I shall buy three," she said as she selected a pair of barrel cactuses and one succulent. She carried them to the front of the exhibit to pay for them, and then Fletcher offered to carry the box for her. The air was both damp and chilly as they stepped outside.

"Do you think the cactuses can survive the climate in Manhattan?" he asked agreeably.

"I'm about to find out," she said with a smile.

It seemed he'd taken her scandalous news in stride. They wandered through the rose garden, which still looked bleak in the early spring gloom. Just as she was beginning to feel at ease, Fletcher startled her with a question she didn't see coming.

"I'm glad the nuns helped mend your ways," he said with a note of humor in his voice, "but you don't really believe all that chapter and verse nonsense they spout, do you?"

She paused. "What do you mean?"

"Well, retreating from the world to pray, and all that. It seems remarkably self-centered to me. If there is a God, I can't imagine he'd respect a life like that."

Plenty of people thought the same about monastic orders, but it hurt to hear him say it so bluntly. The nuns had created an oasis of beauty and healing in their desert wilderness. Plenty of troubled women sought sanctuary with them while finding a truer connection to God and purpose in the world. Those years had been hard but possibly the most meaningful of her life.

"You don't believe in God?" she asked cautiously.

He gave a polite laugh. "Well, I'm not going to say 'no.' Where would the logic be in that? If He exists and for some inexplicable reason has been hiding for the past two thousand years, it makes sense to go through the motions of faith. And if He doesn't exist, I'm no worse off for holding myself to a code of moral conduct that has served the world well."

"Very logical of you."

He gave a polite nod. "Always."

Their day in the garden was even more stilted after that. How well did she know Fletcher if she hadn't realized their mismatch on such an important issue? He was suitable in so many ways, but this was a problem.

When she arrived home, she set the cactuses on her windowsill.

Arizona was a part of her life she would never forget. Those days in the arid wilderness had helped forge her into the person she was today, and the cactuses would be a lovely reminder of that time.

Her troubled mind was rocked even further by the delivery of the evening mail. It contained only a single letter, but it was from Alex. Her fingers trembled as she opened it.

> *Good evening, Eloise,*
>
> *Tonight an old soldier came to the tavern to claim the wishbone he left in 1862. His visit made me realize how important this tavern is. It is a lodestone that burns in our collective memory, and it drew that man a thousand miles to come save his wishbone before the town disappears.*
>
> *The engineers are skeptical of our ability to get the tavern out of the valley, but Hercules and I will try. We've sunk every dime we have into making it happen. The engineers think we are crazy, but when you love something, price is not an issue. Sometimes love must overrule what reason recommends. I must at least try, or I will forever wonder.*
>
> *I have the same feeling about you. I can't stop hoping that we can recapture what we once had, but this time do it right. You aren't a cuckoo bird, you are my ballast. A more poetic man would compare you to rose petals or moonlight glinting on the water. I can't. My best memories of you are slogging through an ice storm, balancing books, ordering me to toe the line, and I love you for it. I can't help but believe that God plunked us down in that valley for a reason. You make me a better man, and I believe between the two of us, we have a purpose in the world.*

Come back. Come back to the valley and to me. Duval Springs will be gone soon, but we can build a new home from the ground up and make it perfect for both of us.

Love always,
Alex

She was battling tears by the time she finished the letter. It hurt. She loved him, and a piece of her always would. Alex was laughter and vigor and endless summer days. He was braver than she could ever be, but living on the edge and taunting whirlwinds wasn't what she wanted in life. And the one time she had asked anything of him, he told her that a tavern mattered more than her father.

In a perfect world, she would be able to take the best pieces of Alex and meld them with Fletcher's safe and predictable life. But the real world didn't work that way, and she wasn't perfect either. She would resent it if someone suggested she should eliminate pieces of her personality to please another. She would just have to keep searching until she found a man who could provide her with the stability she needed.

She slipped Alex's note into her copy of *Treasure Island*, then tucked them both high up on the top shelf of her closet. Far away and out of sight.

Chapter
THIRTY

By the second week of April, the only building remaining in Duval Springs that was still to be moved was the tavern. The state would soon arrive to demolish the abandoned buildings whose owners had taken the payout and left the valley.

Hercules and his family moved out of the tavern as soon as the dismantling began. Every stone, board, and roof tile had been numbered and plotted. Soon the building would be taken apart like a giant jigsaw puzzle. The windows had already been removed, and tomorrow a crane would lift the roof off, but first Alex needed to unscrew the internal brackets from inside the attic.

He worked alone, for it was dangerous up in the attic. A couple of the floorboards were so old that they split when he put his weight on them, and he didn't want his nephews or Hercules up here. His brother weighed more than he did, and these old boards might protest. Mold, dust, and stale air made it a gritty task.

There wasn't enough room to stand, and Alex's neck ached as he unscrewed the brackets. Footsteps coming up the ladder broke his concentration, and Hercules popped his head through the opening in the floor.

"Don't come any closer," Alex cautioned. "These old planks won't hold us both."

"Then get over here," Hercules said. "I've got news."

The boards creaked as Alex crawled toward the opening. He fought the temptation to sneeze as more dust swirled. "What is it?"

"Word has it that Garrett's been sprung from prison. He's a free man, out on five thousand dollars' bail."

Alex's jaw dropped. "What more proof did they need that he's guilty?"

"The sheriff says there's too many suspects to hold Garrett," Hercules said. "They let him out but are keeping him under house arrest. And they've taken Oscar Ott in for questioning."

"Where did you hear that?"

"Around."

Alex stilled and looked Hercules in the eye. "No, specifically—where did you hear that?" He held his breath. Eloise had long suspected that Hercules was the town snitch. Alex refused to believe it, but Hercules did seem to know everything that went on in the valley.

Hercules smirked. "I heard it from those two gravediggers. They never dug up many graves, but they're sure friendly with the sheriff." A grin broke out across his face. "For pity's sake, why didn't you tell me they were undercover detectives?"

Alex smiled as relief trickled through him. "It was supposed to be a secret."

"Like anything stays a secret in this town." Hercules winked and headed back down the ladder.

Alex returned to work, but as he dismantled the brackets, a nagging question surfaced and wouldn't let him rest.

How did Hercules learn those men were detectives?

❦

Every muscle in Alex's body ached as he crawled out of the attic with two hundred years of dust coating his throat. Hercules and his family had already moved in to the Gilmore Inn, and Alex looked forward to a hot meal with them.

"Any mail for me?" he asked at the front desk. It had been a week since he sent Eloise that letter. He hadn't heard back from her yet, but there were two letters in his slot, and he eyed them in anticipation.

Kasper didn't budge from his chair at the telegraph stand. "You know I'm not paid to deliver postal mail."

The mail slots were within arm's reach of Kasper's station, but Alex was too tired to argue with the world's laziest man. He walked around the counter and grabbed his two letters. A bill from the engineers and another for oxen feed. His heart sank. Had Eloise even gotten his note?

Hercules and a dozen other workers were already chowing down in the dining room, and Alex was about to join them when Marie Trudeau entered the hotel. She walked directly to Kasper, ignoring the sidelong looks sent by some in the dining room.

"Do you have any telegrams for Mr. Garrett? Or other letters? I've been asked to collect everything."

It looked like Hercules was right about Garrett getting out of jail, and Mrs. Trudeau hadn't wasted any time going back to him.

"I've been sending telegrams up to his house as they come in," Kasper said.

"No other notes or messages?" she pressed. "He thinks you might have something."

"Nope."

Willard came out of his office at the sound of Mrs. Trudeau's voice. "I don't know why you're currying favor with Garrett," the normally genial innkeeper said. "Everyone knows he did it. It's just a matter of time before they arrest him again."

Mrs. Trudeau faced Willard, proudly holding up her hand to display a ring with a flashing blue stone. "*That's* why I'm helping him. It is a promise of marriage, and I wouldn't devote myself to any man unless I had complete faith in him." She used her best schoolmarm voice. Except for Willard and Kasper, every person in this room had been in Mrs. Trudeau's classroom at some point and instinctively settled down upon hearing that tone.

Alex braced himself when she turned her attention to him, especially when the starch went out of her and sympathy clouded her face.

"Alex, I've also brought news for you, and you're going to want to be sitting down to hear it."

He went on alert. "Go ahead and tell me now."

"Mr. Garrett told me that Eloise is attending her cousin's wedding tomorrow with that fellow in charge of the reservoir finances, Fletcher Jones."

"She's doing *what?*" he blurted, although he'd heard perfectly well the first time. Fletcher Jones was supposed to be in her past! No wonder she hadn't answered his letter if she was gallivanting around town with that stuffed shirt.

Catcalls followed him as he vaulted upstairs and raced to his room. He'd need money for a train ticket and a fresh shirt. He could change once he was aboard the train.

Hercules awaited him in the lobby, an annoyed look on his face. "Where are you going?"

"New York City. You know why."

"Funny, I heard it was her cousin getting married, not Eloise."

Alex shrugged into his coat. "Would you sit back while some man escorted Sally all over town?"

"I don't know if you noticed, but we're at a critical point in getting the tavern moved. Everyone looks to you for leadership on this kind of thing."

It was true. People were getting tired as the end drew near, and he was the right person to light a fire beneath the troops. Abandoning the tavern gnawed at him, but a man had to have priorities in life.

"The tavern is my family's home," he admitted. "But Eloise is my *family*. I can't stand down. I did that twelve years ago, and I won't give up so easily. Never again."

Hercules gave a reluctant nod of acceptance. "Then go get her."

Eloise and Fletcher sat near the middle of the church during the wedding, but even from here she could see the affection blazing in Nick's eyes as he gazed at his bride. It was a love match, and she ought to be happy for her cousin.

Instead, the sight of Nick and Rosalind kneeling before the altar with clasped hands and open hearts made her wonder if she would ever have a man who adored her that much. Alex claimed to, but time and again he'd taken her for granted. And Fletcher? He sat stiffly beside her, the epitome of well-mannered comportment. He had all the makings of a good husband, but their hearts weren't aligned.

The wedding reception was held at an elegant clubhouse. As they waited in the receiving line, Eloise and Fletcher each commented on how lovely Rosalind looked. In the dining room, they admired the quality of the miniature pastries and the towering cake. When the music began, Fletcher rose and invited her to the dance floor.

"You dance very well," he complimented.

"Thank you."

They danced a waltz, gliding across the floor in perfect tandem.

He was obviously a polished dancer, and she bit her tongue to avoid complimenting him in turn. If they said one more polite thing to each other, she'd shriek like a banshee.

"The string quartet is very good, aren't they?" Fletcher said.

"Yes, excellent." She itched to ask him if he'd ever been reprimanded in school, read a novel he loathed, had a howling weakness. It was on the tip of her tongue to ask if he'd ever done something horrible enough to make his mother cry when she noticed a disturbance in the rear of the hall. It looked like someone was trying to enter the reception without an invitation, and the waiters were blocking him.

Nick noticed and brusquely cut through the dance floor with a fighting expression on his face. "What are you doing here, Duval?" he demanded.

Eloise gasped as she recognized Alex, his hair disheveled and collar askew. Alex didn't even glance at Nick as he pushed through the crowd until he stood before her. Fletcher's arms tightened protectively around her.

"Alex?" she asked, her voice both shocked and bewildered. Had he come all this way for her? It felt like her heart was about to leap out of her chest, but she couldn't really believe he was here.

"Don't do this, Eloise," Alex said, his breath ragged as though he'd run a hundred miles. "Come back home."

"Get out of here," Fletcher said. "She's made her choice, and you don't belong here."

Some waiters materialized and stood at the ready, one looking to Nick for instruction. Nick gave a curt shake of his head. Alex didn't spare them a glance. All he could do was stare at her as though she held the keys to the universe in her hand.

"Come back to the valley, Eloise," Alex said. "We still have work to do and castles to build. Don't throw away everything we have. Not for him."

A man wearing a general's uniform was calm but firm. "Take it outside, gentlemen."

"There won't be any fistfights at my wedding," Nick said.

"We can cart him off to jail until he cools off," the general offered.

Fletcher was quick to agree. "Good idea—"

"Don't you dare," Eloise said. She didn't know why Alex was here, but she simultaneously wanted to protect him and kick him to the moon and back.

"He doesn't deserve you," Alex said passionately.

"And Nick doesn't deserve to have you idiots disrupt his wedding," the general said. "You have five seconds to disperse. Five! Four!"

"Alex, be realistic," Eloise pleaded. "For once in your life, could you please reach deep down inside and dredge up a tiny sliver of logic?"

"There's nothing logical about the way I feel for you. I will wait for you until the stars fall from the sky—"

"Fine, but your five seconds are up," Nick said. "Go outside and start waiting for those stars to fall. You've caused enough commotion in here."

"Let's step out onto the terrace and handle this like rational adults," she said. "Or at least we can pretend to be rational for a few minutes, okay?"

He hadn't torn his eyes off her face, but hope began to gleam behind his eyes, and she felt it too. He flashed her a half-repentant, half-wicked smile. "Right," he agreed. "Rational adults. Let's go."

She led the way, even though Fletcher tried to hold her in place. She twisted away and headed toward the French doors that opened onto a flagstone terrace. She sensed both men following.

"You've made quite a spectacle of yourself," Fletcher accused Alex the moment they stepped onto the terrace.

"That's what a man in love does," Alex said, looking directly at her, hope burning in his eyes.

"Really?" Fletcher drawled. "An intelligent man would have shown affection by pulling out all the stops to prove Mr. Garrett innocent, rather than dithering in a hopeless quest."

Alex snorted. "If Bruce Garrett is innocent, I'll eat my hat."

"It's true, Alex," she said. "Fletcher helped me find proof that Oscar Ott signed for equipment to transport a boxcar off rails three days after the Russians went missing. We have proof." She sent a grateful smile to Fletcher, for he truly had been heroic that day, dropping everything to find evidence of that purchase.

"Are you sure?" Alex sputtered.

"Certain."

Alex winced. "I said I would eat my hat, and I will, Eloise. Just say the word."

She nearly exploded. This was just the sort of stupid, extravagant gesture she was coming to expect from him. "Do you think for a single second that I would enjoy watching you eat your hat?"

"It can be done. I saw a guy in Cuba do it on a dare." Alex looked braced for battle, his chin lifted and face resolute, if a little apprehensive.

A seed of mirth bubbled up inside her, requiring willpower to force it back. She clamped a hand over her mouth, but the fact that Alex would probably do it if she asked was both appalling and hilarious. A snort of laughter escaped, and then she couldn't help it. Peals of laughter broke out, and Alex flashed a knowing grin, laughing alongside her.

"Shall we rejoin the reception?" Fletcher asked, a hint of impatience in his tone.

She ought to, for it was a grand celebration with fine food, an excellent string quartet, and an escort who was gentlemanly and safe.

ELIZABETH CAMDEN

But a hundred miles away was a town with half-built streets
and people fighting for a cause, powered by little but their own
two hands and hope for the future. She glanced at Fletcher. He
had countless fine qualities, but he wasn't the right man for
her. They didn't share the same faith, and he didn't inspire her
to reach beyond her boundaries. They couldn't be a real team.

"I need to return to the valley," she said to him gently. "I have
unfinished work up there."

Fletcher gave the slightest nod. "And you are most assuredly
finished here."

She watched him retreat into the club, a tangled mass of emotions swirling inside. Fletcher had been stable, gentlemanly, and
predictable. Alex was none of those things and never would be.

Even as regret began to cloud the edges of her mind, Alex
pulled her gently into his arms, reading her mind like he always
could. "Shh," he whispered in her ear. "I've got you. You're safe.
We're in this together."

"I don't feel very safe right now." She felt like she'd just
been flung into the deep end of the ocean without a net or life
raft. Alex turned her around, drawing her back against him,
and coaxed her to look through the windows at the glittering
wedding reception in full swing.

"Tell me what you see in there," he said.

"Happy people. Perfect lives."

His arms tightened around her middle, and he whispered in
her ear. "Oh, Eloise, there's no such thing as a perfect life, but
what you and I have is magnificent. It comes with blisters on
our hands and an uncertain future, but even so, it has been a
grand ride, and I don't ever want it to end. I know you wish I
could be more logical. Sometimes I wish you could be a little
more impulsive. But, Eloise, we bring out the best in each other.
Can you doubt that?"

She closed her eyes and leaned back against him. If she rolled the dice and gambled on Alex, she would never be able to change him. She needed to accept his freewheeling ways, just as he accepted her own oddities. Alex was a gamble, and she'd never been a risk-taker.

"I know I've hurt you," he continued. "Over the past eight months I've picked up and moved houses, blasted through bedrock, steamrolled new land . . . and I've gotten a little clumsy. I made the mistake of thinking you were as tough as you looked, but it was always the gentle side of you I loved best."

"Even ballast has feelings." She said it simply, with no bitterness or accusation, and he nodded in acceptance.

"I know, and I can do better. Just don't walk away from us."

On the other side of the French doors, the wedding guests glittered in candlelight as they danced and laughed. Nick and his bride looked dazzling, twirling in an unabashed waltz as though they didn't have a care in the world. But even that was an illusion. Nick had an ulcer from the stress of his job, and Rosalind had a rocky past. They had fought hard to get where they were and still had plenty of challenges ahead.

Then she saw Fletcher holding a petite blond woman as they executed the steps of the waltz. She winced a little, and Alex must have sensed it.

"Are you regretting what just happened?" he asked quietly.

"It's too late for regrets."

He turned her to face him, sympathy radiating from his warm gaze. "You're the one who gambled everything tonight. That's quite a role-reversal for us, isn't it? I'm fully aware that you have walked away from a safe job, a safe man, and a very nice apartment with water and electricity. I know this isn't easy for you. When we get back to Highpoint, there are going to be obstacles everywhere, but if we battle them together, they won't seem so bad."

The fact that he acknowledged her insecurities without

belittling them meant the world to her. And truly, she was strong enough to face whatever happened up there. She stepped closer into the comfort of his arms.

"It's the obstacles that make us stronger," she whispered into his ear.

Life would be so much easier if it could be nothing but a candlelit waltz, but she had chosen her course, and there was no going back.

"Let's take the train home tomorrow," she whispered, and felt him smile against the side of her face.

She prayed she was doing the right thing.

Alex's back was stiff from sleeping on a bench at Grand Central Station. When he parted from Eloise last night, he hadn't let on that he had no money for a hotel and instead simply found a bench at the train station, where he would meet her to return home.

He made his way to the washroom to splash cold water on his face and straighten his rumpled clothes. After purchasing train tickets for himself, Eloise, and her maid, he spent his last dime on a cup of hot coffee and felt ready to face the day. He paced the main terminal, scanning the crowd in search of her. He didn't have long to wait, but his heart sank when he saw her. She came alone, with only a satchel and a slim box in one hand. No trunks of clothing or the maid and baby she adored.

"Let me carry that for you," he said as he reached for the bag. "I thought Tasha and the baby would be with you."

She shook her head. "They've just settled back in to the city. I don't want to ask them to move until . . . well, I don't even know if I'll have a roof over my head in Duval Springs."

He smiled in relief. "The Gilmore Inn still stands. The tavern is in lousy shape, but you can stay at the inn through the end of the month."

They took a seat on a bench, and he finally got a glimpse of what she had in the cardboard box. "Cactuses?" he asked.

"I saw them for sale at the botanical garden and couldn't resist. They remind me of Arizona."

Aside from the one time she'd told him about the convent, she never spoke about those years. He'd assumed she'd hated that period of her life, but maybe not. He'd hated the army at first. He'd been forced into it out of desperation, but over the years he rose to the challenge and became a better man. That sharp detour in his life had been grueling, but he was grateful for it now.

He glanced down at the box. "I like your cactuses. They remind me of you."

"Prickly?"

"Tough. Resilient. Maybe a little bit prickly, but it's part of what makes them so dauntless."

"They're not dauntless," she said. "Cactuses are pure jelly on the inside."

Now he was convinced the cactus was the perfect metaphor for her. Eloise had always been tenderhearted, and he'd forgotten that in the way she'd fought like a gladiator over the past few months. To the outside world she was a relentless force of indefatigable logic, but inside she was pure jelly.

"Eloise!" The shout cut through the din of the train station, and Alex spotted Claude Fitzgerald and Enzo Accardi heading toward them. Both men lugged heavy bags and carried overcoats.

"I didn't realize you'd been sent to the valley as well," Claude said in a confused voice.

"She lives there," Alex said. At least, he hoped she'd be living there, and Eloise didn't deny it.

"Well, Mr. Mayor," Claude said pompously, "May 1 is only

two short weeks away, so Enzo and I are moving in, preparing for the final demolition. Four caseloads of explosives are being loaded onto the train as we speak."

"What a soothing thought," Alex murmured.

"We have a private compartment," Enzo said. "Will you join us? It will be good to see each other again."

"Let's!" Eloise agreed, a little too rapidly for Alex's taste. He would have welcomed the chance to be alone with her, but Eloise was already following the others across the crowded terminal.

The train ride with the two demolition experts was surprisingly enjoyable. It was good to see Enzo again, and even Claude wasn't so unbearable anymore. Perhaps now that Alex had reconciled himself to the loss of the town, it was easier to see humanity in the face of someone he had always considered an enemy. His world had been forever changed, and it was time to make peace. A sense of euphoria came over him while watching Eloise chat with her old colleagues. He loved seeing her happy. He loved that she was coming back to the valley. The world was back on track, and he would handle the challenges as they came. His sense of well-being continued as they arrived in Kingston and boarded a carriage for Duval Springs.

It came to an abrupt end the moment the carriage arrived in Duval Springs and Alex looked out the window.

The tavern was a disaster. He stepped out of the carriage, staring in bewildered horror at the chaos.

"It looks like a bomb exploded," Claude said.

The tavern's roof was gone, and a huge mound of broken boards and tiles lay scattered everywhere. He scanned the yard, looking for Hercules, and finally saw him slumped on a bench in the town square. Sally and a handful of other men were with him.

Alex ran over, the others following. "What happened?" he asked.

Hercules looked sick. "The roof came apart when we tried to lift it off. Everything was going perfectly, but as the crane lowered the roof, it crumbled. One second it was fine, and then it smashed to pieces and crashed to the ground."

Enzo had joined them, concern on his face. "Were the internal trusses in place during the lift?"

"Every one of them," Hercules confirmed.

Enzo sighed. "I'll go have a look, but this seems very odd."

Alex followed Enzo back to the wreckage that had once been the roof of the tavern. Dust still swirled in the air, and he battled a sick feeling as Enzo hunkered down to examine the broken boards. After a few minutes, Enzo headed inside the partially dismantled tavern to get a better look at the exposed framework.

His expression was grim when he emerged. "Where is your brother?"

"Right here," Hercules said.

Enzo guided them to the mound of rubble and pulled a mangled board out to show them. "I'm sorry, my friends," he said gently. "The wood in this tavern is completely riddled with termite tunnels. The roof collapsed under the stress of being moved, and now that I can see it better, the rest of the building has the same problem. None of it can be saved."

The words were a shock. Alex stood motionless, unable to accept what he'd just heard, but Hercules took it badly. He knelt on the ground and buried his face in his hands.

This couldn't be happening. Of all the buildings in town, this was the one they loved the most. It hurt to look at the tavern with its roof ripped off and windows pulled out. It would have been better to burn it all down in a glorious bonfire rather than see it pulled apart in slow mutilation.

"You're going to be all right, Alex," Eloise said.

Anguish twisted his words. "This tavern is the heart and soul of our community. It's who we are."

"No, it's not," she said firmly. "This tavern has witnessed history and joy and tragedy, but it was the *people* who made it historic, not the boards and stones. The tavern doesn't define you. When you get knocked down, you pick yourself up and move on. It's the American way. You don't whine. You don't quit. You pick up and begin again."

Eloise had been doing that all her life. He gathered her close and laid his face on top of her head. His lovely, logical Eloise. His ballast. Everything she said was right, but this was a wound that would hurt for a long time.

Eloise sat in the Gilmore Inn's dining room as the last of the evening dishes were cleared away. Alex had been despondent all through dinner over the loss of the tavern, but it was nothing compared to Hercules, who slumped in the corner and hadn't eaten a bite.

Claude seemed determined to dump salt in their wound by bellyaching over the mess Hercules had made in trying to dismantle the tavern.

"It's going to make our work more difficult," Claude groused. "We could have burned it down in a clean and contained manner had it been left alone. As it is, there's a mess all over the town square for us to clean up. They ought to be charged for it."

"You're not going to charge for it," Eloise said. She no longer worked for the state, but as a citizen of New York, she was entitled to an opinion and wasn't afraid to voice it.

"I can send a few men from the cement factory down to pitch in," Jack Riesel said.

Ever since his company's accountant had fallen under suspicion for colluding in the death of the Russians, Jack had been exceedingly helpful, volunteering on work crews and joining others in communal meals. Oscar was still in jail, but the detectives hadn't stopped looking for evidence. The sheriff had already questioned Jack and his father twice but apparently hadn't found anything incriminating.

"Anything I can do to help," Jack continued with a generous smile. "I'm sure everyone will be willing to pitch in." He looked at Kasper, who lounged on a bench.

"Don't look at me," Kasper said mildly. "I've already contributed my work quota for the week."

Claude gestured to the two gravediggers dining with Eugene Franks, the old soldier who recently returned for his chicken bone. "Why can't they help us with the cleanup? They can—"

"They're not helping," Alex interrupted.

Shortly before dinner, Alex had confided to her that the gravediggers were actually detectives looking for evidence of who had buried that boxcar. How could she have been so blind as not to have noticed those men were no more gravediggers than she was? Silas Roth was as skinny as a bean pole, and the other man had hands softer than hers.

Claude was still disgruntled. "That tavern is a disaster I hadn't accounted for. I say the gravediggers need to help with the mess."

Hercules ignored the conversation and stared moodily into space. Sally stood beside him, patting the baby's back and gently swaying as she surveyed the wreckage of her home through the dining room windows.

"It's all a matter of perspective," the old soldier said as he drew on his pipe. "I was at the battle of Vicksburg. That city was under siege for two months, and the chaos was the real thing. *That* was a mess. This is a little yard cleanup."

"Where are we going to live after we move to the new town?" The question came from Bill, Hercules's fourteen-year-old son.

"I don't know," Hercules said. "For now, we'll stay here in the hotel."

"But what about after those guys burn down the hotel?" Bill pressed, resentment plain in his face as he eyed Claude.

"Dr. Lloyd has a lot of room in his house," Alex said. "Maybe he can put some of us up."

Hercules sighed. "I'd rather just get a new tavern built as soon as possible. I'll find the money somehow."

No one knew what to say. An uncomfortable silence stretched in the dining room.

Bill dug into his pocket and retrieved a crumpled slip of paper. He studied it for a moment before speaking. "The state owes me sixty dollars for moving all those graves. You can have it, if it helps."

Hercules buried his face in his hands and started sobbing. Sally dropped to his side, but his weeping didn't cease. He didn't even lift his head as he spoke through his tears. "That's your money, son. You worked hard for it."

It took a while for Hercules to regain his composure, and Eloise sat helplessly alongside Alex, wishing there was something she could say or do.

Finally, the oldest Duval boy stood. "Well, I had some good news this afternoon," he said, shifting a little.

"Let's hear it," Alex said.

John held up a slim envelope and offered a timid smile. "I got accepted to Harvard. I start in September."

This brought a fresh round of tears from Hercules, but this time they were mingled with laughter as he lunged across the dining room to pull his son into a hug. John's news was exactly what was needed to lift everyone's doldrums and make them look toward the future.

Jack grinned as he put up a pair of fists and pretended to spar with John. "I'm a Yale man down to the Yale-blue blood running in my veins. Welcome to the storied rivalry. May it be a long and bitter one!"

Claude was full of advice about how John should comport himself at Harvard. John hung on every word, even after Claude veered away from advice and into bragging about his own accomplishments at Harvard.

At some point during the bittersweet celebrations, the old soldier rose to seek his bed. "I'll be leaving first thing in the morning, so I'll say my good-byes now," he said to the group that suddenly fell silent. "I didn't expect to find so much comfort in coming back for that chicken bone, but the neighborliness here was something I haven't known for a long time."

Eloise offered to drive him in the morning. All the men had plenty of work in clearing out the last remnants of the town to be saved, but she could take a few hours to drive the old soldier into Kingston.

Everything broke up quickly after that. Jack headed back up the mountain, and Kasper pulled the leather covering over his telegraph machine. One of the gravediggers left "for some fresh air," but the other decided to remain in the dining room to smoke another pipe. Eloise could only hope they knew what they were doing, for loitering around the hotel and socializing didn't seem very productive, and her nagging sense of unease was growing. Even as she headed upstairs for the night, the scar on her back prickled and itched.

Eloise couldn't shake a feeling of sadness as she drove the old soldier into Kingston. His eyes took on a faraway quality as he gazed at Duval Springs a final time before climbing aboard the wagon. The village green was a trampled patch of mud, and vacant lots pockmarked the town square in the bleak spring sunshine.

"The town I loved is already gone," he said.

"Yes," she acknowledged. In two weeks, the remaining buildings would be demolished, but the idyllic town of her childhood had vanished. All that remained was the memory.

An hour later, they arrived at the Kingston train depot. The old soldier carried only a satchel, so he needed no help as he hefted the bag down from the wagon's bench.

"Thank you kindly, young lady," he said as he tipped his hat to her.

Something caught her eye on the covered walkway running the length of the train depot. There weren't many people loitering on the platform, for the train would leave soon, and most of the passengers were already aboard. But the rail-thin figure of the man casually lounging on a bench was familiar. It was Silas Roth, one of the undercover gravediggers. What on earth was he doing here?

"I'll go with you to the ticket window," she said.

"There's no need. I'll be fine, if you want to be on your way."

What she wanted was to know why Silas Roth was at the train station, staring straight ahead, casually gnawing on a toothpick. She scanned the rest of the crowd but didn't spot the other undercover detective.

"Nonsense, I'll go with you," she said as she headed toward the ticket window. In three minutes the ticket had been purchased and the old soldier was ready to board. She followed him to the waiting passenger car, where the door remained open for the last stragglers.

"I've enjoyed your visit," she said as she prepared to say good-bye to this strangely melancholy man. "I know the rest of the town appreciated—"

"Miss Drake!" a voice shouted. It was Kasper Nagy. He wore a tense expression and carried a coat slung over one arm as he hurried toward her. "Miss Drake, thank heavens I've found you in time."

"What's the matter?" It was odd to see the town's famously lazy telegraph operator looking so animated.

"I'm afraid you must go on a journey with me."

Before she could make sense of the strange comment, Silas Roth vaulted off the bench and came striding toward them. "Kasper Nagy, you are under arrest for the murder of twenty-three Russian immigrants in 1903."

Eloise froze, stunned by the statement, but the other detective materialized at Kasper's other side, handcuffs at the ready.

Kasper took a step back, and his anxious expression changed to one of determination. "That won't be possible," he said.

"It's mandatory," the detective said. "No arguing."

"But Miss Drake and I are going on a journey, and you see—" He slipped a pistol from beneath his coat, and a gunshot cracked through the air.

The old soldier toppled and fell, blood blooming across his shirt.

Kasper grabbed Eloise's arm and jammed the barrel of the pistol against her temple. "I regret the demonstration to prove that I am in earnest," he said.

Eloise couldn't breathe, couldn't move.

"Let her go, Kasper," one of the detectives ordered.

"Not until I get where I'm going. You've seen that I have no problem killing a hostage, so if you want her to stay safe, I need the two of you to back up. All the way to the depot wall. Move!"

Both men started inching backward, their eyes still trained on Kasper, but all Eloise could see was the old soldier lying motionless on the ground.

"S-somebody help him," she stammered, but no one moved. Aside from the two detectives, everyone else at the depot had scattered for cover.

"It's no use, Kasper," one of the detectives said. "Oscar Ott has been singing like a bird. He's told us how you ordered him to pay for the equipment to bury the Russians."

The barrel of the gun pressed harder against her temple, and the stink of gunpowder was sickening.

"Fine, guilty as charged," Kasper said. "But you're not going to catch me, because I've got a hostage and you're going to do exactly as I say. I need you to deliver a message to the station-master that this train is to go directly to Milton," he ordered. "There will be no stops between here and Milton, where you will be provided with further instructions."

Kasper jerked her backward, and a whimper escaped her throat. He whispered in her ear. "Easy does it, you'll be fine. Just keep following orders."

The stubble of his whiskers against her cheek made her flesh crawl. She managed to nod as he dragged her backward, and prayers from the convent ran through her mind. *Lord, have mercy . . . Christ, have mercy . . . Holy Mary, pray for me. . . .*

The two detectives gaped as Kasper hauled her inside an open boxcar filled with stacks of lumber, still using her body as a shield. The detectives had followed at a careful distance, keeping their hands raised.

"You can let her go now, Kasper."

He shook his head. "Deliver my instructions. If this train isn't moving in three minutes, I shoot her ear off."

The two men conferred for a moment before one of them raced to the depot office. Over the next few moments, uniformed train officials darted across the platform, scurrying to make arrangements. The old soldier hadn't moved from where he sprawled on the ground, and no one went to help him.

At last, one of the detectives stepped forward, both hands in the air. "Okay, the train is going to Milton. Now let her go."

Kasper shook his head. "Miss Drake is my insurance policy. You'll learn more in Milton."

"Be reasonable," the detective said. "We can't let this train leave with her aboard."

Kasper slid the gun barrel behind the shell of her ear, pushing it forward. "She doesn't really need this ear," he called out. "You have ten seconds to start moving, otherwise I'll demonstrate another show of force. Miss Drake has two ears and lots of fingers and toes."

She'd have fallen if the arm around her waist wasn't so firm, but finally there was a jerk, and the train began moving, inching its way out of the station. The gun was still jammed to her ear, and she'd never felt so helpless as the train pulled away and the two detectives slid into the distance. The boxcar door was still open as they left the railyard, then passed a series of warehouses and an open field. A group of boys played stickball in an empty lot. The rest of the world carried on while the old soldier was dead and a madman had a gun to her head.

"Let's step back," Kasper said. Stacks of lumber filled the space behind them, but she obeyed as much as possible. The door of the boxcar was still wide open, adding to her trepidation.

"In a few minutes, we're both going to jump," he said.

"Jump where?"

"Jump *off*, Miss Drake. You didn't really think we're going to Milton, did you?"

She blanched. The train was moving at full speed, and the countryside flew past at an alarming rate. Kingston was gone, and now they were in the middle of unbroken forest. Kasper clung to the open frame of the door with one hand but still aimed the gun at her with the other. Wind ruffled his hair as he scrutinized the countryside ahead of him.

"In one more minute, you are going to jump," he said. "I'll follow the moment you're off. Don't try anything stupid. Remember, if you play by the rules, you'll be fine."

How could he know where they were? The barren trees flying past the open door all looked the same to her, but soon the forest thinned. Sunlight glinted on water through the trees, so they had to be close to the river. Gravel covered the raised track bed, and it would be awful to land on it.

"Now, Miss Drake." Kasper held the gun straight at her. "Jump now with everything intact, or I shoot off your ear and then you jump. Your choice, but make it quick."

This was going to hurt, but Kasper took a step closer to her. *Lord, have mercy. Christ, have mercy.*

She held her breath and jumped. Her knees banged hard, and her hands slammed against the gravel. She tumbled down the embankment, helpless against the momentum. Even after her body stopped rolling, everything kept whirling. She pushed onto all fours, tugging her skirts aside to scramble upright. Could she make it to the woods before Kasper got his gun?

It was pointless. There'd be no cover in the barren forest, and Kasper was already on his feet, his gun back in hand. A trickle of blood tracked down his face, much like the blood on both her palms. The gravel roadbed hadn't been kind to either of them.

"Very good, Miss Drake," he panted. "Now we're heading for the river, and after a few hours of good behavior, you'll be set free. Keep your hands in plain view as we walk. Don't try any heroics."

"I'm an accountant," she said. "We don't do heroics."

Heroism was easier to imagine when reading *Treasure Island* or *Ivanhoe*. Right now she felt like a whipped dog as she trudged into the forest, her feet sinking into mucky soil with each step. She scanned the land on either side of her, desperate for a sign of civilization, but there was nothing aside from a squirrel racing through the carpet of decaying leaves. Her entire body hurt, and a cut on her lip leaked a salty tang of blood.

"Why did you shoot the old soldier?" she asked, her voice

shaking as they walked farther into the woods. The sight of that kind man sprawled on the platform would haunt her forever. "You didn't have to do that."

"I didn't want to, but the train station was under surveillance. They were planning to arrest me, and I needed to get out."

"What makes you think they were about to arrest you?"

Kasper let out a whoosh of breath, and suddenly she sensed he was as exhausted as she was. "I eavesdrop on the wires, you know that," he said as though she were a simpleton. "Those detectives were using a telegraph station at Kingston and didn't realize I could hear every word. They wired the Russian embassy in Washington that a person from Finland was about to be arrested for the deaths of twenty-three Russian citizens, and asked if they wanted me deported to Russia. So I needed to get out, and fast. I'm sorry about the old soldier, but it was him or me."

By now they were nearing the river, over a mile wide with choppy gray water and no sign of a town on either side. A flat-bottomed barge waited along the riverbank in the distance. She froze, for a man on the barge took a cigar from his mouth and sent them a brief wave.

"Don't get your hopes up," Kasper said. "It's only Jack, and we're in this together."

A fresh round of fear gripped her, for it would be impossible to escape, now that there were two captors. "Were you the town snitch?" she asked as they walked toward the barge.

"*Snitch* has such a derogatory connotation," Kasper said. "A snitch is nothing more than a purveyor of information. It's a service, if you will."

She detected the trace of his accent again, and Eloise had the sensation she was walking alongside the man who had written the incriminating message on the back of the Garrett scrip. Tasha had said the Russian note was badly written, probably because Kasper wasn't a native speaker of the language, merely a man who grew up in Russian-occupied Finland.

Jack Riesel lowered a wooden plank for them to board when they drew alongside the barge. He tossed a cigar over the side, and Eloise recognized the cedar-scented tobacco from the night she'd been shot. How many times since that night had she smiled and worked alongside Jack, never realizing he was the one hunting her that night? He always had a peppermint stick in his mouth when she was with him, but it seemed he liked cigars when doing dirty work. A chill raced through her, but she mustn't let on that she suspected him.

"Welcome aboard," Jack said with a regretful smile. "I apologize for all the trouble this morning. You certainly don't deserve any of it, but in a few hours everything will be over, and we'll set you free. That's the plan, so long as you cooperate. Okay, Eloise?"

His face was soft and open, but his breath reeked of the cedar-scented cigar.

A glance around the barge didn't reveal much. A wheelhouse enclosed the captain's wheel and pumps. It was a working barge, with barrels, piles of rope, and casks of fuel on the deck. Only a few things looked incongruous. Stacked alongside the wheelhouse were some fine leather trunks and traveling bags. She glanced at Kasper, whose face had turned grim.

"All my worldly goods, packed and ready to accompany me back to Finland," he said bitterly.

"Finland?"

"I can hardly remain in the United States, can I? Those gravediggers are about to put all the pieces together."

"Did you mean to kill the Russians?"

Kasper shot a glare at Jack, who answered her question. "What happened was exactly what was written on that piece of scrip. It was an accident. We didn't mean for them to be seriously hurt."

"Except that you blamed Bruce Garrett for it, when it was you all along."

Jack was defensive in his reply. "I was the enforcer during the strike, and I was good at it. Accidents happen. I tried to cover it up so no one would ever know, and the note Kasper wrote on the scrip was only an insurance policy should the boxcar be discovered. Neither of us wanted what happened. Everything would have been fine if that stretch of land hadn't been seized by the state for development."

She wished he wasn't telling her all this. It meant they probably didn't intend to let her survive this trip.

"Forgive me, but I must ask you to step inside the hold," Jack said. "I assure you, as soon as Kasper and I are safely out of the country, you will be released to go about your business. We don't want to hurt you, and in a little less than twelve hours, we will all be free."

Jack held open the door to the hold. Built alongside the back of the wheelhouse, it was little more than a closet lined with shelves of tinned food and coils of rope hanging from pegs. There were no windows, and it would be pitch-black inside.

"Don't make me go in there," she stammered through suddenly chattering teeth. "I'll be good. I won't try to escape."

"I know you'll be good, because you'll be locked in the storage hold. We won't be able to guard you all night long," Kasper said. "Now get inside, or I'll be required to demonstrate another show of force."

Her mouth went dry. A true hero would make a valiant lunge for freedom rather than obediently walk into captivity, but she wasn't much of a hero. Her heart sank as she eyed the lock on the door. The iron bolt was thicker than her thumb and secured by a heavy padlock. It would be impossible to escape once she was locked inside.

Kasper sighed. "You have such pretty ears too. Jack? Brace yourself, I'm about to perform an unpleasant task."

"I'll go!" she said.

Five seconds later she stood in the musty closet and listened to the bolt slide shut and the padlock click into place. She was trapped. It was pitch-black in here, and there was no way out.

ercules shook off his despondency from the previous evening and came to Alex with a surprising suggestion.

"The McGregor house has been sitting empty ever since they moved to Albany in December. How about we jack it up and move it to Highpoint for us to live in? It will save the state the cost of knocking it down."

Why not? There didn't seem to be any reason for the state to deny them an abandoned house, but Alex knew better than to expect reason whenever government bureaucracies were involved. Eloise was expected back within the hour from driving the old soldier into Kingston, and he'd ask about their odds of getting the house. The prospect of living in a *real* house for the first time in his life was immensely appealing.

"Let's go look," he said, excitement burgeoning inside.

They sprinted to the east side of town, where the two-story house sat on an abandoned street. They had to break in through a window, since the front door had been locked. Their footsteps echoed on the hardwood floors as they moved through barren rooms stripped of furniture and the embellishments that made a house a home. But Alex didn't see barren rooms. He saw gathering places where children would laugh and come of age.

He and Hercules walked each room, envisioning which pieces of furniture from the tavern could be moved here. Outside, the sky clouded over and rain began to fall, making the interior even gloomier, but every inch of this house brimmed with possibility. Heedless of the rain, they circled the house to measure the foundation and inspect the windows. Everything about this building was well-made and likely to survive the move. They wouldn't have time to build a basement, but if they acted fast, they could get this house moved in time.

It was late in the afternoon before they made it back to the town square. The nonstop drizzle meant Alex was likely to find the demolition crew in the hotel. He and Hercules were accustomed to working through the rain, but he'd bet his bottom dollar that Claude would have set up shop in the hotel's dining room.

He was right. Claude and Enzo sat before mounds of paperwork, completely ignoring the telegraph machine that rattled unattended.

"Where's Kasper?" Alex asked. Kasper was the only person who knew how to operate the telegraph, and he hadn't set up the Morse inker to catch messages.

"No idea," Willard said. "Whoever is on the other end of that message has been persistent. It keeps going off every few minutes, and it's been driving me insane. I'm tempted to yank the wire from the wall."

"What about Eloise, is she back yet?"

Willard shook his head. "Nope, and she promised to bring us back a chocolate torte from the bakery in Kingston."

It was worrisome. Eloise should have returned by now, but maybe she had decided to wait for the rain to stop. In the meantime, he needed to make arrangements to save the McGregor place. They might be able to buy a few more days.

"Enzo!" he said in a hearty voice. "Let's talk about the order of demolition. You probably aren't going to get to the east side of town for a while, right?"

Before Enzo could reply, a pounding of footsteps was followed by the hotel door nearly being torn off its hinges. Bruce Garrett stormed into the lobby, his face a thundercloud.

"Saddle up every able-bodied man you can find," he ordered. "Kasper Nagy killed the old soldier and made a run for it. He's kidnapped Eloise too."

Alex listened in disbelief as Bruce relayed the story. The sheriff in Kingston had placed a telephone call to Garrett's mansion, telling them that Kasper Nagy had made a daring escape when the detectives tried to arrest him for the death of the Russians. Garrett admitted that Kasper had also been the town snitch, with excellent access to everyone's secrets as the only telegraph operator in town. He'd eavesdropped at the hotel and carried out a lot of dirty work for both Garrett and Theodore Riesel over the years.

Alex didn't care about ancient history. None of that mattered until they got Eloise back.

Garrett's voice was frustrated as he continued talking. "Kasper left a set of demands to be met at the Milton depot, but when the train stopped, there was no sign of either Kasper or Eloise. They bailed off the train somewhere in the thirty miles of wilderness between Kingston and Milton."

The stop at Milton had obviously been a ruse, but figuring out Kasper's plan would be a complicated guessing game. Unless Alex could find some clues.

"Do you have a key for this safe?" he asked Willard as he yanked the cuckoo clock that covered it from the wall.

Willard shook his head. "It's Western Union property. Kasper has the only key."

"Forget keys," Hercules said. "We've got sledgehammers."

Two minutes later they had retrieved sledgehammers and crowbars from the yard outside. Alex extracted the safe from the hole in the wall, struggling to balance the heavy metal box as he lowered it to the floor with a thud.

"Have at it," he told Hercules.

Hercules hefted the sledgehammer high, bringing it down on the rim of the safe with an earsplitting clang. It wasn't the strongest safe, and after a dozen blows, the door no longer fit neatly inside the frame. Alex wiggled a crowbar into the crack, and after a few more blows from the sledgehammer, they were able to pry the door open.

Alex pulled out stacks of paper, most of it run-of-the-mill forms for Western Union, but some papers didn't fit. A map of the Hudson River with markings. An advertisement for a steamship due to sail for Rotterdam *tomorrow*. A separate page contained ticket prices and the port of embarkation in New York.

"Kasper is heading for New York City, and it looks like he's doing it via the Hudson."

The train Kasper had dragged Eloise onto ran alongside the Hudson River for miles, and they'd obviously bailed out well before Milton. Eloise would be a useful hostage all the way to Manhattan, but after that, her survival didn't look good.

"I want my daughter back," Garrett declared. "I don't care what it takes."

"Daughter?" Claude asked. "I thought she was only your—"

"She's my *daughter*," Garrett interrupted. "Nothing in my life has made me prouder than that girl, and I want her back."

Part of Alex wished Eloise could hear that declaration, but the most important thing was getting her back. He focused on the map and saw an excellent spot to intercept a ship well before it reached Manhattan.

"West Point," he said, pointing to the map. "He won't be

expecting an attack there, and the folks at the military academy will be able to help. Let's get started."

Even trapped inside the hold, Eloise could hear the argument raging between Kasper and Jack. With her ear pressed against the wood, sound transferred almost as well as if she were in the room.

"Ten thousand dollars is plenty to set yourself up in style in Finland," Jack said.

"But it's *Finland*," Kasper growled. "It's under the boot of the Russians, and it's freezing year-round. I need another ten thousand to buy my silence for good."

"And you'll get it, but you'll have to wait until the quarry is mine."

Her mouth went dry. It was the third time Jack had implied he would soon own the quarry, and she wondered if this was related to the legal documents Bruce had been working on regarding the inheritance of his property.

"With luck, Garrett will still swing for killing the Russians," Jack said. "If he wiggles off the hook . . . well, accidents happen all the time. Especially in quarries with blasting and rock slides."

Her heart sank. Jack intended to waltz back into town and continue life as before. That could only happen if she was dead, and he planned on taking Bruce out soon too.

"When?" Kasper demanded. "Don't think I can't stir up trouble for you even if I'm in Finland."

"An accident now would look suspicious," Jack said. "I'll be sure it happens within a year or two. First we take care of the little problem, then I'll go after the big problem. The little problem will be an excellent hostage until you're safely out of the country. So far she hasn't been any trouble at all."

Her heart pounded so fast she went dizzy. Once she and Bruce were dead, the quarry would go directly to Jack. Conversation halted, and soon Eloise smelled the reek of cedar-scented cigar. She clamped a hand over her mouth to keep from gagging, but the conversation had come to an end.

She was probably going to die tonight, and her life was full of regrets.

No . . . actually, it wasn't. All in all, she was mostly proud of her life. She'd done well by Tasha and the baby. She'd gotten her accounting certification and done honorable work for companies who needed her help.

Her only real regret was Alex. They had been perfect together, even though they were complete opposites. He sparked a bold streak in her, while she helped tame his wildest impulses, and she had loved every moment of it. Alex had been right. They *were* one for the ages, and she regretted it had taken her this long to realize it.

And she regretted that, in Jack Riesel's words, his "little problem" had been no trouble at all.

It was time to make some trouble. This wasn't how her story was going to end. The cavalry wasn't coming. If she was going to be rescued, she'd have to do it herself. A calm, cold determination took root as she pressed her ear to the side of the closet again to listen.

To her surprise, she heard the distinct sound of a man's snore. The scent of cedar tobacco was back, which meant Jack was awake and had lit another cigar. It was probably dark by now, but she'd gleaned enough from their earlier conversation to know that Jack expected to arrive in the port of New York at seven o'clock in the morning.

There was no getting through the heavy lock on the door, so another way had to be found. She'd already explored every square inch of the closet, running her palms over the walls, ropes, wires, and tie-downs hanging from the pegs. A toolbox rested on the floor. She carefully handled the equipment, but most of it was useless. Loose bolts, screws, a roll of string, but no sign of a hammer that might serve as a weapon. She found a nail rolling at the bottom of the box, a big one, at least three inches long. Maybe she could use it to defend herself? If she wrapped it in cloth, she'd have a better grasp and could jab one of the men.

She sighed and rolled her eyes, imagining how pathetic she'd seem trying to take on two gun-toting men with a single nail.

What would a hero from her adventure novels do? It was the dead of night, and one of her captors was asleep. Any hero worth his salt would say now was the time to act. He wouldn't stand in a closet and fret over looking foolish while brandishing a nail for defense. If he couldn't pick the lock on the door, he would use a broadsword to hack his way out through the middle. She didn't have a broadsword and couldn't afford the noise even if she did.

But the door had hinges.

And she had tools.

She smiled so widely that it split the cut on her lip. With the nail and the heel of her boot, she could tap the pin from each of the hinges.

It didn't take long to wiggle out of her boots and position the nail beneath the base of the first hinge. She tapped the nail with her boot heel, the dull thud barely making any noise. Two minutes later the pin popped free. She repeated the procedure until only a single hinge held the door in place.

She would need to move fast once the door was off. Then she'd have to swim for freedom. Would she remember how? It had been twelve years since she'd last swum, but it was her only hope of escaping this barge. The water would be freezing, and her velvet gown would get waterlogged and slow her down. She slipped out of her jacket and skirt, all the way down to her skivvies. Gooseflesh puckered her skin, and she wasn't even in the water yet.

She leaned her forehead against the door. *Please, God, I've made a lot of mistakes, but I've tried to live a good and worthy life. Thank you for the gift of the convent. Thank you for giving me a father here on earth, even if he isn't perfect. I'm not either. And thank you for Alex. He taught me to swim so that maybe I'll survive this night. And if you could help me lift this door off its hinges without making a huge racket, I'd truly appreciate it. Amen.*

It was now or never.

She held her breath as she tapped the pin from the final hinge, then knelt and worked her fingers beneath the crack at the bottom of the door. A little wiggle, and the door tipped inward. The lock held fast, but she rotated the door enough to squeeze through the opening.

It was almost pitch-black outside as well, with only a sliver of moonlight glinting on the water. Forest covered most of the shoreline, and cold air surrounded her as she crept toward the rim of the barge. There was no sign of civilization except for a few lights twinkling over a mile away. Could she wait until the barge was closer to the lights?

"Hey!" Jack roared. "How did you get out here?"

He stood only yards away, and the time for thinking was over. She jumped.

It was freezing! She dog-paddled furiously to keep her head above water. Jack threw his cigar at her, and the glowing tip fizzled out only inches from her face.

"Kasper, wake up!" he screamed. "She's getting away and I can't swim!"

She wasn't moving fast enough with the dog paddle. Fabric wafted around her, and the water was so icy that her muscles started seizing up.

Alex's voice sounded in her mind. *Swim! Don't dog-paddle—swim. You know how. I taught you.*

"Right," she muttered, and quit dog-paddling. She put her face in the water, lifted her hips and feet, and propelled herself forward, swimming in smooth, confident strokes. She didn't look back, couldn't worry about what was going on behind her. Voices yelled and shouted, but she kept her face in the water and swam for her life.

Her lungs felt ready to burst, but she didn't stop, just kept moving. After a long while, she slowed to catch her breath, and her feet sank. Mercifully, her toes touched smooth, slimy rocks. She was almost to shore! A renewed jolt of energy prompted her to flatten out and start swimming again.

"Halt!" The commanding voice echoed across the water, and she panicked, ducking beneath the surface to hide.

Then she realized the voice had come from the land, not behind her. She lifted her head and swiped water from her eyes. The silhouette of a man standing on shore had a rifle aimed straight at her.

"Don't shoot!" she implored. "I need help."

"Get out of the water, ma'am," the voice ordered.

She planted her feet on the rocks, and this time the water only came to her shoulders. She raised both hands in the universal sign of surrender and started slogging forward. More men rushed to join the first. There were four of them, all with rifles trained straight at her.

They were all in uniform. Their faces were young but fierce and determined, and as she blinked the water from her eyes, she recognized their uniform. They were cadets from the United States Military Academy at West Point.

She was safe.

THIRTY-FOUR

lex stood on the shore of the campus at West Point, his soul frozen as he watched the grim operation in the middle of the river before him. After Alex alerted West Point about the escaping barge, the campus went on alert and sent their cadets to patrol the shoreline for several miles in both directions. Alex and Garrett had taken the train to West Point, where the navy's revenue cutter service had been deployed to intercept all passing boats at Constitution Island. The cutter service was designed to waylay smugglers, and they had plenty of experience stopping and boarding boats.

There had only been one boat all night long, a barge belonging to the Riesels. The slow-moving barge had been stopped more than an hour ago, but there was no sign of Eloise on board.

"Let me have the binoculars," Alex said to Garrett, whose face was grim as he handed them over. Torches on the barge illuminated the deck, where Kasper Nagy and Jack Riesel sat on opposite ends of the barge, handcuffed and helpless while being independently questioned by military personnel.

Jack Riesel. Learning that a friend was behind the death of the Russians and the sabotage was a stab in the back. Someday soon it would hurt, but it hadn't yet sunk in. All he could do right now was think of Eloise, and it looked bad for her. The first sailors to search the barge reported no sign of a hostage, and both Kasper and Jack swore that Eloise had jumped. A convenient excuse. A man who could so easily murder the old soldier would have no qualms about shooting a hostage once she was no longer useful. Eloise was probably dead and on the bottom of the river by now.

"I want on that ship," Garrett said when the officer in charge approached them.

"We can't have civilians on board while the investigation continues," the officer said. "I assure you, no stone will be left unturned."

"I'll be more effective at getting the truth out of those men if I have to rip them open to do it!" Garrett snapped.

Alex lowered the binoculars as the arguing continued, but it faded into the background. *Oh, Eloise*. Had she been frightened? Angry? It didn't seem possible that a woman like her could be snuffed out so quickly. She had been a diamond. A heroine worthy of Shakespeare or Sophocles or one of the Old Testament female warriors.

A flare launched from the far side of the campus. It was from land, not the river, and the officers on the shore looked over in concern. There was yelling and shouting in the distance, and a crowd of people were heading this way. Alex strained to hear what they were saying. There was so much shouting and confusion, but finally one voice rose above the others.

"We found her!" someone hollered.

Alex dropped the binoculars and ran. A throng of people clustered beneath a streetlamp, and they were cheering. Did he just see a flash of red? So many men and soldiers congregated beneath the light, but in the middle was someone with sopping wet red hair.

"Back away," he ordered, and like magic, the cadets stepped back.

Could it be Eloise? She looked like a drowned puppy, with wet hair, bare feet, and a cadet's wool coat draped around her shoulders. It was only battlefield training that kept him standing on his feet.

"Eloise?" She looked nothing like the prim, flawlessly tailored woman of the past few months, but it was her, and she beamed the most radiant smile as she ran into his arms. He clasped her to him but then didn't move a muscle. If he moved, this dream might end, for it couldn't be real. But she felt real. The smell and prickle of wet wool felt real. He buried his face in her neck and couldn't let her go, for she was alive and safe. He'd never let her go again.

Thank you, God. He didn't understand how Eloise had managed to get herself off that barge, but surely God had been with them this night.

"Stand aside. I need to see my daughter," a gruff voice said.

Alex smiled against the side of Eloise's face, reluctant to let her go, but if Garrett was willing to openly acknowledge Eloise, Alex needed to stop resenting the man so much. He pulled back to gaze down into her face.

"Your father is here too," he said, and he stood back to let Garrett pull Eloise into a mighty bear hug.

The next few minutes were a blur as Eloise recounted how she had gotten the hinges off the door and swum to freedom. She had come ashore almost a mile upstream, where patrolling cadets spotted her. One of the sailors from the cutter service commended her, saying that by getting off the barge before they stormed the ship, she had been safer and prevented her captors from using her as a hostage.

Exhaustion clouded the edges of Alex's mind, but he heard a growl from Eloise's stomach. She looked a little embarrassed as she clamped an arm across her stomach, but it had been a long time since either of them had eaten. A lieutenant offered to bring her some food if she was too hungry to wait for breakfast.

"What time is breakfast served?" Eloise asked.

"Seven o'clock, ma'am."

She glanced at the clock tower and nodded. "I can wait the four hours."

The lieutenant quirked a brow. "Seven o'clock is only three hours away."

She sagged. "Normally I'm really good at math. Truly. I'm an accountant."

Alex circled her with an arm. "We'd be grateful for something to eat," he said, and the officer led them across campus toward a dining hall.

Garrett tried to follow, but all it took was a few softly spoken words from Eloise to cause him to stand down. Alex couldn't hear what was said, but Garrett gave a grudging nod and stepped back to give them privacy. It looked like Alex would have to make peace with his old rival, but for now he needed to be alone with Eloise.

Ten minutes later they were in the cadet mess hall, gorging on the best-tasting cheese sandwiches in the history of mankind. Was it just that they were famished, or was there something truly magical about tonight? The mess hall was cavernous, with slate floors and flags hanging along the stone walls. Every noise they made bounced and echoed in the castle-like hall, and it felt like they were the only two people in the world.

He did his best to tell Eloise what had gone on during the past several hours, how Garrett had put out word in the valley that his daughter was in trouble, and offered a ridiculous reward for anyone willing to help save her.

She frowned at him. "I hope he didn't offer too much, because I kind of saved myself."

"That you did," Alex said with a smile. "But let me repeat—he promised a rich reward to anyone who helped save *his daughter*. He's shouting it from the mountaintops. Didn't you hear him outside?"

The words penetrated, and Eloise's face warmed. "That feels pretty good."

"I think he was terrified he'd made the biggest mistake of his life by denying you all these years. Frankly, none of us expected you'd be able to get yourself out of that fix without help. Miss Drake, despite your protestations of being a humble accountant, I find—"

"Stop right there," she said. "The test I had to pass to get certified was eye-watering. There's nothing humble about being a CPA."

He bit back a smile. "My apologies. Despite your exhaustive, impressive, and sometimes tedious work as an accountant, you persist in behaving like a protagonist out of a boy's adventure tale."

Her shoulders sagged, and it looked as if she felt aches and pains in every muscle in her body. "I know, and I wish it would stop."

"Truly?"

"Truly! I want to live by the rules. I want daily schedules and to know what I'm having for dinner tonight and what I will wear to work tomorrow. I want a list of every task expected of me, and I shall systematically slay each item."

"Eloise . . . I want those things for you too."

"Really? It seems like you want to tear your hair out every time I break out the rule books."

He smiled and shook his head. "You're my ballast. We couldn't have moved that town without your tedious schedules and attention to detail. We need you. *I need you.* I've needed you to help keep me grounded since I was eighteen years old.

Despite your fleeting lapses into heroism, I love your solid, finicky strength."

Over the past twelve hours, he'd castigated himself for all the things he should have done to make Eloise know she was loved and cherished. He wouldn't wait another day, not another minute to start making those things happen.

He got up from his chair and then down on one knee. The scrape of the chair echoed off the ceiling, and he swallowed hard. "I think I'm twelve years overdue on this."

She stopped him. "It's been a long day for us both. Don't let irrational emotion make you say something you don't mean. Be logical."

He grabbed her hand and looked up into her eyes. "This is the most logical thing I've ever done. We were written in the stars long ago, and it's time to do things right. Eloise, will you marry me?"

She fell to her knees so that they were face to face. They were complete opposites, but over the past eight months, they'd soared alongside each other and accomplished wonderful things.

She reached up to cup his face between her palms. "Bruce may have a heart attack and the world may stop spinning on its axis, but I would be honored to marry you."

For once in her life, Eloise felt sorry for Oscar Ott.

During the following week, she worked alongside the detectives to unsnarl the financial records at the cement factory and figure out how Kasper Nagy's blackmailing scheme worked. They met in a stark room in the Kingston sheriff's office. A table, four walls, four chairs, and stacks of accounting ledgers.

Oscar was walked out of his jail cell and asked to explain his accounting system. He was covered in a sheen of perspiration, and his eyes were frantic. "I don't know anything!" he whined. "I just did what Jack and Kasper told me to do. I didn't know they were siphoning money from the company." He looked at Eloise. "You know how complicated things can be. How they can trick you. Tell them!"

He was a pitiful sight. It was impossible to know what caused Oscar's sense of inferiority that drove him to be so nasty, but she would no longer let this unhappy man hurt her. After careful study of the books, Eloise concluded Oscar probably didn't understand the fraudulent system Jack designed to keep funneling blackmail money to Kasper. Oscar's lack of formal training was probably why Jack had kept him on board all these years.

More work with the detectives unraveled the rest of the scheme. Kasper had been the town snitch for decades, collecting a healthy stipend from both Bruce and Theodore Riesel for passing along gossip he gleaned while eavesdropping at the hotel. When Jack needed help covering up the accidental death of the Russians, he turned to Kasper, a man with no scruples, a rudimentary knowledge of the Russian language, and who was willing to do anything for a dollar. In return, Kasper gave his service to "Pomo," which meant *boss* in Kasper's native Finnish—for a price. Kasper had also told Jack about the conversation between her and Alex the day they made maple candy. When it looked like Eloise stood to inherit half the fortune Jack had always assumed would be his alone, they tried for an accidental shooting to remove her from the scene.

Bruce had never finished breaking the complicated trust regarding the inheritance of the two companies, and since Jack was going to jail for the rest of his life, it looked like Eloise was going to someday inherit both the cement factory and a limestone quarry.

She'd been horrified, but Alex was over the moon. "You don't have to actually run the place," he said. "Hire Boomer or someone else who knows what they're doing. I'm just happy the companies will be in good hands."

God willing, she wouldn't have to worry about it for years to come, for Bruce was still in excellent health, and ever since announcing his engagement to Marie Trudeau, he seemed ten years younger. Eloise wasn't sure what the next few years held in store for them all, but she had faith they would be good ones. She was going to marry the man she loved and live in a new town with a bright future.

But tonight, it was time to say good-bye to the old town. Bruce had arranged a huge celebration for anyone who wanted to watch the final demolition of Duval Springs from the terrace of his home. His household staff was here, as was Marie, but most people chose to watch from Highpoint, where a similar gathering was being held to witness the town's final hours. Eloise brought her telescope out onto the terrace, and Marie set out sandwiches, fruit, and pastries. Alex looked like he was bracing for a battle as he stood at the edge of the terrace, hands in his pockets, gazing down at Duval Springs.

"How are you doing?" Eloise asked.

He shrugged. "I'm okay. Sort of." He flashed her a wink. "No matter what, I'm not going to cry in front of Garrett."

She wasn't so sure about that. Alex usually got misty at times like these, and he'd been emotional all day. She wished this final farewell could be over so they could start their new life in Highpoint. To her relief, Bruce and all his staff were respectful as they began gathering on the terrace. Moose even offered Alex a handshake.

"I have good memories of the harvest festivals down there," he said. "I used to be part of the barbershop quartet."

Alex nodded. "I remember."

Even the housekeeper had a story. "My father had a wishbone in the tavern during the Civil War. We still have it in the family."

Alex blinked a little faster as the memories started getting to him. Eloise slid her hand into his and squeezed. He squeezed back.

"Thanks, ballast," he whispered to her.

Even from up here, Duval Springs looked terrible with over half its buildings gone and every tree in the town already cut down and burned. The old elm tree where Alex had carved their initials was gone. Teams of real gravediggers had moved the rest of the cemetery. Smaller buildings had been knocked down and the rubble gathered into mounds. Larger buildings would be burned in place with their windows propped open to allow for air circulation to help the flames. The Gilmore Inn had been set with accelerants to ensure all four floors would be properly engulfed.

Moose peered through the telescope. "Enzo is getting ready to set off the fuses," he said. "Come look!"

"I can't take it," Alex whispered, and remained motionless as he watched the beginning of the fire through pained eyes.

This was going to be hard, but witnessing the town's final moments was a way to bid farewell to a place that represented the best of America. Nothing lasted forever, and Duval Springs had a grand run.

"There's the first flame," Moose said from his position at the telescope. Even through the naked eye, it didn't take long to spot the orange line creeping up the column of the Gilmore Inn. The accelerants kicked in, and the other columns soon caught, and then the underside of the balcony was quickly engulfed. Marie came to stand on Alex's other side.

"It is the last hour of the last day," she said gently.

Alex gave a ragged sigh and lost the battle. He collapsed into a chair and started bawling like a baby. After a few minutes, he got control and wiped his face. "I'm so glad you're here," he told Marie. "Thank you. A thousand times, thank you."

"For what?" she asked.

"For being the best teacher I ever had. For staying with us until the end."

Tears spilled down Marie's face too. "We were all lucky to have been at a place like Duval Springs."

Other buildings were soon lit, but it was the four-story inn that was the most spectacular as flames poured from the open windows. Everyone stood in dazed fascination as the fire spread throughout the town. Even from here, Eloise could smell the burning wood.

Someone tilted the telescope toward Highpoint. "Look over there! Dr. Lloyd is smooching Rebecca Wiggin in the bandstand."

"I don't believe it," Alex said. He darted to the telescope and focused the knob. "Eloise, you've got to see this." He beckoned her to the telescope.

She hesitated. "I don't think it's right to spy on people."

Alex pulled away from the telescope to shoot her a teasing grin. "Listen to you! Didn't you spy on the entire town of Duval Springs for years?"

She could hardly deny it, but she still lifted her chin and refused to look. No one else was so prudish. Even Marie took a peek at the creamery lady sharing an unseemly kiss with the town's bachelor doctor. Small towns would always have their scandal and nosy neighbors, and Highpoint was following in the tradition.

After an hour, most of the buildings in the town square were smoldering piles of charred wood, but far more interesting were the ongoing developments over at Highpoint. Alex moved the telescope to the other side of the terrace so people could watch the children at Highpoint play crack-the-whip on the town square, and Hercules had people lined up to bob for apples.

Duval Springs was in the past. It was time to look toward the future in Highpoint.

Epilogue

June 1915

*I*ncessant knocking on his bedroom door woke Alex. It was only four o'clock in the morning, but as the hotel's manager, he didn't have the luxury of ignoring it. Eloise still slumbered, so he padded quietly to the door to crack it open. Nick and Rosalind Drake were on the other side, both fully dressed and looking anxious.

"What's wrong?" Alex asked.

"Nothing, but we need you to open the kitchen," Nick said. "We need breakfast. It's going to be a long day."

Alex smothered a laugh. "I know. That's why I'd like a few more hours of sleep. Go back to bed."

"Can't," Nick said. "We open the pipes today, and I've got a team ready to do a final inspection before we start."

After eight years, millions of dollars, and thousands of uprooted lives, the reservoir was filled and ready to begin operations. For years the reservoir had been a vast pit in the ground, surrounded by cranes, earthmoving equipment, and thousands of construction workers. Now the finished reservoir looked like a natural lake, sparkling like a gem in their secluded valley. When they turned the taps on later today, water would begin flowing toward New York City for the first time.

"Please," Rosalind said. "I know it's early, but we've got a crew of hungry men and need to be on the job within the hour."

Alex nodded. "I'm doing it for you, not for him."

At least Rosalind said *please*. Alex still sometimes resented the city workers who had invaded their lives, but he couldn't help being a little proud of the reservoir. It was a testament to the human spirit that they could transform the earth in such a manner.

When he returned to his bedroom after opening the kitchen, Eloise was up and getting dressed, looking almost as anxious as Nick and Rosalind.

"Hurry," she said. "We need to set up the tables on the lawn, then start carrying out the food. We're expecting two thousand people for the celebration today, and they'll be here soon."

Eloise loved planning these town festivals, and as the mayor's wife, she got to attend every one of them. She was still a perfectionist, and it was that quality that had helped them create a first-rate hotel in Highpoint. Their town needed a hotel, and since Willard Gilmore had moved to Albany, Alex and Eloise had stepped up to the plate and built one. They had owned and operated it since the first year of their marriage.

By noon, people from all over the valley gathered on the banks of the new Ashokan Reservoir. Children played in the nearby field, adults ate and gossiped, and everyone took part in judging the pie contest. Each year since the clearing of the valley, the displaced residents scattered around the state gathered for a reunion, but today was special. Today the festival would be held on the banks of a beautiful lake that had been born of their sacrifices.

From the corner of his eye, Alex spotted a couple of teenaged boys tugging off their shirts, and when they kicked off their shoes, he knew exactly what they were up to.

He darted to the water's edge to stop them. "You boys know the rules against swimming in the reservoir."

After all, the city had posted dozens of signs prohibiting swimming and boating. Alex usually looked the other way when local boys stole a quick swim, for ducks and fish certainly made themselves at home in the lake. The water would go through plenty of filtration and treatment before it arrived at the city, so the rules seemed a little pointless to him.

And if he and Eloise sometimes slipped out for a forbidden moonlit dip of their own? Well, let the city come arrest them. He didn't intend to quit.

"Oh, come on," one of the boys grumbled.

Alex leaned closer and lowered his voice. "Wait until the journalists and photographers are gone. Then you can have at it," he said with a wink.

It was approaching the noon hour, and Alex loped over to join Eloise, who was burping their youngest son over her shoulder. Eloise had a limitless supply of patience, which was good, because they'd had four sons in the last seven years, and they were a handful. At the moment they only had the baby to tend with, for Hercules had taken the older boys and Blessed Joy to watch the engineers open the inlet gates.

"Brace yourself," he murmured to Eloise.

The clock was about to strike the noon hour, and Nick had warned the entire town of what would happen at twelve o'clock. Even so, the blast of the steam whistles was overwhelming. Ducks startled into flight, and Alex covered the baby's ears. Every steam whistle, siren, and horn stationed along the reservoir blared, signaling that the taps had been turned on.

The whistles bellowed throughout the valley for a solid minute. At this very moment, the first gallon of water had been released to begin its hundred-mile journey to New York City. Some of the crowd clapped and cheered, and others covered their ears and waited for the earsplitting assault to end.

"Good boy," Alex crooned to the baby when the whistles fell silent, for little Jacob had only let out a few whimpers and now smiled at him with a gummy, toothless grin.

Alex's ears were still ringing ten minutes later when Nick and Rosalind rolled up in their automobile, both smiling wide. Hercules and the children clambered out of the back seat.

"Pipes open!" Nick roared as he vaulted from the car. He reached over the lunch table and began stuffing his pockets with apples, muffins, and a wedge of cheese. At Eloise's frown of disapproval, he shrugged defensively. "What? It's going to be a long day. I'm driving ninety-five miles to make inspections of the aqueduct all along the way. This time tomorrow, the water is going to be at New York City. Are you ready, Rosalind?"

"Let's go," she replied. Rosalind had to scurry to keep up with Nick's long-legged stride, but soon the two of them were back in their automobile, the bonnet folded back and their faces to the wind as they set off to race the water to New York City.

Blessed Joy watched Nick's departure, her six-year-old face covered in awe. "I want to be a plumber when I grow up."

"Last week you wanted to be a ballerina," Hercules said.

"She can be anything she wants to be," Eloise said.

It was what they told all the children living in Highpoint, even though Alex hoped they wouldn't be lured away by the temptations of the city. As the mayor of Highpoint, maybe he was biased, but this valley was the best place in the world. He grabbed Blessed Joy's hand to walk her over to the edge of the water and hunkered down beside her.

"Do you see that buoy out there in the middle of the lake?" he asked, pointing to a distant speck. "That's where the tavern was. That's where you were born."

"In Duval Springs?" Joy asked.

"Yes, in Duval Springs." The lake was so huge it was hard to know exactly where Duval Springs had been located, but its memories were forever engraved on his heart.

Blessed Joy ran off to show the spot to Ilya, who resented being pulled away from the pie contest for something so pointless as admiring a distant buoy. Most of the children weren't interested in the idyllic village that once flourished here. Someday they might want to know more about the history of this place, and if they did, he would be ready to teach them.

Maybe that was the nature of progress. Why dwell on the way life used to be? The sacrifices of the past were already fading away, even for him. Someday people would probably even take this reservoir for granted and never realize the sacrifices made by thousands of people to make this engineering miracle possible.

Wind coming off the lake ruffled his hair as he gazed at the buoy bobbing in the sunshine. He dwelled on the past because he loved it, because it was part of his soul, and he never wanted to forget those days, even though they were gone forever. The end of Duval Springs had been hard, but helping his people survive that time would always be his proudest accomplishment.

Eloise slid up alongside him, wrapping an arm around his waist as she gazed out at the lake. "I used to stare down at that town with such envy," she said. "Now all that's left is a buoy."

Her comment triggered the romantic in him. He had fought hard for Duval Springs, but in losing it, he'd found something better. He leaned over to whisper in her ear. "That town tempted the princess down from the mountaintop. I'll be forever grateful for that."

The detour that had been thrown into their lives ended up guiding him and Eloise exactly where they were meant to be. He pulled his wife and baby close and thanked God for the unexpected detours in their lives.

Historical Note

*D*uval Springs is a fictional town, but it's modeled. on the collective experience of several towns that were dismantled to build the Ashokan Reservoir. Some of the smaller towns relocated to higher ground, but most people took their payouts and moved to nearby villages. Urban legend claims that when the water level in the reservoir is low, chimneys and church steeples from the drowned villages break the surface of the water. There is no truth to the myth, as all buildings, cemeteries, railroads, and vegetation were completely removed before hollowing out the basin of the reservoir. Today only a few historic markers along the edge of the water commemorate the vanished towns of Ashton, Boiceville, Brodhead Bridge, Brown's Station, Olive Branch, Olive City, and West Hurley.

Beginning in 1913 and continuing until the late twentieth century, an annual Labor Day reunion of the displaced residents and their families was held at the reservoir. In 1985, Mayor Ed Koch of New York City sent a proclamation to be read aloud at one of these reunions, which was attended by five of the surviving displaced people. The proclamation read:

"The aqueduct system that supplies water to New York City is one of the wonders of the modern world. . . . It is appropriate indeed to remember and honor the sacrifices of our fellow New Yorkers upstate who helped make our water supply possible. Every day of the year since 1905, the people of New York City have raised their glasses in a toast to you—and in those glasses is the best water in the world."

Questions for Discussion

1. At the end of the novel, Alex is trying to educate the next generation about the past. Are there things you wish the younger people in your lives had a better appreciation for? What is the best way to teach them?

2. Bruce drove Alex out of town to split him away from Eloise. Why did he do this rather than force Eloise and Alex into a shotgun wedding? Although his methods were harsh, was his decision to discourage their romance the right one?

3. Eloise has the steadfast skills of a planner, while Alex is a dreamer. She reflects, "It was simply the way God had made them, and the world needed both sorts to succeed." Do you agree with her?

4. At one point Eloise predicts that if she and Alex had married when they were young, it would have been a disaster. What do you think?

5. Shortly after the dead bodies are found, Eloise proclaims, "I can't abandon someone, even if the worst is true. *Especially* if the worst is true." How do you feel about supporting a loved one if they had committed a terrible offense?

6. Eloise often harkens back to swashbuckling heroes of adventure novels and ultimately draws upon their bravery when she helps move the town. Have you ever been inspired to embark on an action based on fictional characters?

7. Do you think Eloise chose the right man? Why?

8. When Eloise is at Nick's wedding, she looks through the terrace window to see an idyllic image of people dancing and laughing. She characterizes them as happy people living perfect lives. Are there times when you observe people from afar and feel your own life comes up short? How realistic is that?

9. Did you guess the villains before the end? Were there any plot twists that took you by surprise?

10. Eloise overcompensates for her history of being rejected by making herself overly helpful to people. Are there any upsides to this?

11. Eloise concludes that most of Oscar Ott's nasty comments were rooted in unhappiness and insecurity. Do you agree?

Elizabeth Camden is the author of twelve historical novels and has been honored with both the RITA Award and the Christy Award. With a master's in history and a master's in library science, she is a research librarian by day and scribbles away on her next novel by night. She lives with her husband in Florida. Learn more at www.elizabethcamden.com.

Sign Up for Elizabeth's Newsletter!

Keep up to date with Elizabeth's news on book releases and events by signing up for her email list at elizabethcamden.com.

More from Elizabeth Camden!

Dr. Rosalind Werner is at the forefront of a groundbreaking new water technology—if only she can get support for her work. Nicholas Drake, Commissioner of Water for New York, is skeptical—and surprised by his reaction to Rosalind. While they fight against their own attraction, they stand on opposite sides of a battle that will impact thousands of lives.

A Daring Venture

BETHANYHOUSE

You May Also Enjoy . . .

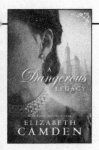

Telegraph operator Lucy Drake is a master of Morse code, but the presence of Sir Colin Beckwith at a rival news agency puts her livelihood at risk. When Colin's reputation is jeopardized, Lucy agrees to help in exchange for his assistance in recovering her family's stolen fortune. However, the web of treachery they're diving into is more dangerous than they know.

A Dangerous Legacy by Elizabeth Camden

Naval officer Ryan Gallagher broke Jenny's heart six years ago when he abruptly disappeared. Now he's returned but refuses to discuss what happened. Furious, Jenny has no notion of the impossible situation Ryan is in. With lives still at risk, he can't tell Jenny the truth about his overseas mission—but he can't bear to lose her again either.

To the Farthest Shores by Elizabeth Camden

Renowned artist Stella West has quit her career and moved to Boston to solve the mysterious death of her sister. But she soon realizes she is in need of a well-connected ally. Fortunately, magazine owner Romulus White has been trying to hire her for years. Sparks fly when Stella and Romulus join forces, but will their investigation cost them everything?

From This Moment by Elizabeth Camden

BETHANYHOUSE

More Historical Fiction from Bethany House Publishers

With a Mohawk mother and a French father in 1759 Montreal, Catherine Duval finds it easiest to remain neutral among warring sides. But when her British ex-fiancé, Samuel, is taken prisoner by her father, he claims to have information that could end the war. At last, she must choose who to fight for. Is she willing to commit treason for the greater good?

Between Two Shores by Jocelyn Green
jocelyngreen.com

After her grandfather's death, Emmaline discovers her supposedly deceased father actually lives in Canada. Shocked, she decides to go to him. Accompanied by her friend Jonathan, who harbors a secret love for her, Emmaline arrives in Toronto—to her father's dismay. Will she give up, or will she stay? And will Jonathan have the courage to tell her the truth?

The Highest of Hopes by Susan Anne Mason
CANADIAN CROSSINGS #2
susanannemason.com

In spring 1918, British Lieutenant Colin Mabry receives an urgent message from a woman he once loved but thought dead. Feeling the need to redeem himself, he travels to France—only to find the woman's half-sister, Johanna, who believes her sister is alive and the prisoner of a German spy. As they seek answers across Europe, danger lies at every turn.

Far Side of the Sea by Kate Breslin
katebreslin.com

BETHANYHOUSE